Praise for

"From page one, *Dead Silence* grabs readers by the lapels and doesn't let go until the last, satisfying page. Unique and tension-filled. My kind of thriller."

—Creston Mapes, bestselling author

"Robin Caroll's suspense *Dead Silence* kept me reading until the last page. With crafty twists and everyone a suspect, she takes her strong heroine Elise Carmichael on a heart-wrenching search for the truth. When Elise sees something she shouldn't have and then hears her powerful mother-in-law, a senator in Arkansas, has been murdered, she's shocked. Soon the killer comes after Elise and threatens her and her deaf son. With little help from the authorities, Elise takes matters into her own hands. As the danger escalates, Elise will do anything to save her son and find out the truth. A pulse-racing story that could have been ripped from the current headlines. Another winner from Robin Caroll."

—Lenora Worth, 2019 RITA® finalist

"Robin Caroll has done it again! From the first page to the last, I couldn't read Elise and Sawyer's story fast enough. Caroll kept me guessing until the very end. Is it wrong to hope her next book comes out soon so I can get my Robin Caroll fix again?"

—Kathleen Y'Barbo, *Publishers Weekly* bestselling author of *The Black Midnight* and *Chisholm Trail Bride*

"Caroll's *Dead Silence* is a heart-stopping novel that had me on the edge of my seat. The unusual premise and great characters make this a standout. Highly recommended!"

—Colleen Coble, author of *One Little Lie* and the Lavender Tide series

"Robin Caroll hits it out of the park with *Dead Silence*. I've been a member of the hard of hearing/deaf community for 30 plus years and am fluent in ASL. Therefore, I feel qualified to say that Robin nails the deaf culture in a way that hearing people rarely can. Not only that, but the story itself is wonderfully well done. Don't read this one at night if you have to work the next day, because you won't be able to put it down until you turn the last page."

—Lynette Eason, bestselling, award-winning author of the Blue Justice series

"Take a clever set-up, a delightful little boy, a beleaguered heroine, add a murder or three, and you have a recipe for hours of fun reading. It's no mystery why *Dead Silence* will please."

—Gayle Roper, author of *Lost and Found, Hide and Seek*

"Robin Caroll is one of my absolute favorite, must-read authors. I'm in awe of her writing and can't wait to read ANYTHING she writes. *Highly recommended!*"

—Carrie Stuart Parks, award-winning, bestselling author

"Robin Caroll is a master storyteller. She brings such amazing nuances to her characters to make them larger than life. And this story is one of her best. *Dead Silence* will touch your heart *and* keep your mind guessing, what's next!"

—Dineen Miller, multi-published and award-winning author

DEAD SILENCE

DEAD SILENCE

ROBIN CAROLL

SHILOH RUN PRESS
An Imprint of Barbour Publishing, Inc.

Print ISBN 978-1-64352-331-6

eBook Editions:
Adobe Digital Edition (.epub) 978-1-64352-593-8
Kindle and MobiPocket Edition (.prc) 978-1-64352-594-5

Cover Design: Kirk DouPonce, DogEared Design

Published by Shiloh Run Press, an imprint of Barbour Publishing, Inc., 1810 Barbour Drive, Uhrichsville, Ohio 44683, www.shilohrunpress.com

Our mission is to inspire the world with the life-changing message of the Bible.

 Member of the
Evangelical Christian
Publishers Association

Printed in the United States of America.

For Case…..
You're my Raylan and Boyd all rolled into one.
—We dug coal together.

CHAPTER ONE

"Stop worrying. Lilliana York will be taken care of tonight. Permanently. Just as you instructed."

Elise Carmichael froze in her path across the polished lobby floor of the Arkansas Federal Courthouse. Had she read that security guard's lips correctly? She turned to get a better look at his mouth. He stood off in the corner almost, his back facing the wall of glass, out of reach of the security camera that faced the front entrance. The storm clouds over Little Rock had intensified, making the early April afternoon even darker.

"You just make sure the money's ready to be wired as soon as it's done." The guard shoved the cell phone into his back pants pocket, nodded at the man who stood adjacent to him, then moved to join the other guards at the entrance by the metal detector. She recognized him as belonging, but didn't know his name. The other man, she didn't recognize at all.

This had to be some kind of joke. Surely this couldn't be real. Senator Lilliana York was very prominent and formidable. And, yes, aggressive. Elise should know since Lilliana was her mother-in-law. She had to tell—

Her ringtone blasted from the side pocket of her purse. Elise jerked it free and stared at the display and knew she had to take the call. She watched the guard laugh at something one of the others said, leaning casually against the bag X-ray machine. "Hey, Hallie. Look I'll be here a little longer—"

Hallie talked over her. "It's Sawyer. We're on our way to the hospital now."

Elise's world stopped spinning. Her heart stalled before free-falling to her toes. "What's wrong?"

"He fell while we were at the park. Someone called 911, and we're in an ambulance on the way to Children's right now."

Elise's pulse pounded in her head. "I'm on my way." She fled past the guards and out the front door.

The first raindrops pelted against her as she sprinted toward the paid lot where she'd parked. She didn't have an umbrella, but it didn't matter. All that mattered was getting to the hospital to check on her son.

A fall could mean so many things. Head injury. . .neck injury. . . broken leg. . .so many possible scenarios. She might be considered overprotective of Sawyer, but that was certainly justified. He might—

The slick sidewalk stole her footing. Her knees grazed over the pebbled surface of the unforgiving concrete that dug into the tender flesh. Blood puckered on both knees. Elise moved to stand, realizing then she hadn't just slipped, but her heel had broken off her right pump. She wobbled, then kicked off the shoes.

Everything in her cried, in pain or anguish or just from sheer frustration.

"Hey, are you okay?" One of the scads of young attorneys who tried to make a name for themselves day in and day out rushed toward her, his briefcase over his head.

Rain slushed down into her eyes and she swiped her face. "I'm fine, I think. My heel broke." Elise picked up her soaked bag from the ground.

Thunder boomed in the massive clouds overhead.

"Where's your car?" He held his briefcase over her head, standing very close to her.

She could feel his body heat. Panic filled her chest. "I'm fine. Thanks. I appreciate it, but I'm good." She turned, leaving her shoes on the sidewalk, and sprinted toward the lot with her car.

The attorney hollered after her, but the now rising wind snatched his words away before she could make them out. It didn't matter. She didn't want help. She just wanted to get to the hospital. Get to Sawyer.

She fumbled in her bag for her car keys as she headed toward her car. Why couldn't she find them? She felt all around, but the keys weren't there. Elise slammed her purse on the hood and fumbled about. The rain soaked her and her purse and everything inside. Still no keys.

"Hey." The young attorney stood behind her. She turned quickly.

He still held the briefcase over his head with his right hand, but his left hand held out her keys. "I called after you to let you know you dropped these, but I guess you couldn't hear me."

Thunder rumbled and lightning flashed. The earth shook.

Elise took the offered keys and used the remote to unlock the doors. "Sorry. I just need to get to the hospital. My son's been injured."

"Oh. Okay. Well, I hope he's okay." He took a step backward. "You, um, left your shoes, too, but I couldn't grab them."

"That's okay. Thanks for bringing me my keys." She opened the driver's door and slipped behind the steering wheel. She locked the doors, then started the engine. The windshield fogged up, but she could see the attorney shake his head at her, then turn and jog back the way he'd come.

Elise turned on the defroster and waited for the windshield to clear. She flipped the windshield wipers to high and grabbed her cell from her purse. Thank goodness she hadn't busted her phone screen again. She stuck the phone in the console and put on her seatbelt. She glanced in the rearview mirror and gasped.

No wonder the guy had looked so wary of her—she was a complete mess. The rain had plastered her long, brown hair to her head. Wet, her blond highlights were barely visible and looked more like gray streaks. Her mascara had run in the rain, and when she'd wiped her face, she'd smeared it across her cheeks.

She reached into the console and pulled out some leftover napkins from the fast food takeout she'd gotten Sawyer just the other day. She rubbed away the makeup as best she could, but traces still remained. It didn't matter. Getting to Sawyer did. She balled up the napkin and tossed it in the passenger's seat.

The defroster had done its job and cleared the windshield, so Elise eased the car out of the parking lot onto the main street. She paid extra careful attention to the traffic, not only because of the weather, but also because she seemed to be having the worst luck today.

Her knees burned, and at the red light she inspected their condition. Still bleeding from the cuts, and the skin around the tears was already starting to turn colors. Lovely. She used the balled-up napkin to dab at the blood.

She arrived at Children's Hospital safely, parked in the lot closest to the Emergency Room, and then started to get out of the car when she noticed her dirty bare feet. No way they'd let her into a hospital barefoot. Elise turned and dug around in the back seat. Sure enough, she found the slides she kept in the car in case she had to run any errands after work and didn't want to wear heels. Not the prettiest or most stylish, but they were shoes.

Kind of.

Elise slipped them on and grabbed her phone and purse, locked the car, then rushed into the hospital. A quick glance around the waiting room and no sign of Hallie or Sawyer. She went to the counter.

"May I help you?" The receptionist, with her scrubs covered with little smiling emojis, didn't react to Elise's haphazard appearance. She even offered a calming smile.

"Sawyer Carmichael. He was brought in by ambulance. I'm his mother."

"Just a moment, Mrs. Carmichael." She typed on the computer.

Elise balled her hands to avoid tapping her fingers on the counter and glanced around the waiting room. A young girl, probably no more than eighteen or nineteen held a crying baby. A couple on the opposite side of the room sat and watched a toddler playing with the table of Legos. A woman sobbed as she held a man's hand while an infant slept in a carrier in the chair beside him.

"Come on back, Mrs. Carmichael. I'll take you to your son." The nurse had moved from behind the counter to stand beside her.

Elise nodded and followed the young woman through a maze of halls into an exam room. She spied Sawyer lying on the bed, his face almost as pale as the white sheet covering him. Elise pulled him into her arms, kissing his head, then leaned back and began to sign to him. "What happened?"

He looked at Hallie, who answered for him. "He was playing at the park and he fell off the gym thing. He landed on his wrist and bumped his head."

Elise noticed for the first time Sawyer's right wrist. It was swollen and bluish.

"One of the other parents at the park called 911. They don't think he has a concussion, but just took X-rays of his wrist. I'm so sorry, Elise."

The school had let out early for an in-service date, so a lot of the parents had planned to take their kids to the park to enjoy the pretty, early-April weather. Sawyer had been elated when Elise had agreed to let Hallie take him to the park to play with his friends.

"It's not your fault. Kids play and kids get hurt." Elise pushed down the panic threatening to make her puke and signed to Sawyer. "Does it hurt badly?"

He nodded.

"I'm sorry." If only she could take the pain for him, she would. In a heartbeat. At only seven, he'd already been through so much.

He made the sign for *I love you* with his left hand.

"I love you too, honey." She kissed his head.

"What happened to your knees?" Hallie asked. She looked into Elise's face. "What happened to you, period?"

"I got caught in the rain. My shoe broke, and apparently my makeup is not waterproof." She automatically signed as she talked. It was habit and she always did it around Sawyer, even though he could read lips almost as well as she did.

A dark-haired woman in a white coat walked in and offered her hand to Elise. "I'm Dr. Martin." A nurse, this one wearing panda scrubs, followed her in.

"Elise Carmichael. How is Sawyer?"

"I don't think he has a concussion, but he might have a little knot on the back of his head tomorrow, and possibly a headache." The doctor glanced over at Sawyer. "Unfortunately, his wrist is broken in two places. I'll need to do a reduction and then we'll put it in a cast." She looked back at Elise. "He'll be in a cast for six to eight weeks, depending upon how he heals."

Elise blinked back the tears. "Dr. Martin, I'm assuming you know Sawyer is deaf. He needs both hands to communicate."

"I understand, but there's no other way. If we don't keep his wrist immobile, the bones might not heal in proper alignment, which could cause more pain and difficulty as he tries to sign later." Dr. Martin smiled at her. "I can only imagine how devastating this is, but I assure you, this is the only treatment option."

Elise nodded.

"Now, for the reduction, we'll use local anesthesia. We'll need you to fill out some forms. Christi here will go over them with you, then we'll get Sawyer set up so you can get out of here."

"Thank you."

Almost two hours and a lot of teeth grinding and tear shedding later, Elise loaded Sawyer into the back seat of her car while Hallie stowed his bag in the floorboard of the back seat. The rain had stopped, thankfully, but now night had crept in.

"I'll drop you off at Pinnacle Park to pick up your car." Elise eased the car out of the Children's Hospital parking lot, then steered onto I-630 west.

"Elise, again, I'm so sorry." Hallie glanced in the back seat at Sawyer, whose eyes had already closed. "He was playing on the gym and the next thing I knew, he was on the ground. It was like his fall happened in slow motion and I just couldn't get to him quickly enough."

"It happens. It could just as easily have happened when I was with him at the park." She cut her eyes over to the young woman beside her. Hallie was only twenty-four, but had been watching Sawyer for three years, ever since Elise met her at the Arkansas School for the Deaf where Hallie worked part time. "You can stop beating yourself up. I don't blame you."

Hallie nodded, then stared out the window into the darkness. "I just feel so bad for him."

"Me too." Elise glanced in her rearview mirror. Sawyer's head had rolled against the window and his mouth hung open. Elise's heart ached just looking at him. He was her entire life. If anything ever happened to him. . .no, she wouldn't go down that road. Not again. Not tonight.

"I can come earlier tomorrow, if you want. I'm sure you won't want to send him to school. I'll be happy to stay with him."

The trial Elise was working was still underway, which meant she had to work tomorrow. All she wanted to do was crash on the couch with Sawyer and watch comedies, but she couldn't. This trial had been going on all week and was set to end tomorrow. With a deaf defendant, Elise's interpreting was mandatory. She couldn't back out at the last minute. "I'd appreciate it. Thanks." Over the weekend, she'd see how he did. Dr. Martin had said he could return to school on Monday, with the excuse for his limited physical activity, but Elise would play it by ear.

Elise turned the car on Highway 10, also known as Cantrell Road, heading into West Little Rock. Pinnacle Park sat at the bottom of the cone-shaped peak of Pinnacle Mountain, which stood more than a thousand feet above the Arkansas River Valley. The mountain was a popular hiking attraction with its more than forty miles of trails, but the playground and picnic tables at the park drew kids of all ages.

She pulled into the lot beside Hallie's little compact. "I'll see you in the morning."

"Good night." Hallie slipped out and gently shut the door so as not to wake up Sawyer.

Elise waited until Hallie started her engine and turned on her headlights before she backed out and headed toward home. Sawyer never woke up. It might have been the medication they'd given him in the emergency room. Or it could be that he was just plumb exhausted.

She carried him and his bag inside the house, and still he didn't stir. Elise ran a hand over his hair as she tucked him in. His hair, so much like Judson's had been. . .another pang washed over her, surprising her that even after five years, the pain still had such sting. Elise kissed Sawyer's forehead, then silently closed his bedroom door.

Once in her own shower, she released the tears she'd smothered earlier. Fear, anxiety, and flat-out panic washed away with the shampoo and vanilla-scented body wash. Elise didn't bother to dry her hair, exhaustion tugging down every muscle in her entire body. She crawled into bed alone and stared at the ceiling.

Tomorrow had to be better.

CHAPTER TWO

"Does it hurt worse this morning?" Elise signed to Sawyer.

He nodded.

"The doctor said you could have an ibuprofen for the pain, but you need to eat something first. Pancakes? Waffles? Oatmeal?"

Sawyer tried to sign back, but not being able to use his right hand prevented his attempt. He let out a groan.

"Don't get frustrated. I know it stinks, but we'll figure it out. If all else fails, you can use your iPad program." She ruffled his bedhead hair. "For now, just nod or shake your head. Pancakes?"

He shook his head.

"Waffles?"

He nodded.

"Then waffles it is." She turned on the waffle maker and pulled out the ingredients. "Hallie will be here soon to stay with you all day. That'll be cool, right?"

A nod.

She whipped the milk and eggs together before adding to the mix. Elise used the ladle to pour batter into the maker, then looked back at her son. "Juice?"

He wrinkled his nose and shook his head.

Elise chuckled. "Chocolate milk?"

He grinned and nodded.

"Okay then." She snatched a glass and the milk.

The lights in the house flashed.

Sawyer scooted off the barstool at the kitchen island and ran to the front door. The light dimmed, then brightened as the front door was opened and closed.

"Good morning." Hallie joined Elise in the kitchen. "How'd you sleep?" She signed as she spoke.

"Surprisingly, well." Elise spoke with her back to Sawyer and didn't sign. "I only woke up like ten times to go check on him." She pulled the waffles off the iron, swabbed butter over them, then poured warmed syrup over the plate before setting it in front of her son.

Hallie grinned.

"Do you want a waffle?" Elise signed and asked Hallie.

"I'll make it myself. You can go finish getting ready for work."

"Thanks." Elise snatched Sawyer's fork that he'd just put waffles on and bit off the bite.

He laughed, but grabbed the fork back.

Elise ruffled his hair and winked at Hallie before retreating to her bedroom. She scrutinized herself, deciding that today would definitely be a minimal day. Hey, that's what casual Fridays were all about, right? Not in the courtroom. She grinned at herself, then wound her hair up into a bun and swiped on a little makeup: just eyeliner, mascara, and lip gloss. She studied her reflection in the mirror. Not too bad. . .considering.

She studied her knees. They had little rough spots where the concrete had broken the skin, but they were both dark bluish already. Nope, no dress today. She dabbed a little Betadine on her knees before turning on the TV in her bedroom. She always liked to catch the weather before she decided what to wear.

She turned up the volume before stepping into her closet to find slacks and a shirt. The weather came on the local news, forecasting a chilly April day with another chance of rain. Elise grabbed her black blazer and tossed it on the bed. Now, for shoes.

Sitting on the floor, she dug around for her short dress boots. Where had she worn them last?

"The time is eight-oh-two."

Elise grabbed the low heels and stood. She didn't have time to search for the boots. Court started at nine thirty this morning, and she couldn't be late. Not for the last day of the trial. She slipped on the shoes and went to the bed to grab the blazer.

"A recap of this morning's headlines: United States senator, Lilliana York, was found dead early this morning."

Elise sank to sitting on the bed and punched up the volume with the remote, her eyes glued to the television.

A professional headshot of her mother-in-law filled the screen while the morning news reporter spoke. "Found in her Little Rock home this morning by her husband, Noland, US Senator Lilliana York had been shot twice. Authorities are investigating the shooting and have no additional comment at this time."

Elise's heart pounded against her ribs.

"A Little Rock native, Lilliana graduated from Joe T. Robinson High School and went on to the University of Arkansas in Fayetteville while completing her pre-law requirements. She returned home to Little Rock and graduated from Bowman Law School in Little Rock in 1977. She began working for the Arkansas District Attorney's office that same year."

A video of the senator began to play on the screen as the reporter spoke again.

"Decades of experience as a successful attorney helped guide Lilliana's approach to governing. She was committed to seeing justice served, in and out of the courtroom."

"As the daughter of a United States Marine lieutenant colonel, Lilliana learned at an early age about the sacrifices of our men and women in uniform, as well as the unique challenges military families face. Her and her first husband's son, Judson, was an active Marine until the time of his death—which was in the line of duty, just five years ago. Lilliana brought those values with her to Washington where she was committed to enhancing the quality of life for both our veterans and their families."

Photos of Lilliana and her children, Mary Ellen and Judson, rolled over the television screen. Elise's heart caught at the sight of her husband as a young man. His smile still struck her speechless. Not a single day went by that she didn't miss him with all of her heart.

"Lilliana became a widow seventeen years ago. She knew what it took to be a single mother and did it well, until remarrying Noland York four years ago. Senator Lilliana York was sixty-one years old at the time of her death."

The screen filled with the other Arkansas US senator, Grady Boone. "It's appalling that this happened in our city's capital, in our own homes. This is why we must support more stringent gun control laws, so we can protect our homes, our loved ones, why, our very lives." He pointed his bony finger into the camera, his comb-over plastered to his head so even the wind didn't disturb a single hair.

The camera focused back on the reporter. "We'll keep you updated as the story develops, but again, United States Senator Lilliana York was found murdered in her Little Rock home this morning, shot twice." She smiled into the camera. "Stay tuned as Casey has traffic right after these messages."

Elise turned off the television, trying to ignore the tight burning in her chest. With Sawyer getting rushed to the hospital, she'd totally forgotten about the security guard's phone call. Certainly understandable that her mind would focus on her child, but now Lilliana was dead.

Could she have prevented it had she told someone?

Her stomach roiled. Technically, she was considered an officer of the court. As such, she had an obligation to report potential crimes.

But her son had been injured and she'd honestly not thought about that guard again. Until now.

Well, she could do something today. She could identify the security guard. The call might not have had anything to do with Lilliana being shot, but that wasn't her job to determine. That was the police's.

She would report what she knew and let them handle it as they saw fit. That would be her due diligence.

While she and Lilliana hadn't been close since Judson's death, Elise couldn't help but wonder why Noland or Mary Ellen hadn't called. She and Mary Ellen were still close, despite Lilliana's discouraging Mary Ellen from being so involved. Elise made a mental note to call her sister-in-law as soon as she could.

With a plan of action in her mind, she turned off her bedroom light and went back into the kitchen. She kissed Sawyer goodbye and told Hallie to avoid letting Sawyer see the news because of his grandmother's death. She wanted to be the one to break the news to him. Elise and Lilliana might not have been close, but they'd put aside differences to make sure Sawyer knew his father's side of the family and had a relationship with his grandmother and aunt. He would take the news of Lilliana's death hard. Elise sighed in dread over having to tell him and headed out to the garage.

Once the case was given to the jury, the court would release Elise. She'd go over to the US Attorney's Office and report what she'd "heard" from the security guard's phone call, then she could get back home to Sawyer and break the news to him. It was going to be another trying day.

She turned on the radio as she drove. All the local stations were updating with news about Lilliana's death. Some stations reported that their sources thought it had been a break-in gone wrong. Some interviewed suggested the senator had stepped on the wrong toes and the shooting was retaliation.

Elise turned off the radio, her palms sweating against the steering wheel. While she didn't know for sure the guard had been responsible, she had that gut feeling. Her breathing hitched as she exited off the interstate into the downtown area. It hadn't been a break-in gone wrong, but it could have been retaliation. Lilliana had certainly managed to make several politicians and lobbyists angry enough to strike out at her.

What had she inadvertently gotten herself into?

Slipping her earbud into place, Elise called Mary Ellen's cell. Her sister-in-law answered on the second ring.

"Oh Elise. . ." Mary Ellen sniffed.

"I'm so sorry. I just heard on the news." Elise entered the interstate, heading toward downtown.

"It's horrible. I just got into town this morning. How's Sawyer taking the news?"

"I haven't told him yet. It's the last day of a court case I'm on so I have to be in court. I plan on telling him as soon as I get home."

"You don't think someone will say something to him at school?" Concern seeped into Mary Ellen's voice.

Right. She didn't know. "He's not at school today. He had an accident at the park yesterday and broke his wrist. It's in a cast. He's at home with Hallie today."

"Oh, mercy me, it's all so horrible. Mom's death, now poor Sawyer's wrist—how can he sign one-handed?"

"He can't. We're working out a manner of communicating, but he gets frustrated easily, rightly so." Elise eased into the right lane as the morning traffic nearly had everything at a standstill. Common in Little Rock on a weekday morning.

"That poor baby. And then you'll have to tell him about his grandmother." Mary Ellen sniffed again.

Elise picked her next words carefully. "The news said she was shot?"

"Twice. It was awful. Noland found her. The police say a silencer—excuse me, a suppressor, was used."

"So that's why he didn't hear the shots." Elise spoke aloud, but her thoughts were jumbled as she inched her car toward the exit.

"I guess. The FBI showed up this morning, booting out the local authorities. Right now, they're questioning Noland about their marriage, if there was a pre-nup, where he was at the time of her death. Crazy stuff like did he habitually take sleeping pills, what is the status of Mom's life insurance policies. . .it's surreal."

The spouse was always the first suspect. "They're just doing their job to rule him out as a suspect."

"Like Noland would hurt a fly."

Elise smiled to herself. Noland was the most unassuming man she'd ever met. He was perfectly suited to be Lilliana's husband. Where she was outgoing and demanding, Noland was quiet and had the heart of a servant. One of the reasons why he'd been a trusted member of the press. "I'm guessing they'll figure that out for themselves rather quickly." She took the exit and made her way toward the courthouse.

"They want me to come in today to give my statement. I wasn't even here." Mary Ellen had moved to Eureka Springs years ago to intern at Turpentine Creek Wildlife Rescue. She had just finished her stint in the veterinarian program, and at thirty-one, had finally come into her own.

"Just a formality, I'm sure." Elise turned into her pre-paid parking space. "I just got to work. Why don't we plan to have lunch at my place tomorrow? It'll give you a break and Sawyer would love to see you."

"That sounds great. I'll come by your place around one? Noland and I can't make any arrangements until the coroner releases Mom's body, which is who knows when."

The coroner? Elise didn't bother asking. "Sounds good. Love you, Mary Ellen."

"Love you too. Thanks."

Elise disconnected the call and tossed her earbuds into the console. She took a moment to breathe deeply after she turned off the engine. She closed her eyes and sent up a prayer.

It was going to be a very, very long day.

CHAPTER THREE

"Court is adjourned." The judge's gavel hit, sending a bang of finality.

The bailiff moved to stand in front of the judge's station. "All rise."

Everyone in the courtroom stood silently as the judge retired to his chambers, but as soon as the door closed, all the voices blended together to echo in the federal courtroom.

Elise grabbed her belongings and wove around people to exit through the massive doors of the courtroom. She usually lingered a little, visiting with the various court reporters, but not today. She had to go talk with Sawyer and deliver the crushing news. It would be the first time he'd lost someone he could remember. When Judson had died, Sawyer had been a mere toddler, understanding nothing. He had no clear memories of his father, only the photos and videos she shared with him constantly. But Lilliana? He was close to his Grams, and this was going to hurt. If only Elise could take on the pain for him.

But first, she had to talk to the US Attorney's Office.

She hesitated as she walked toward the courthouse's main exit. At the security station her gaze jerked over each face—some she knew, some she didn't—but she didn't spy the one face she was looking for. The US Attorney's Office was only a block or so from the federal courthouse, so she headed toward the exit.

"Excuse me, Elise Carmichael?"

She turned toward the woman's voice. The dirty-blond woman in a black suit smiled, revealing a row of perfectly straight, bleached-white teeth. "You are Elise Carmichael, right?" Her blue eyes blinked inno-cently under clumpless eyelashes.

Elise wasn't fooled. She knew the look. Dark suit, disarming smile, and another suit beside her. Definitely FBI. "I am."

The woman pulled out the familiar badge and flashed it in Elise's face. "I'm Agent Wright and this is my partner, Agent Rodriguez."

He smiled. His teeth too were bleached white and perfectly straight. Was that a prerequisite for agents? One of the perks of employment?

"We have a few questions regarding your mother-in-law's death, if you don't mind."

Elise sighed. If she told them what she'd seen, it would save her a trip to the US Attorney's Office. She nodded.

"Follow us, please."

She fell into step behind the woman. Agent Rodriguez followed her. She'd just agreed to speak with them; did they think she was going to bolt? Some of the security guards she knew stared as they led her down the hall to where rooms were available for private meetings. She'd never felt more like a criminal.

Agent Wright opened one of the doors and motioned her inside. Elise took a seat at the conference table. The agents sat across from her. Agent Rodriguez opened a padfolio she hadn't noticed tucked under his arm, as it blended so perfectly with the standard bureau-style suit.

"Would you like a glass of water before we start?" Agent Wright came across as so solicitous.

"No, thank you." Elise knew better. This wasn't her first time around FBI tactics. She'd been a translator one too many times with the FBI questioning witnesses. Not with these agents, but they were almost interchangeable in the way they spoke, acted, and looked. Quantico should be very proud.

But Elise wanted to get this over with and get to Sawyer. "Before you ask me anything, there's something I need to tell you."

"Okay."

It was hard to miss the sideways glances the agents stole at one another. Elise let out a breath. They weren't very discreet. "Yesterday as I was leaving the courthouse, I noticed one of the security guards on a cell phone in the corner behind the security area."

Both agents nodded in sync.

"I read his lips to say: 'Lilliana York will be taken care of tonight. Permanently. Just as you instructed. You just make sure the money's ready to be wired as soon as it's done.'"

Agent Wright pushed one of her wavy locks behind her ear. "Are you sure?"

Elise hesitated, then nodded. "Lip reading isn't a perfect science, of course. People have different shapes of mouth, different ways of forming their words, and then there's each person's accent to take into account. It changes the way the person forms words."

"So, you're not sure that's what was actually said?" Agent Rodriguez asked.

Elise carefully considered his question. "One hundred percent? No. No one can be. But I've been in speech lessons and studying lip reading and ASL for the last seven years. I'm pretty certain that's what he said."

"Who all did you report this to?" Agent Wright asked.

Now Elise resisted the urge to squirm under their scrutiny. "Well, no one."

"What?" The agents' shock was in unison as was their question.

"I saw the guard, then my phone rang, and my sitter told me my son had fallen at the park and had been taken by ambulance to the hospital, so I ran to get there, but it was raining and I broke a heel, and I fell and my knees took a beating, but I ran to my car anyway only to find that my keys had fallen out of my purse when I fell so I couldn't find them, but a young attorney had followed me and had them, so I rushed to the hospital. My son's wrist was broken and he's deaf so needs both hands to sign, but won't be able to." She finally stopped to draw in a breath.

An uncomfortable silence filled the highly air-conditioned room. Maybe she should have accepted that offer of water.

"Maybe we can pull the security camera footage," Agent Rodriguez spoke more to his fellow agent than Elise.

"You can try, but where they stood, the cameras couldn't reach. Those cameras face the front entrance, not behind the security checkpoint," Elise offered.

"I can only imagine how stressed you had to have been worrying over your son." Agent Wright flashed that high-wattage smile at her. "Is he okay?"

Elise nodded. "He'll be in a cast for about two months, which will make communicating difficult, but we'll manage."

"So he's at home?"

"We got home about ten or so last night."

The two agents made eye contact.

Agent Rodriguez turned to her. "When you got home, did you call anyone about what you lip-read?"

Elise swallowed against a dry mouth before shaking her head. "I didn't." She held up her hands in mock defense. "I should have, I know, and initially when I saw the guard's conversation, I intended to tell someone in the US Attorney's Office. Then I got the call about Sawyer. My mind was completely focused on my son. Once he was tucked into bed, exhaustion kicked in. I took a shower and crawled into bed myself. I didn't think about the call again until this morning when I turned on the news."

An exaggerated silence ensued.

"Let me make sure I have this right." Agent Rodriguez clicked his pen on the table as he stared at the writing pad. "You lip-read a threat on a US senator's life, but then got a call that your son had been taken to the hospital, so told no one. Once you returned home from the hospital, you were so exhausted you didn't think to call any law enforcement authority to report what you'd read?"

It sounded bad, she knew, but she could only state what happened. "That's right."

"Did you perhaps call your mother-in-law and tell her? Warn her, maybe?" Agent Wright asked.

Elise shook her head. She could only offer up the truth. "I told you, I was exhausted and fell into bed after a shower. I didn't even think about the guard's call until this morning's news."

Another pregnant pause filled the space over the conference table.

"I understand that you and your mother-in-law weren't exactly close?" Agent Wright asked, but Agent Rodriguez was the one writing.

Cute. Elise knew they would try different tactics to try and get her to open up, but she had nothing to hide. "We weren't."

A moment of silence passed as the agents waited for her to elaborate. She didn't.

Agent Wright leaned back in her chair. "Why is that exactly?"

No sense not telling them now. They could ask several people and find out the truth. Elise licked her lips. "She didn't exactly think I was the best choice for her son's wife."

Agent Rodriguez crossed his arms over his chest while Agent Wright leaned forward. "What's the story behind that?"

Elise really wished she had that water right now. "When I met Judson, I was doing some modeling. Mainly for magazines and local ads. Women's wear, sunglasses, and swimsuits. At that time, I had no desire to go to college or anything that would *better myself*, according to Lilliana. But Judson and I met, and sparks flew. We had a whirlwind romance and fell deeply in love with one another."

Oh, how they'd loved each other. Judson had swept her off her feet. Loved her with a passion she'd only read about in romance novels. He could make her forget any and everything with just a look. He stole her words and breath when he smiled at her. And his touch? Oh, my. . .that could make her melt into a puddle in his hands.

Agent Wright snapped her back to the present. "The senator

didn't approve, I take it?"

Elise shook her head. "It wasn't just me that she resented, it was that her son would throw away the life she'd planned for him, to be with me." Elise smiled softly. "But that's what she never understood—I supported every single decision Judson made. I never held him back, nor ever would. I too wanted only the best for him. He was that good of a man."

"Did it get better after you got married? Had your son?" Agent Wright asked.

Elise shrugged. "She accepted our marriage, of course. She played nice for his sake, but also let everyone know how little she thought of me. It infuriated Judson, but I figured in time, she'd come around. Then we had Sawyer." Elise smiled.

The first time she had held Sawyer and saw Judson's eyes, Elise knew her heart would never be the same. The dimples were just like Judson's. The shape of his nose. The way he scrunched his face just before he cried.

"Did the senator lessen her disapproval after you gave her a grandson?" Agent Rodriguez asked.

Elise tilted her head ever so slightly. "Lilliana was smitten with Sawyer. She doted on him. Loves him very much." She paused, letting various memories wash over her. "She spent as much time as possible with him. Especially when Judson was deployed."

"I understand your husband was killed in the line of duty. I'm very sorry for your loss." Agent Wright almost sounded sincere.

"Yes. It devastated me. Still does." Why had she turned down the offer of a glass of water?

Agent Wright let a moment pass before she asked, "How did you and the senator get along after that?"

Oh, what a loaded question that was. "Well, since Lilliana resented me to begin with, Judson's death did nothing to improve her feelings toward me. However, she clung to Sawyer even more. Mary Ellen and I both felt that she needed Sawyer to help her in the grief process, so

I encouraged their close bond. Despite our differences, Lilliana was Sawyer's grandmother and I wanted him to stay close with his father's family. His roots, so to speak."

"Mary Ellen. . .the senator's daughter?" Agent Rodriguez interrupted.

As if they didn't know since they'd asked her to come in and give a statement. "Yes. Mary Ellen and I have always been friends since we met when Judson and I started dating. She understood how Lilliana could be. . .hmm. . .trying at times."

Agent Wright raised a single eyebrow as she stole a glance at her partner. "So Mary Ellen and the senator were at odds?"

Elise snorted and locked stares with Agent Wright. "Do you know any girl who hasn't been at odds with her mother at least once in her life?" She shook her head. "I meant that Mary Ellen understood how high Lilliana's expectations were for her children and how crushing it could be when those expectations weren't met to Lilliana's standards."

"Mary Ellen doesn't meet her mother's expectations? Was their relationship strained?" Agent Rodriguez asked.

Elise shook her head. They were deliberately being obtuse and trying to put words in her mouth. "No. I mean, I know that Lilliana had wanted Mary Ellen to go into law like she had, but Mary Ellen always wanted a different path."

"What kind of different path?" Agent Wright asked.

"Mary Ellen has always been a type of crusader, which is a trait she got directly from Lilliana, although neither of them would ever recognize it or admit it if they did." Elise smiled. Mary Ellen would rather someone tell her she was ugly than to tell her she was like her mother in any way. "Don't get me wrong, Mary Ellen has always loved and respected Lilliana, but instead of becoming a lawyer to fight injustices, her path was to stand up for those who can't stand up for themselves. Primarily animals who need saving."

It had taken her some time to find her path. Elise remembered Judson trying to intervene on his sister's behalf many times against their mother. Like when Lilliana pulled all the funding for Mary Ellen's college because she hadn't declared a pre-law major. One reason why it took so long for Mary Ellen to get her veterinary degree.

"Mary Ellen currently works at a large cat refuge in Eureka Springs, right?" Agent Rodriguez asked.

Elise nodded. "She does."

"I'm guessing the senator didn't like that much?" Agent Rodriguez flashed those pearly whites at her again.

But it was Elise's turn to smile. "Actually, Lilliana did. Since the federal animal protection laws were enabled, this gave Lilliana another leg up. Her daughter being a proponent of animal protection. She could try to push the bills for the large exotic animals' protection and use Mary Ellen much like she used Judson for her military stances."

"Are you saying the senator used her children for her political gain?" Agent Wright wore a shocked expression.

Elise chuckled. "Every politician will use whatever they can for their or their party's gain. Doesn't everyone know this?" She shook her head. "Lilliana was no different."

"So last night, you said you were in bed by ten or so?" Agent Rodriguez asked.

Elise sighed. "Yes."

"Can anyone verify that?" he asked.

"No, not even my son, who was asleep."

Agent Wright pressed her lips together, but was silent.

"Would you recognize the security guard again if you saw him?" Agent Rodriguez asked.

"Yes, and before you ask, I didn't see him on duty today. I know because I looked as I came in. Also, there was another man close to the guard, not in any uniform. He was in a business suit, but a better one than the ones the FB—just better ones that you see from the junior attorneys in the courthouse. I didn't recognize him at all. But when the security guard hung up the phone, he nodded at that man, who nodded back."

"Would you recognize him again if you saw him?"

She nodded. "It wasn't that his face was familiar, but it was distinctive." She let out a heavy sigh. "I don't know how else to explain it."

"But you're certain he was with the guard?"

Elise shook her head. "I said I didn't know, only that he nodded to the man, who nodded back, when he got off the phone."

Agent Rodriguez nodded. "But the guard was standing close enough for the man to hear his side of the conversation? He wasn't trying to put space between them or anything?"

"No, they were standing about two feet from each other." That made sense. If the guard didn't care that the man overheard, then the man was most likely with the guard. Elise stood. "Now, I really need to get home and tell my son that his grandmother is dead."

Both agents nodded in tandem. Agent Rodriguez handed her a business card. "Both of our contact information is on there. We'll get the security guard employee records and be in contact soon for a photo lineup."

She took the card and nodded.

"Please don't make any plans to leave town in the near future. At least not until you clear it through our office," Agent Wright said.

"Where would I go?" Elise didn't wait for any reply before she left. The question was rhetorical anyway, because if she had the means, she would take Sawyer as far away from Little Rock as she could.

Probably what she should have done five years ago when Judson died.

CHAPTER FOUR

"Is it feeling any better?" Elise spoke and signed to Sawyer. Hallie had just left and Elise sat with her son on the couch.

He lifted a shoulder, did that adorable face scrunch, then waggled his left hand.

Oh, her heart.

"Come over here. I have something to tell you." She opened her arms after signing.

He scooted next to her, but frowned.

She ruffled his hair and grinned. "No, you aren't in trouble."

Sawyer cocked his head to the side.

If there were any way she could take her baby's pain, she would in a heartbeat. Since she couldn't, she needed to be as gentle as she could.

"Something's happened to Nana."

His eyes widened a little, causing her heart to hiccup, and he roughly made the sign for *what*.

She took a deep breath and picked her words carefully. "I'm so sorry, honey, but Nana died last night."

He pressed his lips together and his eyes filled with moisture. He put his hands together and used his left hand to make the twisting motion for *how*.

Why, God? Why did she have to shatter her sweet baby's innocence when he was only seven? He'd already been through so much in his young life, why this? Why now?

But she couldn't lie to him. Wouldn't. It was all over the news, so it wouldn't do her any good anyway. "She was shot."

The tears spilled out of his eyes and trailed down his sweet cheeks. She pulled him in and hugged him tightly. She kissed his head as she rocked him. His sobs shook his entire little body. It was so unfair. Once again, she silently railed at God in anguish over her son's pain.

He pushed away from her embrace and met her gaze. With his left hand, he made the sign for *why*.

"We don't know yet. The FBI is investigating."

A myriad of different expressions crossed his face in a matter of seconds.

Elise wanted to reach out to him, hold him, make all the pain go away, but Sawyer had never liked to be babied, even when he was younger. She loved that about her son, but at times, she wished he'd just let her over-mother him.

He jumped from the couch and ran down the hall to his room, his socked feet padding on the wooden floor. His door slammed with a resounding boom. She normally wouldn't tolerate such an outburst, but for this. . .yeah, he could slam all the doors he wanted.

She sighed, then headed to the kitchen to stir the spaghetti sauce Hallie had been thoughtful enough to start for their supper. She knew Elise liked to slowly simmer the homemade jarred sauce for several hours because it let all the freshly added herbs be soaked into the meat. Despite the enticing aroma that wafted under her nose when she lifted the lid, Elise didn't feel much like eating and she was pretty sure it'd be hours before Sawyer was ready to eat anything.

The lights flashed and the doorbell rang simultaneously. She moved to the front door and bounced up on the tips of her toes to look through the peephole. The two FBI agents stood on the porch. She glanced over her shoulder—Sawyer hadn't come out of his bedroom—and tugged open the door. "Agents."

Agent Rodriguez held up his little padfolio. "We have the security guard's photos for you to look at."

She opened the door wider and motioned them toward the living room. Maybe if they caught the person responsible for Lilliana's murder, it would bring some comfort to Sawyer, Mary Ellen, and Noland.

Once they were settled, the agents on the couch and Elise in her recliner, Agent Rodriguez handed her a stapled stack of three pages. "Here are the photos of all the security guards employed at the courthouse. Take your time and look them over carefully. If you see the man you saw on the phone, just give us the number under his photo. If you don't see him, just let us know that too."

Elise nodded and studied the six photos on the first page. He wasn't there. She flipped to the second page.

"Take all the time that you need," Agent Wright said.

She nodded, but studied the pictures of the six faces on the second page. He wasn't there. She turned to the third and last page, and there he was, smiling up at her. "Number three."

The two agents locked stares. "Are you sure?" Agent Rodriguez asked.

"Yes." Even though she'd lip-read his conversation at a profile view, there was no question in her mind that this was the man.

"What percentage of sure are you?" Agent Wright asked.

"One hundred." Not even ninety-nine point nine. "I'm positive that's him."

Agent Rodriguez took the papers from her and stood. "Thank you. And I'm assuming you didn't recognize the man who had been with this guard."

Elise stood along with Agent Wright. "Who is he? I know he's not a new guard because I recognized him but didn't know his name. Is the other man a new security guard that just wasn't working yesterday?"

"I'm sorry, we can't give out that kind of information." Agent Wright led the way to the front door. "We'll be in touch if we have any further questions."

They rushed to their car before Elise could ask anything more.

She shut and locked the door behind them, then went to get a bottled water. She understood they couldn't tell her his name, but at least she'd done what she could to help the investigation along. The cold water felt good going down. Maybe she should take Sawyer a bottle. He was probably over his crying jag by now, so the water would be good for him.

But he'd be even more upset if she invaded his space if he wasn't finished crying. No, she'd give him all the time he needed. When he was ready, he'd come out.

The knock on the front door startled her. Everyone used the doorbell, well, everyone who knew a deaf person lived here. Knocking didn't activate the alert light flashes.

Elise stood on tiptoe to look out the peephole Judson had demanded they have. Mary Ellen stood on the stoop, staring right back at Elise. She quickly unbolted the door. "Mary Ellen, why didn't you ring the doorbell."

"Because I want to talk to you and I don't want Sawyer to hear. Can you come sit on the porch?" The edge in Mary Ellen's voice was unmistakable.

Elise glanced over her shoulder and didn't see Sawyer, so she stepped out onto the porch and pulled the door almost closed behind her. She sat on the swing Judson had given her for her first Mother's Day. "What's going on?"

Mary Ellen leaned against the front rail, facing Elise. "Did you lip-read someone making a threat of sorts against Mom and not tell anyone?" Red crept into her cheeks.

The FBI sure wasted no time in trying to pit people against each other. Elise quickly explained what happened. "I'm so sorry. I honestly didn't even think about that call until this morning when I saw the news."

Mary Ellen stood still, but her breathing was a little erratic. "You didn't even call Mom?"

"I honestly thought nothing more once I got the call that Sawyer was hurt. All I could think was to get to him. Once I got to the hospital, all my thoughts were focused on him. Even after I tucked him in, I was so beat that I just collapsed in my bed." She blinked at her sister-in-law. "Surely you can understand that."

"I do. I do." Mary Ellen moved to the other side of the swing and sat. "It's just. . .well, the way the agents said it, the implication was that you chose not to notify anyone because of your strained relationship with Mom."

Elise reached over and laid a hand over Mary Ellen's. "Not even close. If I wouldn't have gotten Hallie's call about Sawyer, I would have told someone right then. Once I heard about Sawyer, every other part of my brain shut down."

"I should have known those agents were just trying to. . . I don't even know." She ran her hand through her copperish-colored hair and used her toe to set the swing in motion.

Elise settled back in the swing. "They just left. Had me do a photograph lineup to identify the guard I saw make the threat on the phone."

Mary Ellen jerked her leg, jarring the fluid swinging. "Did you? I mean, did you see him? Identify him?"

Elise nodded. "I'm guessing they will go question him now, or bring him to their office to intimidate during their questioning."

"They should. If you said you saw him make threatening remarks against Mom, then I have no doubt that he did."

Elise smiled at Mary Ellen's loyalty. "Well, I had no doubt it was him. Hopefully, they'll get answers soon."

Mary Ellen rested back in the swing. "They also told me that you insinuated there were some serious issues between me and Mom."

Why did the FBI insist on such a standard of interrogation? "I hope you know that's not true. I did tell them how we both had times of difficulty because of how high your mother's expectations were. Not just for you and me, but Judson as well."

"*Difficulties* is a polite way of saying how Mom put us through the ringer so many times."

Elise tilted her head. "True, but I don't think she ever did it to be mean. I think she just had a plan in mind and if anyone deviated from it, she needed time to adjust."

"Again, you're being polite."

"I don't want to speak ill of the dead. Yes, Lilliana could be a handful, but I refuse to believe she did it out of meanness or spite."

"Well, there were times I wasn't too sure about that." Mary Ellen shook her head.

Elise wasn't going to go down this trail. Mary Ellen was processing grief and was, understandably, emotional. "I did tell the agents how much you working at the refuge had pleased her."

Mary Ellen snorted. "Let's be honest, she was only pleased because it fed into her political stance."

"Hey, at least you met her approval regardless of the reason."

"You know Mom was proud of you getting your degree and being such an advocate for the deaf."

Elise chuckled. "Because that also fed into her political stance."

Mary Ellen joined in the laughter. "There is that." She let out a long, heavy breath. "She wouldn't have been such a bully if Jud hadn't died."

"He didn't tolerate her brashness; that's a fact."

"She wasn't that way when Dad was alive, either."

"I wish I could have met him." Elise had heard so many wonderful stories from Judson about their father.

"He would've loved you."

"Really?" It was the same thing Judson had told her many times.

Mary Ellen nodded. "Oh, yeah. He loved me and Jud to distraction. We always knew that. And if someone made one of us happy, they became a quick favorite of Dad's. He would've only had to see Jud light up when you walked into a room to fall in love with you."

Elise blinked away the tears burning her eyes. "Judson said many times that he wished I could have met him."

"And Dad would have eaten Sawyer up, even more than Mom."

They both swung on the porch in silence, lost in memories and thoughts, hopes and shattered dreams.

The front door creaked open, then Sawyer shot into Mary Ellen's arms. She kissed his head frantically as tears filled her eyes.

It was obvious Mary Ellen needed her nephew's comfort and Sawyer needed his aunt's. Elise pushed off the swing and stood. "I need to go check the spaghetti. You should eat with us, Mary Ellen. Y'all come in when you're ready." She went inside and shut the door, tears filling her own eyes.

Her hands shook as she pulled pasta from the shelf and put a pot of water on to boil, then set the table. It was going to be an emotional time for all of them. Perhaps she should take herself off the trial roster for a little while. Spend time with Sawyer and Mary Ellen. At least until after the funeral, whenever that would be.

Just before the pasta was ready to drain, Mary Ellen and Sawyer came in, both bearing matching tear-streaked cheeks. "What can I do to help?" Mary Ellen asked and signed.

Elise smiled. "Can you pour the drinks, please?" She turned to Sawyer and signed. "Can you put the shaky cheese on the table?"

He grinned and nodded, weaving around his aunt to the refrigerator.

Mary Ellen winked at Elise. "He's going to be okay, you know," she whispered.

"I know."

The kitchen suddenly seemed brighter as the three of them sat down and ate. There were some sad moments, but many smiles. Elise felt good about where they were and how Sawyer was handling Lilliana's death. At least for tonight, there was peace and calmness.

After supper, Mary Ellen kissed Sawyer goodbye and Elise sent him off to shower. Elise walked Mary Ellen toward the front door.

"Thanks for inviting me to stay for supper, especially since I was loaded for bear when I got here."

Elise gave her a hug. "I know the FBI is just trying to do their job, and I want them to find out who killed Lilliana and see them brought to justice, but I do question their tactics."

"Yeah, but I should've known better. I shouldn't have been such a jerk to you."

Elise chuckled and looped arms with her sister-in-law as they reached the door. "You weren't a jerk, but if you had been, you're entitled. You're dealing with a lot. How's Noland holding up?"

Mary Ellen shrugged. "He's confused. He wants us to plan the funeral but the coroner had to do an autopsy so he can't claim the body yet. He should be able to tomorrow." She leaned against the door and faced Elise. "And the media are like ants at a picnic. Seriously, they hound him, even when he goes to get the mail. It's ridiculous."

"That's horrible, but I guess expected. She was a prominent US senator."

"I know. I probably shouldn't come for lunch. Noland wants to go to the funeral home mid-morning."

"I understand. Let me know if there's anything you need me to do."

"Thanks, Elise. Anyway, tonight was nice. Being here with you and Sawyer always makes me happy. Thanks."

"Anytime. You know that." Elise gave Mary Ellen another quick hug before she opened the front door.

She spied the box on the step as soon as Mary Ellen did.

"What's this?" Mary Ellen picked up the wrapped shoebox and handed it to Elise.

"I don't know." The box wasn't heavy. She rested it on her forearm as she removed the lid and peered inside.

She dropped the box and the lid and took a step backward.

The dead rat rolled out of the tissue paper onto the porch.

"What in the world?" Mary Ellen asked.

Elise's mind spun as she stared at the dead rat. "The question is, who else did the FBI tell about what I saw?"

"What do you mean?"

Elise locked gazes with her sister-in-law. "A rat." She glanced back down at the dead rodent. "Someone's warning me that rats don't meet a happy ending."

CHAPTER FIVE

Had she already added the vanilla? Elise couldn't remember. She added a teaspoon. Even if she had, that extra bit wouldn't make them too sweet. She glanced over her shoulder and made sure Sawyer was still watching Saturday morning cartoons in the living room before whipping the waffle mix.

She yawned wide as she poured a half cup of the batter into the waffle maker and clicked it closed. Elise hadn't got much sleep last night, tossing and turning half the night—getting up to check the doors and on Sawyer the other half. That rat. . .she got the message loud and clear—someone knew she'd "heard" what the guard said and was warning her to keep quiet. The only way someone could know was through the investigation's FBI agents. They were the only ones she'd told. Now someone else knew and wanted her to keep her mouth shut. She'd gone over every possible option as she'd lain in her bed last night. The ceiling fan had provided no answers.

As she pulled the waffles onto a plate and slathered it with softened butter, she still didn't know if she should tell the FBI about the rat, or call the sheriff's office. Or maybe she should just be more vigilant and wait. Besides, she couldn't do either with Sawyer underfoot. He was much too attuned to her moods, and since he could lip read eavesdropping was as common for him as it was for her. That would give her until Monday to decide what to do. Maybe then she'd know what was best. Maybe by then they'd have had time to question the security officer.

After she made their breakfast, she turned off the cartoons on the television so Sawyer could come eat. At least he looked like he'd slept okay.

"Does it hurt less today?" She nodded at his wrist.

He wrinkled his nose, but nodded before taking a big bite. Syrup dripped down his chin, and they both laughed.

Laughing was good. Normal. She'd take normal.

She took a sip of her coffee and watched him over the rim. So much like Judson. It seemed like every day, he grew to look like his father just a little bit more. Elise was going to have her hands full when he became a teenager.

Sawyer knocked on the table, and she jerked her gaze to him. He pointed at her phone on the table beside her, vibrating. His inability to hear made his other senses more attentive.

She took a minute to register the caller ID before answering. "Hey, Hallie."

"Hi. How's Sawyer?"

Elise glanced across the table to her smirking son who shoved waffles into his mouth like a man who hadn't eaten in a week. "Apparently, hungry." She chuckled. "He's devouring waffles at the moment."

"How'd he take the news about his grandmother?"

"As well as can be expected."

"I thought maybe, if you didn't mind, I could take him to a matinee this morning? The new action hero movie is showing."

"Sure. He'd probably love that." Elise stared at Sawyer, who was staring at her lips. "Although, with as much as he's eating, he might not want to go see a movie. He might be so full he'll need to stay home and take a nap."

His face tightened.

Hallie laughed. "He's eavesdropping again, huh?"

"Yep."

Sawyer made a pouting face, which made Elise laugh all the more.

"I'll swing by and pick him up in about thirty minutes?"

Elise turned so Sawyer couldn't see her face. "He'll be ready. Thanks, Hallie." She put her phone back on the table and took another deliberately slow drink of coffee. She caught his wave in her peripheral vision, but pretended not to see.

Sawyer rapped the table, harder than before. She slowly looked at him. He roughly signed, one handed, "Can I go?"

She grinned. "You have to clean up and get dressed. Hallie will be here in about half an hour."

Sawyer shoved the last bite into his mouth, then scrambled to take his plate to the counter and hurry off toward his room.

Elise carried her plate and Sawyer's glass and loaded the dishwasher. As she did, she realized she would now have the time to contact the sheriff's office or FBI without having to worry about Sawyer. She glanced at the ceiling. Great. *Now* You decide to send me a sign? After everything else, *this* is what causes You to act?

She hurried to help Sawyer get dressed since he hadn't had time to learn how to get around the nuances of putting on clothes with a cast. He'd just finished brushing his teeth when the lights flashed and the doorbell chimed.

Elise followed Sawyer to the door. He opened it and hugged Hallie. She held a brightly wrapped box. He reached for it.

Hallie handed it to Elise, then signed to Sawyer. "Sorry, buddy. It's not from me." She looked at Elise. "It was in front of the door when I got here."

Another rat? Elise forced a smile and set the box on top of the entry shelf, out of Sawyer's reach. She hugged Sawyer. "You have a good time, okay?"

He looked at the box, then back at Elise before making the sign—kind of—for *what*.

"Oh, someone just needed to drop something off for me. Probably work related." She forced the smile and stood, locking stares with Hallie.

It took a moment for the younger woman to catch on. "Well, we need to be off if we're going to get a good seat. And get our buttery popcorn."

Sawyer grabbed his iPad from the living room. He took it everywhere because it had his type-to-voice program for when he interacted with people who didn't know sign language.

"Thanks again, Hallie." Elise watched them get seatbelts fastened, and waved as they drove off. She shut and locked the door, then grabbed the box and set it on the counter. She refreshed her coffee and took a sip, staring at that box.

Everything in her wanted to just take the whole thing, unopened, and toss it in the trash can outside. Yet, she couldn't. She had to know what was inside. Probably just another rat, but she needed to know. Especially if she was going to law enforcement.

Maybe she shouldn't open it. She could be messing up evidence.

No, Hallie had handled it and Elise had already touched it. Her prints were already there.

She set down her coffee cup and hovered over the box. It was smaller than the one the rat was in. It'd been lighter too. Much lighter. This one was wrapped in different paper. Brighter. More cheerful. Like a birthday present.

Elise took another sip of her coffee. If it was another dead rat, she didn't want it in her house for another minute. She set down her cup, then carefully lifted the lid from the box and peered inside.

Tissue paper looked to be wrapped around whatever was lying in the box.

Elise's heartbeat quickened. She let out a long, slow exhale, but her pulse still pounded like she'd just run a marathon.

Oh, this was just ridiculous.

She jerked the tissue paper aside to find a doll. A hand-made-type doll. Almost like a Raggedy Ann doll, but without the smile. This one didn't have a mouth. Well, a regular mouth. There was a thin, red line for a mouth, but three big Xs had been sewn over the mouth. The dress the doll wore was tattered and torn. A small piece of paper laid on top of the doll's stomach. It read: *Snitches Get Stitches.*

Elise grabbed her coffee cup and took a step backward. Now she knew she had to tell the FBI. Sure, she'd rather talk to the locals, but this was proof-positive that it was connected to Lilliana's murder and what she'd told the agents.

No better time than the present.

She put the lid back on the box with the horridly evil doll, double-checked the front door to make sure it was locked before she headed to take a quick shower and get dressed. She turned on the news as she brushed her teeth, listening to the morning recaps. According to the weather, it would be a cool April day to enjoy.

Maybe she could take Sawyer to the park this afternoon. Make a picnic late lunch or early dinner.

She'd barely finished brushing her hair when the lights flashed.

Her stomach balled into a knot.

What if it was another box? What if whoever sent the box was going to act?

The lights flashed again and the doorbell chimed.

She reached into the top of her closet and pulled out Judson's 9mm semi-automatic. Elise put her finger on the safety as she headed to the front door. She stood on tiptoe to look out the peephole.

Agents Wright and Rodriguez, looking rather annoyed, stood on the porch.

Elise shoved the gun onto the top shelf, then unlocked and opened the door. "Sorry. I just got out of the shower." As if it wasn't obvious with her wet hair curling against her face. "What can I do for you, agents?"

"We've received some information regarding the senator's case," Agent Wright said. "May we come inside?"

"Why not?" Elise opened the door wider and motioned the two into the house. "I'm getting a cup of coffee. Would either of you like one?" She turned and headed into the kitchen before waiting for an answer.

"Yes, please." Agent Rodriguez followed her into the kitchen.

Agent Wright was on his heels. "You have a very nice home." Her gaze roved over every viewable area.

"Thanks. Judson and I loved it the first time we saw it." She pulled another mug from the cabinet and poured. "How do you take your coffee?" she asked Agent Rodriguez.

"Black." He took the cup she offered him. "Thank you."

Agent Wright was staring at the box on the counter. "A birthday?"

If it didn't apply to the case, Elise would have snapped at the agent. But it did apply. "No." She set her mug on the counter and looked Agent Rodriguez square in the eye. "I do have a question for you two."

"Yes?" Agent Rodriguez set his coffee down and leaned against the counter.

"Who all did you tell about what I'd told you about the guard?"

"Excuse me?" Agent Wright had the audacity to act indignant.

"Who. Did. You. Tell?" Had they not told someone, then she wouldn't be getting dead rats and demonic-looking dolls.

"This is an ongoing investigation, Mrs. Carmichael," started Agent Rodriguez. "We can't provide you with confidential information."

"I don't think you keep much of anything confidential," Elise interrupted. "You see, I only told you two. Not a single other person. I mean, I know you told Mary Ellen Carmichael because she came to see me. But who else did you tell?"

"Why?" Agent Rodriguez asked.

Her hip dug into the edge of the wooden island in the center of the kitchen. "Because I know I only told you two, but you apparently had no qualms telling Mary Ellen and others. I'd like to know who else you told."

"It's none of your business," Agent Wright said.

"Actually, it is." Elise pushed off the island and flipped the top back off the box. She shoved the box to the female agent. "Because you've put me in the crosshairs of someone who wants me to be quiet. I got that this morning."

The agents used a pen to move the tissue paper and read the note.

Elise crossed her arms over her chest. " 'Snitches get stitches.' Pretty clear to me that somebody else knows what I saw."

"Where did you get this?" Agent Rodriguez asked.

"It was left on my front porch this morning. At least it's better than last night's delivery."

"Last night's?" Agent Rodriguez straightened and stared at her. "You received something else last night?"

She nodded. "It was a shoebox, bigger than this one, wrapped in plainer paper. Only there wasn't a doll inside. It was a dead rat."

"Where is it now?" Agent Rodriguez asked.

"In the trash can outside."

"You threw it away?" His eyes widened.

Elise dropped her hands into balls at her side. "I wasn't going to keep a dead rat in my house. Not with my son here."

"Where is your son now, Mrs. Carmichael?" Agent Wright joined the conversation.

"He's at a movie with his sitter. She's the one who found the box and brought it in this morning. Luckily, I was able to keep her and Sawyer from opening it."

"It's evidence in an ongoing investigation. We'll need to take this as well as the other box and rat." Agent Wright pulled out her cell and stepped into the corner.

"Be my guest."

As Agent Wright made a call, Agent Rodriguez studied her. "Why didn't you call us last night when you got the box?"

"I was debating." Elise grabbed her coffee and took a sip. "I didn't want it to be connected to Lilliana's death, but I knew it was. Still, some part of me wanted to just push it away and pretend like it will all go away."

"You know that won't happen, right?" Agent Rodriguez's tone had softened considerably.

"I realized that after I got the doll. I was actually getting ready to call you and tell you about it. Maybe it's from the security guard I identified, warning me to keep my mouth shut."

Agent Wright joined them and spoke to her partner as she put on latex gloves and pulled out a bag. "The lab is waiting for us to bring in the evidence. They'll get right on trying to pull prints or DNA." She put the box with the doll and note in the big bag, then turned to Elise. "I'm assuming as a translator for the court, your fingerprints are on file?"

Elise nodded.

"We might need a DNA sample as well."

Elise nodded again.

"You really should have called us immediately," Agent Wright chastised as she closed the bag with an evidence label and popped off the latex gloves, slipping them into her pocket.

"To be fair, can you blame me for hesitating? I mean, I tell you what I saw and within hours, not only is my sister-in-law in the know and at my door, but someone else knows and is sending me dead rats. To my home! Wouldn't that make you hesitant to offer up anything?"

Before Agent Wright could respond, Agent Rodriguez intervened. "Now, for the reason we came by. . ."

"You mean you didn't come just to check on me?" Elise set her cup on the counter. She knew she sounded bitter, but Agent Wright's attitude really wore on her nerves.

Agent Rodriguez spoke in an even tone. "The security guard you identified yesterday, Marcus Tate."

"Oh, now you're going to give me his name. Why the sudden change of heart? Because now I'm getting threats for telling you what I saw him say on the phone?" Sarcasm was her defense mechanism against the metallic burn searing up the back of her throat.

"We went to question him yesterday afternoon, but he wasn't at work or home. We followed the lead you gave us from what you'd lip-read him say. His financials indicate a large amount of money was wired into his account yesterday morning."

"Proof I wasn't lying." While she felt vindicated in a way, Elise also knew that they wouldn't be telling her this without a reason.

"Yes. A unit was set outside his home to alert our team when he returned. The alert came in about seven thirty last night. Two of our agents were sent to his home to pick him up and bring him in for questioning. They arrived on-site at approximately nine, and found him in his home, shot dead." Agent Wright crossed her arms over her chest.

Just when she thought there might be some answers... "Someone murdered him to cover their trail."

Agent Rodriguez nodded. "That's our working theory."

Elise shook her head. While she was disappointed, of course, she really couldn't see a reason for them to show up to tell her this. "So he couldn't have sent the boxes to me? At least not the one this morning."

"No." Agent Rodriguez shrugged. "We're working the investigation of his cell records and tracing the wired money into his account. We'll find out all the dirty little details."

Elise still failed to see how this meant anything to her. She nodded, waiting for them to get to whatever they wanted with her.

She didn't have to wait but a minute before Agent Wright let her know. "Our tech has been working on the senator's phone. Pulling data, seeing who and what she had been calling and texting."

What did that have to do with her? Elise shrugged.

"Apparently, the last email she sent was to your iPad. Several files were sent, then were deleted off of her phone."

"To me?" Lilliana never sent her anything. She only called to discuss Sawyer. "She never sent me anything."

"It was traced back to your iPad, Mrs. Carmichael." Agent Wright peered at her cell. "Your IP address, the iPad registered in your name with this number." She flipped the phone around so Elise could see.

"Oh, that's Sawyer's iPad." She looked up at the agents. "Why would Lilliana send files to Sawyer then delete them?"

"That's what we'd like to know."

CHAPTER SIX

Agents Rodriguez and Wright stared at her with accusation in their stance.

Elise didn't care. She'd had enough of their attitudes, innuendoes, but mostly their blanket disregard for hers and Sawyer's safety. She leaned against the kitchen island. "Lilliana and Sawyer rarely emailed. They chatted through Messenger mostly. I can't ever recall a time she sent Sawyer any files. Even when she shared photographs, it was through the app and not email."

"Well, we'll still need to take the iPad." Agent Wright wore her smirk like a badge.

"Sorry, you can't."

Agent Wright crossed her arms over her chest. "You know we can get a warrant."

Elise shrugged. "Be that as it may, you can't have it now."

"Fine. Then we'll get a warrant and be back." Agent Wright lifted the evidence bag and turned toward the door.

"Good luck with that." Elise moved into the hallway as well. "That iPad runs Sawyer's text-to-talk program, which I believe, is protected by the Americans with Disabilities Act. I'm sure you should inform the judge of that, because I'm certainly about to call a lawyer and inform them."

"Whoa. Let's just wait a minute." Agent Rodriguez finally joined them in the conversation, as he stepped into the hallway. "We all want the same thing here—to find out who murdered the senator. That's the primary objective."

Elise shook her head. "No, that's *your* primary objective. Mine is keeping my son safe, which you apparently aren't concerned with." The more she thought about it, the madder she got. These agents had shared information with heaven only knew, and now she'd received two tangible threats at her home. Just steps away from the room where her son slept. "You know what, I think you both should leave. I'll hire an attorney and send you his or her contact information as soon as possible so you'll know who to reach out to if you have any more questions for me."

"There's no need for—" Agent Rodriguez held out his hands, palms outward.

"No, there shouldn't be any need, but there is." Elise's steps to the front door punctuated her words. "You've put me and my son in harm's way. I'll be telling the attorney that as well." She gripped the doorknob and opened the door.

"Let's all just calm down for a moment."

She had to give it to Agent Rodriguez—he was doing his level best. But Elise knew her rights and she also wasn't intimidated by badges. "I'm very calm, and since I've invoked my right to have representation, you need to leave."

He and his partner exchanged a look.

Elise held the door open wide. "Now. Please. Thank you."

They could think whatever they want, but they knew she was right. Without another word, both left. She shut the door, locking the deadbolt, then leaned her full weight against the smooth wood. Now she had to find a lawyer, and fast. Not an easy feat on a Saturday, but Elise knew the FBI agents, especially Agent Wright, would move quickly to get that warrant. Thank goodness Sawyer had taken his iPad.

She glanced at her watch. They would still be in the movie. Elise moved quickly to her phone and texted Hallie. PLEASE TAKE SAWYER TO GET SOME LUNCH OR SOMETHING. I HAVE AN IMPORTANT ERRAND

OR TWO TO RUN AND WON'T BE HOME UNTIL THREE OR LATER. That should give her time.

Just as she was about to look up a number, her cell phone rang in her hand. She nearly dropped it before she could answer it.

"Hello, Elise?" Noland's voice sounded as shaky as Elise felt.

"Hi, Noland." She mentally kicked herself for not having called him yet to offer her condolences. "I'm sorry I haven't called. I'm so sorry about Lilliana. It's just horrible."

"That it is. Mary Ellen and I will be making arrangements this afternoon. I just wondered if you'd like to come with us and help? I know you and Lilliana weren't very close, but she loved Sawyer with everything she had and was always so thankful to you for allowing her such constant and easy access to him."

"He doted on her as well and I'm grateful for the relationship they shared, but I think you and Mary Ellen should make the arrangements as you feel best. That's what Lilliana would want. Mary Ellen will let me know when the services are. Sawyer and I will definitely be there." Something she hadn't really thought about until this exact moment: her son going to his first funeral that he'd remember. He hadn't remembered anything about Judson's, which was both a blessing and a curse.

"Of course. I understand that the FBI has been questioning you as well? They've been asking me questions about our marriage, Lilliana's life insurance, and the like. I know they're doing their job, but it sure feels like they want to tie it up all nicely with the husband, but that's just not going to happen. I loved her." His voice cracked.

Elise's heart went out to him. "They've gone about things the wrong way, in my opinion. As a matter of fact, I just kicked them out until I obtain counsel. The FBI agents took something I told them during questioning and let others know. Now I'm getting threats here at the house. I need to protect myself and Sawyer."

"Threats? You two should come stay here at the house. Mary Ellen's staying here as well until everything is concluded."

Elise bit her tongue not to bring up that Lilliana had been murdered in that exact home. "I appreciate that, but everything here is set up for Sawyer's convenience. I don't want to disrupt his life more than it already is."

"I completely understand, Elise."

She let out a little breath. "Let me know if there's anything I can do for you, Noland."

"I will. Mary Ellen will give you all the funeral arrangement information as soon as we conclude everything."

"Thanks, Noland." She disconnected the call, then quickly looked up the number for the attorney she most respected since working in the federal courthouse. Sure enough, there was an emergency contact number. This wasn't necessarily life or death exactly, but Elise called the number anyway. After a brief explanation, she set an appointment to meet with Arabella Morris in a little over an hour.

After she changed clothes and swiped on a little makeup, Elise checked her phone. A text message from Hallie assured her that Sawyer wouldn't be home until about four.

Perfect.

She left home, after being careful to check and make sure all the doors were locked, and headed downtown where most all the law firms were conveniently located in proximity to the courthouses. Since it was the weekend, metered parking was free. Elise parked just a few spaces down from Arabella Morris's office.

Elise hoped Arabella would take her case. The late-thirties lawyer had a reputation for being one of the best. She was short and slim with a bob cut that suited her round face and black as midnight hair. Elise had been in the courtroom with most all of the local attorneys at one time or another, but had always been impressed with Arabella. The woman could be cutthroat, leveling a witness on cross-examination with a single glance, but she was also passionate in fighting for her clients. Elise had never seen her ruffled. Not even once. No matter what a witness said on the stand, Arabella nodded as if it was the answer she'd been expecting.

Arabella Morris defined calm, cool, and collected.

Elise smoothed her pants as she got out of the vintage Dodge Charger and locked the doors. Judson had been so excited to find the old car for sale and snapped it up immediately. He'd lovingly restored "Cha Cha," as he'd named her, back to her original beautiful state. Elise refused to consider getting rid of the old girl now, despite being offered top dollar several times.

A blast of cool air hit Elise as she opened the door to Arabella's law firm. The lights were out in the reception area. "Hello," she called out.

"Back here." Arabella met her at the door to the hallway. "On weekends when we're just working here, we leave the front unmanned." She shook Elise's hand with a firm grip. "Come on back." Without waiting for a reply, she led the way down the hall to an ordinary, no-nonsense conference room.

Papers were strewn over one end of the table. Arabella motioned to the other end. "Have a seat." She took the chair at the end of the table. Elise sat beside her. "So," Arabella began as she pulled a legal pad and pen to her. "What's going on?"

Elise quickly brought Arabella up to speed. The attorney took rapid notes as Elise spoke. When Elise was finished, she looked at what she'd written and tapped her pen on the pad, filling the silence with little *thwatting* noises. "You haven't checked the iPad to see if an email was received from Lilliana?"

Elise shook her head. "It's been a crazy week. Usually, I clean out all the spam mail once a month. We've never used the email really on the iPad. I can't remember the last time we got an email that wasn't trying to sell us something or give us funds from a foreign entity."

Chuckling under her breath, Arabella nodded. "I hear you there."

Thwat. Thwat. Thwat. The pen against the pad of paper again.

"And your son didn't mention seeing an alert or anything?"

Again, Elise shook her head. "I've turned off notifications on most all of the programs except his talk to text and his learning apps, so no, he wouldn't have gotten any type of alert if she sent him an email."

Arabella nodded, but kept her head bent over the legal pad. "They just volunteered the information about Marcus Tate?"

Elise nodded. "Is that unusual?"

"Well, in my experience, FBI agents usually keep things really tight to their chest in their investigations. Especially specifics of how they're proceeding with the investigation—pulling cell records and tracing the money wire."

"Maybe they told me that because I'm the one who mentioned money. Repeating what I saw the guard say on the phone."

Arabella grabbed her pen. "Perhaps. Or maybe they were trying to get more information from you."

"Me? I don't know anything more than what I told them. I was completely honest with them and answered their questions to the best of my ability." Were they going to come after her? Elise knew all too well that many times, innocent people were charged with something they didn't even do.

Arabella smiled. "I'm sure you did. It's just that their actions seem to be quite the contradiction, which concerns me."

Maybe they were just inept? Elise could sure believe that, especially Agent Wright, who seemed to wear the chip on her shoulder like a badge of courage or something. "What does that mean? For my case?"

Thwat. Thwat.

"I'm not really sure. I've never dealt with these two specific agents before. I'll have to call my contact in the bureau and see what I can learn." She stared off into space for a moment before moving her gaze back to Elise. "There was nothing else in the box with the rat or the doll besides the note?"

"Nothing else."

"And they took both of them?"

Elise nodded. "I saw Agent Wright take the one with the doll. I'm assuming she grabbed the rat one out of the trash before they left."

"Hmm."

Thwat. Thwat. Thwat.

"Okay, first things first. There's a chance they'll get a judge on the phone to sign off on the warrant since this is a US senator we're talking about. Yes, ADA laws protect deaf persons, and with your son's recent injury and being further handicapped, I would bet there'd be some parameters so the iPad would be back to him within twenty-four or forty-eight hours."

"So I have to give it to them, just like that?" She would hate to have to hand it over to Agent Wright and her smug little smile.

"If they serve you with a warrant, yes. But when they show up, be it today, tomorrow, or Monday, I want you to call me immediately." She handed Elise a business card. "That has my cell on it. If you get my voice mail, leave me a message and then text me too. I want to see the warrant before you give them anything, even if you have to snap a picture with your cell and message it to me."

"Does this mean you're taking my case?" Elise let the flame of hope flare in her chest.

Arabella chuckled and shook her head. "That was a given from the time I spoke with you on the phone. I don't just meet with people on a Saturday for giggles. I know you from the courthouse. I've always been impressed with your professionalism." She shrugged. "Besides, I was in the JAG Corps and I knew of your husband. Sometimes, things just feel right and I decide to take a case before I even know all the details."

Elise smiled, lighter as if some of the weight that she'd been bearing had slipped off her shoulders. "Okay. So, if I check the iPad tonight and see the email from Lilliana, I shouldn't delete it or anything?"

Arabella shook her head. "No way. They'd charge you with interfering in a federal investigation. You get the warrant, you call me. Once I see the warrant, that'll determine what they're working on, and maybe by then I'll have some info from my contact at the bureau on these agents." She glanced at her watch. "My contact is probably working today and I might be able to get a jump on them before they get a warrant. I'll also try to get a heads-up from a clerk friend of mine of which judge they're hounding for the warrant. Might be useful information."

"Okay. Call you when they show up. Got it." At least there was a plan now. Elise felt more proactive than reactive.

"I would suggest something else."

"What?"

"A digital camera over your front door that is motion activated."

Elise sat up straight in the wooden chair. That feeling of taking charge was a false sense of security. "You think I need that?"

Arabella nodded. "If it were me—a single mom and my son, I'd consider getting a full security system with that camera. And not just because of this case. In today's world, there's no telling what can and does happen. We have mass shootings by people with agendas, an opioid epidemic going on, and who knows what else. We have to keep ourselves and our families safe."

"True." Elise hadn't considered a security system before. When Judson was still alive, there was no need, but Arabella was right. The world had gone crazy lately, from politics to prejudices—real and perceived. Now, with the rat and doll. . . Why, she'd just pulled out Judson's gun today. She should have considered an added layer of protection before now. She would definitely check into a security system on Monday.

But first, she had a very specific question. "About the email Lilliana supposedly sent. . ."

"Yes?"

Elise worried the edge of Arabella's business card with her thumbnail. "Say when Sawyer comes home this afternoon and there's no warrant served yet, can I check and see if an email from Lilliana was received on his iPad?"

Arabella winked as she smiled. "That electronic device is yours.

You can look at anything in there that you wish until you are legally notified you can't." She smiled wider. "You can even forward things to yourself or download them. Save them to review as you'd like even."

Elise knew she'd admired Arabella before, now she really liked her. "Because that would be within my legal rights, correct?"

"Yes. Until you are legally notified otherwise, that iPad and all the information on it is your property. Since you have been made aware of the importance of some possible data, I would strongly urge you not to delete anything." She stood. "Other than that, you are within your rights to share and copy as you see fit. Unless and until you are told otherwise by a legal decree of some sort."

Standing as well, Elise shook Arabella's hand. "Thank you for everything. I guess I should call and tell the FBI that you are my attorney of record now?"

Arabella shook her head. "Not needed. I'll call and get it on the record."

Elise slowly exhaled. "Thanks so much. It really helps just to know I'm not standing alone against the FBI." She never thought she'd be on this end of an investigation.

Arabella led her toward the door. "I know this is all almost over-bearing, especially for a single mom who's had a lot thrown at you recently. I get it, but let's just take things one step at a time, okay?"

"I will. I'll call as soon as they show up with the warrant."

Elise walked into the sunshine. A gentle breeze whisked around the corner of the building, almost like a kiss on her cheek. She would check the iPad as Hallie brought Sawyer home and if Lilliana had sent something, she would download and back it up.

Whatever it could be.

CHAPTER SEVEN

Grocery shopping wasn't for the faint of heart.

Elise had planned a quick stop to get bread, milk, and eggs, but in the middle of the store, she realized she had no idea of what she had in her fridge or freezer at the moment. So she had to expand her shopping to meats, vegetables, and fruits. Her plan of fifteen minutes in and out had been extended into nearly an hour.

Sometimes, adulting was a royal pain, like a dull headache with its constant pounding.

She pulled up in her driveway, easing around Hallie's car and into the garage. She pushed the button to close the garage and checked her watch—4:11. Wow, the time had really flown by today. She grabbed an armful of all the plastic bags and headed to the door to the kitchen, juggling her load to open the door. "Hello?" she called out.

Hallie rushed to help her. "Are there more bags I can help you with?"

"No, this is it. Sorry I'm late."

"No big deal. We haven't been here long. Sawyer's putting his new action figure from the movie in his case in his room. I figured your appointment ran long. Must have been important since you didn't lock the front door." She set the bags she'd taken from Elise on the counter. "Now I understand what held you up. Grocery stores are awful on the weekend."

Elise nodded, but her mind replayed Hallie's words. "I locked the front door. It was unlocked when you got here?" Her heartbeat picked up its pace.

"Yeah, but you probably just thought you locked it but didn't. I've done that so many times." Hallie pulled the refrigerated items out and put them in the fridge. "No big deal."

Only it was, and Elise was sure she'd locked the door. Hadn't she? Surely she had, with everything going on. But as she replayed her actions before she left, she wasn't exactly one hundred percent positive she'd really locked the door.

She absentmindedly put away the rest of the groceries, her mind going over her exit again and again. Each time, she remembered locking the door, but had she really? Sure, she was on alert now because of Arabella's security system suggestion, but had she been diligent before? Had she locked the door?

Hallie was right, it really didn't matter. Apparently no one had broken in or anything since they were all inside and okay. Yet, she couldn't take any chances, and she had to be honest. "Hallie, I need to tell you something that might make you not want to come and watch Sawyer for a bit."

Elise quickly filled her sitter and friend in on what had been going on. "I'm going to call Monday about getting an alarm system and camera installed, but I wanted to let you know so you could decide what to do. And please know that I will totally understand if you need to not come here until this mess is all settled. No hard feelings on my end at all."

Hallie shook her head. "Sawyer is like family to me. You too Elise. Dead rats and dolls don't scare me. I'm here for the long haul—good and bad, for as long as you let me."

Elise hugged her, blinking back the tears. This young woman was such a dear, and her dedication to Sawyer made Elise love her all the more. "Thank you," she whispered before she pulled back.

"Of course." She tilted her head to the side as she often did when making a decision. "We had only just gotten here like five or so minutes before you got here. Maybe we should check the house, just to be safe."

"Good idea." Elise opened the pantry door and peered inside. Nothing.

Hallie peeked into the laundry room. "Clear."

Elise grinned. Hallie was a cop show addict. It was amusing to hear her using their lingo. She shook her head and moved to the living room closet. Nothing inside.

Stepping out of the guest bathroom, Hallie shook her head.

The guest bedroom as well as its closet were all clear. Elise was starting to feel a bit silly. Despite what she thought, she probably just hadn't locked the door in her rush to get to her appointment with Arabella. She plastered what she hoped was a cheerful smile on her face as she opened the door to Sawyer's room.

He sat on the very edge of the foot of his bed, his ramrod-straight back to the door.

Elise took a few steps forward to touch his shoulder. "Hey, Saw—" She froze as she spied the snake coiled on the bed, a mere three feet away from her son.

Sawyer glanced at her, then back at the snake, as if mesmerized. She took a slow step toward her son. The snake coiled itself tighter, lifting its menacing head onto its body.

Oh, merciful Jesus.

The blood in her veins turned icy. She forced her breathing to slow as she calculated the distance between Sawyer and the snake. Without thinking more, Elise reached out and grabbed her son, spinning to put her back to the snake as she flung Sawyer into Hallie's arms as she'd just entered the room.

A quick glance over her shoulder to be sure the snake was still on the bed, and Elise shoved Hallie and Sawyer out of the room, shutting the door behind them.

"What was that?" Hallie said and signed.

"Are you okay?" Elise knelt before her son and signed with shaky hands. "Did it bite you? Are you all right?"

He nodded, but his face was so pale.

"Are you sure you weren't bitten?"

Sawyer signed that he wasn't.

Elise pulled him into her arms and stood, carrying him down the hall on weak legs, Hallie on her heels. Her heart raced, but she forced herself not to have a mental breakdown before sitting on the couch in the living room, cradling Sawyer in her arms. If anything ever happened to him. . .

"I'm going to call someone to come get that. . .well, to come remove it and make sure there aren't any others." Hallie pulled her cell from her pocket. "I can't imagine how he got in here. I mean, I know spring brings them out, but man." She got up and went into the kitchen to make the call.

Elise could only taste the metallic tinge on her tongue. She held on to Sawyer and kept kissing his head.

He allowed it for a few more minutes, then wiggled out of her lap, clumsily making the sign for "all right."

She ruffled his hair and smiled. "That scared me." Her breathing slowed back into a regular rhythm.

He pointed to himself and nodded.

"I bet." Lord, but she was thankful he hadn't been bitten. Thankful too that she'd gone to check on him when she did. The snake would have eventually moved and then. . .well, she didn't want to consider what could have happened. She shivered.

"They're sending someone right over, they said. They asked what kind of snake it was and I told them all I knew was *alive*."

"I have no idea what kind it is either. Didn't stay to check."

Hallie chuckled. "Me either. Anyway, they said someone will be here real soon since no one was out on a call."

"Thank you." Elise let out another slow breath.

"That was some quick moving in there, Elise."

"Pure instinct."

Sawyer lifted the remote and curled up on the couch as some cartoon filled the television. He tugged the throw from the back of the couch and snuggled down.

Elise chuckled as relief washed over her. "Good thing kids are so resilient."

"Let's go get some iced tea. I know I could use something to drink." Hallie led the way into the kitchen.

Elise kissed Sawyer's head again, signed they'd just be in the kitchen, then followed Hallie. "I certainly need something to wash this coppery taste out of my mouth for sure."

"Funny how fear has a metal taste, isn't it?" Hallie pulled out two glasses from the cabinet. "I never really thought about it, but fear and blood both taste metallic-y."

Elise grabbed the pitcher of tea from the fridge and began to pour. "Must be some strange chemical reaction the body has to the rush of adrenaline." It didn't matter. She didn't like the feeling or the experiences that caused it.

"Must be."

They drank in silence for several minutes. Elise couldn't get past her fear of something happening to Sawyer. Sure, every mother worried over her child's safety, but Elise felt she fretted even more. Not because he was deaf, although that did bring its own set of challenges, but because of having lost Judson as she had. Her heart had nearly ripped apart when the military men had showed up at her door. It was needing to be there, and be strong for Sawyer that kept her going. Gave her a purpose, a reason to get up every morning. Without her son, Elise honestly didn't know how she would have forced herself to go on.

The doorbell rang and lights flashed.

Elise shot to her feet, then let out another calming breath. "Wow, that was quick." She opened the door and shook hands with the wildlife retrieval man who introduced himself as Muldoon, and his partner beside him as Roger.

"Kinda early for snakes to be making appearances in homes, but with the hit of warmer weather we've had last week, guess it's possible."

Muldoon said as he followed Elise down the hall to Sawyer's room.

"Do you have a basement? That's usually how they get in," Roger explained.

"No, no basement." Which brought up the question, how, exactly, did the snake get in the house? Specifically, in Sawyer's room.

"You said on the phone you didn't know what kind of snake it was?" Elise nodded. "I'm sorry, no."

"Not to worry, we'll figure it out." Muldoon nodded at the closed door. "In here?" He took the pole-looking thing from Roger.

She nodded and shivered.

"Don't worry, ma'am, Muldoon's the best. He'll get it and we'll check the house to make sure it didn't bring any family or friends with it." Roger grinned, then opened the door to Sawyer's room. He and Muldoon disappeared inside.

Elise turned to find Sawyer and Hallie in the hall behind her. Sawyer's eyes were big with awe. "No, sir," she signed and said. "You are not going any closer." Yep, kids were not only resilient, but also bordered on insane.

Disappointment crossed his face.

"I mean it, Sawyer. Snakes are poisonous." She led them back to the living room. "You stay here and watch your cartoons."

He pouted, but she shook her head and went to the kitchen and retrieved her tea. The cool liquid was refreshing, and the hint of mint killed out all the copper taste. Just what she needed.

In minutes, Muldoon and Roger came out of Sawyer's room. Muldoon carried what looked like a burlap bag. "We got him, ma'am. I'll put him away in our truck while Roger does a walk-through, okay?"

"Of course." Just seeing the bag with the bulge inside, knowing that it was the snake that had been so close to her baby...she shivered.

Twenty minutes later, both men returned to the kitchen. "The house is all clear, ma'am. No sign of any other snakes or anything else, for that matter," Roger said.

Elise reached for her purse and pulled out her checkbook. Whatever price they quoted her, it was well worth it just for her peace of mind. "Thank you. How much do I owe you?"

Roger handed her an invoice, and she wrote the check. She handed it to him, smiling. "Again, thank you so much. And your promptness is greatly appreciated."

"Ma'am, that's something else. Our promptness."

"What?" She put her checkbook back into her purse and pushed it on the counter.

"We were able to come fast because there's not a big issue with snakes out right now. Actually, there's no issue."

Elise rubbed her upper arms. "What does that mean?"

"Well, that was a copperhead. They're common in the area, so that's not a big deal, but this early in the season?"

Apprehension squeezed her chest. "What?"

Muldoon shrugged. "Copperheads usually aren't out and active this early in the year. When we get calls this early in the season, it's usually someone's pet snake that got out."

"I assure you, we have no pet snakes."

Muldoon chuckled. "I don't know many people who would have a copperhead as a pet, even if they liked snakes."

"Then. . ." The hairs on the back of her neck drew to attention.

Roger handed her a receipt. "We looked all over and can find no point of entry. None of the usual ones, so to speak."

"What are you saying?" She could hear her pulse in her ears.

"Is it possible, even remotely, that someone brought that snake in here? Because we can't find any other way for him to have gotten in here."

"And he's a bit sluggish," Muldoon added. "He was easy to catch because he was slow. That usually indicates he wasn't already active on his own."

Heat crept up Elise's spine. "It is possible that someone could've put the snake in here. I'll look into it." Elise stood and led them to the front door, lucky her knees didn't wobble. "Thank you again." She shut the door behind them, making sure to lock the knob and turn the deadbolt.

Elise couldn't think. Her head throbbed. This wasn't a dead rat or a doll left on her front porch. This was a deadly snake *in* her house. In *Sawyer's* bed.

The threats had just escalated.

CHAPTER EIGHT

"My question is, should I call the FBI and tell them? I've lived here over seven years and never had a snake so much as in my yard before. Even the exterminator or whatever said it was more likely someone brought it in." Elise paced the confines of the kitchen as she spoke on the phone.

"Well, legally speaking, there's no evidence that your house was broken into. If you left the door unlocked, that's not breaking and entering. Nothing is missing, so there wasn't a theft. There was no note or warning, so no confirmed threat by a person." Arabella's voice had a calming effect. "You can't prove anything, so I'm afraid by contacting the agents, you might escalate their getting a warrant. I called my contact at the bureau and you're right, Agent Rodriguez is a good one, but Agent Wright is newer and trying to make a name for herself. They are going to try and get a warrant, so I listed myself as attorney of record. That doesn't mean they'll notify me before serving you with a warrant, but at least they know you have legal representation."

Oh, man. With the snake, she'd forgotten about checking the iPad. She'd do that as soon as she got off the phone. "So, I just do nothing?" The image of that snake coiled up to Sawyer made her blood run cold.

"Get a security system. Today. That's my strongest piece of advice. The local hardware store has the self-monitoring ones that you can set up yourself. At least you'd have known if someone opened your door. You'd have an event log. And a camera for the front door."

"Okay. I'll go to the store. Thanks, Arabella. Sorry to have disturbed you."

"No problem. That's what I'm here for."

Elise checked on Sawyer watching television in the living room, same place he'd settled again after Hallie left. She headed down the hall to his room, stopping outside his bedroom door. She just couldn't shake the image of the snake.

Well, she couldn't just avoid his room forever. She let out a huff and opened the door. Nothing. No snake. No movement. Nothing. She didn't know whether to be relieved or more suspicious.

First things first. She grabbed up his bedding—sheets, comforter, pillows—and carried them to the laundry room. No way could Sawyer sleep on those things after a snake had been lying in wait for him. She shoved in half the load into the washer, adding extra detergent, before she headed back to his room.

Her heart hiccupped a little as she reentered, but it wasn't as bad as before. She glanced to his desk and found his iPad charging, as usual. She glanced over her shoulder, not really knowing why, before she put in the password and opened the tablet. She clicked on the mail icon. Sure enough, there was an email from Lilliana.

Elise's mouth went dry. This was the last communication from Lilliana before she was murdered. And she'd sent it to Sawyer.

Again, Elise looked over her shoulder as butterflies swarmed her stomach.

She opened the email, and her confusion grew. There was no message, just a couple of files attached. Remembering what Arabella had said, Elise forwarded the entire email to herself, waited to make sure it'd been sent, then deleted the record of the forward. The FBI could probably determine she'd forwarded it to herself, but it wouldn't be immediately obvious. It didn't matter anyway—her lawyer said she was within her legal right to do what she wanted.

After plugging the iPad back in to continue charging, Elise went into the living room. "Hey, we need to run to the hardware store. Put your shoes on, please," she signed.

"Can we pick up pizza for dinner?" Sawyer's signing was rough because of his cast, but it was clear enough that Elise could understand after a moment.

Or maybe she just knew her son's unquenchable appetite of late. She grinned. "Depends on how good you are."

He actually rolled his eyes as he went to get his sneakers.

Elise balled her hands at her side, resisting the urge to hold him tight and never let him go. He was growing up so very fast. Soon, he'd be in middle school, then high school, then a blink later, he'd be off to college. Just the thought sent jabs into her heart.

Sawyer returned with his iPad, and she blinked away the emotional tears threatening to leak. She made sure she locked and turned the deadbolt before getting settled in the car and heading to Home Depot.

While Sawyer played a game on his iPad, Elise spoke with a store employee about the pros and cons of each of the security systems they carried. It took a while to make a decision, but ultimately, she chose the SkyLink because of its ease of setup and monitoring. She bought the base system, then added in two external cameras that were activated by motion, two additional motion sensors, and two additional interior cameras. The clerk had assured her that setup was a snap. He was also kind enough to alert her to buy the large packs of batteries in both triple-A and double-A size.

Loaded with boxes and confidence, Elise and Sawyer picked up pizza, then headed toward home. Elise felt like she was finally taking charge of the situation. Hiring Arabella had been the first step, now she was being proactive about protecting her son and herself.

Her cell phone rang. Elise glanced at the caller ID, then answered the call, putting it on speaker. "Hey, Mary Ellen."

"Where are you and Sawyer? I dropped by the house, but you obviously aren't here."

"We're on our way home. Stay there. We have plenty of pizza and should be there in less than five minutes."

"Okay."

Elise signed to Sawyer. "Mary Ellen is at the house. She's going to have pizza with us."

"Yes!" But he didn't really need to sign—the smile on his face said he was more than happy to see his aunt again.

Minutes later, Elise turned into the driveway and opened the garage. Mary Ellen followed them inside. "Didn't mean to question you, I was just worried when you weren't here."

"Don't be silly. You can help carry in." Elise passed the pizza box to Sawyer, then loaded her and Mary Ellen's arms.

"Um, what's all this?" Mary Ellen followed Elise into the house after Elise shut the garage door.

Elise quickly explained what had transpired since they'd last talked as she unloaded the boxes onto the kitchen counter. "Arabella was right—I need a security system. Should have installed one after Judson died."

"Wow. And you can't report the snake incident?" Mary Ellen helped Sawyer put a slice of pizza on his plate.

Elise grabbed glasses from the cabinet, then the iced tea from the fridge. She didn't sign and made sure her back was to Sawyer. "Arabella's right about that too. I have no proof anyone entered the house illegally, with or without the snake. But once we get the cameras hooked up, we'll be able to stop someone in their tracks if they try to enter. And if they want to leave a nasty little present on the porch, we'll have them on video." She turned and slid a glass to Sawyer, smiling as her son didn't wait to sit at the island before he took a huge bite.

"So you're going to set it up tonight?" Mary Ellen took a glass from Elise.

"As soon as we're finished eating." She took a bite of the slice of pizza Mary Ellen had put on her plate, not a bit ashamed of how wonderful it tasted.

"Want some help?"

"I'd love it." Elise swallowed.

"Funny that the FBI hasn't contacted me or Noland about the security guard being found dead."

"Yeah. I would think they would've told you." Then again, nothing they did seemed textbook FBI policy in Elise's opinion.

"I mean, I'm Mom's daughter and Noland is her husband."

"Did they tell you about the files Lilliana sent Sawyer?" Elise took another bite of her pizza.

"No. What files?" Mary Ellen set down her water bottle.

Elise explained.

"So what are the files?"

"I don't know yet. I haven't looked. I'm waiting until Sawyer isn't around to check."

Mary Ellen nodded. "But if there's a clue about who killed Mom..."

"I know." Elise nodded. "I'll check them soon. If there's anything obvious on there about her murder, I'll let Arabella know and we'll go from there."

Mary Ellen shook her head. "I just can't imagine what Mom would have sent."

Elise nodded. "Once I have a chance to look at them, I can let you know what they are." She couldn't explain it to Mary Ellen, but she didn't want to look at the files with her sister-in-law, just on the off-chance that they might have something to do with Judson. Not that that made any sense, but Elise couldn't think of anything else Lilliana would have sent to Sawyer's iPad.

Mary Ellen finished her last bite of pizza. "I'm a little surprised the FBI didn't tell me or Noland about the files. They seem to thrive on stirring the pot."

"Oh, I hear you. There's a lot that I think they've handled wrong. When all is said and done, I plan to file a formal complaint on the manner in which they handled this case."

"Me too." Mary Ellen swiped a paper napkin across her mouth

and took a long pull from her water bottle.

Changing the subject, but not really, Elise asked, "So, how did the arrangements go?"

The early crow's feet at the corners of Mary Ellen's eyes drooped. "It was long. There are so many rituals expected of a sitting US senator, with her involvement in so many various groups, organizations, and committees." She shook her head. "Poor Noland. He wanted to incorporate all of Mom's wishes and those of her groups and stuff, but if we included everything each entity wanted, the funeral would last hours upon hours."

"I'm sorry." Elise remembered how Lilliana had helped coordinate the military honors for Judson's funeral. It had been quite the undertaking.

"It's okay. At least it's done. Funeral will be Tuesday at noon."

"Why don't you let me and Sawyer order the casket spray? It would mean a lot to us."

"Really?"

Elise nodded. "She helped me so much with Judson's funeral. Sawyer adored her and she doted on him."

"He misses her." Mary Ellen took a bite of pizza.

"He does. After the funeral, it'll get worse because the day-to-day living without a loved one is the hardest." She smiled at her sister-in-law. "But you know that."

Mary Ellen reached out and squeezed her hand. "I do." She took her last bite of pizza.

"Her favorite flowers were carnations, right?"

"How'd you remember that?" Mary Ellen smiled.

"I remember Judson telling me, explaining that Lilliana thought the extravagance of roses was only because of public perception. She told him that carnations lasted longer, smelled just as sweet, and were a fraction of the cost of the roses he sent me." Elise grinned at the memory.

Mary Ellen chuckled. "That sounds like Mom. She liked getting the biggest bang for her buck, that's for sure."

"I'll make sure the casket spray is all carnations."

"Thank you, Elise."

"Of course." Elise took their plates and glasses to the sink and rinsed them. Mary Ellen took them from her and put them in the dishwasher.

After Elise wiped the counter, she dried her hands. "Let's get started setting this baby up." She moved to the box with the base system.

The Home Depot worker had been honest in his assessment—the SkyLink system was quick and easy to set up, using only a few tools and several batteries. Elise stood and watched the various cameras on her iPhone. "This is really cool."

Mary Ellen looked over her shoulder. "You can see every point of entry with all the cameras."

Elise nodded. "And the alarm will sound and I'll get a notification on my phone if any of those windows or doors are opened. Even the sensor on the garage door is monitored."

"That should give you peace of mind." Mary Ellen smiled at her.

Elise took a moment to evaluate herself. "It does."

"Good." Mary Ellen grabbed her car keys from the kitchen counter. "Well, I need to get back to Mom's—I mean, Noland's. I don't want to keep him up too late and although he won't admit it, he won't go to sleep until I'm home."

Elise gave her sister-in-law a hug. "Thanks for everything, Mary Ellen."

Mary Ellen squeezed her back. "No problem." She took a step back. "How about you go to church with us in the morning? It'd mean a lot to Noland for us all to be there."

A big lump crawled up Elise's throat and stuck there. She didn't want to go to Lilliana's church. She didn't even want to go to her and Sawyer's church. It'd been hit and miss for years, ever since Judson died. She felt like a hypocrite going—she believed in God and Jesus and all of the Good News Gospel, but she was still so angry. She'd lost so much, but more than that, her precious son had lost his father, never had hearing, had to struggle. . .and now, his grandmother.

"Please. I'd like you and Sawyer to be there." Mary Ellen rarely asked for something more than once.

"Okay. Services still start at eight thirty?"

Mary Ellen nodded and gave her another quick hug. "Yes, and thank you. It means a lot." She let Elise go. "I'll see you in the morning." She went into the living room where Sawyer was back in front of the television and gave him a hug and signed that she would see him tomorrow morning at church.

Sawyer glanced up at his mom, who nodded. He grinned at his aunt and gave her another hug.

At least she'd made the right decision this time.

After seeing Mary Ellen out, Elise sent Sawyer to take his bath. She took all the boxes to the garage and put them in the recycling container. Back inside, she set the new alarm system. A sense of security that she hadn't felt since Judson died settled over her. She'd sleep soundly tonight.

Remembering she'd stripped Sawyer's bed, Elise quickly made it with fresh sheets and comforter, finishing just as Sawyer came barreling in and jumped on his bed. They did their nighttime snuggling, he closed his eyes to pray, then a final kiss before Elise turned out his light and cracked his door.

It'd been a long day. Elise took a quick shower and got ready for bed. As she crawled under the covers, she spied her laptop on Judson's bedside table, blinking green with its full charge.

She set her pillows against the wooden headboard and pulled the computer on her lap. She accessed her email and found the forward from Sawyer's iPad. She clicked to open the first attachment.

A photo of a woman holding a baby loaded. The woman looked to be barely eighteen. The baby wasn't yet a year old. No note on the photo. Nothing. But by the clarity of the photo and the clothing and hairstyle of the woman, the photo couldn't have been taken more than a few years ago.

Elise closed the picture and clicked on the second attachment.

A lab result loaded. Elise stared, trying to figure it out. The best she could determine, it was a DNA test, dated a couple of years ago. Linked to a crime, maybe? Had Lilliana gotten this DNA evidence linking a specific person to a crime and they killed her for it?

If so, why on earth would she send it to her grandson?

CHAPTER NINE

The seemingly constant breeze pushed the clouds across the sky like striped balls on a pool table. The sun peeked in and out from behind them, shining down on the high steeple of the church sitting front and center in west Little Rock. This was the church Lilliana had taken Judson and Mary Ellen to when they were little. The church where she'd married Noland. The church where Judson and Elise had also said their vows and where Sawyer had been christened.

Elise's mixed emotions about attending services tangled even more as she pulled into the parking lot. There were news vans parked under the few shaded areas, crews with cameras outside. Waiting. Like vultures. Anxiety clawed about in the pit of her stomach as she glanced at her son in the back seat. He was playing on his handheld Nintendo, oblivious they'd even arrived.

Elise drove farther down the parking lot, grateful that she hadn't piqued the interest of the news crews. Yet.

Of course they were here to encroach on Lilliana's family during their grieving process. No doubt that the murder of a US senator was news. Elise knew they were only trying to do their job, but to be at the family's church just two days after her murder? Well, that was just trying to pull on people's emotions and get better ratings. Elise didn't like it. She never had, but now Sawyer, as Lilliana's only grandchild, would be a target for those reporters.

Her cell vibrated in the console. Elise snatched it up. "Hey, Mary Ellen."

"Hey. I just saw you drive past. Isn't this place a circus?"

Surely Mary Ellen realized why it was a circus. "Yeah, but not my monkeys."

"Go around to the side of the building, by the nursery. Nobody's out there. Park there and come in through the children's wing so you won't be stopped."

"Will do. On my way." She turned the corner and found a parking place, then got Sawyer's attention. "Do you want to go into big church or children's?"

He crinkled his nose and tilted his head for a moment, the made a one-handed attempt at signing, "Children's."

She smiled and nodded. "Leave your Nintendo in the car, but don't forget your iPad," she signed. He did as instructed without argument—a real rarity these days, then followed her out of the car. She grabbed his hand as they shut the doors. She made sure to lock it via the remote fob before heading toward the double glass doors. Maybe this would keep him out of all the reporters' line of vision. Hey, this could work, getting him in and out without interference.

Mary Ellen waited for them just inside the doors. She hugged Sawyer first, then Elise. "Thank you for coming," she both said and signed.

"Sawyer's going to go to children's church this morning." Elise too signed as she spoke.

He tucked his little iPad under his arm and led the way down the hall to the area reserved for children his age. Elise was a little surprised he remembered. It'd been a while since she'd brought him. Well, Lilliana had taken him off and on for the past handful of months.

"Thanks for coming." Mary Ellen looped her arm through Elise's. "I didn't realize it was going to be such a madhouse. At least Pastor won't let the news crews inside. He said he felt strange turning anyone away from God's house, but knew they were only here to watch us. I know he would normally let them in, just to give every opportunity for someone to hear the Good News, but he's being very considerate for our sakes."

"Funny how everyone wants separation of church and state until they can use it to benefit themselves. Then you see everyone camped out in churches' parking lots. Anything to get a good story."

"Yeah. We've even seen some of Mom's colleagues here today, who Noland says aren't members of this church. It's kind of nice for them to be here as a show of solidarity."

"Or be seen here to gain approval in the voting public's eye."

Mary Ellen stopped Elise and faced her. "Are you really that cynical?"

"I'm sorry. I'm in a foul mood. Ever since I saw the news vans and knew they were trying to prey on the family's grief. . .well, it just makes me angry."

Mary Ellen smiled. "I know. I feel like that a lot too. But Mom played the same game so well herself, I guess it doesn't bother me quite as much."

They fell back into step as they reached the room where Sawyer's age group of kids met. Elise signed him in, making sure to put in bold that he was deaf, and took the verification card from the worker. She was going to give him a hug and tell him goodbye, but he was already playing with two other boys. Elise smiled, thankful yet again for the resilience of children. His talk to text program also broke a lot of ice with kids too.

She and Mary Ellen headed to the main sanctuary, quickly found Noland near the front, and slid in beside him. Elise squeezed his hand. "How're you doing?"

"I'm okay. Really. Now that the arrangements are made, I can breathe a little easier. I think once the service is over and the news has a newer topic to report on, I'll be able to start tackling my emotions."

Elise smiled. "I'm here for you, Noland. Through it all."

"You and Mary Ellen have been very good to me. I love you girls as if you were my own."

She gave him a sideways hug just as the pastor made his way to the pulpit.

"Welcome, everyone. Looks like we have a full house today."

People shifted in their seats, checking out everyone around them. Elise did the same. She didn't know what was usual, but this morning there were very few empty spaces in the pews. Death made funny bed partners, it seemed.

And there Elise saw them—Agent Wright and Agent Rodriguez, sitting several rows back, on the end of the pew closest to the west wall, not the aisle. Were they here to speak to her or Mary Ellen or Noland? Someone else? Here for security? They didn't seem the type.

Yep, death surely made funny bed partners.

The pastor continued, his voice booming against the rafters of the high, wooden ceiling. "It saddens me that we have lost Lilliana York. She was a special person and a longtime member of this church, but I'll save my words for her service. However, I'm proud to see so many here today in a show of support, respect, and love for Lilliana's family as they seek solace here in the midst of their grief. Let us all bow our heads to offer up a prayer for this family."

Although she wouldn't want to admit it and doing so made her feel guilty, Elise tuned out the pastor's prayer as she sat on the cushioned wooden pew. All last night, despite feeling safer because of the security system, details from the numerous trials she'd translated for flitted across her mind.

The FBI didn't have a motive for her murder yet. It was obvious the security guard, Marcus Tate, had been working for someone to kill Lilliana. Did the FBI even know who that person was? Was that why Agents Wright and Rodriguez were here? Could the murderer be here, in this very room?

It was no secret that murderers often returned to the scene of the crime, drawn there to see how others reacted to their handiwork. Coming to the victim's family church to get an up close and personal view of their grief would probably be even better.

The pastor concluded his prayer and instructed the congregation to stand. The worship leader led the first lyrics of "Amazing Grace."

Elise looked over her shoulder and spied the agents. Neither were singing, but both were looking around, as if inventorying everyone in attendance. Agent Rodriguez's glance locked with Elise's. He gave her a shaky smile. She turned back to the front and sang the chorus with everyone else. "...I once was lost, but now am found. T'was blind but now I see."

Noland shook beside her. Elise noticed the tears trailing down his cheeks. She put her arm around him and hugged. She felt the stares on them. Some of the people behind him put hands on his shoulders. He ducked his head and sobbed. Elise didn't know if the others' touch, or even hers, was comforting to him. Either way, she felt like maybe he shouldn't have come today. No one should have their fresh and raw grief on such a public display.

He reached up and patted each hand on him, as well as Elise. Maybe it was comforting to him. Maybe, in his experience, his church family gave him comfort during such a trying time. When Judson had died, all Elise wanted to do was cuddle Sawyer in bed alone. She certainly didn't want her raw emotions on stage for everyone to see. But, maybe Noland was different. Everyone did grieve in their own way, none more right or wrong than any other.

Grief was grief, no matter how you dealt with it. The pain was gut-wrenching. If these people gave Noland comfort, she would sit right here with him and let these people in, no matter how uncomfortable it made her.

The pastor started his sermon on Psalm 94:14: "For the Lord will not forsake his people; he will not abandon his heritage."

Elise tuned out the pastor's voice and words. *The Lord will not forsake his people.* Really? Elise sure felt like God had forsaken people sometimes. Yes, she knew people had to die here on earth. She got it. And she understood that not all deaths, as a matter of fact the majority of deaths, weren't peaceful in the passing. She got that. She accepted death as a part of life, even when Judson died. Her parents died. Even now, when Lilliana was dead. She accepted the violent path to death, understanding people died in military duty. . .in car accidents. . .and even in violent crimes. And yes, while painful, the families who loved those who died would grieve—adults and children alike. It wasn't pleasant, but most everyone would experience grief at some time in their life.

No, what she couldn't understand and what made the whole *"the Lord will not forsake his people"* bit hard for Elise to swallow was how wasn't Sawyer forsaken when he was born deaf? He was an innocent child, having done not a single thing wrong, not able to even comprehend what sin was at his birth, yet sound had been stolen from him before his first breath. How wasn't that being forsaken?

Suddenly the congregation stood, ripping Elise from her thoughts. She stood alongside Noland and Mary Ellen and sang the closing hymn. She glanced over her shoulder to find both the agents had already left. In a strange way, she understood. If she had been able to leave, she would've, but she couldn't leave Noland and Mary Ellen.

The church service concluded and soon everyone was standing. So many people came by to hug them, people Elise had never seen before in her life. As uncomfortable as it made her, it seemed to make Noland smile, so she endured as much as she could before she whispered to Mary Ellen, "I'm going to go get Sawyer."

"Oh, don't bother. They now bring the little ones to the narthex to meet their parents."

Great. He'd be right here where everyone could see him. Every instinct in Elise told her to run. She started weaving her way through the people to get out of the sanctuary. If she caught him soon enough, she could walk him back to the children's wing and they could exit out the door they'd entered. If she moved quickly enough.

Mary Ellen grabbed her arm. "Hey, I said they bring them here."

"I'll meet him and then we can go out the doors we came in." Elise swallowed the panic from her voice as she tugged away her arm.

Mary Ellen didn't release her. "Elise, it's okay. They bring them here and match them to the card they gave you. They lock off the children's wing after service, so you couldn't go out that way anyway. It's a safety feature. I'm parked right out front and will drive you to your car. Just slow down. We need to wait on Noland. He rode with me."

There'd be no way to keep Sawyer out of sight. So far, the news hadn't contacted them, which suited Elise just fine. But if they saw him at church. . .well, all bets were off.

She broke free from Mary Ellen when she spied her son with the other kids. She rushed to him, putting on a smile so as to not alarm him in any way. "Did you have fun?" She signed only.

He grinned back and nodded, waving his Bible coloring sheet.

Mary Ellen and Noland came up behind them. Sawyer hugged them both, very tight and longer than usual. He'd always been a sensitive child; he probably knew they needed the extra contact today.

Noland led them out of the building. Sure enough, the news reporters and camera crew were on the edge of the church grounds, microphones at the ready. But they were focused on the man gripping a woman's hand and holding court on the edge of the parking lot.

"It is my intention to not rest until the murder of Lilliana York is solved. No person should fear going home, to their own personal sanctuary." He spied Noland from the corner of his eye and turned. He pulled Noland to his side before anyone could protest. "Dear Noland. May I offer my most sincere condolences on the loss of your beloved wife? My own wife and I are just outraged at this horrible event."

Extra microphones were pitched near Noland's face. "Um, thank you, Senator Boone. Your kind words are such a balm in this most stormy time."

Ah, that's why he looked familiar to Elise. He was the other US senator from Arkansas, Grady Boone, who had been making noise about a path to the oval office during the next presidential election. He'd been the one on television commenting after Lilliana's murder.

Noland took a side step to move away from the man.

But the politician wasn't finished his grandstanding. "Anything you need, you let us know." Senator Boone turned back to the cameras. "This is why it's imperative that we, as Americans, define and enforce more stringent and thorough gun control laws."

Seemed like he was going to keep using Lilliana's murder to push his political agenda on gun control. Elise shook her hand and tightened her grip on Sawyer. Did this man know no bounds?

Mary Ellen eased her hand to Noland's arm and gently tugged him back to her. Elise flanked Noland's other side, with Sawyer also protected. The foursome made their way to Mary Ellen's car waiting in the parking lot. Some of the reporters hounded behind them. For the first time, Elise was truly thankful that Sawyer was deaf.

"Mrs. Carmichael, how is your son handling his grandmother's murder?"

"Has the FBI updated the family with any progress on the investigation?"

"Did he hurt his arm in reaction to the news about his grandmother?"

Elise knew she should ignore them. Knew she should just get into Mary Ellen's car with the others now that they'd reached it. Knew she shouldn't even give the time of day.

Knowing and doing were two different things.

Once everyone else was in the car, Elise stood by the door next to where her son sat waiting. She looked at the little group of reporters. She couldn't stop the words. "You should all be ashamed of yourself. Not only hounding a widow, a woman grieving the loss of her mother, but a young, deaf child? Seriously? Where do you draw the line?" She paused for a moment, realizing she should shut up and get in the car. She'd never been good at keeping quiet though.

"To imply he hurt himself for any reason is insulting. He is a child. Seven years old." She shook her head. "How do you people sleep at night? Why must you take a grieving family seeking consolation of their loss with their church family and turn it into a three-ring circus? For what? Ratings?" Elise slipped into the seat beside Sawyer and slammed the door shut.

Mary Ellen silently eased the car out of the parking space and headed to where Elise had parked.

"I'm sorry. I know I should've kept my big mouth shut, but—"

Noland twisted from his seat next to Mary Ellen. "Don't you dare apologize, Elise. They were hounding about Sawyer. One of the reasons I was happy to give up my press credentials—everyone seems to care more about a scoop and scandal than just giving the people the facts and letting them make up their own minds. You handled them better than I ever could have, and I appreciate what you said." He grinned. "And now I really appreciate you having come today. I feel like I must owe you and Sawyer lunch, at the very least." He looked to Mary Ellen. "What do you say, Mary Ellen?"

Mary Ellen smiled and caught Elise's stare in the rearview mirror. "I think lunch sounds just about perfect for today. How about Copeland's? You can follow us in your own car and leave straight from there."

CHAPTER TEN

The greeter sat them quicker than Elise had anticipated for a Sunday after-church lunch. Granted it was right near the bar area, but that kind of made them even more isolated. Right now, that's what Elise wanted. She loved Copeland's, the southern chain restaurant that served Creole-Cajun classics. The food always made Elise happy.

They settled into their table, placed their drink and food orders; then as the waitress left, Sawyer pulled out his handheld Nintendo and looked at his mom and waved it.

He was so cute, and he'd been such a trooper after church. Elise nodded and was rewarded with a huge grin before he ducked his head and was lost in the world of gaming.

The waitress delivered their drinks, then rushed off. The cool iced tea felt good going down Elise's throat. She shouldn't have gotten so riled up at those reporters, but she hadn't been able to help herself. They were leeches.

"Did y'all notice the two FBI agents at church this morning?" Elise asked after making sure Sawyer wasn't eavesdropping.

"No. What were they doing there?" Noland's hand shook as he lifted his glass. "They are bordering on harassment."

"I'm guessing they were there to see if anyone unusual was there." Elise didn't want to go into her theory because she certainly didn't want to alarm or scare neither Noland nor Mary Ellen, but she did want them to be cautious.

"Unusual? You mean like the press and the politicians and the scum who would use Mom's murder for their own purpose?"

Elise nodded. "Like anybody. I guess it's common practice in an investigation."

"I bet they'll be at the funeral Tuesday too." Mary Ellen sighed and took a sip of her soft drink.

"Is there any way we can prevent that, I wonder." Noland dabbed his mouth with the linen napkin.

"It would only make them more determined to come, would be my guess." Elise shrugged. "Besides, maybe they'll see someone there they've already linked to the crime somewhat."

"I'm not holding my breath." Noland turned to Mary Ellen and asked her about the responsive reading portion of the morning's worship segment.

While Noland and Mary Ellen went over the attributes of the pastor's service, Elise's attention went to the televisions hanging over the bar. One was set to the sports channel, but the other was set on a news station. Both were silent.

Elise's hand froze mid-drink as that other US senator, with Noland at his side, filled the screen. She interrupted Noland and Mary Ellen's ongoing discussion. "I know that Lilliana and I spoke mainly of Sawyer and things relating to him, but I was a little shocked that she was friends with him." Elise nodded toward the television. "I know she didn't support gun control, but the way he's positioned next to you, Noland, it makes it appear as if you're in support of his statements."

"Of course you know I'm not. Politicians are trained how to angle themselves with someone to get the best shot for the camera." Noland shook his head. "It's all a game to them, and it's such a sad time in history that they all use any and everything to get a leg up in a poll or in the race."

"Mom detested Grady Boone in particular."

Elise jerked her attention to her sister-in-law. "Really? Why's that?"

Mary Ellen shrugged. "She called him a womanizer and the worst kind—one who uses his position to seduce younger women and then pay them off to keep their torrid relationships quiet. It made Mom sick."

"I can imagine." Elise might not have been Lilliana's biggest fan on a personal level, but she did respect most all of the stances her mother-in-law took. Protecting the rights of women was one of Lilliana's big ones. It was probably the women vote that won her the election.

"When Mom heard that he was making his way toward the presidency, she about flipped. I remember one time we were on the phone and Mom said she'd do everything in her power to see that he never made inroads to the White House. She believed he was worse than any president we've ever had, and you know that's saying a lot."

The waitress delivered their food and refilled their drinks. The table was silent except for the sounds of chewing and murmurs of appreciation for the food. Before long they'd finished the meal, and despite arguing with Noland, he paid the check and they all headed outside.

The sun shone brighter than it had earlier. Maybe she and Sawyer should go home and take naps. That sure sounded good about now.

Before she could say goodbye to Noland and Mary Ellen, Sawyer tapped her arm and pointed at her purse. She smiled and shook her head as she dug around for her cell. She'd forgotten to turn the volume back on after they'd left church. She pulled it out, and the smile slid off her face.

It was the SkyLink app, and the front door camera had been activated by the motion detector. She clicked on the camera and waited the five to ten seconds it took for the live feed to load.

"What is it?" Mary Ellen moved closer to her as they slowly made their way to the parking lot where they had parked side by side.

Not wanting to alarm Sawyer, Elise forced herself to smile as she showed her sister-in-law the screen as they stopped at their vehicles.

Both women leaned against the front of Elise's Charger and stared at her cell screen as a person in a hooded jacket stood at the door, trying the knob. Hat pulled low, obscuring a view of the face, Hoodie turned, holding a box that Elise hadn't noticed before. A box that looked suspiciously like the two Elise had received.

Hoodie jerked his head toward the street, right then left. He quickly set the box on the front step then turned and trotted down the front walkway.

"Hope we can see what kind of vehicle he gets in," Mary Ellen whispered.

Elise ran her finger over the cell's screen, adjusting the camera as far as the line of vision could reach.

The hooded figure jotted across the street and turned out of the camera's reach.

Elise readjusted the camera's focus. The box sat right there, on the front step. Just waiting for her. The shrimp po' boy that had been so scrumptious going down now threatened to reverse route.

Mary Ellen turned so her back was to Sawyer, speaking to Elise in just barely above a whisper. "Call the police...the FBI agents. You can meet them there and let them open the box. We can take Sawyer back to Noland's and hang out."

Elise wanted nothing more than to take Sawyer and run, just to go away. To where, she had no idea. No plan. She wanted everything to go back to normal. She wanted Lilliana's murder solved and the persons responsible brought to justice.

Well, Marcus Tate the security guard, had already been dealt his hand of justice.

Mary Ellen added, "Or I can drop Noland and Sawyer off at Mom's and then meet you back at your place. We can call the FBI then. Whatever you want to do, Elise."

Elise pressed her lips together, still staring at the box.

Mary Ellen touched her arm. "Elise?"

She nodded.

Mary Ellen turned around and smiled. "Hey Noland, feel like having a television watching buddy spend the afternoon with you today?" She raised her gaze to her stepfather's face.

Noland looked at Mary Ellen, then at Elise, then back at Mary Ellen. The questions burned in his eyes, but Mary Ellen tilted her head slightly toward Sawyer.

"I'd love to have Sawyer come hang with me. There are a couple of good movies on I've been wanting to watch," Noland said and signed, turning to Sawyer. "Are you up for that?"

Sawyer grinned wide and nodded.

"Great. I'll drive y'all home, then head back to Elise's to—" Mary Ellen's hands froze mid-sign.

Elise didn't miss a beat as she quickly signed, "Mary Ellen's stuck with helping me clean out my closet." She paused and looked at her son. "Unless you want to?"

He shook his head and walked to Mary Ellen's car.

Elise followed, giving him a big hug and kiss, then got in her car.

"Hey, wait on me to get there to do anything, unless the FBI is there. Don't go in alone, and don't open that box alone," Mary Ellen all but hissed.

Elise shut the door and started the car, her mind whirling so fast it was a wonder she wasn't dizzy.

Since Marcus Tate was already dead, the only other person who could be doing this to her would be the man she saw with Tate when he was on the phone. She didn't even know who he was! To threaten her now made no sense. She'd already told the FBI everything she knew, so why keep threatening her?

Unless he thought she knew something else.

Bile burned the back of her throat. What if she did know something and wasn't even aware of it? Maybe she'd seen someone she shouldn't have. She replayed that afternoon in her mind.

Tate's words in the call. He hung up. Nodded at the other man, who nodded back.

Had there been anyone else around? Someone maybe she wouldn't have even taken note of?

She'd gotten the call from Hallie and didn't remember seeing much of anything. She'd broken her heel, fallen, then ran to her car. The young lawyer type who'd given her keys back to her—could he be involved?

Elise's heartbeat pounded as she drove west, out of the capital city's limits. She had seen that man's face up close. Even in the rain, she could instantly recall his features. If he was involved, he would recognize her car. Maybe he'd checked out information on her and that's how he knew where she lived.

She didn't recall seeing anyone else until she got to the hospital and saw Hallie and Sawyer. No one on the way home. Nothing else out of place.

Elise pulled into her driveway and pushed the button to open the garage, but didn't pull in. She inched up until she could see the box on the step. She wanted to speed away and not come back until it was gone, but knew she couldn't.

She put Cha Cha into Park and scrolled through her phone until she found the contact information for Agent Rodriguez. He had, at least, smiled at her in church. He'd also had the decency to look a little embarrassed at getting caught there. He was better than Agent Wright, at least as far as Elise was concerned.

She pressed the screen and the phone dialed Agent Rodriguez's cell phone.

He answered on the second ring. "Agent Rodriguez."

"Yes, this is Elise Carmichael."

"Yes, ma'am. What can I do for you?" There was the slightest hesitation in his voice, as if he expected her to call him out on the church visit.

"I've received another box. At my house."

"What's inside?"

"I don't know. I haven't opened it yet. Haven't even touched it.

The person delivered it and my new security system's camera alerted me. I'm sitting in my car in my driveway." For no apparent reason, the urge to cry nearly choked her. She couldn't make sense of it. Not only was she not the crying type, she certainly shouldn't cry in front of a man who was trying to disrupt her life more than it already was.

"Don't touch it. We'll be there immediately." The connection died.

Elise deactivated the security system, then slipped the phone into her purse and turned off the car's engine. He'd said *they* would be here soon. Great. That meant Agent Wright would be in attendance as well. Lovely. Just more to make Elise's day all that much better.

She scratched her knee, wishing she were out of the dress she'd been wearing way too long on a weekend and into her faded and worn jeans. At least Sawyer was safe and out of harm's way.

For the moment.

CHAPTER ELEVEN

"Have you touched the box?" Agent Wright practically jumped out of the car before her partner brought the vehicle to a complete stop.

Elise ignored her, crossing her arms over her chest as she leaned against the bricks lining the walkway up the stairs. Mary Ellen had arrived just moments ago. Together the two women sat on the ledge and waited.

"I'll ask again." Agent Wright stood on the bottom step. "Have you touched the box?"

Elise cut her eyes to the woman. "No. Agent Rodriguez told me not to, so I didn't. I haven't even gone in the house. I opened the garage and parked, then Mary Ellen and I sat here to make sure the box wasn't disturbed until he could get here."

Speaking of the agent, he loped up the walkway to join them, slipping latex gloves on as he stopped beside his partner. "What have we got?"

Elise nodded to the box as she pushed off the brick ledge. "As I was leaving lunch after church this morning, I received an alert on my cell from my security system that the camera there had been activated." She pointed to the camera partially hidden in the eaves over the front door. "We saw a person wearing a hoodie at the front door. At first, I didn't see the box. They tried the knob on the door, but it was locked. They took a step back, and that's when I noticed the box. They looked around—I'm guessing to see if anyone was watching, and apparently not since they set the box down and took off."

"Could you see what vehicle they got in?" Agent Rodriguez asked. Elise shook her head. "I adjusted the camera as far as the line of vision could reach, but the person moved farther away."

"I didn't know you had a security camera." Agent Wright's tone came out practically accusing. "You didn't mention it before. Do you have the video from the last two boxes you say were delivered?"

That she *said* were delivered? As if she would make it up? "No. I just got the security system set up yesterday. I didn't have it when the other two boxes were delivered. Because of the boxes, and not knowing who else you told, which has put me and my son in harm's way, is why I had to buy a security system." Maybe if they did their job correctly, there wouldn't have even been a need.

Her mind flashed to the newscast from a couple of weeks ago about another school shooting, then the image of Sawyer filled her mind's eye. Maybe not an immediate need, but she was thankful Arabella had made the suggestion when she did. And that she'd listened.

"Can you forward me a copy of the video?" Agent Rodriguez sat on the stair beside the box.

Again Elise nodded. "To the email on your business card?"

"That'd be fine."

She pulled out her cell, tapped a few times, and then pocketed her phone again. "Done."

"So, let's take a look here." He lifted his gloved hands to the box, easing it closer and turning it. "Do you see anything familiar or the like?" he asked Elise.

Glancing at the box, she shook her head. "Like before, I don't recognize anything special about the wrapping paper or anything." Her pulse kicked up a notch and her mouth went dry. A dead rat. . .a cryptic doll. . .a snake. . .now what?

Slowly and ever so carefully, Agent Rodriguez lifted the lid and handed it to his partner, who slipped it into the waiting evidence bag she held.

Whatever was in the box was wrapped up in the familiar tissue paper. White and plain with no identifying marks.

Elise held her breath as he gently pushed the delicate paper aside.

A thin stack of photos were nestled inside. Agent Rodriguez lifted them, then immediately handed them to his partner before Elise could make out what they were. He stood and handed Elise a pair of latex gloves from his pocket.

"What are these for?" She took the gloves without waiting for his reply and put them on.

Agent Rodriguez ushered Mary Ellen up the stairs, giving space to his partner and Elise.

Agent Wright stood and moved off the steps into the brightness from the sun. "Come see, Mrs. Carmichael."

Heartbeat pounding against her chest, Elise did.

"Are these you?" Agent Wright handed her the handful of photographs.

Elise took them and turned them around to look at them.

Her heart swan-dived to her stomach, riding waves of nausea.

The pictures were indeed of her. A silhouette of her in her shower. Taken from the angle of her bedroom.

He had been in her house, and she hadn't even known. He could have killed her. . .Sawyer! Oh mercy, he could have hurt Sawyer, or taken him, or even killed—

"Elise, is this you?" Agent Wright's voice had softened.

With tears burning her eyes, she nodded. That metallic sensation burnt the back of her throat again.

"Can you try to figure out when these might have been taken?" Agent Wright asked.

"There's no window in my bathroom. He took that from inside my house. Looking into the bathroom from inside my bedroom." She had never felt more sick.

"I understand. This is very upsetting and traumatic." Agent Wright truly sounded compassionate. "But please see if you can pinpoint when these might have been taken."

Elise licked her lips and took the pictures back with her hands shaking. She gave herself a mental shake and forced herself to focus.

The light was dim, which was how she preferred her evening showers. "They all look to have been taken at night when I don't use the overhead light in the bathroom."

"Good. What else?" Agent Wright's voice came out softer than Elise had ever heard it. Soothing. It did actually help calm Elise's tangled nerves.

She focused back on the pictures. No clothes laid on the floor, but that wasn't at all unusual. Elise had always been a stickler about putting clothes in the hamper. It made laundry day easier and she loved a neat and tidy home. Laundry. . .

Elise lifted the photos closer to see them better. She squinted. Which towel hung on the hook outside the shower door?

"Anything?" Agent Wright asked.

"Hang on." Was it a bath sheet or regular towel?

She squinted. Not a bath sheet. Definitely a regular towel. Was that red or black? So hard to tell in the dim light. Wait, red. It was red. "Friday night." She lifted her gaze to the agent's. "These were taken Friday night."

"Are you sure?"

Elise nodded. "I use white towels every morning, but in the evenings, I rotate my towels so that some colors aren't more vivid than others. Black on Mondays, blue on Tuesdays, gold on Wednesdays, hunter green on Thursdays, red on Fridays, and bath sheets on Saturdays and Sundays. So this is a red towel, so it was definitely taken on Friday."

"OCD much?" Agent Wright mumbled under her breath.

And just like that, Elise's reconsideration of the woman dissipated. "Yes, I'm a bit OCD, but seems like it's useful to your investigation right now, isn't it?"

Agent Wright's cheeks pinked up. "Anything else you notice about the picture? Anything you can tell us?"

Elise looked back at the photographs, tilting her head as she tried to study it without emotion. "From the angle, I'd say he had to be standing opposite the wall the built-in vanity is, closer to my closet." He'd been so close. To her. To Sawyer.

And she hadn't even had a clue.

"Wait." Agent Wright grabbed one of the pictures and flipped it over. There was a label stuck to the back. Clearly a label made on one of those crafter's handheld label makers.

Elise shifted to stand closer to the agent to read alongside her.

I SEE YOU. I CAN ALWAYS GET TO YOU AND YOUR SON. SAY NOTHING ELSE.

Agent Wright took the photographs and moved beside Agent Rodriguez. They turned from Mary Ellen and spoke in whispers.

"What is it?" Mary Ellen joined her in the sunlight. "Mr. Agent Man over there wouldn't tell me a thing."

"It's pictures of me in the shower."

"Oh heavens! A peeping Tom on top of everything else? That's just downright creepy." Mary Ellen put an arm around Elise. "Good thing you now have the security system."

Yes, that did, in fact, give her the strength to not run away. "There was also a warning on the back of one of them. Warning me to keep my mouth shut or he could get to me and Sawyer."

Mary Ellen squeezed her into a hug. "It's okay now."

Yes, she and Sawyer were okay, at least for now, but she wasn't going to hold her breath. She wasn't going to just sit around and let the FBI run the investigation, which they clearly had no regard for her or Sawyer's well-being. Right now, she needed to think. . .to rationalize the facts and see what was what, at least the best that she could. "Okay. The pictures were taken Friday night."

"The night after Mom was killed."

Elise nodded, but her mind whirred with the information she knew. "The night after I'd told the FBI about what I'd seen. The same night the security guard, Marcus Tate, was murdered."

"Which, by the way, the FBI finally did come and tell me and Noland that he'd been killed. Asked us crazy questions too, like did we know him—did we know if Mom knew him, and if so, how well—had he ever been to the house—did we ever recall seeing Mom and him together? . . .that kind of stuff."

Elise shook her head. "I'm not sure what their gig is." They had to have an angle, but she sure couldn't figure out what their plan was. It baffled the mind.

Mary Ellen shrugged. "Okay, anyway, back to the topic at hand. The pictures of you were taken Friday night."

"Mary Ellen, he was in my house! In my bedroom. Sawyer was just down the hall, asleep. This guy could have hurt us, done something awful t—"

Her sister-in-law cut Elise off. "Don't. Don't even go there. Yes, he was in your home. Yes, horrible things could've happened, but they didn't. He could have taken pictures of Sawyer, but he didn't, so he probably didn't even go into Sawyer's room. Only yours, for whatever reason besides to scare you into doing whatever he wants. Sawyer is safe. You're safe. And now you have a security system that adds another level of protection for you both."

"I know, I know." But Elise couldn't get it out of her mind. He was right there. So close, and she'd been blissfully unaware of the danger.

The two FBI agents came back to them. "We'll get this evidence processed and see if we can find any prints or DNA or anything," Agent Rodriguez said.

Elise nodded.

"Is there anything else?" The snippiness had crept back into Agent Wright's voice.

Elise could snap back with the best of them, especially when her son was in danger. "Anything else? You mean aside from my mother-in-law having been murdered in her own home and no one seems to have even a clue as to who shot her and why? Or, do you mean like me and my son being put in danger in the first place because you two told someone I'd lip-read what that guard said? You mean anything else like that?"

"Now, now." Agent Rodriguez took a step away from his partner, in Elise's direction.

Elise held up her hands as if fending off the agents. "No. I made a mistake in even calling you and reporting this. You probably won't find any evidence. You've got it, and I've sent the video to you, so please, just go."

"Mrs. Carmichael—" Agent Rodriguez started.

"Don't 'Mrs. Carmichael' me. I'm done." She picked up her purse from where she'd left it on the ledge, and unlocked the front door. "Come on, Mary Ellen."

Her sister-in-law threw the agents a look, then followed Elise into the house.

It gave Elise great satisfaction, more than it really should have, to slam the door shut on the FBI agents and lock the deadbolt.

Chapter Twelve

Elise glanced at her phone for the umpteenth time since dropping Sawyer off at school Monday morning. It'd only been an hour or so, but she desperately wanted him to be okay. Despite her offer to let him stay home from school, he'd been adamant he wanted to go. While she admired his dedication to his schoolwork—or maybe it was more to show off his cool cast to his friends—if she was being honest, she'd have to admit that she would rather he have stayed home with her. Yet, he'd gone, taking Hallie's hand as she dropped him off. She shouldn't worry. Hallie was there and knew what was going on and would do everything to protect him, but still. . .

She grabbed the papers off the printer. After she'd talked with Mary Ellen last night, she'd decided to do a little research on the files Lilliana had sent to Sawyer's iPad. She'd forwarded the documents to Mary Ellen this morning. Maybe between the two of them, they could make some heads or tails of what the files were and why on earth Lilliana would have sent them to Sawyer. Mary Ellen would make sure Noland ate something for breakfast—she said he hadn't been eating well since Lilliana's murder—then she would head over to Elise's. They were going to put their heads together and see what they could figure out.

The first paper off the printer was the photo. The woman didn't look familiar, nor did the baby. Elise took in the background. The picture had definitely been taken in someone's house. It looked like they sat in a kitchen, at one of those retro-styled, red vinyl kitchen chairs with chrome. She could almost make out a microwave cart behind them. But it wasn't Lilliana's house or Elise's. She hadn't been to Mary Ellen's place in Eureka Springs, but the style wasn't Mary Ellen's.

So who was this woman and baby? Was it a family member of Lilliana's? It couldn't be. Why on earth would she have sent a family photo to Sawyer's iPad in such a cryptic way? It made no sense. If it was, Mary Ellen would be sure to recognize them, and they could go from there.

Elise set the printout of the picture down, staring at it as she sipped her coffee. The next file, the lab results, lay beside the picture. Definitely DNA results, but for whom? Why did Lilliana have it? It was dated a couple of years ago, so why was it so important now?

Certainly Lilliana had to have known she was about to be murdered when she sent the files to Sawyer. This was basically her last act, so it had to be important. But why send it to Sawyer?

Elise took another sip of her strong, black coffee. She knew that Sawyer wouldn't check the email. She must have known that the FBI would be able to trace her sending it and recover it, even though she deleted it off her phone before she was shot. She'd taken a risk in sending the email.

Maybe she sent it to Sawyer so the FBI would get the files. That made sense. She would know that Sawyer wouldn't check the email. Elise didn't except maybe once a month. So Lilliana must have known the files would be safe until the FBI came looking.

A big risk for someone who was about to be murdered.

She looked at the lab results again. What was the name of the lab company? If she could make that out, surely that would be a good starting place. Was that DNAncestors? Yeah, she thought it might be. The logo looked like the one on the television commercials.

The lights flashed and the doorbell rang.

Elise grabbed her cell phone and quickly activated SkyLink, then the front door camera. A young woman, vaguely familiar, stood waiting. Elise went to the door, but didn't open it immediately. "May I help you?" she stated loudly.

"Mrs. Carmichael? Elise Carmichael?"

Standing on tiptoe, Elise looked through the peephole. It was clearer than the camera's live feed. The woman was maybe all of five feet, with long, dark hair that waved down her back. Her big, brown eyes were spellbinding even through a door's peephole.

Elise opened the door a little wider than a crack. "What do you want?"

"I'm Wesson Kelly, with the *Gazette*."

Of course, the media. "Not interested." Elise pushed the door, but the young woman shoved the toe of her boot inside.

"Please, Mrs. Carmichael. I was outside the church yesterday and I heard what you said. You're right, we acted very badly. I, for one, am very sorry."

Elise didn't slam the door and break the woman's toe, which she'd originally considered. It took a lot of gumption to show up and apologize. "Thank you. I appreciate that." She looked the girl up and down. What was this Wesson Kelly's game? "But I'm not going to give you an interview or anything. I'm certainly not going to give you access to anyone in my family." Especially not Sawyer.

"No, ma'am. I understand."

"Well, you have to want something. You could have apologized with a phone call. What is it?"

"May I come inside? I waited until you'd taken your son to school."

Elise narrowed her eyes. "Are you following me?"

"No, ma'am. Not at all." But her cheeks reddened. "I parked across the street, down a bit, and waited until you came back."

"I've been back for over an hour."

Her face reddened even more. "Yes, ma'am. I was trying to build up my courage to come ring your bell. I wanted—want to talk to you. To apologize, of course, but also to talk with you about Senator York's murder investigation. After yesterday, though, I was a little scared you'd kick me off your porch and back to the curb. I was ready to run if you opened the door and yelled at me again."

The beginnings of a grin tickled the edges of Elise's lips. The girl seemed honest at least. Elise had to admit she was more than a little curious as to what this Wesson Kelly had to say about Lilliana's murder investigation. She opened the door. "I just made a pot of coffee. Would you like a cup?"

"Oh yes, ma'am, please."

"Come on in." She waited until Wesson stood beside her before she shut and locked the door. "Follow me." She led the way to the kitchen, poured a cup of coffee, then slid it on the island in front of Wesson. "Sugar's there and if you need cream, you'll have to make do with the milk in the fridge."

"No, I take it black, but thank you."

At least she had good taste in coffee. "So, you've apologized and I've accepted. What else did you want to discuss about Lilliana's case?"

Wesson took a sip of the coffee, then set down the cup. She wrapped her hands around the mug, as if she were trying to warm herself, although this April morning was rather warm. "I've got a few sources who tell me that you've been receiving some very disturbing boxes in relation to the case. Is this true?"

Elise peered across the island at the younger woman, trying to get a read on her. She was a tough one though. It was her eyes. They were dark pools of melted chocolate. "Is this conversation off the record or whatever? Just between us two?"

Wesson nodded. "Yes, ma'am, unless or until you tell me otherwise."

Elise paused. Apparently the FBI wasn't keeping anything regarding her and the investigation confidential, so what could it hurt? Maybe she could play quid pro quo and get information on her own. "Yes, I've gotten a few boxes that contained disturbing items." A rat, a doll with a warning, and photographs of her in her own shower with another warning. . .yeah, she'd call those disturbing.

"Can you tell me what's been in the boxes?"

"I'd rather not just yet." Again, things that only she and the FBI knew had gotten out. Well, Mary Ellen knew, but she wouldn't tell anyone, not even Noland. "Where are you getting your information?"

Wesson hesitated. "I can't name my source, of course, but my source is affiliated with the bureau."

Elise *knew* the leak was with the FBI!

"But my source is not in any way responsible for any deliveries to you. I'm one hundred percent positive about that."

Fair enough. Elise took another sip of coffee.

"Will you tell me how those boxes are connected to the case?" Wesson shook her head and spoke before Elise could reply. "I also hear that you lip-read a conversation the security guard had in which he insinuates he'll take care—meaning kill—Senator York. Is that correct?"

Elise paused only a moment before she nodded.

"Do you think this is why you've gotten the boxes?"

Elise took another sip of coffee. "I do. All of the boxes contained some sort of warning in some way. Warning me to keep quiet. I can only assume that refers to the one-sided phone conversation I eavesdropped."

"I would agree. However, unless you know who the guard was speaking to, there should be no one needing you to keep quiet now. Especially since the guard himself was murdered on Friday."

Elise smiled, then lifted her cup. "Therein is the question then, isn't it?"

"It just doesn't make a lot of sense. I could understand the guard would want you to keep quiet about what you saw him say on the phone, but once he was murdered, you shouldn't be a threat to anyone else, unless you know who the guard was talking to." Wesson sat straighter in the bar stool at the island. "Do you know who the guard was talking to?"

Elise shook her head. "I don't, but sure wish I did. That would make the investigation move along much quicker and all those involved in killing Lilliana could be brought to justice." Then there'd be no more threats against her and Sawyer.

"Then what do you think of the continued threats? If it wasn't the guard, then who is sending you those boxes?"

"Again, that's a good question to which I don't have an answer." Elise went and refilled her coffee cup, then topped off Wesson's. "I'll let you in on a little clue too: I'm pretty certain the FBI hasn't the foggiest notion either." She put the carafe back on the warmer and returned to her barstool across from Wesson.

The young reporter worried her bottom lip between her rows of teeth. "It doesn't make sense."

"It doesn't." Well, not unless you counted the files Lilliana had sent to Sawyer's iPad. Was it possible the FBI hadn't leaked that bit of information? "What else does your source tell you?"

"That the agents working the case tried today to get a warrant for a particular thing you have that is possibly connected to the case, but that two judges turned them down."

That was new. Elise smiled. "Really?"

Wesson nodded. "Did you know they were trying to get a warrant?"

Elise nodded.

"But you didn't know they'd been denied?"

"I didn't know that. I mean, my attorney said a judge might be cautious because of the specifics, but you never know."

Wesson nodded again. "Will you tell me what specific item they want to get their hands on?"

"I'm not really ready to say at this time. My attorney has told me not to say anything." Not exactly, but she was pretty sure Arabella wouldn't be pleased with her providing information to the media. Even though Wesson did seem different. Or was she just going to burn Elise? "No offense, but you're young and I don't recognize you from any time before. Why are you here, asking questions?"

"That's fair." Wesson sipped her coffee then set it down with a resounding thud. "I am young, and a woman to boot. According to my supervisors, I don't have the experience, suaveness, or contacts to report on the political scene." She shrugged. "But this has always been my dream. I've wanted to be a journalist for as long as I can remember. I studied hard and graduated *magna cum laude* from University of Arkansas here in Little Rock. I interned every chance I got, and grabbed every opportunity to work on a paper. One summer, I even cleaned bathrooms and emptied trash. I know I have to pay my dues before I can move up the ladder and eventually get to cover the White House, but I'm trying."

Elise stared at Wesson, whose dreams were so big. She related. At one time, before she met Judson and had Sawyer, she'd dreamed of being the next big supermodel. She wanted to walk the runway at fashion week in Paris, France. To model the top designer's lines, wearing the funky makeup and crazy hairstyles.

She didn't regret the choice she'd made of giving up her dream to be a wife to Judson and mother to Sawyer—not in the least. She'd loved being a wife, and to the man she loved with all her heart. When they found out she was pregnant with Sawyer, they were both over-the-moon happy. Oh the many, many nights they'd lain in bed and talked until the wee hours about the plans they had for their baby. Their baby would know nothing but love from the moment he was born. Their baby would have doting parents who spent time with him.

The dream crashed when Judson was killed, but still, Elise didn't regret giving up modeling. Even though the pain of losing Judson still nearly strangled her at times, it was all worth it to have Sawyer.

Wesson pulled Elise from her thoughts. "I know it might sound silly, but that's my dream."

Elise smiled. "Dreams are never silly. We have to dream and dream big, and chase those dreams with everything we have."

Wesson nodded. "That's what I'm trying to do. That's why I'm here. I was at the church yesterday on my own. The paper didn't send me to cover the case. Matter of fact, the reporter assigned to the case wasn't too happy to see me there. Luckily, I was able to duck away." She grinned behind her blush. "But then I heard what you said, and I felt so bad. When I was in college, I swore I'd be a good reporter, only reporting the facts. I'd never planned on playing on someone's grief, and I did. You put me in my place."

Elise chuckled. "Well, I might've been a little harsher than I should have."

"No, you were right. We were being vultures and shouldn't have hounded you and your family. Certainly not your son."

"What did you hope to accomplish by coming here?"

Wesson blushed and lifted a shoulder. "I thought maybe by just being direct and only using any information you said I could report, you might prefer that over being followed by pesky reporters. Like the guy with the camera who was hiding in the bushes along your driveway when you got home."

CHAPTER THIRTEEN

Elise froze. "What man in the bushes?"

"Just a guy with a camera in the bushes."

The photographs someone took of her in the shower raced across Elise's mind. She leveled her voice and chose her words carefully. "I didn't see any man. Did you recognize him? Can you describe him?"

"He was maybe five eight or nine, possibly about one fifty or so. He wore a pair of dark jeans, black tennis shoes, and a dark gray hoodie. I figure he was some freelance photographer hoping to sell photos to one of the tabloid rags. I didn't recognize him, but mainly because he had the hood up that covered his head, which I did think was a little weird since it's been so warm this morning." Wesson's face reddened. "Oh no. He wasn't a freelancer, was he?"

Elise slowly shook her head. The description matched the security camera's image of the guy leaving the box on her doorstep.

"I should have called the police, shouldn't I?" Wesson's face was redder than a summer tomato.

"Maybe. I don't know." The answer was yes, she should have, but Elise could read the sincere anguish on the poor girl's face. "Did you happen to see him get in a vehicle?"

Wesson shook her head. "I watched you go into the house, then tried to work up my courage to come to your door."

"Anything at all would be helpful. Please, think." Elise gripped the mug so tight that it was a wonder it didn't explode in her hands and splash coffee everywhere.

Wesson closed her eyes and did a little rock on the barstool. A second passed.

Two seconds.

Three.

Her eyes shot open and she stared at Elise. "He got into a silver Ford. A Focus, I think, but I can't be sure. He headed south on your street, away from your house."

Finally! Something that maybe could help down the road. At least it was something of a lead, which is more than Elise could give credit to the FBI for.

"I'm sorry, Mrs. Carmichael. If I had realized, I would have called 911 or hollered out at you." Wesson's voice was thick, as if full of tears. "I didn't see him until you pulled into the driveway. When you were in the garage, he stood and I'm guessing took some pictures, then ducked back into the bushes while your garage door closed. He left right after that, so like I said, I thought he was just a freelance photographer." She shook her head. "I should have known better, with hearing about the packages sent to you. I'm so sorry, Mrs. Carmichael." Tears pooled in Wesson's big eyes.

"It's okay." Elise resisted the urge to walk around the island and hug the younger woman. She was, after all, still a reporter and hadn't yet proven to be trustworthy. All this could be an act to get more info, but Elise didn't think so. "First things first, my name is Elise, use it. Second, you couldn't have known and in your line of work, it would be a natural assumption if you saw a man in the bushes with a camera that you would think he was a freelance photographer. You saw him leave, so you knew I wasn't in imminent danger, so you naturally wouldn't have called the police." Especially because she would've had to explain what she was doing there herself.

"You're too kind. I feel like I messed up."

The doorbell rang and the lights flashed. Both Elise and Wesson jumped before Elise pulled out her cell and checked the camera on the SkyLink app. "It's just my sister-in-law. I'll be back in a minute."

Elise opened the door and pulled Mary Ellen inside. She quickly brought Mary Ellen up to speed about Wesson as she locked the door, then led the way into the kitchen. "Mary Ellen Carmichael, meet Wesson Kelly. Wesson, my sister-in-law, Mary Ellen."

"I was just telling Mary Ellen about the man in the bushes that you saw. Since it is a lead, I'm going to call the FBI and let them know. I'll have to give them your name as well." Elise reached for her cell.

"I understand." Wesson took another sip of coffee.

Elise called Agent Rodriguez, who answered immediately.

"Mrs. Carmichael?"

Elise quickly explained about what Wesson had seen.

"We'll be right over."

Elise smiled at Wesson. "They said they'd be right over, but who really knows what that means?"

Wesson nodded. "Mrs.—Elise, I'm so sorry for what you're going through." She cut her eyes to Mary Ellen. "And your family."

"Thank you." Elise took a moment to make her decision. "Let me explain to you what was in the boxes."

She had just finished telling Wesson everything, except for the documents Lilliana had sent to Sawyer's iPad, when her cell phone chimed with an alert from the motion detector at the front door. A second or two later, the doorbell rang and the lights flashed.

Wesson physically jumped.

Elise chuckled. "It's okay. You get used to the feature for families with deaf members since they can't hear the doorbell. It's a little surprising until you get used to it."

Wesson nodded. "But very smart."

"Just a minute, it's likely the FBI." Elise headed to the front door and peered through the peephole. Sure enough, Agent Wright and Agent Rodriguez stood on the porch with another woman. Agent Rodriguez wore a concerned expression while Agent Wright looked like she'd been sucking on lemons all morning. The other woman was taller than average, probably about five nine, with wavy dirty blond hair cut at her shoulders. She carried a large case.

Elise unlocked and opened the door. "Agents."

"Mrs. Carmichael, this is Connie Parson, our sketch artist."

Elise smiled at Connie, whose ready returning smile came across as easy and genuine. Elise waved them inside, then shut and locked the door behind them. She led them into the kitchen where the young reporter waited. "Agent Rodriguez, Agent Wright, and Ms. Parson, this is Wesson Kelly with the *Gazette*, and you know my sister-in-law, Mary Ellen."

"I'm so sorry I didn't call 911 earlier. I just didn't think there was anything more than some photographer trying to make a buck."

Agent Rodriguez stood next to Wesson at the kitchen island. "It's okay. You're telling us now." He glanced up at Elise. "I'll take Ms. Kelly's statement. Why don't you ladies go into the living room?"

Agent Wright nodded, then led Elise, Mary Ellen, and Connie into the living room. Elise and Connie sat on the couch, Mary Ellen took one of the overstuffed chairs, while Agent Wright stood. Hovering. "We brought Connie along to work with you on the sketch of who you saw with the guard during his phone call."

At least they were doing something. "Oh. Okay." She smiled at the sketch artist. "I don't know much about what I saw of him. I was rushed and then I had a call come in that—"

"Don't you worry. Just relax. I'm going to ask you questions and you just answer me." She opened her case and pulled out several items: drawing board, pencils, erasers, circle template, paper. . . "This drawing will only be as good as your memory. It will not be a portrait. An innocent person will not be arrested from this. Your name will not be on the drawing. The worst that can happen is we'll spend some time together. We can stop at any time if you need a break. Okay?"

Elise exhaled and nodded. She'd seen sketches on television and of course, in various court cases she'd translated in, but never knew the process of how they came to be. This would be interesting.

Connie flashed her ready smile again. "I need you to tell me what happened. I need you to start at the beginning and don't leave anything out, even if you think it's unimportant."

When Elise had finished telling her everything she remembered, she leaned back into the couch, closing her eyes to bring up a mental picture of the man who she now was almost positive had been with Marcus Tate in the corner of the security area of the federal courthouse.

"We'll start with the basics. What would you guess his age range to be?"

Still keeping her eyes closed, Elise gauged her mental image. "About thirty-five to forty."

"Good. What was his race?" Connie not only had an easy and ready smile, but a soothing voice too. Very calming, which played well into her chosen profession.

"He was white." Elise opened her eyes and looked at Connie. "I mean, he was Caucasian but looked tan."

Connie nodded. "Hair color and style?"

Elise closed her eyes again to bring up her mental image. "Short, cropped hair, like a military or policeman's cut." She focused on the sketch artist. "It was a little darker than your hair."

"What about his height, weight, or build?" Connie asked.

"I'm guessing about five foot nine or ten, very fit and cut. No muffin top on him." Elise smiled.

"Lucky him." Connie chuckled. "What about your overall impression?"

"Oh." Elise closed her eyes, then opened them after a moment. "He seemed focused. Intent. He stared at Marcus Tate the entire time I saw them together."

"Good." Connie moved her materials around. "If this guy had a job, what kind of job would he have? Banker? Truck driver? Student? Street person?"

Hmm. That was a tough one.

"It doesn't have to be his actual profession or even close, just what is your guess from his appearance?"

"Well, the way he stood, I'd say military or law enforcement. The haircut backs that up. He seemed to stand with confidence, like the witnesses I see on the stand who know what they're saying is the truth. But..."

"But what?"

How to explain? It was more of a feeling than his actual appearance. "I don't know. Yes, he had the stance and carried himself like a cop or officer or something, but there was something else. I don't know. An arrogance of some sort?"

"How does someone look arrogant?" Agent Wright interrupted.

Connie gave her a level stare, but Elise wasn't going to let any agent be chide and rude in her own home. "Look in the mirror and I bet you can figure it out."

Connie snorted and Mary Ellen chuckled.

"That's not amusing." Agent Wright glared. "We need to focus on the task at hand: the sketch."

Sighing, Connie gave a slight shake of her head before looking back at Elise. "What was his most outstanding feature? A scar? Glasses? Tattoo? Beard or mustache?"

Elise shook her head. "I wasn't close enough to him to see any scars or tattoos. He didn't wear glasses, nor did he have any facial hair that I could see."

"Okay, just his most outstanding feature."

"His jawline."

Connie straightened in her seat. "His jawline?"

Heat pressed against Elise's cheeks. "You know how you read in romance novels and movie synopses that some guy has a chiseled jaw? I always thought that was stupid until I think about this guy's jawline. It *was* chiseled, as romanticized as that sounds."

Connie gave a little laugh under her breath. "Hey, we all need some romance in our life, no matter how silly or far away."

Elise grinned.

"What was he wearing?"

"A suit. Not from the department store rack like some of the law enforcement I see taking the stand, but not ultraexpensive like some of the higher-priced attorneys wear. Definitely wasn't tailored to his build."

Connie nodded. "I know you said you weren't close enough to see scars or tattoos, but what about a mannerism? Like constantly fiddling with a button or something?"

Elise fought to remember the details. "No, nothing that I noticed."

Connie handed her a large binder. "Go through this book and find people who kind of look like the person you saw. Give me the number underneath the face and tell me what you notice about the face that looks like the man you saw. Like the nose on B-3, the mouth of C-5, like that."

Elise flipped through the binder, which contained about forty or fifty pictures. The pictures were numbered A-1, B-12, etc. and there were sixteen photos per page. Elise went through the book and gave numbers with what matched from the person in the book to the man she saw with Marcus Tate. Connie began to sketch, her pencils making soothing scraping noises against the paper.

Agent Wright paced as Elise, Mary Ellen, and Connie were silent, except for the times Connie would ask for clarification over a part of the face, like was the nose thinner than the picture, or were the eyes bigger. . .stuff like that.

The female agent stopped pacing, hovering over Connie's shoulder, but staring at Elise. "Funny that you let a reporter into your home." Agent Wright crossed her arms over her chest and leaned against the back of the couch. "Especially since I heard you ripped into the reporters yesterday."

The woman's snide behavior knew no bounds. Elise glanced up and met the agent's glare. "Heard? You mean physically, since you were at the church. Which, I don't ever recall having seen you in services there before. Do you attend there often?"

Connie gave a little snicker under her breath. Elise knew she had liked her instantly.

Mary Ellen snorted.

"So who is Wesson Kelly to you?" Agent Wright ignored Elise's question and Mary Ellen's response, but cut her eyes down to Connie. "I can't fathom why you let a member of the press into your home."

"I'm sure you can't." Elise didn't offer anything else. She didn't owe the FBI any explanation about whom she invited into her home.

Connie interrupted. "What about the forehead? Wider or narrower?"

Elise glanced at the drawing. "Wider by about a fourth of an inch, maybe a little less, but much taller. Like an inch taller. Lots of space between his eyebrows and hairline."

Connie nodded and kept sketching.

"So, why did you?" Agent Wright pressed.

Elise let out a very audible sigh and glanced at the agent. "Why did I what?"

Agent Wright narrowed her eyes. "Why did you let Wesson Kelly into your home? Does she know something you'd rather her not report on?"

"No, nothing of the sort. There's no blackmail going on if that's what you were insinuating. I let her in because I wanted to. Since it's my house, I believe I can invite in any guest I'd like."

Elise focused back on Connie's hand moving the pencil over the sketchbook. She could almost hear Agent Wright grinding her teeth.

Connie hesitated. "What about the jawline? Since you feel it's his prominent feature, I want to make sure I have it right."

Elise studied it. "It's more, defined here. Stronger." She pointed to the place she meant. "There's no softness to the line, at least not from a distance. Maybe it's different up close, but it looked like a cut line to me."

"Got it." Connie went back to sketching.

Of course Agent Wright just couldn't let them work in peace. "You know, we caught Senator Boone's press conference after church, where Noland stood beside him." Agent Wright paused.

Elise remained silent.

"Everyone we've spoken to commented on how much Senator York was against Senator Boone on most every topic. Some imply that there were also personal reasons the two clashed."

Again, Elise remained silent.

Connie kept sketching, but she'd raised an eyebrow as she drew.

Agent Wright sat on the edge of the chair facing the couch. "Do you have any insight on that?"

Elise leveled her gaze at the agent. "No. You already know Lilliana and I weren't close and almost all of our discussions were about Sawyer, so why on earth would you think I have any insight in her business dealings or who she did or didn't like?" The woman was on a fishing expedition, and Elise wasn't going to bait the hook for her.

"Mmm-hmm." Agent Wright shot back to standing, turning to stare at Mary Ellen. "What about you, Mary Ellen? What would you say your mother's relationship with Senator Boone was like?"

Before Mary Ellen could answer, Elise's temper kicked in. These agents, well, Agent Wright needed a push, or rather a hard shove. "Do *you* have anything new on the case? A suspect? A lead? Anything?"

"I can't discuss an open investigation."

Elise nodded. "Yeah, I know. I just find it amusing that the only leads you seem to get are the ones me or my family provide for you."

"Maybe you're more involved than you've led us to believe? Is that why you won't provide the iPad?"

Ah, but she wasn't offended. This woman was just trying to get a rise out of them. Elise wasn't going to let it happen. "No, but hey, feel free to follow up on me and waste more time."

"I—" Agent Wright started.

Connie interrupted. "Here, how's this?" She turned the drawing around to face Elise. "Is it close to what you remember him looking like?"

Elise took the picture and stared. "Wow." Sure, it wasn't exact, but it came really, really close. "That's pretty good."

"On a one-to-ten scale, with one not close and ten being perfect, how close does this come to your memory?" Connie asked.

"Eight and a half to nine." She met the artist's gaze. "You're really talented."

"Thank you." Connie nodded. "What can I do to make it a nine?"

Elise studied the picture. "Is there a way to harden his eyes? I remember that. Even from a distance, his eyes looked hard."

Connie took the picture back and picked up a pencil.

Agent Rodriguez came into the living room. "Ms. Kelly has agreed to sit with Connie as well and give a description of the man she saw with the camera, even though she says she doesn't remember much." He patted the artist's shoulder. "Connie has a way of helping witnesses remember details they didn't think they'd remember."

Elise smiled. "She's good. You know, I've had composites entered into evidence in some of the cases I've been a translator for, but I never knew how they came about. This has been most interesting."

"It's a neat process, and when you have someone as experienced as Connie, it's a lot easier."

Connie swatted at him. "Is that a polite way of calling me old?"

He grinned and held his hands up in mock surrender. "No, ma'am. Not me. My momma didn't raise a fool."

Connie chuckled. "Smart of you to listen to your momma."

He chuckled and took his partner by the elbow. They moved a few feet away and spoke quietly.

Connie handed the drawing back to Elise. "What about now?"

"Wow." Connie had shaded around the eyes, giving them more of a hooded look. Elise slowly nodded. "This is definitely a ten on how I remember him." She pulled out her cell and snapped a quick picture while the agents spoke to each other in whispers.

Connie nodded and gathered her supplies. "My work here is done. I'll go start with Ms. Kelly now." She left the room with a final nudge against Agent Rodriguez's shoulder as she passed them. Both agents returned to Elise and Mary Ellen.

Elise handed the drawing to Agent Rodriguez. "That's the man I saw with Marcus Tate."

He looked at the picture, then back at Elise. "Are you sure?"

She nodded as his face paled before he handed it to Agent Wright. "I'm positive. Why?"

Agent Wright handed the drawing back to her partner.

He looked at it again, then slowly shook his head. "I know him."

Chapter Fourteen

Silence invaded the room. Everyone stared at Agent Rodriguez.

"I mean, I don't know him, know him, but I recognize him." Agent Rodriguez took a seat where Connie had been and looked at his partner and passed her the drawing. "Don't you?"

Agent Wright took the paper and stared. She lifted her shoulders just a little bit. "I think I've seen him before, but I can't be sure, nor can I place from where." She handed the paper back to Agent Rodriguez. "So who is he?"

"I'm pretty certain he's with Capitol Police." Agent Rodriguez leaned back on the couch.

Elise sucked in air. "Capitol Police? As in, the officers who provide security for the US Capitol or our state capitol?"

"Someone who might have been on Mom's protection detail?" Mary Ellen asked.

"I'm not sure, but I think he checked in with us a year or so ago from the US Capitol." Agent Rodriguez nodded. "Yeah, I'm pretty sure that's where I've seen him before."

Elise sank farther into the couch. "Okay, but what is he doing here in Little Rock? It's a long way from Washington."

Agent Wright dropped into the chair facing the couch. "It's complicated. Everybody assumes everyone in politics has a Secret Service detail. That's far from the truth."

Agent Rodriguez crossed his legs at the ankles. "Secret Service is usually reserved for presidents, past and present, and their families, as well as main candidates running for president."

"And the vice president and his family too," Agent Wright added.

Agent Rodriguez nodded. "Right. They'll also have temporary details provided to foreign heads of state while visiting the United States."

He continued. "The US Capitol Police protect members of Congress twenty-four hours a day when they are in the Capitol building, but it's a different story once they are back in their districts. Key leaders in the House and Senate have the protection of US Capitol Police on a constant basis: the House Speaker, House and Senate Majority and Minority Leaders, and House and Senate whips."

Mary Ellen rubbed her lip. "Forgive me, but it's been a long time since I took Political Science, and Mom and I tried not to talk politics at home very often. Can you remind me what a whip is and why they'd have constant protection from the Capitol Police."

"Whips are basically party enforcers." Agent Wright inched to the edge of the chair. "They ensure party discipline, mostly making sure that members of the party vote according to the party platform, rather than according to their own individual ideology or the will of the voters of the district to which they were elected."

Elise sunk deeper into the couch. "That explains so much of the problems with politics today. Each party elects a whip to enforce their party platform rather than what the people actually want. It's a sad state, and most voters today don't even know about whips."

Agent Wright looked back at her partner. "You think this guy is Capitol Police here on security detail?"

Agent Rodriguez shrugged. "Maybe. Or maybe he's changed jobs."

Maybe, but unlikely. One didn't exactly go from guarding the nation's capital to hanging out in Arkansas, of all places. Elise once again brought up his image in her mind. "He *was* at a federal courthouse when I saw him."

Agent Rodriguez nodded. "Right. With a state capitol security guard."

"Who ended up murdering my mother." Mary Ellen's voice was barely a whisper.

Elise somewhat enjoyed being a party to the agents' discussion, but hated that Mary Ellen had to deal with the grief. "If he's with any law enforcement or security detail, his photo should be stored, right? So you could get his name and address and details."

Agent Wright cut her eyes to Elise, as if remembering she was there. "We'll run the drawing through our database and see if anything pops."

That would waste time. Elise couldn't see the logic in wasting any more time than had already passed. "If you already have an idea of where you recognize him from, wouldn't it skip some steps and save some time to look at the Capitol Police first?"

Agent Rodriguez straightened in his space on the couch. "We have procedures we have to follow, Mrs. Carmichael."

"What's more important than solving my mother's murder?"

Elise could relate to Mary Ellen's frustration. She was most interested in getting the case closed, the guilty parties brought to justice, so she and Sawyer could breathe easier. "You're talking about the murder of a US senator. I understand about procedures and policies, trust me, I was married to a Marine so I get it. But I also understand the importance of catching everyone involved with the conspiracy to murder a US senator. And if this man *is* Capitol Police, then the political implications run even deeper than a state capitol security officer committing the murder alone."

Agent Wright again wore her sucking-sour-lemons expression. "We'll run our investigation according to the bureau's protocol in a situation like this."

Could the woman be any more frustrating? Elise pushed off the couch and looked down at the agents. "Every minute you waste following procedure is another minute my son and I are in danger. If this guy is Capitol Police and was involved with Marcus Tate here, I feel fairly certain that he didn't follow any protocol in obtaining *my* information. He obviously has my address and details about me." She popped her hand to her hip, but resisted the urge to wag a finger. "Which he had no way of even knowing what I saw Marcus Tate say except through *your* office."

Agent Rodriguez stood, as did his partner. "Mrs. Carmichael, I understand how upset you must be, but—"

Elise was all but shaking. "Upset? You think this is upset? No, this is fear and anger pushing me to protect my son. I had to go get a security system for protection because of information I told *you*. That was roughly seven hundred bucks just to give me basic protection for my home and family. The threat was brought on because of information released in one way or another from your office. This isn't upset. You haven't even seen an idea of what I'm like when I'm upset." Right now, she just wanted to scream.

Loud and long.

Mary Ellen stood beside her.

Agent Wright slipped her smirk back on. "Maybe had you informed someone of Tate's call earlier, all of this would be a moot point because Senator York could still be alive."

"Monica," Agent Rodriguez hissed.

Mary Ellen sucked in air.

Really shaking now, Elise went to the front door and slung it open. "Leave. Now." Her legs were even shaking as the rage coursed through her.

The agents crossed the room. Agent Rodriguez got to the door first. "Mrs. Carmichael, my partner was out of line with that statement. She didn't—"

But Elise was over the woman. A hundred percent over it. She pointed out the open door. "Get out, right now."

"Connie is still working with Ms. Kelly," Agent Rodriguez started. She had to hand it to him, he tried his best.

Too bad he was partnered with. . .with. . .such a poor excuse of a human being. "Connie can stay until she's done or she can leave now, that's up to her." She wagged her finger between the two agents. "But you two, you are leaving my house now."

"Hey, you called us, remember?" Agent Wright clearly had no idea of the imminent danger she faced every time she opened her mouth.

"I won't make that mistake again, I can assure you." Elise again waved them out the front door.

Agent Rodriguez shook his head. "No, if something else happens, you need to—"

"Out. I'm not discussing anything else with you. If you don't leave, I will contact my attorney and law enforcement. Do you want Connie to stay and finish or leave now?"

Agent Rodriguez crossed the threshold, pulling his partner with him. "Let her finish. We can wait in the car."

"Wait in the car? Do you realize how warm it's gotten?" Agent Wright asked her partner before turning back to Elise. "Why won't you let us see that iPad, Mrs. Carmichael? What are you hiding or who are you protecting?"

Elise shut the door on them, but mainly Agent Wright.

As if she could have prevented Lilliana's murder. *Pfft*. If she'd called Lilliana and told her, her mother-in-law would have waved it off as a prank or irrelevant. If she had called law enforcement, they most likely would have immediately contacted Lilliana, who would have waved it off and disregarded.

Unless she didn't.

No, she wouldn't go back down that road. Yes, she should have told someone, but she'd been so distracted. . .and she could send them the files from the iPad, but Agent Wright would use whatever she possibly could against Elise. Arabella would protect her, but had been adamant about making them get a warrant.

However, she couldn't help but wonder—if she had called the

police, would they have gone to Lilliana and Noland's and just their mere presence there have prevented that murder? At least for that night?

No, she couldn't allow herself to play the *what-if* game. She wasn't going to follow the rabbit trail again.

"Elise, we can't change the past. Don't beat yourself up." Mary Ellen offered her a sideways hug.

But Mary Ellen didn't absolve her. Did Mary Ellen think that if Elise had called, her mother would still be alive? It was a question Elise wasn't ready to ask because she didn't know if she could take the answer.

Elise strode into the kitchen, having to tell herself not to stomp, and poured herself another cup of coffee. Mary Ellen followed and grabbed a bottle of water from the fridge.

"On a one to ten scale, with one not close and ten being perfect, how close does this come to your memory?" Connie asked Wesson, turning her drawing to the young reporter.

"An eight or nine maybe. It looks like him as I remember."

"What can I do to make it a nine?" Connie looked up and winked at Elise.

"Nothing. I mean, it's as I remember him." Wesson lifted the picture and showed Elise. "Do you recognize him?"

Since the agents were cooling their heels in the car, Elise took her time studying the sketch. It looked like the man she'd seen on her security feed, the one who'd left the box of pictures of her. It had to be the same guy. Surely there wasn't more than just one leaving her threats.

Elise passed the sketch to Mary Ellen who glanced at it and shrugged. "Doesn't look familiar to me. I can ask Noland if you want."

Shaking her head, Elise handed the paper back to Connie. "There's no need to upset Noland. I doubt he'd recognize anybody right now."

"What about you, Elise? Anything familiar?" Wesson asked.

Elise shrugged. "He looks like the guy who left me those boxes on my front porch that my security video recorded."

Connie packed up her things. "Could you let Dennis know I'm done?"

"He and Agent Wright are waiting for you in the car." Elise took a sip of coffee.

"In the car? Why would they go out there?" Connie zipped up her bag.

Elise wrinkled her nose. "Because I made them get out of my house."

Both Wesson and Connie gasped in unison, then Connie gave a little chuckle. "I'm sure it was Monica's fault."

Elise nodded. "That woman is something else. She's the embodiment of the saying 'The FBI stands for Federal Bureau of Idiots.'"

Wesson laughed. "She is quite the rude one, isn't she?"

Mary Ellen shook her head. "Rude doesn't even begin to cover how she treated Elise."

Connie stood. "That one is a handful. I feel sorry for Dennis having been partnered with her. He didn't want her, but nobody else did either. I personally think they assigned her to Dennis in hopes that some of his tact and diplomacy would rub off on her. I don't think it's working."

"Clearly not." Elise could see very little redeeming about the woman, and couldn't feel too sorry for Agent Rodriguez because he could always take charge of every interview or such.

"She's one of the reasons people have such disdain for the FBI," Mary Ellen offered.

"Well, I better not keep them waiting." Connie lifted her bag, but hesitated and patted Elise's shoulder. "It's not my place to say, but I'll say my piece anyway. Give Dennis a chance. He might be saddled with the woman as a partner, but overall, he's a good agent. And a good man to boot. Those are rare these days. He digs and digs until he gets to the truth." She glanced up and nodded at Mary Ellen. "He won't stop digging until he finds out the truth about what happened to your mother."

Connie shuffled toward the front door, walking uneven as she toted her bag of art supplies. Elise followed.

Agent Rodriguez was out of the car in a flash as Connie and Elise emerged. He took Connie's case from her before she could descend the steps. She handed him the drawing. "Ms. Kelly says it's pretty close to what she recalls." Connie gave Elise a final look and smile over her shoulder, then joined Agent Wright in the car.

He looked at the picture Connie had drawn. "Do you recognize him?"

Elise shook her head. "Not in person, but he looks a lot like the man on my security video. I sent you the file."

"I'll review it as soon as we get back." He ran a hand over his cropped black hair. "Look, about before. . . I'm really sorry for what Agent Wright insinuated."

"That wasn't an insinuation, that was a blatant accusation of blame. You know it and so do I."

"She shouldn't have said it, either way, and I'm sorry."

Elise leaned against the side of the doorjamb. "I have to wonder why you're always the one making apologies on her behalf. She should be professional enough to know how to speak to witnesses. But she lacks all sense of professionalism and that makes her a liability to the bureau. I can't imagine why they haven't let her go yet."

Agent Rodriguez's cheeks reddened. "She just hasn't learned the art of subtlety very well yet."

Elise laughed out loud. "Yet? How long has she been an agent?"

"Less than five years."

"But more than two, right?"

He nodded.

"Then she should have learned at least the basics." Elise pointed toward the car. "That woman. . .well, let's just say she hasn't mastered much in her communication and interrogation skills. I'm not just saying that. I see agents on the stand all the time. In my professional opinion as to how witnesses come across, I would strongly urge you to never put that woman on a stand."

He smiled and gave a curt nod. "Duly noted." He hesitated a moment. "If anything else happens, do call."

"Thank you, Agent Rodriguez." Elise watched him turn and head back to the car, his shoulders slightly slumped. Agent Wright stared at her through narrowed eyes as her partner drove the car away.

Funny that neither agent asked for the iPad files. Not even once. Maybe the judges squelching their warrant moved that to the back burner, even though it seemed to be the only lead they had on the murder itself. Or maybe Arabella had laid down the law that unless they had a warrant, that demand was off-limits.

What Lilliana had sent was the only direct link to the case. All the rest of this was threats against her for speaking out about what she'd seen. Yes, that was linked to the murder, but whatever Lilliana had sent had been important enough to be the last real act of her life. . .surely that was paramount to finding out what these files were and how they linked to Lilliana and her killer.

Elise went back inside where Wesson and Mary Ellen waited.

"So now what?" the young reporter asked as Elise plopped down on the couch. Wesson slumped down on the other side while Mary Ellen took a chair.

"Now the FBI does whatever they're going to do." Elise shrugged. "Whatever that is."

Wesson studied her for a moment. "What are you going to do?"

The edges of Elise's mouth turned up into a slight smile. The girl was smart, and as far as she could determine, eager. If she was trustworthy remained to be seen, but for now, Elise would give Wesson the benefit of the doubt. She'd take the chance. "How would you like to help me on my investigation into Lilliana's murder?"

Wesson's dark eyes widened to big circles. "Yes. Whatever I can do to help, the answer is yes."

"You're going to investigate Mom's murder?" Mary Ellen set her water bottle on the coaster. "You didn't tell me."

Elise sat up straight on the couch. "I decided that I can't leave something this important to the FBI, who seems to do nothing but follow leads we give them."

"I'm in, then." Mary Ellen crossed her arms over her chest. "I'm with you a hundred percent."

Elise smiled at her sister-in-law, then looked back at Wesson. "I won't promise you an exclusive. Actually, I can't even promise you an interview or that you can publish any details. Still interested?"

Wesson slowly nodded. "I'm not going to lie and say I wouldn't be disappointed because I would—I mean, it's every reporter's dream to get an exclusive or scoop, but I still want to help. I need all the experience I can get in investigating."

"Even if you can't discuss it with anyone until after the fact? After everything's already been reported?"

"It'd be hard, but yes."

Elise's gut instinct told her to trust Wesson. "Okay. What the agents wanted to get a warrant for is my son's iPad." She quickly explained everything. To both Mary Ellen and Wesson's credit, neither interrupted, and Wesson didn't try to sneak taking notes or record the conversation.

"What were the files Mom sent? I can't imagine her sending something so important to Sawyer's iPad."

Elise jumped up and ran and got her laptop, then plopped down on the couch between Wesson and Mary Ellen. "These were the two files."

She opened the first one and the picture filled the laptop screen.

"Do you know who they are?" Wesson tilted the screen to remove the glare.

Elise shook her head. "I have no idea. I don't think I've ever seen the woman or the room before, and babies kind of look like all babies or no one in particular." She shifted the screen for Mary Ellen to have a better view. "What about you?"

Mary Ellen slowly shook her head. "I don't recognize either, but there is something vaguely familiar about the picture. I just don't know what."

Wesson leaned in closer. "Let's break it down. I don't see any background image that might have some significance."

"I didn't either. What about you, Mary Ellen?"

Again, Mary Ellen slowly shook her head. "No, but again, there's something familiar, I just can't place it."

"Maybe it'll come to you in a bit." Elise closed the file and opened the lab results. "This was the other file."

Wesson straightened a little. "Lab results from. . .where?"

Elise tapped the logo.

"DNAncestry? It's DNA test results?"

"I'm not sure, but that's their logo, right?"

Wesson nodded. "Looks like the one I've seen. But whose results are these?"

"That's part of the mystery. There's no name, only an account number, and it's dated a couple of years ago. I guess they use only account numbers to protect people's privacy." Elise shrugged before looking at Mary Ellen. "Any idea why your mom would have DNA test results?"

Mary Ellen shook her head. "Mom didn't even like DNAncestry. She thought family lines should be kept by family and shared with each new generation."

Elise nodded. "I remember Judson had a booklet with y'alls family ancestors going back forever it seemed."

Wesson tapped the screen. "They didn't give you the name when you called?"

"I haven't had a chance to call yet."

Wesson's eyes widened and she pulled her cell from her pocket. "We should call now. Before the FBI get the warrant and get this.

Once they do, all this information will be harder to get, if we can even get it at all."

Elise smiled at Wesson's enthusiasm as well as her automatic use of *we*. "Start your investigating skills."

"Really? I can make the call?" The young reporter practically bounced in her seat on the couch.

Elise chuckled out loud, and glanced at Mary Ellen, who nodded. "Yes, you can make the call. Put it on speaker."

Wesson looked up the number, then waited while it dialed. Once a connection was made, she pressed the screen to activate the speaker and set the phone on the coffee table. "Hello. I'm calling about test results, please."

"One moment and I'll connect you with that department."

A click sounded, then an annoying voice over of the lab's menu of services offered.

Wesson pulled out a pen and little stenographer's notebook. She blushed. "Hey, we might not get a second chance so I want to make sure we get it all."

Elise nodded.

"Results, how may I help you?"

"Yes ma'am, I'm looking at the lab results that were sent and am a little confused."

"How may I help?" The woman at the lab sounded bored.

"Let me give you the account number to pull up." Wesson read the numbers aloud.

"Just a moment." Sounds of typing came through the connection. At least it wasn't the lab promo they'd just heard.

"Yes, Mrs. Poe, I have your record up in front of me. It looks pretty straightforward, even though it's older than most people call about."

Wesson was quick on her feet. "Yes, we're finally getting around to reviewing everything. Can you tell me what these results mean, exactly?"

The woman on the phone sighed. "The match between your son and the sample you gave us resulted in a ninety nine point two percentage that he is the father."

"So, to be clear, the paternity results show that my son is the son of the sample I provided?"

"Yes, ma'am."

Elise went back to the picture of the woman with the baby. Must be a boy and the woman must be Mrs. Poe. It had to be.

"Just because everything has been a bit crazy in my life, and I want to make sure records are secure, can you tell me if I listed the name correlating to the sample?"

"No—" There was a hesitation over the connection. "Mrs. Poe, because we do take our clients' privacy very seriously, I'm going to need you to give me more information to verify your identity. If you'll just—"

"Thank you for your assistance." Wesson disconnected the call and stared at Elise. "I'm betting that girl in the photo is Mrs. Poe and her baby's father denied him."

Elise looked at her sister-in-law. "Does the name Poe ring any bells to you?"

Mary Ellen wrinkled her brow, then let out a hiss. "This is so frustrating. I don't know a Poe, but like the picture, something is familiar about the name. I just can't make the connection."

Elise studied the picture while nodding slowly. "It'll probably come to you when you aren't trying to remember. What I'm most curious about is why did Lilliana have this and send it as her last act on this earth? Who is it, and how do they connect to Lilliana?"

Chapter Fifteen

This was getting them nowhere.

Elise stood and stretched. "I think we've exhausted all of the online searches we can do."

Wesson sat up from the couch and put her cell in her pocket. "My battery's almost dead anyway. I'll go into the office and see if I can find anything in the paper's archives about a Mrs. Poe."

"Smart. Mary Ellen and I can ask Noland and see if the name rings any bells to him." Doubtful because she just couldn't see Lilliana sharing secrets with anyone. Actually, Elise was having the hardest time grasping that Lilliana had a secret of any magnitude. Especially something that would be enough to be murdered over.

She needed to figure out the connection. The sooner the better.

She had just seen Wesson out when her cell rang. She checked the caller ID. "Arabella?"

"Hi, Elise. Did you have a run-in with the FBI agents again?"

That was fast. "Kind of. Did someone call and tattle on me?" Elise was so tired of the attitude of Agent Wright. She had to be the one to make the call.

"They're claiming your attitude and behavior is suspicious. I'm a little concerned that they might use that to get the warrant and even list you as a suspect."

Elise sank into a barstool. "A suspect? I would never—"

"I know," Arabella interrupted. "But everyone is a suspect who was close to the senator, and there's no denying you two weren't exactly on the best terms. And then there's the life insurance policy."

Life insurance policy? "What are you talking about? What policy?"

"They didn't tell you?" Arabella's voice carried the weight of incredulous shock.

Mary Ellen tossed her water bottle in the recycling bin before grabbing another from the fridge.

"Who didn't tell me what?" Elise's heart seemed to beat in peanut butter even as she asked the question.

"The FBI. Of course they didn't tell you." Arabella sighed very loudly. "Senator York had several life insurance policies. Most listed her husband and daughter as beneficiaries, but she had a policy that names Sawyer the beneficiary with you as the custodian of the account until Sawyer reaches legal age."

Elise stared at Mary Ellen as she took a seat in the barstool catty-corner to her. That was sweet of Lilliana to make sure her grandson would have a little nest egg. "He is her grandson, and they loved each other, so I can see her leaving him a little security." It made sense, and it also made sense that Lilliana would've never told her.

"Little? Oh no, Elise. It's not a little policy."

Probably enough to cover his college then, which actually was more than generous of her mother-in-law. "How much?"

"Two million dollars."

Elise nearly choked on her own spit. "Two million dollars? Are you serious?"

Mary Ellen stared at her intently.

"Very much so. And with that sum, it screams motive for murder. Especially since you didn't mention it to the agents."

"I didn't know about the policy. Not a thing. Lilliana never told me."

Mary Ellen tilted her head.

Arabella continued. "I understand, but it's there nonetheless."

This was going from bad to worse. "What should I do?"

"Maybe we should show some goodwill."

Elise figured she'd shown some serious goodwill in not full-blown lashing out at Agent Wright, but apparently, Arabella had something else in mind. "Like what?"

"Since you already have the files the senator sent you, why don't you offer to let the FBI pull everything off the iPad?"

What? "But I thought we didn't—"

"Elise, the decision is yours, of course, but there is no harm in letting them have it. It actually shows there's nothing there for you to hide." Arabella paused. "Um, is there?"

Elise quickly told her attorney what the two files contained.

"So," Arabella continued, "it would show you have nothing to hide and are going the extra mile to assist in the investigation."

"But it's the way Sawyer communicates outside of school."

Mary Ellen took a long swig, nearly drinking half the water in the bottle.

"And you can stipulate that they can only have the iPad for the time while Sawyer is in school," Arabella offered.

Elise chewed her bottom lip. "You think this is what I should do?"

"The decision is yours, of course, but I do think it will go a long way in moving along the investigation—away from you as a suspect and toward finding the real killer, which will keep you and your son safe."

Elise glanced at Mary Ellen who continued to stare with questions in her expression. "Okay. What do I need to do?"

"I'll call the FBI and work it out. What times would work best for you for them to pick up and return? I'll specify those times. Since you're offering, you hold the power."

Elise nodded, even though Arabella couldn't see her. "I get back from taking Sawyer to school at eight. They can pick up then, but I'd need it back before I leave to pick him up at three."

"That should be plenty of time."

Something else clicked in Elise's brain. "Arabella, can I make a specific request?"

"Like what?"

"I don't care who picks up and brings back the iPad, as long as it isn't Agent Wright."

"Of course, I can stipulate that. Is there any specific reason?"

Elise avoided Mary Ellen's stare. "She said that had I called someone earlier, Lilliana would still be alive."

"Wow, that's pretty unprofessional."

"Exactly. I don't know what her deal is against me, but I don't want her here."

"I understand completely. I'll make the call now and will either call or text you later to confirm."

"Thanks, Arabella." Elise disconnected the call and brought Mary Ellen up to speed on the details of the conversation.

"You know that you aren't responsible for Mom's death, right? Whoever shot her is responsible."

Elise lifted a single shoulder. "I appreciate that, Mary Ellen."

"It's the truth. You didn't pull the trigger, so you didn't kill her. You didn't hire the guard to kill her, so you aren't to blame."

"But if I had called—"

Mary Ellen reached out and took her hand. "We can't know what would've happened. What if I had been home? Could I have stopped whoever shot her?" She shook her head. "We can't beat ourselves up over the unknown. We just have to let go of any guilt we feel and move on, praying that we'll see justice for Mom on this side of paradise."

Elise wished she could have the faith of her sister-in-law, but she wasn't going to get into a theological discussion at the moment. Instead, she squeezed Mary Ellen's hand and smiled.

"I did have a thought while you were on the phone." Mary Ellen grabbed another water bottle from the fridge and passed it to Elise before she took another drink of hers.

"What's that?" Elise opened the bottle and took a sip.

"That paternity test had to be really important to Mom for her to have it, but also for her to have sent it."

"Right."

Mary Ellen half shrugged, half leaned. "What if it's about Noland?"

"What?" Elise had just taken another sip and nearly spit it across the kitchen island. "Noland?"

Mary Ellen held up her hand. "Hear me out. I mean, think about it. Noland was in the press corps and traveled a lot. He never married until he met Mom and supposedly never had children. What if the DNA test has nothing to do with why Mom was killed? What if it's about Noland and a child he fathered?"

"Why would Lilliana send that to Sawyer's iPad?"

"I don't know, but I do know Mom was big on family. You know that. She wouldn't have wanted something like this to get out and cause a scandal for the family. Maybe she knew you'd find it and would work to solve the puzzle."

It was farfetched, but also possible. "Then the files would have nothing to do with her murder."

Mary Ellen nodded. "Not that I can see."

"But Mary Ellen, the DNA test is only a few years old. That would mean that he fathered a child while married to your mom. I can't see Noland cheating."

Mary Ellen held up a finger. "The test is a few years old. It says nothing about the age of the child or the sample. The kid could be our age for all we know, but the paternity test was just run a few years ago. Maybe when Mom got the kid's DNA."

"Don't you think she would have told Noland?" Elise still couldn't wrap her mind around the scenario.

"Maybe she did. We won't know until we ask." Mary Ellen shrugged. "Maybe she didn't. Maybe she was looking into the woman to find out more about her before she told Noland. I just know if Mom found out Noland had a child, she'd tell him."

Elise chewed her bottom lip. "Maybe. What if the woman didn't want Noland or anyone else to know? What if she had passed the child off as someone else's baby? That could be motive enough for murder to keep her secret, right?"

"Could be." Mary Ellen finished her water in one big gulp. "I don't know. I just can't make heads or tails of this. It's all very unlike Mom. She wasn't secretive, you know that. That's why she couldn't stand lobbyists, because they play both sides of the aisle. She was all about blowing the whistle on what was wrong or immoral, at least in her opinion."

Elise couldn't help but grin wryly. "Oh, I know all too well. She was one of the most opinionated people I've ever met."

Mary Ellen laughed. "And she wondered why I haven't married yet. Sheesh, she'd chase away any man I got serious with in mere moments." She shook her head. "I don't know how you put up with her sometimes."

Elise sobered. "Because of your brother. Judson made up for every snide comment, rude remark, or condescending quip she ever made. He made me feel like it was just us against the world, his mother included." She smiled at the memories. "He loved away every concern or doubt she ever presented me with, so it was more than worth it to stay and put up with her."

"Yeah, Jud was always able to rise above her snideness, even when we were kids. He would do the same for me, telling me things to make me laugh and feel better. Like Mom's bun was pulled back too tight and made her brain collapse. Or she had a bad case of constipation and was just full of it." Mary Ellen laughed.

Elise chuckled too. "Yeah, he was the best at making jokes to ease a tense situation."

"I miss him," Mary Ellen whispered.

"Oh, me too. I still miss him so much that I feel like part of me died with him. If it wasn't for having Sawyer, I don't know what I'd do."

Mary Ellen reached out and squeezed Elise's hand. "I'm here for you whenever you need to talk."

"I know." Elise swiped at the few tears that had escaped. "But back to the paternity test. You really think it could be about a child of Noland's?"

"Well, there's really no way to know unless we ask. He'll either tell us what's what, or he'll be clueless. Either way, we'll have an idea of whether it was personal or not to Mom."

"True. If it's about Noland and has nothing to do with her murder, then I have to wonder if she was working on a project or bill or something that might have gotten her killed."

Mary Ellen nodded. "Well, when we ask Noland, if he's clueless, then we can go through Mom's office at the house. She kept a lot of her files there, some duplicates of what she was working on. She also had a lot of correspondence brought to the house. She didn't like clutter at her office, and she was never sure about the security of what was kept at her office at the capitol."

Elise glanced at the clock. "We'll need to hurry. I only have three hours or so before I have to go get Sawyer."

"Then why are we sitting here wasting time?" Mary Ellen tossed the water bottles into the recycling bin and grabbed her purse. "Let's go."

Chapter Sixteen

"Maybe we shouldn't just blurt out about the paternity test." Elise locked her car, parked behind Mary Ellen's in the circular drive at Lilliana and Noland's house.

"Well, give me a little credit. I kind of planned on easing into it." Mary Ellen unlocked the front door and stepped over the threshold. "Noland?"

"In here." Noland stuck his head out of the sitting room. "Well, hello, Elise. I didn't know you were coming over."

"It wasn't planned." Elise went and hugged the man. In spite of Lilliana's attitude toward her, Noland had always been nothing but nice to her. "How are you?" She followed him into the sitting room and sat next to him on the couch.

He muted the local news on the television. "I think I'm doing as well as can be expected. After tomorrow's service, I think I'll be okay."

Elise nodded. "I remember. It's hard to get through the service when you just want to curl up with your grief."

"Exactly." He slapped the side of his thigh. "So what are you girls up to?"

Mary Ellen sat in the rocker next to the couch, but before she could say anything, Elise grabbed the remote from the coffee table and turned the sound back on.

The screen filled with the sketch Connie had made of the man Elise had seen with Marcus Tate. The newscaster's voice seemed to boom. "This is a sketch of a person of interest in the murder of

Senator Lilliana York. This person is wanted for questioning. If you recognize him, please contact law enforcement at the number on the bottom of the screen."

"Wow, they got that out fast," Mary Ellen said.

Noland looked at Elise. "Did you help with that sketch?"

Elise slowly nodded. "He's the man I saw with the security guard on the phone."

"Good. I hope someone recognizes him," Noland said.

"Me too." Elise wiped her hands on her jeans. Why her palms were so sweaty, she had no idea.

"Is that what you girls came to tell me?"

Mary Ellen straightened in the rocking chair. "Noland, we need to ask you something a little difficult."

"What's that?" He looked back and forth between Mary Ellen and Elise. "Has the FBI found out anything? Has an arrest been made?"

"No, it's nothing like that." Elise took a deep breath. "Just before Lilliana's time of death, she sent files to Sawyer's iPad, then deleted them off of her phone."

"Files? To Sawyer? Of what?" Noland suddenly looked every bit of his sixty-three years, with the circles under his eyes drooping into his cheekbones. The gauntness of his cheeks was only highlighted by the paleness of his skin.

Elise laid a hand on his, Mary Ellen doing the same with his other hand. "There were two files. One is a picture of a woman holding a baby. The other is a DNA paternity test with a woman named Mrs. Poe. Does this mean anything to you?"

Noland shook his head, the tufts of hair above his ears gently swaying. "No. Should it? Does it have something to do with why Lilliana was murdered? Who is this Poe woman?"

"We don't know." Elise glanced at her sister-in-law.

Mary Ellen licked her lips. "Noland, is it possible Mom had that information because it related to you? I mean, I guess Poe could be just the name the woman gave the clinic."

Noland straightened, paused, then burst out laughing.

Elise and Mary Ellen stared at one another, then Noland. Had he lost his mind?

"Oh, girls," he managed between cackles. "This is rich."

"I don't understand," Mary Ellen began, her brows furrowing.

"You think Lilliana might have run a paternity test on someone thinking I might be the father?"

Mary Ellen shrugged. "I think it's possible."

Elise nodded. "No judgment here, Noland. We just have to check every possibility."

"Well, you'd be checking up on a possible miracle for me to have fathered a child." Noland continued to chuckle. "You see, I had a very serious case of mumps as a teen and I'm afraid the high temperatures left me sterile. I couldn't father a child if I'd wanted, which was a big part of the reason why I never married until later in life. Lilliana knew all this."

Oh, the heartbreak. Elise rested a hand on his shoulder. "I'm so sorry."

"I made peace with it years ago. As a young reporter, it was probably best I couldn't have children. I was out of the country a lot. It would have been quite the burden on any woman I might have had a child with." He sighed. "So, that paternity test has nothing to do with me."

"Then we're back to square one." Elise scooted back on the couch.

Mary Ellen clapped her hands, the sound echoing in the small sitting room. "Well, we can at least go through Mom's office here. See if we can find anything about a woman named Poe. Or maybe at least get a working list of her projects or bills."

Noland ran a hand over his thinning hair. "Why are you girls doing this? Isn't the FBI running their investigation?"

Elise frowned. "I'm sorry, but I don't have much faith in them, and every day they don't catch someone is another day Sawyer and I are at risk."

"What do you mean?" Noland asked.

Elise realized she hadn't told Noland about all of the threats. With a slow breath, she filled him in on everything that had transpired, including working with Wesson Kelly.

"I had no idea. Are you sure you and Sawyer don't want to come stay here with me and Mary Ellen? There's safety in numbers."

"I appreciate that, I truly do, but Sawyer is more comfortable at home, and now that I have the security system, we're pretty safe."

He shook his head. "It bothers me that someone was in your house though. Do you have a weapon for protection?"

Elise had to smile. "Now, Noland, I was married to Judson. I have his service handgun. I keep it locked up for Sawyer's safety, of course, but I know how to use it. Judson made sure of that."

"That makes me feel a little better. Maybe you should keep it close, especially at night."

"I will."

"You know, I'm not much help in a lot of things, but digging around I'm good at. I can use some of my old contacts and see what I can find out about your reporter."

Elise smiled. "You don't have to do that, Noland."

"I want to. Makes me feel like I'm doing something. I want to find out who killed Lilliana, who was determined enough to come into our home, our sanctuary, and shoot her. Any little thing I can do to help that along, I'm in."

Elise nodded. She could certainly understand the sentiment. Feeling helpless after losing someone was one of the worst emotions. She knew that well. "Okay, I'd appreciate it. Especially knowing if she's trustworthy. I think she is, but my gauge could be way off." She glanced to Mary Ellen. "So, Lilliana's office?"

Mary Ellen stood and led the way.

Lilliana's home office was not a reflection of her office in the capitol. This room held a bookcase filled with family photos, unlike the staged political pictures in her other office. There were handmade gifts from Sawyer on her credenza and a nice fluffy chair with throw pillow and blanket in front of the gas fireplace.

"I'll start with the files on her desk, the ones the FBI didn't take anyway, and you can start on the file cabinet." Mary Ellen sat in her mother's leather chair behind the beautifully carved cherrywood desk.

"I can't believe they'd leave anything. One would think they'd take everything." Elise opened the top drawer of the five-drawer wooden file cabinet.

"You'd think. They did take a lot of files, and her computer."

Elise started flipping through files. "And obviously her phone."

"Yeah." Mary Ellen moved papers around the desk. "Elise, do you have any idea what we're looking for here?"

Exasperation forced out a sigh. "I don't know exactly. Something with the name Poe on it. Or anything that looks like it's out of place."

"As if we'd know what was out of place," Mary Ellen mumbled.

It did seem farfetched, but Elise refused to just give up. There had to be some lead somewhere.

But two and a half hours and an entire desk and filing cabinet later, there still wasn't a lead to be found.

"I was so sure we'd find something here in Mom's office." Mary Ellen slid the credenza door shut.

Elise shared her frustration. "I thought so too." She glanced at the clock. "I've got to go get Sawyer from school."

"I'll keep looking around the house. If it was something really important, maybe Mom didn't keep it in her office."

"Maybe not." Elise gave her sister-in-law a quick hug, waved at Noland as she passed the sitting room on the way out, and then headed to Sawyer's school.

The beautiful April sun shone down on Little Rock, but a gentle breeze held the higher temperature at bay. A perfect spring day.

Elise drove with the windows down, soaking in the tranquility of the afternoon.

She turned on West Markham Street and hit a traffic jam like she'd never seen on that road, not even when the Clintons were in town during his presidency.

Great. Sawyer would panic if he didn't see her as soon as school let out. Elise dug around in her purse and found her cell phone. Somehow, she'd put her phone on silent. As she saw the four missed calls from Hallie and two voice messages from the school, her heart squeezed. She tapped the screen to play back the messages.

"Mrs. Carmichael, this is Anna Carol Smith. I don't want to alarm you, but a man claiming to be Sawyer's uncle tried to check him out. We, of course, knew this was not the case, so we didn't allow him to pick up Sawyer and we phoned the police. The man left before the police got here, but we will need you to come into the office to pick up Sawyer this afternoon."

The vise on Elise's heart tightened as she moved on to the next message. "Mrs. Carmichael, it's Anna Carol again. After speaking with Hallie Newsom, the police are treating this as an attempted kidnapping. The school is in shutdown mode. Every parent must come into the office to pick up their children. Please come as soon as you receive this message. The police want to speak with you."

She quickly called Hallie, who answered on the first ring. "Elise, he's okay. He's sitting with me in the counselor's office."

The tension in every nerve in Elise's body lessened just a little. "Thank you, Hallie. I must've put my phone on silent somehow."

"It's okay. He's fine. The office pulled his record when the guy came in and asked to check Sawyer out. As soon as they saw no man was authorized, they phoned the police. The guy must've figured out something was up because he left before the police could get here."

Panic nearly choked her. All she wanted was to hold her son in her arms. "I'm stuck in traffic."

"It's because the school's in lockdown and the police are here, verifying every child is picked up by an authorized person."

"I'm so sorry." Tears filled her eyes and her voice.

"Hey, Elise, it's okay. I told the police what has been going on with the threats and such, so they're taking this very seriously. The important thing is Sawyer is fine. He's here in the office, playing on his iPad."

"I'll get there as soon as I can." She wanted to be there now. Until she could see Sawyer and hold him, she would worry.

"It'll take a little time. Don't worry. I'm not going to leave him. I'll be here until you pick him up."

"Thanks, Hallie." She disconnected the call and continued the slow process of making her way to the school.

Her mind went to all the crazy places it shouldn't. What if the school hadn't been diligent and let some strange man take Sawyer? Would Sawyer have gone with him? She had gone over standard safety rules and regulations with her son when he started school, but would he really follow her instructions? She'd seen all the documentaries about kids who had been well versed in being safe follow a stranger to find a puppy or kitten or the like. Would Sawyer?

If the man had gotten Sawyer, what would he have done? Elise's mouth went dry as the Mohave Desert. Used him as leverage to control Elise? But for what? She didn't know anything more than she'd already told the FBI. It wasn't like she knew something else. . .

The sketch!

The FBI had put it on the noon news. Was the man who tried to pick up Sawyer the same man she'd seen with Marcus Tate?

A man connected to Lilliana's murder?

Elise's hands trembled and she gripped the steering wheel tighter. Had she inadvertently made Sawyer even more of a target?

Nausea came in waves. This couldn't be happening. Maybe she should take Sawyer and just go somewhere far away. Somewhere no one would know where they were. Where nobody could find them. She could tell Sawyer it was a vacation. She could take a leave from work. It wasn't busy now anyway—she wasn't even scheduled on any court docket until Friday, and she'd already taken off for Lilliana's funeral.

A car tried to merge into Elise's lane, but she inched up. He threw her a sign, but she ignored him. All that mattered was getting to Sawyer as quickly as she could. If it wouldn't cause more of a jam, she would've already abandoned the car and ran the block or so to the school.

Running. Judson had always said running toward trouble to stand up for what was right was what set the men apart from the cowards. Right now, she didn't care that she wanted, desperately, to act as a coward. Anything to keep their son safe.

Finally, she made it to the school. She inched up out of the road and pulled almost over the curb of the parking lot. She locked the car, then ran to the office door, past two news crews talking to nervous parents in the line to pick up their children, their identification in hand to show the uniformed police officers at the door.

Elise pushed past the parents.

"Ma'am, you'll need to go to the back of the line and wait," the female police officer said.

"I'm Elise Carmichael."

"Oh. Yes." The male officer looked at the female one. "I'll take her back." He glanced back at Elise. "Do you have identification?"

She dug in her purse and pulled out her driver's license.

He glanced at it then nodded. "Follow me."

Elise shoved her wallet back into her purse and followed the officer into the office. The school secretary, Mrs. Smith, stood as they walked by. "Oh Mrs. Carmichael. We had no idea. I'm so sorry for what you're going through."

"Thank you." Elise's reply was automatic because she really had no idea what she was thanking the woman for? Stopping a stranger from taking her son, maybe? She should hug the tar out of the woman.

The officer stopped outside one of the offices and opened the door. "Here you go, ma'am."

She stepped inside, expecting to see Hallie and Sawyer, but instead found Agents Wright and Rodriguez along with two other suited men.

"Where's Sawyer?" Panic crawled up her throat, its claws digging in.

"He's fine. Come on in and have a seat." Agent Rodriguez motioned toward the chairs. "This is Special Agent Lionel Eaton and Agent Fred Brewer. They head up the missing children investigations."

"I want to see my son. Now." Elise couldn't stop the trembling.

"In just a moment, Mrs. Carmichael. We'd like to ask you a few questions first," one of the agents said.

Elise didn't know if it was the special one or the other, but she really didn't care. "No, I want to see my son first."

"He's okay, Elise." Agent Rodriguez used that calming voice of his.

It didn't work this time. Elise turned around and opened the door and stepped out into the hall. "Hallie," she called, raising her voice a little. "Hallie." She raised her voice even more.

A door across the hall opened and Hallie stuck her head out. "Hey, Elise. We're in here."

Elise ignored all the FBI agents and nearly knocked over Hallie to get into the room with her son.

He lounged in an overstuffed chair, leg hanging over the arm, and played intently on a game on his iPad. He didn't even look up as she entered until she scooped him into a hug. He squirmed out of her embrace, his cheeks blushing.

She didn't care that she embarrassed him. She kissed his forehead before she straightened and turned to Hallie. She gave the young woman a big hug as well. "Thank you for staying with him," she whispered.

"Of course." Hallie grinned.

"Now that you've seen your son, can we go and talk in the other room?" one of the new agents asked.

Elise glanced at Sawyer's head, already bent back over his iPad, his focus totally on his game. She didn't want to let him out of her sight. Maybe not ever again. "We can talk in here." She crossed her arms over her chest, knowing it was a defensive posture but also knowing she wasn't required to go to any specific place to answer their questions.

One of the agents threw a pointed look at Sawyer. "It might be better if we talked in another room."

"Maybe, but it's okay. My son is deaf, Agent. . .I'm sorry I forgot your name. As long as he's into his game, he won't read lips. We're fine to talk in here."

"It's Special Agent Lionel Eaton, Mrs. Carmichael. I really think it best if we go into the other room."

Before Elise could say anything, Hallie jumped in. "I'll stay with Sawyer, Elise. You know I won't let anything happen to him."

Elise let out a long breath. "Thanks, Hallie." She squatted in front of her son and signed, "I have to go talk to these men for a minute. Hallie is going to stay with you. Okay?"

He nodded. She planted a kiss on the top of his head and stood. Might as well get it over and done with.

"Let's go," she said to no one in particular.

CHAPTER SEVENTEEN

They led her back into the room the officer had originally taken her to. Smaller than the counselor's office where Sawyer and Hallie waited, but it sufficed. Elise didn't plan to be detained longer than necessary. Especially not with Agent Wright in the room.

She sat where the special agent indicated. The rest of the group sat around her. "Mrs. Carmichael, I've gotten the details of the case where you and your son are involved from Agents Wright and Rodriguez. What would you like to tell me about the case?"

"Tell you what about the case?" Seriously?

"I'd like to hear it from you. If you don't mind." He smiled, and Elise was sure he was used to charming people.

She wasn't in a being-charmed mood. "Well, in a nutshell, as a lip-reader, I eavesdrop without even realizing it." She continued, relating everything she thought important and ended with, "Now, since the sketch of the man I saw with Marcus Tate ran on the noon news, there was an attempted kidnapping of my son."

"You think the two are connected?" Special Agent Man asked.

Was he kidding? "Yes, I do. I think all these threats against me and my son are directly related to what I saw and that I have told the FBI. The only people who knew I spoke with the FBI and did the sketch are my sister-in-law and the FBI. There's obviously a leak in your bureau that's put me and my son in danger, and I'm not so sure I should talk to any of you anymore." She hesitated. "At least, not without my lawyer present."

"Why do you think you need your lawyer present, Mrs. Carmichael?"

Mercy, they were going to drive her insane with their calming voices and monotone questions. "Because every time I speak to any FBI agent, it seems me and my son are placed in more danger."

"In what way?"

The urge to throat-punch the man curled her hands into fists. "The threats have escalated from deliveries to stalking me to now attempted kidnapping. I'd say each level is more dangerous than the previous, wouldn't you?" She stood. "Look, I've told you what I know. About this, I know nothing more than what I've been told. I honestly can't think of anything else that might help your case. If I do, I have Agent Rodriguez's number. All I want to do right now is take my son and go home. Enjoy a quiet dinner together before relaxing. Is that too much to ask?"

"The security cameras here at the school caught the man's image," Agent Rodriguez interrupted.

That stopped her short. "And?"

"He looks like the sketch Connie drew from your description of the man you saw with Tate."

She nodded. "The sketch that was on the news at noon today, right?"

He slowly nodded. He pulled out his cell and turned it to her. "It's a little grainy, but does this guy look like the person you saw with Marcus Tate?"

She glanced at the picture. "Maybe. It's hard to tell. I focus mainly on the mouth and lips, and well, I just don't know. The angle. . . I can't say. It looks like him, but I can't be sure." She passed his cell phone back to him.

A surge of adrenaline pulsated throughout her body. Every time she talked to the FBI, the threats against her and Sawyer escalated. This one could have been catastrophic, and she didn't want to think about that—she couldn't.

"Were you able to tell anything else about him?" she asked. "The man who tried to take my son?"

Agent Rodriguez nodded. "We got a partial license plate on the car he left in. He was driving a silver Ford."

"A Ford Focus?" she asked.

Special Agent Whatever lost his perfect composure for a moment. "How'd you know that? Do you know someone who drives a silver Ford Focus?"

Elise shook her head. "Wesson Kelly said that's what she thought the man in the bushes outside my home got into." She faced Agent Rodriguez. "Which would indicate that all my delivered boxes and threats and this attempted kidnapping are all the same person—the man I saw with Marcus Tate."

"It would seem so." Agent Rodriguez suddenly found the floor very interesting.

"And it also seems that every time I speak with the FBI and try to help on the case, it only puts me and my son in more danger."

"Mrs. Carmichael, your attorney has contacted us in regards to allowing us to pull files off your son's iPad. The files the senator sent. According to her, we can have the iPad from nine until three tomorrow." Special Agent What's-His-Face took over the conversation.

She nodded. Thank goodness she and Arabella had already spoken about this. It certainly was a goodwill gesture now.

"I'm wondering if perhaps we might go ahead and take the iPad today and return it tomorrow. In the interest of speeding up the process of the investigation, of course." The Special Agent smiled, but the sincerity didn't move past his mouth.

Elise wasn't in a generous mood to begin with. "That won't work. As I'm sure my attorney explained, my son's talk to text program is on that iPad. You can have someone pick it up tomorrow morning at nine, as planned." She stood. "Now, if that's all, I'd like to take my son and go home. It's been quite a long day."

"Well—" The special agent started.

Elise cut him off. "Good. Thank you." She moved to the door and flung it open, went across the hall and got Sawyer. With a nod to Hallie, she took Sawyer's hand and led him out of the school.

"Mrs. Carmichael!" Anna Carol Smith called out.

Elise paused and looked at the school secretary over her shoulder. "Yes?"

"We. . .I mean, the principal. . .the board. . .well, they thought perhaps you might feel Sawyer is safer at home for a few days. Until this blows over, of course."

Because they didn't want bad publicity or the liability. While bitter, Elise understood. Besides, it wasn't the secretary's fault. But it wasn't Sawyer's either. "Yes. I agree. Thank you, Mrs. Smith."

She turned back and continued leading Sawyer out of the school.

"What's going on?" Sawyer roughly signed once they were in the car.

She didn't want to lie to him, but didn't want to scare him either. The chances that there wouldn't be discussion of this were slim to none. Honesty was the best policy. "It seems someone tried to check you out of school without my permission." Her hands only trembled a little as she signed.

"Who?"

She shook her head. "I don't know."

"Why?"

Elise sighed before she replied. "I saw someone say something about committing a crime. When I reported it to the police, the person got angry. He's been trying to scare me into keeping quiet."

Sawyer's eyes widened.

She hated taking away his child innocence, but she needed him to be cautious. Alert. On guard against someone trying to take him. "So you need to be careful. Only go somewhere with me or Hallie."

"Or Mary Ellen," he signed.

She smiled and nodded. "Yes, or Mary Ellen or Noland."

He stared out the window with a pensive expression. She

recognized the expression of her son processing information. She chewed her bottom lip. If only she could make this all go away for his sake...

"Are you scared?" Sawyer signed with his one hand.

Oh, her sweet boy. "Only when it comes to you. I mean it, Sawyer, you can't go off with anybody you don't know, no matter what they say. Okay?"

He nodded, his little face drawn.

She had to make light of something so heavy now that he understood. She reached over and ruffled his hair. "Okay, I don't feel like cooking tonight. How about we grab a burger and fries on our way home?"

His little face lit up like Christmas morning. "And shakes?"

It was true—children were resilient. And for that, she was thankful. She laughed. "Yes, of course, shakes too." At least she could always count on his stomach to remain constant.

After running through a drive-thru and picking up fast food, which she told herself was okay every once in a while, they made it home. She parked in the garage and disabled the alarm after she'd shut the garage door behind them. Having the SkyLink system gave her the sense of security she hadn't felt all day. But now, here in her home, eating burgers and fries with Sawyer while they watched a movie on DVD, she felt safe, and it was a very good and welcome feeling after the day she'd had.

When Judson was alive, she always felt safe and secure. Even when he was deployed, she still held that sense of refuge he provided. Their home had always felt like a sanctuary to her. While whoever was threatening her might rattle her now, she refused to let him steal the peaceful joy of the house with all the beautiful memories she'd shared with Judson here.

She'd just tucked Sawyer into bed and walked into her own room when her cell phone rang. Her heart clenched for a moment until she recognized the caller ID. "Hey, Wesson."

"Is this a bad time? I don't want to intrude on yours and your son's time."

"No, he just went to bed." Elise kicked off her shoes and pulled out her pajamas, setting them on the hamper in the bathroom.

"Are you okay? I heard what happened. Well, everyone did. It was on the five o'clock news."

Well, at least Sawyer hadn't seen it. Although, he probably would've thought it was cool. "He's okay, that's all that matters. What all did they show on the news?" Elise reached for her towels to put on the hook. She hesitated a moment. Was her color coding of her towels OCD like Agent Wright had accused? Nah, she just liked things a certain way. Judson had never minded, and he was the least OCD person she had ever known. She put the towels on the hook with a little more force than necessary. "What all did they report?"

Wesson let out a sigh before answering. "They mainly showed the line of parents outside the school, a couple of interviews with parents, and then that sketch of the guy, and asked anyone who recognized him to call blah blah blah."

Elise pulled out a makeup remover wipe and rubbed it across her face. She could just bet none of the above would get her votes to PTO president, not that she wanted to be.

"One station got a little clip of you and your son walking out of the school. They had that as the lead to their story."

Great. Maybe it was a good thing that the school didn't want Sawyer attending for the next couple of days. At least here at home, she could keep him close. She wadded the wipe into a tight ball and tossed it into the trashcan. "Well, that can't be helped, I suppose."

"Look, another reason I called is to give you a heads-up that the paper is running a story about the incident at the school tomorrow too. I didn't break my promise. I had nothing to do with the story, but it *is* news and linked to the murder of the senator."

"I understand. I know you didn't tell them anything." Not that she really knew, but she felt pretty positive. "It's okay."

"I appreciate that because I know how hard this is for you. On a more positive note, the final reason that I called you. I found out something on our mysterious Mrs. Poe."

Elise leaned against the bathroom doorjamb. "What?"

"I need to verify everything, of course, but I'm pretty positive this is her. Alice Poe, twenty-six years old, lived here in Little Rock until almost three years ago when she moved and just kind of disappeared."

Alice Poe. "I've never heard her name mentioned. How does she connect in any way to Lilliana?" Elise leaned against the edge of the vanity.

"She was a political science major at the University of Arkansas in Little Rock. Graduated four years ago. She got a position at the state capitol. Nothing big, just mainly a gopher type of entry-level job."

"Getting her foot in the door." Elise nodded, although Wesson couldn't see her. "Did she work with Lilliana?"

"I haven't found that out yet. What I do know is that everyone said she had promise, then suddenly, without much warning, Alice quit her job and moved. No one seemed to know where she went. It was like she fell off the map or something."

"You have no idea where she is?"

"I haven't started digging too hard. I just wanted you to know what I'd found out so far."

Elise chewed her bottom lip. "How can you be sure this Alice Poe is the same woman in the picture or on the DNA results?" Although, the woman in the picture looked to be about the right age.

"I'm not sure yet. I just did some searches for females with the last name of Poe that worked in the capitol building with Senator York for the last five to ten years. I don't know if they were even in contact with each other at this point. Like I said, I'm just starting to really look into her."

So maybe this was a dead end.

Or maybe it was a lead.

At least Wesson was trying. "Good work. And thanks for letting me know."

"Of course. I'll call you if I come up with anything else."

Elise ended the call and stepped into the shower, possibilities swarming her mind. If the paternity test wasn't for Noland, then whom? Why would Lilliana have the results and why would she send them to the iPad?

More questions than answers tucked Elise into bed, settling her in for a restless night's sleep. She had a funeral to attend in the morning.

CHAPTER EIGHTEEN

The morning sun sneaked in through Elise's windows earlier than she would have liked. The last cobwebs of sleep slipped away, just out of her grasp, and reality came crashing in. Today they would lay Lilliana to rest.

So many memories flooded Elise, riding on the rays of sunshine filtering in, as if defying the beautiful April morning with a permanent ending coming for one of the family. Lilliana wasn't an easy woman to love, but Elise respected her for raising the man she had loved so fiercely. Judson wouldn't have been the honorable man that Elise had fallen for had Lilliana not raised him as she did.

And Lilliana had loved Sawyer. Anyone who saw them together could see the special bond between them. She always made time to spend with him and never made him feel like his deafness was a handicap. She tossed away the airs of senator when she was around Sawyer and was just a regular grandmother. Elise loved and respected her for that more than she'd realized.

Today they would bury her next to her first husband and Judson, and they would honor her memory.

Sawyer came running into her room. "You are late to wake up," he clumsily signed.

She grinned as she pulled him into bed with her and held him tight before signing, "We're not late. Nana's funeral is today. Remember."

His happy face fell and he slowly nodded.

Her heart caught. "It's okay to be sad, honey. We'll all miss her."

His signing with one hand was still rough, but Elise could easily make out his reply, "I love her and miss her."

"Me too, honey."

"Do we have to go?"

Oh to be able to just curl up with him and let the world pass them by. But no, she had to teach her son to be honorable like his father. Just like Lilliana had done. "Yes, honey, we do. I know you'll be sad, but we need to say goodbye to her. Honor her memory. That's what funerals are all about."

"Like Daddy's was?"

Elise let out a slow breath. "Yes, honey, like Daddy's. Funerals are to honor their memories and show support for the family and friends left behind."

"Like Noland and Mary Ellen?"

"Yes, like Noland and Mary Ellen." She smiled. "And you."

"You too?"

She nodded. "Me too." She kicked off the covers and got out of bed. "How about we make waffles for breakfast?"

His little face lit up again as he jumped out of bed. His bare feet padded down the hall toward the kitchen.

Elise followed at a slower pace. Today would be very hard on Sawyer, and she wished she could take away the pain she knew he would feel. She hoped the press would be barred from the service and the cemetery. Too bad she couldn't bar the FBI.

Oh no! She'd forgotten about them coming to get Sawyer's iPad. She glanced at the clock and realized she only had a few minutes before one of them would show up. Elise quickly dressed, then stopped by Sawyer's room and grabbed his tablet before heading into the kitchen. She'd just finished pouring the chocolate milk when the lights flashed and the doorbell rang. She noticed the time illuminated on the microwave clock. They were punctual if nothing else.

She signed for Sawyer to stay in the kitchen, then carried the iPad to the door. She looked out the peephole and saw Agent Rodriguez standing alone on her porch. At least she didn't have to face Agent Wright this morning. Good thing because she certainly didn't feel up to that. She unlocked and opened the door.

"Good morning, Mrs. Carmichael." Agent Rodriguez smiled.

She couldn't help smiling back, but she didn't invite him in. She handed him the iPad. "I removed the security passcode so you should have no problem accessing the data on all of the iPad. I expect everything to be in working order when it's returned this afternoon."

"Of course. We're not trying to hurt you or your son, Mrs. Carmichael. We truly are working the case and investigating what happened to your mother-in-law."

"I can help you with that, Agent. She was shot. Murdered. Her funeral is today."

His face never changed expression. "Yes, ma'am, I know. But we're doing our best to solve the case and bring the responsible party or parties to justice."

"This is your best?"

"There's a lot to the investigation you aren't aware of, Mrs. Carmichael, information we can't share with you."

"Yet someone keeps sharing my information. I wonder why that is, Agent Rodriguez."

He had the decency to blush. "We're also working to find out how that information was released."

"Mmm-hmm." She glanced out to his car parked on the curb. Agent Wright sat inside. Of course. "Well, if there's nothing else then, I'll see you this afternoon when you return the iPad."

"Thank you for doing this, Mrs. Carmichael."

She didn't reply, just shut and locked the door. She couldn't waste any more time on their investigation. She had her own investigation, and her son, who needed his mom to make waffles at the moment.

After breakfast, Elise sent Sawyer into the bath to shower. She went into his closet and pulled out the little suit she'd bought him a month ago to wear for Easter Sunday when they went to Lilliana's for a big brunch and Easter egg hunt. Now he would wear it to bury his Nana.

She laid the suit out on the bed, along with socks and put his dress shoes on the floor. She'd help him with the tie after he was dressed. She refused a clip-on because Judson had been adamant that a real man always wore a double Windsor knot. He'd taught Elise how to tie one so she could teach Sawyer in case he was deployed when their son would need to learn to tie his tie.

If only they could have known that the first time she would ever tie the double Windsor for Sawyer would be for his father's funeral. Now she and Sawyer were facing another funeral.

She stared at the ceiling. *Why, God? Why? Sawyer has to fight harder for everything in his life. You took his father, now his grandmother? Why? What did he ever do to deserve any of this?*

As usual, there was no response. No booming voice from the heavens. Not even the quiet, still voice. Nothing but silence. She was getting used to that. Maybe that's why she had stopped praying pretty much altogether. If God couldn't take her anger, then He shouldn't have invoked it. At least, that's what she told herself.

After her own shower, she dressed in the same dress she'd worn to Judson's service. A simple black A-line dress. Nothing fancy. No frills, no ruffles, much like Judson's service had been. Even though his service was with full military honors, it was simple and heartfelt, like he would have wanted. Lilliana had wanted a little more fanfare, but Elise had stood firm. She could only hope that Mary Ellen and Noland hadn't let anyone railroad them into something super elaborate for Lilliana's service. Then again, she might have wanted that. At least the casket spray would be lovely and understated with its one hundred carnations in red, white, and blue. Fitting for a US senator, but also not outrageously extravagant.

Elise applied her makeup with a very light hand as well. She needed to be supportive for Mary Ellen and Noland and Sawyer, and the chance of tears was high. No sense smearing makeup for any reporter cameras that might be lurking about.

She finished helping Sawyer get ready, then drove them over to Noland and Lilliana's house. Noland and Mary Ellen had been quite adamant that she and Sawyer ride in the family limo to the church with them. Elise would have preferred driving herself so they could come home right after the service, but there was no way she'd deny Mary Ellen and Noland.

News vans were already parked on the road in front of Lilliana's house. A single police car was stationed there as well, keeping the camera crew and reporters off of the property.

She gripped Sawyer's hand tightly as they entered the house. It felt strange to be here, all dressed up, without Lilliana. It was her house, after all, and the decor and furnishings were all her. The only room on the bottom floor that looked welcoming was the sitting room. Probably why Noland was there most often. Elise couldn't help but wonder if Noland and Mary Ellen would put the house up for sale soon. She couldn't imagine Noland rambling about in the big old house alone, and Mary Ellen was happy in Eureka Springs.

"Aren't you handsome?" Mary Ellen signed before she scooped Sawyer up into a bear hug, burying her face in the crook of his neck. It was going to be one of those days.

Elise turned as Noland came into the foyer wearing his black suit. "How're you doing?" She gave him a side hug, noticing he'd lost a little weight.

"I'll be glad when today is over, to be honest. I've fielded more calls than ever. I'm just praying that the media and Lil's fellow politicians don't turn today into a circus."

"We passed news crews camped on the road. At least there was a Little Rock Police Department cruiser out there to keep them at bay." Elise gave his arm a gentle squeeze. Yes, he'd definitely lost weight. She remembered how it was. She'd lost almost fifteen pounds after Judson died. She just couldn't eat. Couldn't keep anything down. If it hadn't been for having to make sure Sawyer ate, she probably would have wasted away.

Mary Ellen let Sawyer go. He hugged Noland, tears in his little eyes.

"I almost hired security to make sure the press wouldn't be allowed in to the cemetery, but realized that the politicians would come anyway, whether they were truly associates of Mom's or not."

"It's all about appearances to them." Elise remembered well how many did some gesturing when Judson died, to get in Lilliana's good graces. Elise didn't know if any of their ploys worked or not. She hadn't cared.

"I try really hard to remember that Mom played the game too." Mary Ellen smoothed the black skirt she wore. "And not be offended by their grandstanding."

"I don't recall Lilliana ever using the death of a colleague to support her political stance on an issue," Elise said.

"She didn't." Noland released Sawyer. "After Judson died, she said she would never use a death to further any platform."

So maybe she'd been hurt back then. It was all such a blur to Elise. The service itself, the before and after. . .all she could recall was the overwhelming loss she'd felt.

A knock sounded on the front door.

"That must be the driver. I guess they're ready." Mary Ellen smoothed her black blouse this time.

Elise did remember the feeling that her clothes were all wrong. That the material itched against her skin in an annoying way, like petting a cat the wrong way. A good way to get scratched. She wrapped an arm around her sister-in-law. "You can do this. I'll help you get through it."

Mary Ellen hugged her, really hugged her hard. "Thank you."

Elise looped her arm through Mary Ellen's and took Sawyer's hand in her other. "Let's do this."

They walked to the front door where Noland waited. The four of them made their way out of the house and ducked into the waiting limo. Elise could hear the press calling out to Noland and Mary Ellen. The limo driver shut the door behind them, blocking out the reporters.

The ride to the church was made in silence. Sawyer stared out the window while the adults were all lost in their own thoughts. Elise could only remember the last time she'd been in a family limo on the way to a funeral. The grief and pain crept up behind her, almost knocking the air out of her.

No, she needed to be strong for Noland and Mary Ellen. Their grief was fresh and raw and would be on display today. She would do what she could to protect them. And Sawyer, of course.

The limo eased up to the side entrance of the church. The driver opened their door, and the pastor waited to greet them. He hugged Noland, then Mary Ellen, then Sawyer, before reaching Elise. She held out her hand to shake his. He shook her hand. "Mrs. Carmichael, I'm so sorry for your loss." She nodded, but didn't feel anything as he closed the door behind her.

He led them into the sanctuary, where the coffin sat on the pedestal in the front. Framed photos of Lilliana, mixed in with many floral arrangements, covered the entire wall behind the casket and along the sides. It was a beautiful display, and Lilliana would have been pleased.

The pastor showed them to the little area off to the side, completely shielded from view of the main sanctuary pews. "This is for your immediate family only. For privacy." He waved them in. "Is there anyone else you would like to join you?"

Noland and Mary Ellen exchanged a look, then both shook their heads.

"Very well. I'll let the ushers know they may let the mourners in. There's quite a large group already waiting." He scuttled away.

Mourners. Interesting choice of word. Elise would just bet that ninety-nine percent of the people attending the funeral wouldn't mourn Lilliana at all. They either were there to be seen, because they thought it was expected of them, or because they wanted to use her death as some sort of platform for their own gain.

Elise settled back in the pew, Sawyer on one side and Mary Ellen on the other. Let the games begin.

Chapter Nineteen

The cemetery service was shorter than the church service, and in Elise's opinion, much more personal. Despite the police escort, several news vans were parked along the drive with cameramen using zoom lenses to record the family at the gravesite. Elise wanted to scream at them and shove the cameras away, but knew she couldn't. The best she could do was shield Sawyer from the prying eyes of the cameras and press.

The pastor led the graveside group in the twenty-third Psalm, Lilliana's supposed favorite. Elise didn't know if it really was, or if it was the most common. Either way, at least the service would be over soon, even though she and Sawyer would have to go to Noland's for visiting with everyone. While she supposed it was meant to bring comfort to the family, and to some it might, it had felt like more of a burden to Elise when Judson had died. Thank goodness Lilliana had hosted the visitation at her house, so Elise could retreat to her own home when it all got too much for her to handle.

Elise made a mental note to watch Mary Ellen and Noland carefully and send them to their rooms if they looked like they needed personal space. It was the least Elise could do.

She glanced over her shoulder, past all those seated, past those standing under the canopy, to the very back where Agent Rodriguez and the two new agents stood. No sign of Agent Wright. Maybe she'd been taken off the case. That would be the one bright note on today.

As the pastor began to pray and everyone bowed their heads,

Elise took the opportunity to glance around as unobtrusively as she could, registering each face to memory, especially those she didn't recognize. She wrinkled her nose at the sight of some of the politicians she could only guess were there to be seen. A couple of people she recognized from church. Some she knew to be neighbors of Lilliana and Noland. There were a few who looked familiar, but Elise couldn't place them at the moment. There were a couple who looked like they really didn't belong.

In the back a man and a woman held hands, but were looking around. Their odd demeanor caught Elise's attention. Who were they? An older woman leaning against a younger woman looked out of place as well.

As Elise continued to glance around, she found many people who didn't look as if they should be at Lilliana's funeral, but did she really know her mother-in-law? Maybe these were constituents she'd helped. Or maybe people Lilliana had helped get legislature passed. Perhaps Lilliana had many more acquaintances or friends than Elise had realized.

"Amen." Everyone repeated the pastor's closing word, then lifted their heads.

"Ashes to ashes, dust to dust. We commence this soul to You, Abba God."

Everyone stood. Mary Ellen and Noland seemed to be leaning on one another for support.

The honor guard lifted their rifles and fired their three volleys into the air.

Boom! Boom! Boom!

The echoes of the shots shook Elise's chest. Beside her, Sawyer jumped, looking up at her. He'd never felt such a boom, and it probably scared him a little. She wrapped an arm around him and pulled him against her legs.

The uniformed guard came to stand in front of Noland and Mary Ellen. He saluted, then handed Mary Ellen the folded flag with gloved hands. Tears ran down her cheeks as the guard moved on. She sank back onto the folding metal chair.

Elise sat down beside her, pulling Sawyer back into his chair as well. Noland sat too. Elise grabbed Mary Ellen's hand and squeezed it. Mary Ellen leaned against her. Elise pressed against her, wishing she could give her sister-in-law some comfort and strength. It was hard to watch someone you love grieve.

"I'm okay." Mary Ellen sniffed and shakily stood. Everyone else stood with her.

The pastor came over and shook her hand. She took one of the carnations from the casket spray and turned toward the limo, waiting for Noland to do the same. Elise and Sawyer both followed suit, then together, the four of them walked to the family limo. The driver opened the door and ushered them inside, closing the door before the pack of reporters could reach them.

"Is Nana in heaven with Daddy now?" Sawyer signed.

Elise pulled him into her lap as the driver eased away from the gravesite. She wrapped her arms around him so he could see her signed response. "Yes, honey, Nana is with Daddy in heaven now."

He wiggled out of Elise's lap and onto the limo's seat. "I bet they're having all kinds of fun without me." His broken signing and little pout made the three adults chuckle, breaking the sad tension.

"They probably are, and I'm kind of jealous," Mary Ellen signed with a smile. "I bet Mom is telling your dad all the amazing things you can do and how smart you are."

Sawyer smiled and looked out the window.

"How're you both doing? Honestly?" Elise studied Mary Ellen and Noland's faces, looking for signs of stress.

"I can't believe I lost my composure at the grave. Mom is mortified."

"I think she'd understand, Mary Ellen. It's a hard time and losing a parent is very hard, no matter your age." When she'd lost her parents in an auto accident, Elise had clung to Judson like a drowning person to a life preserver. If he hadn't been there for her. . . "I know she'd understand."

"Of course. You didn't make a scene for appearance's sake. You are grieving. We all are. It's our honest emotions." Noland nodded to punctuate his statement. "Lilliana would understand."

Mary Ellen sniffed again. "She never broke down at Jud's funeral."

Elise's mouth went dry. It was such a blur that she could only recall bits and pieces, and what she did remember was that Lilliana had been in control of her emotions. So much so that Elise had wanted to scream at her, just to get a reaction.

"Not publicly, but she did break down over his death. She told me about it, and she cried many times over the loss in the years of our marriage." Noland's voice was just one level above a whisper.

"Really?" The question was out before Elise could stop it. "I mean, I never knew that."

Noland smiled softly. "That's how Lilliana was. She cried and screamed at the injustice in the privacy of her home, but told me that she'd had to be strong for you and Sawyer and Mary Ellen."

"I never knew either." Mary Ellen's voice cracked.

There were many sides to her mother-in-law that she didn't know about. Elise patted Mary Ellen's knee. "We'll honor her memory at home by being the most gracious hostesses we can."

Mary Ellen smiled. "She would like that."

"Yes, she would." Noland nodded.

Elise would do her best to hold up Mary Ellen and Noland, and to honor Lilliana's memory. Her family would make her proud. But, for now, she had to get them back to the house and through the visitation. None of which would be easy.

The ride back to Noland's was short, but the visitation seemed to go on forever. So many people, all talking and eating. It brought back the memory of Judson's visitation. At least there had been military to break up the monotony. Soon enough, people started going silent and leaving.

"If I have to listen to one more story, I might scream." Mary Ellen handed Elise the last remaining dishes from the living room.

"Is everyone finally gone?" Elise took the dishes, rinsed them, and then stacked them with the others in the full dishwasher.

"Finally. I thought when we sent Noland to go lie down, people would take the hint and leave. It took another thirty minutes of wrapping up all the conversations to get them moving." Mary Ellen plopped down in the kitchen chair. "I'm so glad you started clearing the food because that signaled to people we were shutting down."

"I remember Lilliana doing the same thing at Judson's visitation." Elise smiled as she made a final pass with the washcloth over the counter. "Where's Sawyer?"

"Hiding in the sitting room watching cartoons." Mary Ellen kicked off her black pumps. "I can't tell you how tempted I was to go join him."

"Well, we'll get out of your way and let you get some rest."

"I don't mean to rush you two off. . ."

"I know, but I have to get home because the FBI is supposed to bring back Sawyer's iPad. I'm hoping they might tell me something, anything about the case." Elise leaned against the counter and crossed her arms over her chest.

"I wouldn't hold my breath. I saw them at the funeral, but they didn't come up and speak to me or Noland. Did they seek you out?"

"No, but I wouldn't expect them to. We aren't exactly chummy."

"True." Mary Ellen stood, grabbing her shoes. "I'm planning on calling them tomorrow and asking for an update on Mom's case. As her daughter, I should be kept informed about the investigation. They've done a poor job of that so far."

"Since we stipulated Agent Wright wasn't to pick up or return the iPad, if it's just Agent Rodriguez, maybe he'll tell me something." Elise pushed off the counter. "It's worth a try. The worst he can do is tell me nothing."

"Well, let me know if he gives you any information."

"I will." Elise hugged Mary Ellen and kissed her cheek. "I'll get Sawyer. You get some rest. Whether you think you need it or not, you need to sleep. It's healing for the body."

"Thanks."

"And if you cry in the shower, it helps with the puffy eyes." Elise smiled. "Just passing along a little info as someone who's been there and knows."

Man, did she ever know.

CHAPTER TWENTY

"Can I go out back and play?" Sawyer jumped out of the car as soon as it was parked in the garage. His one-handed signing was getting better.

She turned off the alarm and shut the garage before answering. "What are you going to play with your arm hurt?" Elise could only imagine her son swinging or sliding on the wooden playset Judson had built and falling, hurting himself even worse.

He opened the door and stepped inside the house. "I want to practice my soccer game."

Elise's maternal instincts, which apparently resided in her gut, tightened. He had wanted to try out for the community soccer team, but she hadn't made up her mind yet. She'd been watching him play around in the yard and had to admit he had some smooth moves. Even with the cast, he could practice kicking and popping the ball around. As much as she wanted to keep him safe, she knew he needed to be doing something normal as well as get some of his pent-up energy out. "Okay, but you change into play clothes first."

He grinned and ran to his room.

She shook her head and headed to her room to change. She wanted out of the dress and heels. Funerals weren't just depressing, they went on for far too long and made everyone uncomfortable. Maybe she should reconsider cremation and just arrange for a memorial service someplace. . .no one would have to host anything and no funeral attire. Hmm. Something to think about.

Elise changed into a comfortable romper, hung up her dress, then headed into the kitchen. She glanced out the window and watched Sawyer kicking the soccer ball into the goal from different angles. He'd be devastated if she didn't let him join the community team. Sign-ups were over the next two weeks and he'd brought home flyers from school. There'd also been several different ones mailed to the house. Guess she'd have to decide which seemed the safest and let him play.

A lock of his hair popped down over one eye as he reached his foot out at an angle to make a kick. Elise's heart paused, as it often did as he grew older. He looked so much like Judson that it was almost uncanny. It made Elise smile. She didn't have Judson anymore, but she had a piece of him that she would treasure forever. Judson would be so proud of the boy his son was.

Tears welled in her eyes and she turned away from the window, letting out a sigh. Missing Judson hadn't gotten any easier. She doubted it ever would.

With a shake of her head, Elise opened the fridge and pulled out a bottle of Dr Pepper. She rarely drank sodas at home, trying to set a good example and all, but some days, she needed something more than water. Today was definitely one of those days.

It was so cold and sweet, a true treat.

The doorbell rang and lights flashed.

Elise set down the drink. She glanced into the backyard and saw Sawyer kick the soccer ball into the net, then went to the front door. She popped up and looked through the peephole. Agent Rodriguez stood on the stoop, holding Sawyer's iPad. She unlocked and opened the door.

"Good afternoon, Mrs. Carmichael." He smiled as he spoke.

It was hard not to smile back. "Agent Rodriguez." She reached out for the iPad. "Thank you for being so prompt in returning this."

He set it in her outreached hand, blushing. "Well, your attorney didn't really give us an option of not being prompt."

Elise chuckled. "I bet she didn't." She recalled hers and Mary Ellen's conversation about finding out what was going on with the case. She glanced over his shoulder to his car. It was empty. "I just got a Dr Pepper. Would you like one?"

He hesitated, nodded, and then followed her inside.

She set the iPad on the kitchen island and glanced at Sawyer, still kicking the soccer ball. "I have water, Kool-Aid, juice, and Dr Pepper. What'll you have?"

"Dr Pepper, please."

She grinned as she opened the refrigerator, pulled out a bottle, and passed it to him. She grabbed hers from the counter and led the way into the living room, then took a seat in the chair, curling her feet under her. "So, you know I have to ask, did you find the files Lilliana sent?"

Agent Rodriguez had sat on the couch. "I can't tell you much, but, yes, we did find the files. I'm going to assume you opened the files as well, so you know what they were?"

She resisted the urge to squirm like a child caught cheating on a test. Arabella had assured her that she was within her legal right to do so. "I did."

He sat back on the couch, resting the bottle on his leg. "Let me go ahead and ask you, do you recognize who the woman and baby are in the photograph?"

Elise shook her head. "No clue, and I've studied it. Tried to see if maybe I recognized the place or anything in the picture. Nothing rang a bell to me, nor to Mary Ellen or Noland. All three of us are mystified and have no idea why Lilliana had it."

"So you shared the files with them? With Mary Ellen and Noland?"

Again, she had to remind herself she could do what she wanted with the files on *her* tablet. "Look, I know you think I was trying to hide something by not letting you and your partner have the iPad immediately, but I wasn't. At the time you first mentioned it, I didn't even have a clue that anything by Lilliana had been received."

"But when you did find out, you made it very difficult for us to do our job."

Elise would concede that. "Perhaps I did, but there is a correct way of doing things and an incorrect way. Your partner isn't very adept at recognizing the difference."

"Okay. I don't want to rehash all of that. The important thing is moving forward."

"I agree. I shared the files with Noland and Mary Ellen because if sending those files to a place Lilliana knew would be safe was her last act, I figured it would be important. Her husband and daughter would be the best people to ask about the files."

Elise licked her lips. "Unfortunately, there's nothing about the photograph that seemed to stand out to any of us." She paused, taking a sip of her soda, then decided to turn the tables. "I'm guessing the FBI hasn't a clue who the woman is either?"

"Not as yet." He smiled. "You know I can't really discuss the open investigation with you, Mrs. Carmichael. Especially not investigative details."

She felt the heat in her cheeks. "I know you can't share some things, but I was hoping by letting you have the files off the iPad without a warrant, which I know two judges denied, we might be able to share a little information to help move the investigation along."

He flashed his smile. "Well, let's just say that we're running the photograph through facial recognition software and hope to identify her that way."

"Is that usually successful?" She took another sip of her Dr Pepper.

He crossed an ankle over his opposite thigh. "It all depends. For instance, if the person has a record, that's the easiest confirmation, but that's not the only facial recognition options we have access to. Some places of employment use photo employee IDs. Military. Governments. It varies. All these databases take time to run against. I'm hopeful we'll get a name." He looked more relaxed than Elise had ever noticed. Maybe Agent Wright was bad for more than just a few people. She certainly seemed to rub many, Elise included, the wrong way.

"I hope it pans out. It has to be important for Lilliana to have the presence of mind to send it as her last act." But she kept her mouth shut about the fact that she and Wesson knew it was most likely a woman whose last name was Poe. Or using that name anyway.

He took another sip of his soda. "I can't help but wonder why she sent it to Sawyer. What if he'd just deleted it? I mean, our forensics team is pretty good so they probably would have been able to recover anything, but why send to him?"

Elise had battled that question over and over herself. "I can't say. The only thing I can think is that it was important enough to Lilliana that she wanted it to be safe, to send to someone who wouldn't just delete it."

"But her grandson?"

Elise shrugged. "Lilliana knew Sawyer never checked the email. She knew only I did. Maybe she intended for me to figure it all out." Everyone knew Elise could be almost as bulldoggish about something as Lilliana. Almost.

That was probably just another reason why the two women weren't warm and fuzzy with each other. Both too stubborn over certain issues.

"Have you? Figured it all out?" Agent Rodriguez smiled.

She snorted. "Not hardly. I know Lilliana would never put Sawyer in danger. Whatever that picture and lab results mean, it's important. Vitally so."

"It is confusing. Not just what she sent, but who she sent it to with no explanation." He rubbed the bottom of his bottle on his pants, wiping off the condensation.

"I can only imagine there's no explanation because of lack of time." Elise wished she knew what it meant, but she knew, beyond a doubt, that it was something extremely important. Lilliana would have never sent it to Sawyer's iPad otherwise.

Elise decided to keep pushing the agent to see if she could get any more new information. "Well, we also had no idea why Lilliana would have any DNA results."

He nodded. "That is quite peculiar." He didn't offer anything more.

Should she offer more information? Hmm. He did tell her about the facial recognition. "Mary Ellen and I thought perhaps it was relating to Noland, but that's not an option as he is unable to father children." That would at least stop them from wasting time by trying to see if it was regarding a child of Noland's.

Agent Rodriguez sat up a little straighter on the couch. "Are you positive about that?"

"Well, I'm not a doctor and I didn't look at any medical records, but Mary Ellen and I asked Noland about it and he laughed at us, then told us he was unable to father children. I have no reason not to believe him. There'd be no point in lying now. He really would have nothing to gain."

"You think not?"

"I don't. Lilliana was big on family. Noland knew that. He would never withhold such information from her."

"Unless admitting he had a child that she knew nothing about would give him a motive for murdering his wife if she found out he had a child and he'd lied to her about it."

"Hmm." Elise thought about it for all of a minute or so before she shook her head. "No, that's not Noland. Or Lilliana. If Lilliana truly believed Noland had a child, she would have reached out to the child. She would have definitely told Mary Ellen."

Mary Ellen and Judson had been close, and Lilliana, despite her annoyance with them at times, was always supportive of their sibling bond. It actually seemed to bother her just a little that Mary Ellen would love Elise so, just because Judson did. "No, there's no way Lilliana would have believed Noland had a child and not tell Mary Ellen."

"Perhaps. That is to be determined."

"I guess easy enough to check Noland's medical records. I'm sure he'd provide everything he can to help the investigation. He loved Lilliana very much and wants those responsible for murdering her brought to justice." She took another sip of her soda, but it wasn't near as sweet as before.

"I'm sure he did love her, but in my line of work, I've seen people kill people they love for the strangest reasons. Money is always the first motivator. Like when large life insurance policies are involved." He stared straight at her.

She unwound her feet from under her and set down the bottle on the table. "I don't think that's fair. You know, I just learned that Lilliana had a large life insurance policy that lists Sawyer as the beneficiary. I never knew that."

His eyes widened for only a nanosecond before his composure dropped back in place. "How did you find out?"

Thank goodness Arabella had warned her. "My attorney, of course. I have to admit, I was shocked."

He nodded. "That's quite a lot of money, for a grandchild."

She nodded. "It is. That's why I'm shocked, but not really surprised."

"Oh?"

"Sawyer is Lilliana's only grandchild. They've always had a close relationship that only grew closer when Judson died. It's only natural that she would want him taken care of in the event of her death. Lilliana was a realist if nothing else." Elise let out a humorless chuckle. "She probably assumed I'd never make a lot of money, so Sawyer would need funds for college and a car and maybe even a place to live."

Agent Rodriguez lowered his brows, but didn't comment.

She shook her head. "I think Lilliana was always afraid that after Judson died, I might go back to modeling to pay the bills, and *that* idea scared her. She always thought a profession that depended on your looks was shady."

"I don't get why she would be so down on modeling. Many women have very successful, and lucrative, modeling careers."

Elise pointed. "Ah, but that wasn't using brains or education. As Lilliana told me many times, your looks are a gift from God. Brains and education had to be worked for."

"Sounds like she had a bad experience or something."

"Perhaps, but if she did, I never knew. I think she just resisted the idea that I was making money when I met Judson by posing in bathing suits. I think she wanted someone who appeared a little more. . . um. . .pure to catch her son's attention."

"The heart wants what the heart wants." He lifted his bottle in mock salute.

She did the same and smiled. "That it does." Would her heart ever want anyone after the great love she'd had with Judson? She couldn't imagine ever loving someone as much as Judson, except for Sawyer, of course.

Speaking of Sawyer. . .

Elise stood and grabbed her bottle. "Would you like another?"

Agent Rodriguez stood and shook his head. "No, thank you. I should be heading back to the office. I have an important case I'm working."

She grinned as she walked into the kitchen and dropped her bottle in the recycle bin. He followed suit.

Elise wiped her hands on the dish towel. "Did you find out anything interesting to help the case at the funeral?"

"Not exactly. We'll see." In other words, he wasn't going to tell her.

Fair enough. She didn't tell him about Poe.

Elise glanced out the window into the backyard. She couldn't see Sawyer. The soccer ball lay in the grass. Where was he? She opened the back door and looked around, but couldn't see him anywhere. Had he come inside while she was talking and she hadn't heard him? She took a step on the porch and froze. At the bottom of the porch step sat a box. A very familiar looking box.

"Agent Rodriguez!"

He rushed out beside her. "What is it?"

"Sawyer's not here and there's that." She pointed at the box.

He quickly pulled out gloves from his pocket. After bringing the box inside, he set it on the kitchen island. Slowly, he pulled back the lid.

Inside were many pictures, all of Elise. Talking with Agent Rodriguez and Agent Wright. Standing on the porch with Connie. Different locations, but all had Elise in them. There was an envelope amid them. Agent Rodriguez opened the envelope and pulled out a regular piece of copy paper with a printed out picture of Sawyer. On the bottom of the page, in letters that looked cut out from a magazine, were three words: You Were Warned.

In that moment, Elise's world stopped spinning.

Chapter Twenty-One

Everything blurred in Elise's mind. The world tilted on its axis, her head stuffed with cotton, and she swayed. She was vaguely aware of her legs refusing to hold her upright.

"Whoa." Agent Rodriguez gripped her tightly and half walked, half carried her to the living room. "Easy." He helped ease her down to the couch.

She could hear him talking. . .on the phone? Asking for a team or something. But all she could think about was Sawyer. She closed her eyes and groaned.

The day he was born: so alert in the delivery room, staring at her and Judson and making strong eye contact with them. Taking his first wobbly steps from Judson to her. His first birthday. Second. Third. All the ones after. Hearing his first utterances of da-da and ma-ma and her heart now owned by two men instead of one.

Now he was gone. Taken, because of her. Because she had told the FBI what she'd seen. Because she'd described the man. Because she'd helped in the investigation. Her precious Sawyer. . .

Oh God, please. I don't even know what to say. Just please take care of Sawyer. Bring him back to me, please.

Sobs stole the air from her lungs. She rolled over on the couch, curling into the fetal position. Elise let the darkness overtake her. Welcomed its smothering nothingness all around her.

"Elise, wake up." Mary Ellen's voice cut through the fog of despair squeezing the very life out of her.

Someone shook her. "Wake up. Sawyer needs you."

Sawyer! She blinked open her eyes and sat up. Mary Ellen towered over her, wearing the paleness that Elise could only imagine mirrored her own. "Sawyer's back home?"

Mary Ellen shook her head, sitting on the couch beside her. "Not yet. Agent Rodriguez's team is here setting up. Putting tracers on your phone. Other agents are combing through everything in the backyard and even the front. They got here in less than an hour."

"Wait, how did you—"

"Agent Rodriguez called us and told us what happened. We rushed right over."

"Us?" Her mind wasn't making any connections. It was as if cobwebs of glue were spun in her brain.

"Me and Noland." Mary Ellen put her arm around Elise and squeezed. "Come on, you need to snap out of this."

It was all starting to come back. "How long was I out?" Pictures, the paper with the three words. Elise shot to her feet.

"About an hour or so. We knew you were already exhausted and the shock made you faint, but now. . .well, now you need to act."

Act. Yes. Find Sawyer. "Where is Agent Rodriguez?"

"In the kitchen with his team."

Elise took sure steps into the kitchen. "What is the protocol now? What do I need to do?"

Agent Rodriguez locked stares with her. "We've put a tracer on your home phone. We'll need to monitor your cell as well." He motioned to the other two men sitting at her kitchen table. "These are Agents Hamilton and Warren. They head up our abduction team." Both men nodded at Elise.

She nodded back. "What do I need to do?"

"Be here to answer the call. If one comes in, we'll instruct you what to say." Elise had no idea which agent was which, but she nodded again.

"Okay. What else?"

"That's it for now, ma'am."

This couldn't be all they expected her to do. She needed to be *doing* something.

Noland rushed across the room and pushed a warm mug into her hands. "Oh honey. I made coffee. Go drink this. You know I've been praying since we got the call. I'll make sure everyone has a cup and then will come check on you in the living room. Go sit and drink your coffee."

The doorbell rang and the lights flashed. Elise went to the front door, but another agent stood guard. He had the door open and was moving to close it.

"No, I'm a friend. Ask Elise. She'll tell you."

"I'm sorry. No press."

Elise pulled the door open wide with her free hand. Wesson rushed into the room and hugged Elise, nearly making her spill the coffee Noland had just shoved into her hands. "I'm so sorry. I came as soon as it came across the wire."

"It's okay. She's a friend," Elise told the agent.

Mary Ellen met them in the living room with two cups. "Agent Rodriguez asked us to sit in the living room. He said he'd update us in a few minutes. Hey, Wesson." She passed one of the mugs to the younger reporter.

The three sat on the couch, Elise between the two, letting the heat from the cup warm her hands, which were suddenly ice cold. Matter of fact, her whole body shivered. "I can't believe this is happening. It's like my worst nightmare come to life." She quickly told Wesson and Mary Ellen the details of the box, the pictures, the warning. Her anger began to push aside her pain. She took a sip of coffee, then set her cup on the table. "I can't just sit here and do nothing while my son is out only God knows where." She leaped up, but wasn't sure where to go or what to do.

Mary Ellen took her hand and gently tugged her back down. "Let the FBI do their jobs, Elise. They're trained for this."

Elise's pulse quickened. "My son was kidnapped from my back-yard while an FBI agent was in. My. House." She clenched and unclenched her fists. "Tell me that isn't brazen. To kidnap a kid right under FBI noses."

A thought occurred to her. How this tormenter of hers always seemed to know exactly what she was doing. "Who's to say this person isn't with the FBI himself?"

"You don't mean that," Mary Ellen said.

Elise stared at her sister-in-law. "Maybe I do. Think about it, Mary Ellen. This guy has known every time I've been in contact with the FBI: when I reported the phone call, when I worked with the sketch artist, when they came to question me. . .hey, he even had photos of each of those times. How would he know so quickly of my involvement each and every step of the way if he wasn't an insider?" She snapped her fingers and pointed at Wesson. "Didn't your source say there was a leak in the bureau? Maybe it's not a leak, but it's the person responsible."

Wesson slowly nodded as she set her cup on the table. "He does seem to know everything you do almost as soon as you do it. My source couldn't identify the leak, but maybe if I explain about Saw-yer's kidnapping, that will change. Let me go make the call." Wesson stood, pulled out her cell phone, and walked to the opposite corner of the room.

"Do you think Agent Rodriguez could be involved?" Mary Ellen set her cup on the table beside the other two.

Elise plopped back down on the couch and chewed her bottom lip. Judson had always said she was a good judge of character. From what she'd experienced, the agent hadn't acted devious or anything. "I don't think so. Now, Agent Wright, she'd probably kidnap Sawyer just to prove a point."

"You really think she might be involved?" Mary Ellen's eyes were huge.

"Maybe." She didn't like her, but she didn't think the woman capable of the scheme that Elise had been having to deal with. Although, she could be wrong. "She might be an informant. Feeding information to someone who's actually doing it."

Mary Ellen shook her head. "I don't think so. Yeah, she irritates me and I especially dislike the way she treats and talks to you, but I just can't see her kidnapping Sawyer."

"I just don't know." Elise dipped her head and held it between her hands. "If anything happens to Sawyer. . ."

"Don't even talk that way. Nothing's going to happen to him." Mary Ellen put her arm around Elise and hugged her.

"But bad things do happen. To Judson. To my parents. To your mom. Now to Sawyer." Tears wouldn't be denied and slid down her cheeks.

Mary Ellen hugged her tighter. "I've been praying for God to put a hedge of protection around Sawyer."

Elise snorted and sniffed. "I don't think that helps."

"Of course." Mary Ellen shifted so she could look Elise in the face. "Look, I know you're mad at or disappointed in God. I understand. It's hard to take so much loss and grief and not become bitter. I get it. But honey, God's never left you or forsaken you. He understands your pain and anger all too well. It's okay to rally at Him—none of it catches Him by surprise. He can handle your questions and even your anger."

Hmm.

Mary Ellen handed Elise her mug. "Here, drink this. Despite what you think, the caffeine will help. So will the heat."

Without questioning, Elise took a sip of the coffee, but her mind was going off in a hundred different directions. She took another sip before returning the cup to the table and closing her eyes. *Okay, God, here I am, asking You to protect my son. I know I've been angry at You for a long time, and I'm sorry for lashing out at You. I just am begging You, please bring Sawyer home safely to me. Amen.*

Wesson returned and sat on the end of the couch. "Okay, my source is going to dig around about the leak. She wants to be sure before she gives up a name."

"At least it's something. More than what they are doing." Elise nodded toward the FBI agents taking over her kitchen table.

"That's not fair, Elise. They're following proven protocol and have really been on the ball," Mary Ellen admonished.

But Elise didn't want to be fair. She just wanted to hold Sawyer again. Feel his cheek against hers. Feel his little heart pounding.

Agent Rodriguez rushed into the room. "We've got a lead on the sketch you made. We're going there now to bring the guy in for questioning."

Elise jumped to her feet. "Do you think he has Sawyer?"

"I don't know anything at this point. I'll get word to you as soon as I can."

"If there's a chance Sawyer might be there, I'm going with you." She stepped around the coffee table.

Agent Rodriguez put his hand on her shoulder and stopped her with a gentle but firm grip. "You can't. I'm sorry, Elise, but you can't come. You need to stay here. I promise you, I'll let you know something as soon as I can." He squeezed her shoulder, then turned away and rushed out the door with one of the nameless agents.

Mary Ellen put her arm around Elise and brought her back to the couch. "He said he'd let you know as soon as he could. You trust him, so let him do his job. This could all be over with very soon."

Elise didn't know whether to cry or scream. "If Sawyer is hurt. . ."

"Shh, don't even think that way."

Noland walked into the living room, carrying the carafe of coffee. "Time for refills so I can make a fresh pot." He bent to top off the three cups and lowered his voice. "I heard them say the man's name that matches the sketch is Sam Edwards. The sketch got a hit in facial recognition because he's former Capitol Police."

Way to go, Noland! Elise had thought he was just making coffee for the agents in order to be helpful. "Aren't you the sly one," she whispered back.

He smiled and straightened. "I *was* an investigative reporter for over a decade, you know." He winked at them. "And the connection seems clear because this Sam Edwards is former US Capitol Police in DC, not the state capitol here in Little Rock." Noland carried the carafe back into the kitchen. The sound of water running echoed back to them in the living room.

"Man, I'd love a chance to sit down sometime and pick that man's brain. I bet he could tell some tales. As well as give me some tips and tricks of the trade." Wesson's eyes were on the kitchen door, filled with total admiration.

"That can probably be arranged." Mary Ellen smiled at the young woman.

Elise nodded at the cell in Wesson's hand. "See what you can find out on Sam Edwards. You might just get an exclusive yet."

Wesson's eyes lit up as she opened the search engine and began her search. She plugged in her earbuds and stuck one in her ear. "I'll keep monitoring the police scanners too. Local police might not be aware of any FBI movement and if they're not, there's a chance I can pick up some details."

"Good thinking." Elise nodded, everything in her seemed to be on high alert—her muscles, her nerves, even her hearing. She could make out Noland making small talk to the FBI agents in the kitchen. Every so often, one would chuckle. Their equipment sometimes beeped, sometimes buzzed, but made some sort of constant noise.

"I'm going to run to the bathroom. Can I get you anything while I'm up?" Mary Ellen stood.

Elise shook her head. "Just Sawyer."

Mary Ellen patted her shoulder as she headed down the hall to the bathroom.

If only Judson were here. . .no, if Judson were here, none of this would have happened. She wouldn't have seen that stupid phone call in the first place because she wouldn't have been working in the courthouse.

Did everything happen for a reason? Had everything led her to this place, this time, this situation? What did it all mean?

Two more agents scrambled out of the kitchen and out the front door.

Elise stood. Wesson did as well, gripping her cell phone. Her face seemed pale.

"What's going on?" Elise asked.

"According to the scanner, shots have been fired at a house where FBI agents are reported onsite and involved in the shooting."

Elise's heart slipped to her toes. "Who was shot? Is Sawyer there?"

"I don't know. All I—" She held up a finger and covered her other ear. Her eyes met Elise's.

"What?" Elise's heart beat double time, moving quickly to triple time.

"They've called for backup and an ambulance. There's no report of an officer down."

"Which means?" Elise's hands trembled.

Wesson swallowed loud enough for Elise to hear it. "That some-one is most likely shot and it isn't law enforcement."

CHAPTER TWENTY-TWO

Elise's emotions fast-tracked to near panic in the blink of an eye. She couldn't move, couldn't swallow, almost couldn't breathe.

She took a split second to calm her nerves as best she could. "What's the address?" she asked Wesson.

There was no discussion of which address she wanted, no, demanded. If there was even the slightest chance that Sawyer was there—that he could possibly be hurt. . .she wasn't going to wait in the safety of her home.

"I don't know if that's the smartest move—" Wesson started.

But Elise was having none of it. "I don't care. Give me the address."

Mary Ellen returned from the bathroom. "What's going on?"

"The place where Agent Rodriguez went had shots fired and an ambulance has been called to the scene. I'm telling Wesson to give me the address."

"Wait." Wesson put her hand over the ear with the earbud.

Seconds seemed to slide slow motion off the clock as Elise waited.

One.

Two.

Three.

Four.

Wesson nodded as she listened, then let out a breath. "It's not Sawyer. It was the owner of the house, Sam Edwards. He was shot in the gut and lost consciousness at the scene. He's on his way to the hospital now. Law enforcement is following, hoping to question the guy before he goes into surgery. The agents performed an initial check of the property and reported no sign of Sawyer in the house, or in the guy's car. They've got two forensic teams on their way to see if there's any indication Sawyer was ever in the car or house."

Elise sank back to the couch. As much as she wanted to breathe a sigh of relief, she couldn't. If Sawyer wasn't with the guy she'd seen with Marcus Tate, where was he? Was it possible a third person was involved? The hooded character who kept leaving the boxes? It made sense since a box was left when Sawyer was taken. But who was he? Had he been the person Marcus Tate had been on the phone with?

No, that didn't make sense. Why would whoever he was hire Marcus Tate to kill Lilliana if he was willing to come to her house and leave the warnings, and willing to kidnap a kid? It wasn't logical. So that meant there were four people involved. Marcus Tate, Sam Edwards, the hoodie guy, and the person who called the shots. Marcus Tate was dead and Sam Edwards was shot and accounted for. That left the hoodie guy and the person in charge.

"Elise, are you okay?" Wesson dropped to the chair opposite to where Elise and Mary Ellen sat on the couch.

She worried her bottom lip between her thumb and pointer. "I'm just trying to wrap my mind around the facts." She quickly told them what she'd been thinking.

Mary Ellen nodded. "Yes. Definitely four, at least."

Wesson looked at her phone, and Elise realized the reporter hadn't asked to report on what was happening.

"Hey, go ahead and do what you need to do to get an exclusive. Go to the hospital or whatever."

"Are you sure?" Wesson asked, but stood at the ready.

"Positive. And if you hear anything, call me, okay?"

Wesson nodded. "Of course." She was out the door in the minute it took her to cross the room.

"She'll call as soon as she knows something, you know that." Mary Ellen took a sip of her coffee, then handed the other mug back to Elise. "Drink. It does help."

It hadn't helped her much when Judson had died. Or her parents. But she took a sip to pacify Mary Ellen. Elise appreciated that Mary Ellen and Noland had rushed over and were here for her. She took another sip before setting the coffee down. She needed to try and figure things out.

She got up and grabbed a pad of paper and pen off the desk in front of the big floor-to-ceiling window facing the side yard, then went back to the couch. "We need to figure out a timeline of sorts."

"Okay." Mary Ellen nodded. "So I guess we should start with Mom's murder. That was on Thursday night."

"Actually, we need to start before that. I read Marcus Tate's lips on Thursday afternoon."

"Right. He told the person on the phone to stop worrying that Lilliana would be taken care of that night, permanently, just as instructed, which indicates that the plan had been in place before Thursday. That's the person on the phone, Marcus Tate, and Sam Edwards." Elise jotted the information down on the paper.

"Check. Then, later that night, Marcus Tate shot Mom." Mary Ellen's voice warbled a little.

Elise would move right on. "The next day, I told the FBI what I'd seen Marcus Tate say on the phone. We know for a fact that the FBI told you, but someone said something to the Marcus Tate team. Later on Friday, I identified Marcus Tate from the photo lineup."

Mary Ellen nodded as Elise wrote. "And that night is the night you got the dead rat, right?"

"Yep. And the next day, I got the doll with the snitches get stitches note. So the action that triggered those two threats was my reporting the call to the FBI and identifying Marcus Tate."

"But then, Marcus Tate was murdered. By whom?" Mary Ellen tapped her chin with her forefinger.

Elise looked up from her notes. "I'm going to guess either Sam Edwards, the delivery guy, or the guy calling the shots. My bet is Sam

Edwards, since he was Capitol Police."

"Yeah." Mary Ellen nodded. "That would make sense."

"Then I find the snake in Sawyer's bed on Saturday afternoon. Another warning to keep me quiet, which is another reason my bet is Sam Edwards. I hadn't seen the delivery guy nor the guy on the phone. Sam Edwards knew I had to have seen him to have reported Marcus Tate's phone call. He was trying to scare me into not working with the FBI."

"But that's the day we hooked up the security system, which meant he couldn't have access to you or the house so easily anymore." Mary Ellen took a sip of her coffee.

Elise continued to make notes. "Right, but he had the delivery guy leave me pictures of me in the shower that were taken Friday night. Maybe he didn't realize I would know which day they were taken." Maybe normal people wouldn't. She didn't think she was OCD. Was she? No, she didn't care. Her habit made it easy to identify that the pictures had been taken before the security system was installed.

"Probably thought you'd think they were the night before and scare you."

"Maybe." These guys were good at threats and fear tactics, that much Elise could attest to. "On Monday, I worked with Connie and had a sketch of Sam Edwards drawn. It went live on the news at noon yesterday. That was a big action because Sam Edwards knew he'd been made."

Mary Ellen took another sip of coffee. "Then the funeral this morning."

"And then Sawyer was taken. Now Sam Edwards has been identified and shot, but he apparently wasn't the one who took Sawyer since the FBI didn't find any sign of him at Sam's place." Elise looked over her notes, her anxiety at a dangerous level.

"What're you thinking, Elise?" Mary Ellen set down her cup.

"So the person in charge orders Hoodie to take Sawyer, or hires someone else to do it. And do what? For what purpose?"

"What do you mean?"

Elise set the pad and pen on the coffee table. "I thought Sam Edwards was the one doing all the threats because I could describe him and identify him, right?"

"Yeah."

"But once the sketch hit the news and he knew his time was limited, he should've run, not caring about coming for Sawyer."

"So Hoodie came." Mary Ellen shrugged.

"No, that doesn't make sense. Well, it does. But I'm not sure that guy is smart enough to plan a kidnapping. I mean, I've seen the video and he's cautious, but he also hides in bushes and leaves threats. Not the brightest bulb in the set."

"So he's—what?—gone?"

"Maybe." But that still didn't answer the most important question: Who had Sawyer and where and what did they intend to do with him?

"I see where you're going, but I can't get past where you leave off."

Elise sighed and took a sip of coffee. "Me either. I couldn't pick Delivery Guy out of a lineup, and he should know that because he's never seen me up close either. And I have no idea who the person calling the shots on the phone is."

"So why are you still a threat?" Noland asked from behind them.

Elise shifted and nodded. "Exactly. Why take Sawyer?"

"Maybe you know something you don't realize you know," Mary Ellen said.

"Or. . ." Noland came around and sat in the chair opposite them. "Or maybe that leak at the FBI not only told someone about your lip-reading of Marcus Tate's call, but has also shared about the files and that you have a copy."

"How would they know she has a copy?" Mary Ellen asked.

Noland smiled and shook his head. "Dearest, I can assure you that everyone in the FBI affiliated with the case knows Elise has a copy. Number one, she'd be stupid not to, and they all know she's not stupid. And number two, the forensics team who looked at the iPad could easily see that the files had been forwarded to Elise's email."

Elise's mouth went dry. "So the leak told the person in charge that I have the files Lilliana sent, and that's why they're still coming after me? But I have no idea what those files mean."

"They might not know that," Noland said. "Or they may be worried you will figure out what they mean. The consequences of the truth behind those files must be very serious for them to keep coming after you, but we already knew that because my beloved Lilliana was determined to have those files saved, even as her life was on the line."

That made perfect sense.

Elise nodded. "So, we're back to the files. We need to figure out their importance and that will, hopefully, lead us to who has Sawyer." If they could figure it out in time, she could save Sawyer. That was all that mattered.

"But we still don't have a clue what they're all about." Mary Ellen slowly rocked herself.

"Well, let's work the problem then." Elise grabbed the pen and paper again. At the top, she wrote *picture*, then under it she wrote *DNA results*. "Okay, it's very clear that the picture and the lab work are connected, does everyone agree?"

"Yes." Noland and Mary Ellen spoke in unison.

"Okay, so I think it's safe to assume that the woman in the picture is the mysterious Ms. Poe who had the paternity test run."

"Wait. Did you say Poe?" Noland asked.

Elise realized she hadn't really filled Noland in on what she and Wesson had found out. She quickly remedied that. "Why?"

"I recall overhearing Lilliana on the phone with someone, mentioning a Poe. Let me try to think." Noland closed his eyes and tilted his head back.

Holding her breath, Elise waited. She knew it wasn't easy to recall things under pressure, especially when they were trying hard, but she was having the hardest time being patient.

"Yes. I remember now. It was about a week ago. Late in the evening for her to be on the phone, about ten, which is why I remember paying attention. It was rare that Lilliana took or made calls in our bedroom."

Elise tapped the pen against the pad of paper, forcing herself to let Noland speak at his own pace.

"I distinctively remember her voice—so filled with rage that it trembled. Whomever she was speaking to had made her so very angry."

Elise could be patient no longer. "And you heard her say the name Poe?"

Noland nodded. "Well, not in that conversation. That one ended with her saying, and I quote, '*I have undisputable proof of your actions and I'll expose you. I can assure you, not only will it destroy your reputation, but your political career will die quickly.*'"

Elise stared at Noland. That said nothing about Poe, although if ever there was motive to kill Lilliana, there was a big one.

Noland continued. "She finished that call, then quickly made another. She asked to speak to an Alice Poe. After a few seconds, she said, '*No, that's okay. Please just tell her that Lilliana called to check in on her.*' Then Lilliana put away her phone and finished her nightly routine. When she got into bed, I asked her if everything was okay and she told me it would be."

Elise could barely contain herself. "You said Alice Poe?"

Noland nodded.

"Who's Alice?" Mary Ellen asked.

"A young aide who worked in the state capitol at the same time as Lilliana. We don't know if they knew each other, but Wesson found that Alice is twenty-six. She was a political science major at the University of Arkansas here in Little Rock. According to what Wesson learned, she graduated four years ago and went to work in the capitol, basically as a gopher. Everyone said she had potential. Then out of the blue, three years ago, she just up and left. Moved out of town."

"Why?" Mary Ellen asked.

"Wesson was trying to find that out." Elise's heart stuttered, then beat faster. All of this was very important, she just knew it. She felt it in her bones.

"Where did she move to?" Mary Ellen asked.

"Wesson was working on that too."

"Sounds like this Alice Poe and the threat Lilliana made are the keystone to those files," Noland said. "Let me go try to rustle some of my old contacts and see what I can find out. Discreetly, of course." He moved out of the room.

For the first time since Sawyer had been taken, Elise let hope bloom.

CHAPTER TWENTY-THREE

"Did you get an article?" Mary Ellen stood as Wesson returned.

"I've got a front page, below the fold byline, tomorrow morning. My first." Wesson hugged Elise as she entered the living room, then sat in the chair.

"Congratulations. That's great." Elise meant that, even though she hated how it came to be. "So what's the scoop?"

"Sam Edwards made it out of surgery, barely. The doctors said they lost him twice on the table, but he managed to pull through. He's in a coma, and according to one of the nurses, his prognosis isn't good."

So if he knew who had taken Sawyer and to where, they wouldn't be able to find out. Elise's hope deflated.

"Law enforcement wasn't able to get any type of statement from him in the ambulance, as he lost consciousness when he was shot and never came out of it on the ride to the hospital."

Yet another dead end.

"But, all is not lost." She pulled out a little stenographer's tablet and flipped through pages. "I heard back from some of my sources. Alice Poe. Her leaving three years ago? Finally got confirmation. She was pregnant. She had no family, very few friends, and even less coworkers who knew her beyond just a casual acquaintance. According to the friends she did have, she didn't date and certainly didn't have a boyfriend. Those who were closest to her said she wasn't the type to go out, much less have a physical relationship with a man she didn't know well. So, the pregnancy was a bit of a surprise and she told no one."

"If she didn't tell anyone, how do you know she was pregnant?" Elise asked.

Noland chose that moment to join them, carrying a tray with several bottles of water that he set on the coffee table before sitting in the other chair. "A good journalist never reveals their source."

Wesson smiled at him as she reached for a water. "Very true. But I'll just say that my source is in the medical field and leave it at that."

So that must mean the pregnancy was a definite thing. "So where did she go?"

"I have sources working on that, but nothing yet."

"That's actually why I came in here. Some of my inquiries have placed her still in the state. I'm working on confirmations to get exact locations."

Elise's stomach tightened. "Okay, so here's what I'm thinking. Lilliana found out the guy who fathered Alice's baby had done her wrong. Maybe he abandoned her. Maybe he even said the baby wasn't his. That would make Lilliana angry enough to threaten someone."

Noland nodded. "That it would. And if he was in the political arena in any way, she would use her power to expose him. To ruin him. Lilliana was many things, but she certainly was a woman of power in the Senate."

Mary Ellen inched to the edge of her seat. "I can see Mom wanting to protect the young woman. Especially if she felt the woman had been taken advantage of, or if this guy wasn't just about denying the baby was his, but demanding she get an abortion or something. That would push Mom into full protection mode."

All the random facts started to align. Elise just *knew* they were on the right track now. "If the guy had serious political ambitions and Lilliana threatened to expose him and ruin his reputation, then that's pretty strong motive to have her killed."

"Maybe the guy's married too. That would really make Mom

doubly angry to flat-out threaten him. Especially if the evidence was the paternity results that he's the father of that baby."

Noland nodded. "Which makes it an even stronger motive to have the threat of Lilliana removed."

Elise jotted everything on her notebook. The doorbell rang and lights flashed. Elise was on her feet in a moment, along with two agents, hands on the butts of their guns, who seemed to just appear in the living room. She made it to the door first and snuck a peek through the peephole. "It's Agent Rodriguez." She opened the door as the other agents disappeared into the background as quickly as they'd come forth.

"Is he out of a coma?" Elise greeted the agent.

He ducked inside and shut the door behind him. "I see news travels fast."

Elise didn't reply.

Agent Rodriguez let out a sigh. "He's still in a coma and as far as the doctors are concerned, he most likely will pass away in the next seventy-two hours without regaining consciousness."

Noland passed them on the way to the kitchen. "I'm going to put on a fresh pot of coffee for everyone." He winked at Elise and walked on.

He was a sly one.

Elise led the agent into the living room. He nodded at Mary Ellen, then at Wesson. "At least I know how news travels so fast."

The reporter scowled at him, and he scowled back.

"Agent Rodriguez," one of the other agents called.

He nodded as a way to excuse himself, then headed into the kitchen.

"Okay, well, we figured Sam Edwards was a dead end anyway. We'll just stay positive," Mary Ellen said.

Elise smiled at her. The woman had buried her mother this morning, and here she was, almost twelve hours later, being positive for someone else's sake. "Thank you, Mary Ellen. And Wesson. I don't know what I'd be doing if you two and Noland weren't here for me." Tears burned her eyes. "And for Sawyer."

"Oh honey." Mary Ellen stood and hugged her tight. "I'm praying so hard for Sawyer's quick and safe return. You know that. God's got him."

Elise hugged back, wishing she could have faith like her sister-in-law, but found it extremely hard when she'd been through what she had. Sure, many people had it much worse that she did, but she couldn't speak for them, only herself. And at the moment, she felt very alone and forgotten by God.

Wesson jumped up and hugged her too. "I'm happy to be here and help, and not just for a story. I hate when little kids are used as pawns."

Elise stepped back from both of them. "That's what I don't understand. Why take Sawyer? The note said I was warned, but what does taking him do now? Of course I'd do anything at this point for my son, but what can they want me to do? I already turned the files over to the FBI and whoever's doing this knows that. There was a picture of me giving the iPad to Agent Rodriguez this morning in the box with the warning. What else can they use Sawyer as a pawn to get me to do? I don't know anything else."

"It all comes back to the files again." Wesson sat in the chair, crisscrossing her legs.

Elise dropped to the couch. "I wish Lilliana would have never sent them. It's done nothing but put big targets on both me and Sawyer."

"I'm sorry Mom sent them. I can't imagine why she sent them to Sawyer's tablet rather than mine or Noland's." Mary Ellen sat on the opposite end of the couch from Elise. "I'm sure she had a reason."

"It's not your fault." Elise didn't mean to lash out, but she was angry. Why *had* Lilliana sent the files to Sawyer? She knew he wouldn't check them. She had to know Elise would get them. Surely she didn't plan to put Elise in danger instead of Mary Ellen or Noland. Although, Noland was her husband and Mary Ellen her daughter, while Elise was only related by marriage and they really didn't like one another.

Elise gave herself a mental shake. No, despite their feelings toward each other, Lilliana would have never taken a chance of putting Sawyer in danger of any sort.

So did that mean that Elise was personally connected to this? That was the only logical conclusion. Elise racked her mind and couldn't come up with ever having even met someone named Alice Poe. Not even in passing. "Wait a minute. When did you say Alice Poe went to the University of Arkansas in Little Rock?" she asked Wesson.

Wesson pulled out her little notebook and flipped through pages. "She started about seven or eight years ago. Why?"

"I've been trying to figure out why Lilliana sent the files to me. I'm wondering if she thought there was a personal connection to me."

"Like what?" Mary Ellen asked.

"Like if I'd met Alice at school or something." She went and grabbed her laptop and pulled up the picture of the woman and the baby. "I started back at the same college five years ago, so it's possible our paths crossed." She studied the photo. "I don't recognize her, but that doesn't mean I didn't have a class with her or saw her on campus."

"If that's true, then Mom must have thought you'd act on what she sent."

But she didn't even recognize her. Lilliana had to know that they weren't old friends or anything. So why make the connection? "Or she thought maybe I could relate to Alice because we did go to the same college and we did have young sons. And we are both single mothers." Strong coincidences to some.

"Or maybe Mom just knew you'd keep at it until you figured it out, and once you did, you'd take up what she started and get the guy."

"There is that." Lilliana knew Elise could be just as bullheaded as she was, sometimes more. Especially when it came to children who didn't have fathers.

Would Lilliana have taken the chance to send the files, knowing

Elise would be the one that found them? Was there something obvious they were all missing—something that Elise should have caught and been able to expose the man, without putting Sawyer in danger?

What?

Noland came into the room carrying the tray with coffee and cups. He raised his voice a little louder than normal. "Yes, I know it's after midnight, but I doubt any of us are going to get any sleep, so why not be alert?" He glanced at Elise. "Unless, honey, I can talk you into taking a little rest?"

Elise snorted and shook her head.

"I didn't think so. Here, let me pour everyone a cup." As he leaned over, he lowered his voice to a whisper. "The FBI got a hit on the partial license plate of the Ford Focus. It belongs to one Fred Otto. Little Rock police have a BOLO out for him and will pick him up for questioning as soon as he's located."

"I hope so," Mary Ellen whispered back.

"Do you know a Fred Otto?" Wesson whispered to Elise.

The name didn't ring a single bell for her. Elise shook her head. "Never heard of him." But out of the definite four involved, two of which were out of commission, Elise kind of hoped he was the one who had Sawyer. While he'd delivered threats and taken pictures, he hadn't done anything physically violent. Unlike the person in charge who ordered Lilliana's murder. To think that such an evil and devious person might have Sawyer...

"The police have his home address and are on their way there now. Since it's the middle of the night, they hope to catch him home before he's given any warning that someone might be looking for him."

Elise crossed her fingers, but she noticed Mary Ellen closed her eyes, bowed her head, and her lips went to moving. Praying. Elise guessed it couldn't hurt.

Okay, God, here I am again, asking You to protect my son. Please.

Noland finished pouring the coffee and straightened. "I'll keep you updated as I hear." He headed back into the kitchen.

Elise took a sip of the hot coffee, nearly scalding her tongue, but she barely noticed. Was it possible she was going to get Sawyer back soon? *Please, God, if You're listening, let Sawyer come home safe and sound. And soon.*

"I'll be right back." Wesson headed down the hall to the bathroom, closing the door a little louder than usual.

"I wonder how this Fred Otto is connected." Mary Ellen glanced over her shoulder into the kitchen before commenting. She kept her voice low.

"I'm wondering how they all connect, to be honest." Elise took another sip of coffee. "It was clear to me that Marcus Tate and Sam Edwards knew each other. They were comfortable standing together and being seen together."

"But they didn't work together. Not even in the same state. Marcus here in Little Rock and Sam in DC." Mary Ellen shifted in her seat.

"I don't know. Maybe if they pick up Fred Otto, they'll be able to get answers from him." Elise set down her cup. She didn't need any more caffeine as jumpy as she felt.

Agent Rodriguez came back into the room. "I just thought I'd update you. The hospital just called. Sam Edwards died a few minutes ago. I'm sorry we didn't get the opportunity to question him."

Elise blinked back tears. The frustration at always being a step behind and not knowing what was going on was starting to really get to her. She wanted to go crawl into Sawyer's bed, grab his old stuffed bear, and stay there until he was returned safe and sound.

That just wasn't going to happen though.

"Thanks for letting me know." Elise wondered if he'd give her the information about Fred Otto.

"Of course. I'll let you know if anything else of importance happens on the case." He returned to the kitchen.

So, that was a no that he would give her information not

critical for her to know.

Wesson came back. "You heard Sam Edwards just died? My editor just called so I could amend my article before they go to print in the next hour or so."

"Yeah, Agent Rodriguez just told us." Elise leaned back into the couch. When would this all be over?

Wesson sat between Elise and Mary Ellen on the couch. "Sorry to crowd, but I don't want to be overheard."

"What?" Elise asked.

"I had my source run Sam Edwards and Marcus Tate and Fred Otto to see if there was any connection between the three."

"And?" Elise sat up straight.

"Seems Marcus Tate was married to Sam Edwards's cousin for a few years. They got divorced, but apparently the two men stayed in touch. According to one of my sources, they still went hunting and camping together. Shared a duck hunting lease in Stuttgart even."

It made sense.

"Now, I couldn't find any connection between Sam Edwards and Fred Otto, *but* I did find one between Fred Otto and Marcus Tate. Seems the two are old fishing buddies. They've gone on annual fishing trips together for many years. I couldn't find how they met or anything, but it stands to reason that Marcus Tate was the common link between the three."

And Marcus Tate was dead.

Wesson lowered her voice even more. "I have several of my sources trying to find out if there was anyone else Marcus Tate was close to. It could be that our mysterious fourth person might be linked to Marcus."

And none of it mattered if they couldn't find Sawyer.

Chapter Twenty-Four

The first orange veins of dawn streaked across the April Arkansas sky.

Elise drank her umpteenth cup of coffee on the porch, alone. She'd told them all she needed just a few minutes alone because if she had to sit cooped up in the house without Sawyer for much longer, she was going to scream.

For the first time in a long time, she remembered sitting on this very porch with Judson when she was pregnant, and listening to him read aloud from the Bible. They had so much faith, felt so much promise for their unborn son, and thought the world was theirs.

Oh, how wrong they were.

But when Judson had read scripture to her, his voice and the words soothed her. They'd both taken turns reading the Bible over Sawyer as well when he was an infant, before they'd known he was deaf. Elise allowed a few tears to escape. She'd honestly believed that their son had been as comforted by his daddy's soothing voice as she had, even if he couldn't understand the words. Now she knew he hadn't gotten any comfort.

Now, she had no comfort either.

She wanted to scream. Cry. Stomp her feet. Throw things. Hit something—really, really hard. Yet, she knew none of that would serve any purpose. Except maybe make her feel better temporarily.

The door eased open and both Wesson and Mary Ellen slipped out into the cool morning air, both carrying cups of coffee.

"If we're intruding, we can go back inside," Mary Ellen said.

"It's okay. I just needed a little fresh air and space. I'm good now." Well, not really, but it wasn't their fault.

"I've been praying for peace for you." Mary Ellen smiled and pulled out one of the patio chairs from the table and sat. "I can only imagine how hard this is for you."

"Thank you." Elise smiled as Wesson sat. No sense going into how she didn't feel Mary Ellen's prayers were helping at all.

"Noland's awake and making another pot of coffee." Mary Ellen smiled.

"I'm so glad you made him take a nap. I wish he'd rested more." He'd reluctantly laid down around one thirty, so he'd gotten at least four or so hours.

"You need to rest too," Mary Ellen said.

Elise slowly shook her head. "You know that's not going to happen."

"I had to try."

"And I love you for it."

Wesson's cell lit up. She moved to the yard as she took the call.

"I know your faith has taken a hit, Elise, but know that God loves you and Sawyer so much."

Elise wasn't up to arguing so she just took another sip of coffee. She felt drained. Even worse than when Judson died, because at least she had to appear strong for Sawyer and Lilliana. This wasn't the case now. If anything happened to Sawyer, she'd have no reason to get up in the morning. No reason to carry on.

Wesson came back. "That was one of my sources. First off, the police weren't able to pick up Fred Otto. He wasn't at home. They have someone watching the house. He wasn't at work—he's a stocker at Walmart, but he wasn't scheduled to work anyway, so it's not like he was tipped off that he was wanted for questioning."

Elise nodded. If he wasn't at work, he might be with Sawyer. It'd been too much to hope that he would have Sawyer at his house. He probably was keeping him out at an unknown location to protect his identity.

That's what Elise was going to choose to believe anyway.

Wesson continued. "I heard from my source in the bureau. The FBI leak is most likely a guy named Bob Parker. He's a new guy in the forensics lab and rumor has it, Agent Monica Wright has a crush on him and is trying to do things to catch his attention."

"Which would explain why she shared information with him." The coffee seemed to curdle in Elise's stomach. "Appearing like a big shot agent instead of a lab worker, I'm guessing."

"It would appear. My source says that Monica is very flirty with him, all the time since he was hired, and he hasn't shown much interest in her."

"So what's his connection to Marcus Tate or Sam Edwards or Fred Otto?" Mary Ellen asked.

Wesson shrugged. "I don't know yet, but it seemed suspicious to my source because he was only hired within the last couple of months. My sources say they don't even know if Agent Rodriguez is aware of Monica giving information to Bob, much less why he would share information with anyone else."

"Then maybe we should enlighten him." Elise stood.

"Are you sure that's a good idea? I mean, she's his partner so it may make him angry or upset," Mary Ellen said.

"At this point, I'm past caring about making anyone upset or angry. I want my son back." Elise opened the kitchen door and stuck her head inside. Agent Rodriguez sat with others around the kitchen table. "Agent Rodriguez, may I speak with you out here?"

"Of course." He stood and followed her outside.

She stood with him, but couldn't overlook the sagginess of his shoulders or the way exhaustion clung to him like a too-tight suit.

"What is it?" He leaned against the porch's railing.

"It seems that the leak in the bureau that has gotten some details of my case out of the FBI is through a Bob Parker." Elise watched his face to see if there was any recognition.

There wasn't. "Bob who?"

"Parker. He's a new guy in your forensics lab. Been there only a few months."

The agent crossed his arms over his chest. "And just how, pray tell, has a new guy in our forensics lab received information about your case that has nothing to do with forensic evidence?"

Elise let out a breath and crossed her arms over her chest. "Rumor has it that your partner has a crush on him and shares information. Maybe just to appear to be a big shot agent, I don't know, but that's what I've heard."

"I know you and Monica butt heads but—"

"She's not just saying that because Agent Wright makes her bristle," Wesson interjected. "I'm the one who told Elise."

"And how do you know that, Ms. Kelly?"

"Because I have a source in the bureau who told me." She held up her hand. "Before you start asking, no, I will not tell you who my source is, but this is someone very reliable."

He shook his head. "I can't just take the word of an anonymous source. Not if you're asking me to believe this about my partner."

"Would you rather the alternative?" Mary Ellen interrupted. "That your partner was the one who actually gave information to Sam Edwards or Marcus Tate?"

"You all are wrong. Monica might be rough around the edges, but she would never jeopardize one of our cases." Agent Rodriguez shook his head.

Elise cleared her throat. "We knew there was a leak. Surely you had to know that, even if you hadn't a clue who. I mean, there was just no other way for what I told you and Agent Wright to have gotten to Marcus Tate and Sam Edwards so quickly."

"That's possible, I suppose."

Elise snorted. "Possible? Come on, Agent Rodriguez, they always knew what I did with the FBI as soon as I did it. You have to admit that screams of a leak."

He slowly nodded. "But that doesn't mean Monica was involved."

"Doesn't it?" Elise could appreciate his protection of his partner, but she was someone he was supposed to protect. "Did you tell anyone else what I'd told you?"

"Well, we did tell Mary Ellen, but there was a reason." He had the decency to blush.

"So that we would be at odds and if either of us knew something, we'd spill, right?" Elise asked.

He nodded.

"But other than Mary Ellen, did *you* tell anyone else anything about the case and my involvement in it?" Elise fisted a hand on her hip.

"Well, my supervisor, of course, and fellow agents who were working on certain aspects of the investigation."

"I'd bet you didn't tell nonessential people and I'd even go so far as to say you didn't tell anyone immediately what was going on with the case."

"I didn't."

"Then how in all that is holy do you think the information was dispersed so quickly? Osmosis?" Yeah, she was being sarcastic, but he needed to open his eyes and see the truth.

He didn't reply.

Wesson stood. "Look, my source wouldn't give me a name until the information was verified by several. Just look into it. Bob Parker. Maybe you can find a connection between him and the other guys."

"We're working on making the connections now."

"Let me help you out with that." Elise was tired of the secret game. All of this was just delaying finding Sawyer and bringing him home. "Marcus Tate and Sam Edwards were related by marriage. Even when the marriage ended, they remained friends. Hunting together."

Agent Rodriguez pushed off the porch's rail. "Are you sure?"

"Yes," Wesson answered. "They share a duck hunting lease in Stuttgart. Both of their names are on the lease."

Elise nodded. "Even though you didn't tell me, Fred Otto of the Ford Focus is also connected to Marcus Tate. They're fishing buddies from years ago."

Again he had the decency to blush. "I didn't tell you about Fred Otto because while we hope he's the one who's delivered boxes to you, we don't know that for sure. We're in the process of bringing him in—"

Elise held up her hands. "Yes, I know. You have procedures and protocols, but none of that is bringing my son home. Fred Otto wasn't at home last night, nor was he at work, but he wasn't scheduled to work anyway. If he's the one who actually has Sawyer, I hope he is found quickly and that my son is with him, safe."

A gentle breeze kicked across the yard as the sun broke through the streaks. It was going to be a bright and warm day.

Agent Rodriguez wore a sheepish look. "I'm sorry I can't keep you more informed. We just have to play this close to the vest right now."

"That doesn't matter right now. It seems in some instances, I actually get information before you, and that's okay too, because I'll let you know." Elise wrapped her hands around her arms, hugging herself. "Look, if you don't want to confront your partner, don't. I'm glad she's not here and privy to the information going on here, but I ask that you check into this Bob Parker. There might be a connection there that could lead us to Sawyer if he's not with Fred Otto. Okay?"

The kitchen door opened and an agent stuck his head out. "Sir, you're needed on the radio," he said to Agent Rodriguez, then ducked back inside.

Agent Rodriguez gave a curt nod to Elise. "I'll check into all this." He headed toward the kitchen door.

"That's all I can expect." Because she certainly didn't expect more. It was time for her to stop sitting around waiting. She looked at Wesson and Mary Ellen. "I'm going to take a shower. After that, let's update anything new, then we can form a game plan."

"Game plan?" Mary Ellen stood.

"We're getting just as much information, if not more, than what the FBI is sharing with me. But this is *my* son and I want him back. Now. I'm ready to form a plan to do just that."

"Count me in." Wesson grabbed the coffee cups from the table. "I grabbed a quick shower after I finished the article. Another cup of java and I'll be ready."

"Me too. I want nothing more than for my nephew to be home, safe and sound. If you don't mind, I think I'll run back to Mom's and take a quick shower too. Just to wake me up." Mary Ellen pointed at the cups in Wesson's hands. "I could take a big one of those as well."

Elise stopped. "Mary Ellen, I know you have to be as dead on your feet as I am."

Her sister-in-law shook her head. "I've been able to doze here and there so I'm good. A cool shower and a cup of hot coffee and I'll be ready."

Elise's throat thickened. "I really appreciate you two so much. I can't even put into words how much it means to have you both, and Noland, here for me like this."

"Of course." Mary Ellen smiled. "We're family and that's what family is all about—being there for each other."

Wesson cleared her throat. "I'm not family, but then again, I've never had one. I'm here to help in any way I can. I hope you know it's not just about the byline for me, either."

"I do know, and I appreciate you both. I won't forget this." Elise opened the kitchen door and led the way inside.

Noland was rinsing mugs and sticking them in the dishwasher.

Elise realized he needed a break. "Hey, Noland, Mary Ellen's going to run back to your place for a shower while I get cleaned up. Do you want to go with her?"

"Oh, yes. Please."

Mary Ellen smiled at her stepfather. "Then let's go. We'll come straight back." She turned to look at Elise. "We'll take quick showers, then come straight back. Do you need anything?"

"No, thank you."

Mary Ellen moved to let Wesson put the mugs in the sink. "Then we'll be back soon."

"Oh, go ahead. I know how good it feels to be in clean clothes." Elise grinned.

"Is something going on?" Noland asked.

"Tell you in the car," Mary Ellen whispered. She raised her voice to a normal speaking level and looked at Elise. "We'll be back soon, but call me if anything comes up."

"Or if you think of something we can get you while we're out," Noland added.

"I will. Both of you." Elise gave them a quick hug before they left, then she walked Wesson into the living room. "I shouldn't be long."

Wesson sank onto the couch, kicked off her slides, and snuggled in. "Take your time. I'll be touching base with my contacts."

Elise nodded and headed to her bedroom, determination pounding with every step.

Agent Rodriguez stopped her in the hall. "I just thought I'd update you that we ran a financial inquiry on all of Marcus Tate's accounts. There was no large amount of money wired into his accounts the day Senator York was murdered, or since. We're still tracking though, so maybe something will hit."

Elise nodded. "So the money trail is a dead end too." When were they going to get a break with this case?

"Not yet, but we're still running tracers to see if he had an off-shore account or something similar. Anything that might lead us to who hired him to kill Senator York."

"Thanks for the update." Elise did appreciate his giving her the information that he probably wasn't supposed to tell her. She smiled, then moved on to her bedroom and shut the door.

Hot tears mixed with the hot shower as she slapped the side of the glass stall. She was going to find her son regardless of what the FBI told her to do. Staying put had never been her strongest suit anyway.

Chapter Twenty-Five

"We stopped and grabbed some doughnuts for everyone on our way in." Noland set a box on the coffee table in front of Elise and Wesson. "I'll make a fresh pot of coffee." He carried two other large boxes into the kitchen with him.

Mary Ellen shook her head as she sat in the chair. "He was determined. Besides, he says the agents overlook him when he's feeding them and blending into the background in the kitchen."

"He has a point." Elise opened the doughnuts, her stomach growling. How had she not noticed being so famished? Not the healthiest of breakfast options, but the sugar would give her an energy boost, which she needed. She picked out two chocolate-glazed creations and bit into the still-warm dough. "Mmm. This is good," she muffled.

"Okay, now I have to have one." Wesson sat up and grabbed a regular glazed. "Oh, they're still warm and everything." She took a bite and closed her eyes.

Elise grinned. She knew that feeling, was feeling it now. Her stomach rumbled its appreciation.

Mary Ellen just chuckled and shook her head. "I'm going to go help Noland with the coffee. At least for us."

Elise made quick work of her two doughnuts. She couldn't remember the last time she ate. She needed to take better care of herself. Sawyer would need her when he came back. She was already thinking about the therapy he'd have to deal with. She'd find him a really good child therapist. Hallie could probably recommend someone through the school.

Hallie!

Elise glanced at her watch—seven forty-five. School would be starting soon. She retrieved her cell phone and called Hallie.

Wesson finished off her third doughnut as Mary Ellen returned with the coffee. Both sat on the couch while Elise sat in the chair.

"Hey, Elise. Are you almost here? Yesterday looked like a circus here, but today the coast is clear."

That's when Elise realized no one outside of this house knew Sawyer had been kidnapped. Well, whoever had him, of course. "Hallie, I have some news. Sawyer's been kidnapped."

"What? When?"

Elise quickly brought Hallie up to speed.

"Oh my gosh. Are you okay? Sorry, that was insensitive, of course you aren't okay. Do you need me to come there? I don't know what I can do, but I can sit with you or whatever." Hallie's words tripped over one another.

Despite having to delve into the painful details again, Elise smiled. "Mary Ellen and Noland and a friend are here with me. Along with all the FBI agents."

"I'm so sorry. I didn't know, or I'd have reached out to you."

Didn't know. Elise's stomach knotted. "I know. I've got to go. Just wanted you to know why he wasn't at school today." Her heart nearly choked on the sentence.

"I'll be praying. Call me if you need me for anything."

"Thanks." Elise disconnected the call and looked at Wesson and Mary Ellen and Noland, who'd just brought them all steaming cups of strong, black coffee. "No one knows Sawyer's been kidnapped. I mean, we do, but the public doesn't. What if this Fred Otto does have him and is traveling with him, taking him to the person in charge or just out of town? No one knows to look for him."

"Let's hold a press conference. You can put Sawyer's picture in front of the cameras, make a plea for his safe return, and get people involved. So many people get mobilized when a child is involved." Wesson already had her cell phone in one hand, coffee mug in the other. "I'll call the local stations and get crews here. We can go live at say"—she checked the time—"about nine?"

"That's fine with me." A sense of accomplishment rushed through Elise. Yes! She was finally being proactive in this whole situation, and it felt great. She grabbed a mug and took a sip, letting the heat warm her all the way to her toes.

Noland nodded. "I'll call in a few favors and get some of the outlying news outlets here as well, in case Sawyer is being taken out of town."

Elise glanced at Wesson. "Did you happen to snap a picture of the sketch Connie drew of Fred?"

"Of course." Wesson grinned. "Like I wouldn't?"

"I doubt the FBI is going to let us use their photo or anything, but I want something to put on camera about the one adult we can identify that might have contact with Sawyer." Elise twisted her hands in her lap. Agent Rodriguez was probably going to be very upset about the press conference to begin with, but she didn't have to ask his permission to do what she wanted. Not when it came to finding her son.

Wesson grinned bigger. "Oh, I can do you one better. I'll have my source send me a picture. He's amazing at finding photos people post up on social media." She tapped on her smartphone. "I'll bet he can have several photos to me in minutes. We just print them out and you're all set." She glanced up at Elise. "You *do* have a printer, right?"

"I do. It's color and everything." Elise waggled her eyebrows.

"You'd be surprised at how many people don't have printers anymore. It's all the digital world, baby."

"I know. All the younger people think I'm archaic when I talk about having to buy print cartridges." Elise would never be able to get away from paper copies of everything. Mercy, she didn't even read magazines and newspapers digitally.

Newspapers!

Elise jumped up and opened the front door.

Two agents were at her side in a flash. "Where are you going, Mrs. Carmichael?"

"To get my newspaper." She stared at them. "Is that okay?"

"I'll get it for you, ma'am." The younger agent jogged to her mailbox and pulled out the paper from the yellow box. He handed it to her, not even out of breath.

"Thank you." She took the paper and headed into the living room. The agents shut the door behind her.

If they didn't want her to get her own newspaper, they were really going to flip when she gave a press conference in her front yard.

She sat down and unfolded the paper. Just below the bottom fold she found it:

SUSPECT LINKED TO SENATOR YORK MURDER DIES AFTER SHOOT-OUT. . .*by Adian Mancoff*

Adian Mancoff? This was Wesson's story. Her big career boost. Elise quickly scanned the article. No information that Elise hadn't approved was included. It was well written, factual, and what journalism used to be about: reporting the news without bias or infraction.

"What's the deal?" She waved the paper at Wesson. "Why isn't this your story? Who is Adian Mancoff?"

"Because I've been so publicly linked to you, my editor didn't think it would be wise for the byline to be mine. I gave the story to one of my close friends. Adian used my notes and only what we'd discussed." Wesson gave a little shrug, but disappointment laid in every nuance of her face.

Mary Ellen reached for the newspaper. "That isn't fair."

Wesson shrugged again. "I mean, I can understand. I think my editor was right. Maybe after all is said and done and Sawyer is back home safely, I can write an exposé—a behind the story type of thing."

Elise nodded. "Most definitely. And then you can use all the information."

Wesson's cell rang and she put it to her ear and took a step away.

"It's nice to know that some people still have integrity," Mary Ellen commented. "Especially the media."

"I think that's just who she is. I'm glad we're friends." Elise smiled as Wesson slipped her cell back into her pocket and rejoined them.

"Okay, just heard back from the last one. When I mentioned Senator York's grandson had been kidnapped, all five of the local media were all in. They'll have crews here for a nine o'clock press conference."

"Thanks, Wesson."

"I've got some of the outlying outlets sending crews as well," Noland added.

"Good article." Mary Ellen set the paper on the coffee table. "Has anyone informed the FBI of the conference coming?"

Elise shook her head. "No, and I don't intend to. I don't need to ask permission, and I'm not going to give them time to try and dissuade me, or put a road block up at the end of the subdivision so no news vans can enter."

"Surely they wouldn't do that." Mary Ellen lifted her coffee cup and took a sip.

Elise set her cup on the table. "I wouldn't put anything past them, so I'm not going to give them the opportunity."

"As promised, I've received several photos of Fred Otto. Let me pull the two best and put them on an eight by ten, then we can print it and have it ready for the press conference. We'll need a recent eight by ten of Sawyer too, for you to hold up." Wesson went back to her phone.

"I have that." Sawyer being an only child, there were volumes of pictures of him around the house.

"Have you thought about what you're going to say?" Noland asked.

A tightening in Elise's chest twisted into a ball. "Beyond *please bring my son back*, I haven't a clue." The enormity of what she was about to do hit her and nearly leveled her.

"That's the best place to start." Noland smiled. "You hold up a picture of Sawyer, tell the people he was taken from his own back-yard—that resonates with every parent and gets their attention to listen to the rest of what you have to say."

Elise nodded. She could do that.

"You say his name as many times as you can. Make him a real person. Use his disability, although I know you hate doing that. In this case, use it. Pull the poor deaf child whose Daddy died in the military and whose grandmother, a US senator, was just murdered card. The more sympathy people feel, the more they care, and the more they care, the more involved they'll be willing to get to see Sawyer home safely."

"That makes sense." She despised making any sort of big deal or expecting any type of special consideration because of Sawyer being deaf. Hated even more using that Judson had died in active duty. But to help get her son back, she'd use everything available to her, even if it was a ploy to garner sympathy.

"Sorry to interrupt," Wesson said, "but is your printer the HP one? And is it on?"

"It is, and I never even turn it off."

Wesson shot to her feet. "Where is it?"

"Down the hall, across from my bedroom is the guest room. The printer's in there."

"Great, I'm on it. I'll snag a picture of Sawyer and make a copy too."

Elise smiled. "Thanks, Wesson." She turned back to Noland. "Okay, after I talk about Sawyer, then what?"

"Make sure you really lay it on thick. I know it sounds manip-ulative, and it is, but you need to make every person hearing or watching the conference feel so sympathetic that they are called to action."

"Got it." Elise took a sip of her coffee.

"Everyone who sees Sawyer's picture is going to be moved," Mary Ellen said.

"I forgot to mention to be sure and thank the press for coming. They eat that up, trust me." Noland grinned.

"Yeah, we in the press corps love being thanked." Wesson returned carrying two sheets of paper. "We're kind of shameless in that."

Noland nodded. "Then you can move right into that Fred Otto, and hold up the picture of him, is being sought by the police for questioning in relation to this kidnapping. Be careful not to call him a suspect, just that the police are looking for him. Don't want to border on slander."

This could get dicey. She wanted to just blurt out everything she knew, but realized she couldn't. Doing so could jeopardize the investigation and could even put Sawyer in more danger. She knew that logically, but emotionally, she just wanted to scream and demand her son be brought back home.

"Yeah, but make sure you have his picture right in front of the camera. If you can manage, put Sawyer's picture next to Fred Otto's, like this." Wesson held the two pages side by side. "See, it shows the difference in size and tone, which will also illicit even more empathy from viewers. They'll see that poor, deaf little boy up against this guy."

Mary Ellen joined in. "I know you don't like to share your tough emotions, but you need to let everyone see how vulnerable you are and desperate to get your son back."

"I am desperate to get Sawyer home. That's all I really want." The tears burned so badly and the waves of nausea threatened to toss Elise overboard.

Mary Ellen moved and put her arm around her. "Then show that. Let the people see. Every parent will relate and do what they can to bring Sawyer home."

"Yes! That." Wesson tapped on her phone again. "I'm going to reprint these. We needed a social media tag. This is perfect." She jumped up and went to the guest bedroom.

This was going to turn into a big circus, bigger than the one at the church after Lilliana's murder. But if it helped get Sawyer home, Elise was willing to play with all the monkeys.

"How's this look?" Wesson held up the paper with the picture of Sawyer, only across the bottom in big bold letters was #BringSawyer-Home. "We can monitor the tag, encourage others to share it, make it go viral across the state. Nation even if we need it to."

Elise stared at Sawyer's school picture from last year. He'd wanted to wear the bowtie for his picture. He looked so young and helpless, but so endearing with his crooked smile with a missing front tooth. She never thought she'd look at this picture with a *BringSawyerHome* tag. No one ever thinks their child could be kidnapped. She never did. Even in her job and seeing so much criminal activity did she ever think her family would be touched by such evil.

She'd been so, so wrong.

Chapter Twenty-Six

"There's a lot of press vans parking out front. Crews are getting out and crowding the driveway. Would you know anything about that?" Agent Rodriguez came into the living room, hand on his holster, eyes locked onto Elise's as she stopped pacing.

"It's almost nine." Wesson stood.

Elise straightened and squared up her shoulders. "I do. I invited them here."

Agent Rodriguez's brows lowered. "For what?"

Noland jumped to his feet. "For a press conference about Sawyer. To plea for his safe return and also to appeal to the public if anyone has seen him."

"I'm not sure that's the best—"

Mary Ellen stood and looped her arm through Elise's. "It's time."

"Mrs. Carmichael, we aren't opposed to a press conference, but we should prep you on what to say." Agent Rodriguez moved to block her way to the door.

"I'm a grown woman and quite capable of handling myself at a press conference." She looked from him to the front door. "Are you intending to block my path to my own front door, or is that unintentional?"

"Please, Mrs. Carmichael—"

Elise and her barrage of support moved to walk around him. "I'm tired of waiting for something significant to be done, Agent Rodriguez." She paused and looked over her shoulder at him. "You are more than welcome to join me." She didn't wait for a response as she walked through the front door Noland held open for her. "We'll be right beside you," Noland said.

Wesson handed her the two pictures, then walked on her other side, opposite the side Mary Ellen was on. The three of them reached the end of the driveway where at least fifteen cameras and microphones were jammed in her face. Lights flashed as cameras were hoisted high above their heads. Panic stuck in the back of Elise's throat.

"Back up a little. Give her some space." Agent Rodriguez managed to push back the crowd with just his words and presence.

The butterflies in her stomach calmed that he was there, easing what he could for her, even if she had been a little curt with him. She gave him a subtle smile, then turned toward the cameras. She cleared her throat as microphones and mini recorders were thrust toward her. Mary Ellen squeezed Elise's arm, but took a half step to the right so that Elise was the focus shot.

Wesson held up her hands and everyone went quiet. "Mrs. Carmichael will give her statement, then possibly take a few questions. Please don't interrupt her during her statement as this is an extremely emotional time for her."

Most of the crowd nodded, but thankfully remained quiet.

"I'd first like to thank you all for coming, especially on such short notice. That you members of the press would be so willing to come and help me get the word out about my son's kidnapping, well, I'm thankful."

There was total silence over the throes of reporters and crew.

With shaking hands, Elise held up the picture of Sawyer. "This is my seven year old son, Sawyer. He's a good boy, does extremely well in school. Loves video games, soccer, and eating pizza. Sawyer was also born deaf and mute. He recently hurt his wrist, so it's in a cast, which leaves his ability to communicate with others very limited." She swallowed down the lump lodged in the back of her throat.

"Sawyer was only two years old when his dad died in the line of duty. He was a Marine." She swayed just a little, then remembered not to lock her legs. She bent a knee slightly, then slowly exhaled. "Last week, Sawyer's grandmother, US senator Lilliana York, was murdered in her home."

Elise held out the picture toward the cameras, remembering to keep saying his name, even though it felt so awkward. "Yesterday, after attending his grandmother's funeral and while the FBI was in my home, my son, Sawyer, was taken from our own backyard."

Gasps and *tsking* sounds rippled through the crowd. Adjacent to her, Agent Rodriguez audibly sucked in air. She didn't miss the shocked expression he tossed her way before he masked his face and turned back to the crowd of media.

Elise kept her own rigid posture. No turning back now. "I'd been receiving threats from someone affiliated with Senator York's murder and had been working with the FBI. My son, Sawyer was taken because I worked with the FBI."

More disapproving sounds ran through the crowd, louder this time. It bolstered her resolve. "After my mother-in-law's murder, I came forward with information regarding suspicious activities in relation to her murder. Almost as soon as I did, I began receiving vague threats to keep my mouth shut." Elise struggled to speak slowly and enunciate.

After taking in a long breath and releasing it, Elise continued. "Each time I received a threat, I notified the FBI, and still continued working with them in giving a statement, working with a sketch artist, anything I could do to help. And still I would receive threats to keep quiet."

She shook her head as the crowd inched closer to her. She looked at Wesson, who nodded and touched her elbow.

Elise let out another breath before glancing over to Agent Rodriguez, then back to the crowd. "I have come to believe that some of my information and involvement with the FBI wasn't kept as confidential as I'd originally believed, even when I brought the possible breach up to agents."

Mumbling breezed through the crowd of reporters and crew.

"Whoever took Sawyer was brazen enough to kidnap him from our backyard while the FBI was here." Yes, Agent Rodriguez would be furious and have every right to be, but Elise had told the truth and didn't care about anyone else's disdain. Not when Sawyer's life was on the line.

Elise held up the paper with Fred Otto's photo on it. "This is a man the FBI is interested in speaking with regarding the investigation. His name is Fred Otto."

Movement flurried through the reporters as if choreographed.

She could see Agent Rodriguez making his way to her. Noland had his arm, and Mary Ellen moved to help block, but Elise knew the conference was about to be brought to a screeching halt. She held the papers side by side. "Please, if you know anything about Mr. Otto's or my sweet Sawyer's whereabouts, please contact the local FBI."

Agent Rodriguez had stopped his forward motion. Elise pressed on, not able to withhold her emotions. Tears filled her eyes and overflowed. "Please, please help bring Sawyer back to me. Since widowed, he's my world."

She lowered the pages and signed as she spoke. "Sawyer, if you can see this, know that I love you, honey, and I'm doing everything I can to bring you home. I love you, baby." Sobs overtook her.

Mary Ellen moved and put her arm around Elise, gently moving her to the side a few steps.

Wesson stepped into where Elise had just stood. "As you can imagine, this is very hard on Mrs. Carmichael. We ask for your help in getting the pictures out. We request you put them on all your social media accounts, using the tag #BringSawyerHome." She glanced around. "I'm happy to try and answer any of your questions right now."

"Mrs. Carmichael, what types of threats did you receive?"

Wesson answered for Elise. "Mrs. Carmichael received boxes with warnings such as a dead rat, a doll with a note that snitches get stitches, and photographs taken from inside the home. . .those types of threats."

"How are you involved in the investigation, Mrs. Carmichael?"

Wesson paused. Elise cleared her throat and moved to stand beside her young friend. "I'm a lip-reader, and I saw a conversation that alluded to my mother-in-law, US senator Lilliana York. Once she was murdered, I became a witness of sorts."

"Was Marcus Tate one of the people involved in that conversation? The man who was killed a few nights ago?"

Elise nodded.

"Has the FBI identified the other person in the conversation? Was it him, Fred Otto?"

Elise stood a little straighter. "The other person I saw was identified. Unfortunately, he was also killed. It was not Fred Otto."

"So who is Fred Otto and how is he involved?"

Elise opened her mouth, but Wesson touched her hand. "As Mrs. Carmichael said, Fred Otto is only someone the FBI would like to talk with. He may or may not have information expressly relevant to the investigation. Again, Mrs. Carmichael isn't stating Fred Otto has done anything illegal, only that the FBI need to ask him some questions."

Good thing Wesson was there because Elise just might well have told the world that Fred Otto was the one who delivered the threats and the one Elise was pretty sure had taken Sawyer.

"Again, I beg of you, if anyone has seen Sawyer, or knows anything of his kidnapping, please, please, please call the Little Rock FBI office or the police. You can even call me. I just want my son back." The sobs overtook her again. This time, Mary Ellen and Noland flanked her and led her to the house.

She could hear Wesson winding up the press conference. "Copies of Sawyer's photo are here. If you have any questions regarding the investigation, here is Agent Rodriguez, who has been involved with the case since the beginning."

A barrage of reporters' voices calling out for Agent Rodriguez's attention filled the air. Noland opened the front door and pulled Elise inside. Mary Ellen and Wesson followed, then shut the door.

Every nerve burned into jumbled knots under Elise's skin. She made it to the couch before she broke down in tears. Noland and Mary Ellen sat on either side of her, hugging and rocking her. She couldn't remember the last time she'd felt so raw, like everything in her was exposed to the elements. Even her hair cried out.

Seconds passed. Minutes. Elise couldn't be sure how many. She cried until the tears were dried up, until her sides ached and her chest tightened. Then she sat upright and let out a long breath. "I'm sorry."

"No need to be sorry," Noland said. "We're all bundles of nerves."

Mary Ellen put her hands on either side of Elise's face. "It's going to be okay. Sawyer is going to be all right."

Agony slithered around Elise's heart. "You don't know that."

"I do."

"How?" The word scratched against Elise's throat.

"Because I have faith. You do too, Elise. You're just letting your emotions get in the way of your faith." Mary Ellen's stare was piercing, as if it peered into Elise's very spirit.

Elise tried to shake her head, but Mary Ellen didn't let go of her face. "Think of all the scriptures you clung to when Judson died. You know them. First Peter five. Matthew six. Philippians four. You know to give your concerns to God. It's just hard."

It *was* hard. Maybe that's why she had been so resistant to turn back to God. Putting Sawyer, the one thing, the one person she loved more than anything else in this world, into anyone else's hands besides her own terrified her.

"But it's okay, Elise. God understands. He already knows what you're feeling and what you're most scared of, but you can trust Him." Mary Ellen let go of Elise's face.

"Yet, Judson trusted God with his whole heart, and God took him from me." Fresh tears had found their way to Elise's eyes, and she ducked her head.

"No, God didn't take him. The evil of men who step out of God's will put into motion bad things."

Elise jerked her head back up. "Well, God didn't intervene. He could have prevented Judson's death. He certainly could have prevented Sawyer's deafness. How can the robbing of an innocent baby's ability to hear be attributed to anyone stepping out of God's will?"

Mary Ellen shrugged. "I don't have all the answers, Elise. Not for Sawyer being born deaf, not for the babies with cancer or diseases, not for anything my human mind can't rationalize. I can't explain that, but I do believe God cares for us and wants only the best for us. Only He can see the big picture, today and tomorrow, and knows what we go through today might be preparation for something coming."

Hadn't people said the same thing, or a similar version, to Elise after Judson died? After her parents' accident? It hadn't made her feel better then, and it certainly didn't now.

Mary Ellen gave her a hug, then released her. "I'm praying. Why don't you go splash some water on your face and maybe try to rest for a few minutes?"

Noland stood. "I'm going to put on a pot of soup to feed everyone. You go take a few minutes alone."

Maybe they were right. The crying fit had worn her out. She needed to be ready for when Sawyer came home. She stood. "Maybe just for thirty minutes or so."

She did splash cold water on her face before crawling on top of the bed, covers and all. She'd just rest for a few minutes to let her body conserve some energy.

Elise blinked. Again. And again.

The ceiling fan hummed rhythmically as she watched it, her breathing slowing to almost match its slow cycle.

Okay, God, I'm here. Mary Ellen says it's going to be okay. I want to believe that, I really do, but after losing Judson and Mom and Dad, I'm scared. Yeah, I admit it, I'm scared. But, please, don't let that stop You from keeping Sawyer safe and bringing him back home. Please, God.

CHAPTER TWENTY-SEVEN

One twelve?

Elise blinked and looked at the clock again. One thirteen.

She bolted upright. Had she really been asleep for three hours? Sawyer! What was the latest? Elise washed her face with cold water, then went into the living room. Some of the FBI agents had spilled in from the kitchen. Phones rang and the agents' voices were a constant hum.

"What's going on?" Elise felt like she'd been asleep for days and had woken up in the middle of some alternate reality.

Wesson came beside her. "Ever since the press aired your conference, the FBI has been flooded with tips and sightings."

"Of Sawyer?" Elise's heart arrested.

"A few, but none have led to anything solid yet. But there have been many reports of Fred Otto sightings. The FBI has gotten local law enforcement involved in following through with the reports, so it's not just the public calling in what they think is a tip or sighting, but also conversations between the FBI and law enforcement. It's very busy."

"Why didn't anyone wake me?" Elise felt groggy and out of it.

Mary Ellen shoved a bowl of chicken noodle soup in her hand. "We would have if there had been anything definite to tell you. Go sit in the kitchen with Noland. He's pouring you some tea to go with the soup he made. It's really good, by the way."

"I just feel like I should be doing something." Sawyer was goodness only knew where, in heaven only knew what kind of conditions, and she'd been sleeping and now held a steaming bowl of soup.

"You are." Mary Ellen put her arm around Elise and gently led her to the kitchen. "You're taking care of yourself, replenishing your strength, so you're refreshed and ready to keep doing whatever you need to in order to get Sawyer home." She pulled out a chair in the little alcove where no one else sat, and took the bowl of soup from Elise and set it on the table. "Sit. Eat. Then get back to work."

Elise found herself slinking into the chair as Mary Ellen walked off. She took a bite of the soup. Oh, Mary Ellen was right—the soup was wonderful. And wasn't chicken soup supposed to be really good at restoring key nutrients?

Noland set a glass of iced tea in front of her. "Good, glad to see you're eating. I told Mary Ellen that we would need you to eat, even if we had to force it down your throat. You can't live off coffee and donuts. Believe me, I know. I've tried." He chuckled at himself.

"No force-feeding necessary. This soup is wonderful, Noland. Thank you." She took another big bite.

"Well, good. I'm glad you're enjoying it. Eat up, it's great to keep up your strength and energy."

"Want to sit with me?"

"Actually"—Agent Rodriguez stepped up to the table—"I'd like to have a little chat with you, if you don't mind." He didn't wait for a reply, just took the seat opposite her.

Noland looked from the agent to Elise, clearly waiting for her response before he left.

As much as Elise wanted to avoid the lecture she was sure the FBI agent was going to give her, she didn't want Noland to feel any more awkward than he clearly already did. "It's okay, Noland. Thank you."

"I'll get you some fresh crackers." Noland shot a glare at the agent. "I'll be back in a few minutes."

Elise had to shove another spoonful in her mouth to hide the smile creeping out. How had she never known Noland could be so protective? Better yet, how had she not known what a good cook the man was?

"That was some impromptu press conference, Mrs. Carmichael." The agent crossed his arms over his chest as he leaned back in the chair.

"Oh, I think we're past the formalities. I'm Elise." She took a sip of the iced tea. Whoa, Noland had made it a little on the sweet side with plenty of mint. She wiped her mouth. "I realized that nobody really knew he was missing. How many people might have seen him when he was taken? Or along the route to wherever he was taken? I knew I needed to get the word out. If that messed up your investigation, I'm sorry." But, not really.

"I have no problem with you giving a statement. In fact, we were going to suggest that today. We just usually go over what you should and shouldn't say so that the case isn't jeopardized." His tone clearly implied she'd said something she shouldn't have.

Elise chewed the hunk of chicken and swallowed. "I'm sorry if I said something you didn't approve of, but my concern is not protecting the case. My main concern and focus is on bringing Sawyer home safe and sound. That's it."

"It's not quite that simple."

"To me it is." She took another sip of tea.

"Don't you want whoever murdered your mother-in-law and kidnapped your son to be brought to justice?"

"Yes, but it's not my primary focus. If Sawyer is safely home with me, that's paramount. Those responsible for Lilliana's death and kidnapping Sawyer being brought to justice is icing on the cake, but it's not the main thing to me."

"I understand that, but some of what you said might delay the result you're looking for." He rested his elbows on the table.

"Here are those crackers." Noland set a small pack of Captain's Wafers beside her. "Oh, you finished the soup. Let me get you another bowl."

"No, thank you, Noland. I can't eat any more right now. But thank you."

He paused and looked at Agent Rodriguez, then back at her. "Do you need me to get you anything else?" His look clearly implied he was referring to something akin to a Taser.

She smiled and shook her head. "We're good, Noland. Really, but thank you."

He grabbed her empty soup bowl. "Holler if you want anything." He cut his eyes to Agent Rodriguez. "Or if you need me." He turned away, putting the bowl in the dishwasher.

"Now." Elise turned her attention back to the agent. "What did I say that might delay getting Sawyer back?" She wasn't in a mood to play or mince words. Now that she'd rested and eaten something solid, she had more clarity.

"Naming Fred Otto might make him flee, for starters."

"It could, but maybe not. Maybe someone will have seen him, or if he does try to flee, someone will see him and report it. Or if he does have Sawyer and tries to run off with him, it'll be riskier because now people will notice him and Sawyer."

"I hope that's the way it goes."

"It's not like you haven't already tried to bring him in, right? He's not been home or at work and no one really has a clue where he is, right?"

Agent Rodriguez nodded. "But it could make him take more chances with Sawyer, trying to not be seen."

"True. But every hour Sawyer is gone, the chances of his safe return drop, right? I'm pretty sure I read that somewhere." She drained her tea. The ice cubes clanked against the glass. Elise stared at it, watching the condensation drip to the napkin on the table. Sawyer had been gone for coming up on twenty-four hours.

"Statistically, yes, but this isn't an ordinary kidnapping, Mrs. Carmichael."

Ah, so he wouldn't call her by her first name. Keeping it

professional, not personal. Guess she would do the same, considering the job.

"No, it's not. Sawyer was taken as punishment. To hurt me."

"I don't think so."

She met his stare. "You think not?"

He slowly shook his head. "Why take him? To hurt you? If that's really what they wanted, they'd have killed him. Like they killed Senator York and Marcus Tate. But they didn't. They kidnapped him, which means they took him alive. That screams to me that they're going to use him as leverage to get you to do something, or not do something as the case may be."

She figured there was something else that involved her, even though she had no idea what that could be. "Okay, so there is that. What else did I say that might delay Sawyer's return?" Might as well clear the air.

"The implication that there's a leak in the bureau. My boss already called on it."

"It's true. I know you don't want to believe that about your partner, but it makes everything make sense—how fast they knew everything and the details they knew."

"I'm going to meet with Monica this evening and I'll definitely ask her. In the meantime, I should prepare you that I've requested Bob Parker come here, supposedly to run some forensic tests, when his shift starts." He glanced at his watch. "Which is in about thirty minutes."

"Here? Why?"

Agent Rodriguez lifted a single shoulder. "I want to see how he reacts to being here where Sawyer was kidnapped. Where you are. If he's involved, his conscience should bug him enough that he acts weird and then I can question him."

"So then it's okay what I said on camera then."

Agent Rodriguez slowly shook his head. "Well, that's not necessarily true. When you make public implications like that, well, people in the bureau take offense."

What? "Are you telling me that because I said there was a leak in the FBI without really coming out and saying that, some agents might, what, not work as diligently on my case?" Because if that was the situation, she was about to blow up. "That's why you're bringing Bob Parker here, right?"

"Yes, but what if the leak isn't Bob Parker? What if Ms. Kelly's source has it wrong?"

"But what if it's true. It *is* Bob Parker?"

"Then we will take the appropriate steps."

Elise studied him. "Are you saying that others with the FBI might resent me exposing Bob or your partner and retaliate?"

"No, that's not what I'm saying."

Elise crossed her arms over her chest. "Then what are you saying, exactly? *'People in the bureau take offense.'* What does that mean?"

"Just that you make it hard for them to do their jobs. We take a lot of flak, which isn't warranted all the time."

"But in this case, it is warranted, even if you don't want to admit it."

He let out a very heavy sigh. "I'll admit that there does seem to be the case in this instance, but I won't take hearsay of who is responsible. I'm going to follow through with figuring out who's behind the leak, I guarantee you that."

"That's all we can do, right? Keep following up on everything. Every single lead we can."

Agent Rodriguez pushed to his feet. "Speaking of, I think it's time I get back to get an update. Maybe one of the tips has given us a solid lead."

She nodded and stood as well, grabbing her glass. "Please keep me updated as much as you can."

"I will." He sauntered across the room, taking a seat beside two other agents.

Elise took her glass to the sink and set it down, then wandered back into the living room to join Wesson and Mary Ellen. "What's going on?"

"Right now, they're still sending units out on possible viable leads. Nothing has been confirmed yet, but everyone's hopeful." Mary Ellen inched over to make room for Elise on the couch.

Elise plopped down. With so many calls happening, surely there was at least one good lead. They just had to find it.

Wesson nodded. "On a hunch, I've got my sources checking out those shared duck leases and fishing camps. It might be a place where the group would feel safe taking Sawyer."

"Smart," Elise said. Wesson Kelly might just be a junior reporter, but with the way her mind worked, she would be moving up the ladder quickly. "By the way, Agent Rodriguez informed me that Bob Parker will be coming here, supposedly to do some forensic work, but really, Agent Rodriguez wants to see how he acts here around me, in Sawyer's house."

"That's probably a good thing," Mary Ellen offered. "If he's here, then you know he doesn't have Sawyer."

Maybe. "Or he left Sawyer alone so he wouldn't be under suspicion." Elise hugged herself. She'd taken a nap and eaten hot soup and the house was filled with people. It pained her more than she could put into words to think about her baby alone, maybe hungry, and so scared. Being deaf would make it all so much worse.

"I don't think that's the case." Wesson crossed her legs at the ankles. "I think Fred Otto is the one who is holding Sawyer. I don't know if it's here, or at a camp or a lodge, but I think that's who has Sawyer."

Elise nodded. "I'm still convinced the files Lilliana sent are all tied to everything. The answer is right in front of my face, but I just can't see it."

"I know. I've gone over it all a gazillion times in my head." Mary Ellen leaned back on the couch and closed her eyes. "It literally exhausts me trying to figure it out."

"Hey, that nap did me wonders. Why don't you go crawl up in the guest-room bed and get a few minutes of sleep?" Elise offered.

As if her body reacted on its own, Mary Ellen yawned.

Elise grinned. "See, you can't even argue because you're yawning." She gave her sister-in-law a gentle shove. "Go ahead. Go get some rest. You know we'll wake you if something important comes up."

"Well, I guess I could close my eyes for a little bit." She stood and yawned again, then laughed. "Okay, I'm going."

Elise caught sight of Noland handing out mugs of coffee to the agents. She headed into the kitchen and cornered him. "Hey, I just got Mary Ellen to go lie down. Why don't you go try and get a little rest? You can use Sawyer's room." She caught the hesitation in his eyes. "Maybe something in there will inspire you for another idea about Sawyer."

"Well, I do need to rest a little before the dinner hour rolls around." He dried his hands on the dishtowel. "I'll just take a little doze, then."

"Good. I need you, so I can't have you dead on your feet." She gave him a hug and watched him head down the hall.

Wesson waved her back into the living room. Her eyes were wide as she stood next to the couch.

"What?" Elise joined her.

Wesson leaned close to her before she spoke. "We've found Alice Poe."

Elise's heart lunged. "What?"

Wesson nodded. "Confirmed. She lives in Conway and has a little boy just over two years old."

"Are you positive she's the same one that worked in the court-house here?" Elise asked, but her gut already knew the answer.

"Yep. Double and triple checked. She uses her mother's maiden name as her last name. Guess she couldn't get too far away, but still felt the need to be hidden."

Elise glanced at the agents in the kitchen and entry of the living room. Should she tell them? Agent Rodriguez certainly didn't seem to put much weight into Wesson's sources.

"It's only forty-five minutes away." Wesson shifted her weight from one leg to the other. "We can be there and back in a couple of hours. If we're wrong, it's only time that we would have wasted anyway, sitting here waiting for something. But if we're right, we might get some answers."

Elise hesitated, considering. She truly believed the files were linked to everything that was happening. Wesson had voiced what Elise thought. Going to see this Alice Poe, talking to her and seeing what the connection was, well, that could break the whole case wide open. She let out a slow, cleansing breath. "Let me print out copies of the picture and paternity test to take with us."

"Yes!" Wesson grinned.

"Um, Mrs. Carmichael." Agent Rodriguez stood near the front door.

She faced him.

"News crews are starting to congregate out on your driveway again. Know anything about that?"

Elise and Wesson both rushed to the front windows and peeked through the blinds. Elise shook her head. "I have no idea. I promise you, I didn't call them."

Wesson shook her head as well and stared at the agent. "Me neither."

"Well, then I wonder why they're here," he said.

"Me too." Elise crossed her arms and hugged herself. Had the press gotten some news about Sawyer she hadn't been told yet?

God, please.

Chapter Twenty-Eight

Moments later, the reason for the press's presence was very evident. As those inside Elise's watched through the blinds, a black SUV whipped into the driveway, sending news crews scattering in its wake. Two men opened the back door and US Senator Grady Boone got out. Microphones and cameras were instantly in his face. His smile and hand gestures as if to ward them all away were as smooth and natural as the way his suit jacket fit him.

"Friends, friends, I'm merely here to offer comfort to a scared widow who is missing her son, who happens to be the grandson of my dear fellow senator, Lilliana York, whom we buried just yesterday."

Elise groaned. Mary Ellen and Noland had been adamant that Lilliana had despised him. He would use all of their grief for his political gain. It made Elise sick.

"As I have said many times before, we are a country who needs to get more serious about crime and guns. Senator York was gunned down in her own home. Now, her grandson was kidnapped from his own yard. Where is the justice?"

Maybe he'd just make a statement and then leave. It was the best Elise could hope for.

The man continued, as if he were entitled to hold court on Elise's driveway. "I'm here to tell you, I won't stand for this kind of rampant crime right here in my hometown. Right under the FBI's noses."

Elise glanced at Agent Rodriguez. His jaw clenched so tight that she could see his cheek muscles flexing. She let the little twinge of guilt trickle over her. She'd said the same thing herself. Then again, she was a mother with a missing son and not a United States senator.

"Congress is back in session next week. When I return to DC, I can assure you all that I'll be working very diligently to get some bills backed that will bring security back to our families and a stop to this type of crime happening across our nation: murders, kidnappings, mass shootings. . .it all must end and it must end now." Senator Boone pounded his fist into his other palm.

A couple of the crew members actually clapped, which made the senator smile and nod. "I promise to bring bills to the floor that support stronger gun control. I'll back bills that mean less leniency for violent crimes."

Others joined in the clapping.

Senator Boone's voice rose. "It's time we Americans take back our country. We should be moving forward in peace to resolve the differences on a worldwide level, not putting up with crimes against our fellow Americans, from Americans."

More clapping.

Agent Rodriguez let out a heavy sigh as he stepped away from the windows. While Elise wasn't exactly enthralled with the way the FBI had handled the investigation, it wasn't Agent Rodriguez's fault. She certainly didn't approve of that stupid politician out there using Sawyer and Lilliana to further his own political agenda.

No, it was time to shut him down.

Elise headed for the front door.

"Mrs. Carmichael, I advise you not to go out there. It could be a feeding frenzy with the senator's attitude and words." Agent Rodriguez nodded toward the door.

"But it's my house, my front yard, and it's my son who is missing. I'm not going to let that politician distract from what this is all really about." Elise grabbed the doorknob and swung the door open.

Camera flashes nearly blinded her. Wesson appeared at her side;

without saying a word, the young woman provided much-needed support.

Elise straightened her shoulders and moved to stand beside Senator Boone.

"Dear Mrs. Carmichael," Senator Boone started, putting his arm around her shoulders.

She shrugged off his touch, forcing a smile as she looked at the cameras. "My family and I certainly appreciate everyone's willingness to help find Sawyer and bring him home." She forced a polite smile. "As you can all imagine, we're all exhausted and emotionally spent. Please, keep your eyes open for any sign of my son. Sawyer is the gentlest soul you'll ever meet. If you see him, or have seen him, please contact law enforcement."

"Yes, yes. Everyone, please keep your eyes peeled for any sign of this young boy, who is still grieving his grandmother, my dear Senator York. We all will miss her and the valiant efforts she made while in office."

Elise clenched her teeth to refrain from snapping. She inhaled, then exhaled slowly before she turned to the cameras once again. "Thank you all for coming here again. Now, if you'll excuse me, I must get back to going through the tips that people have already called in."

Wesson stood and held up Sawyer's picture. Elise hadn't even seen her grab it. "Again, this is Mrs. Carmichael's son, Sawyer. Please keep putting his picture on all of your stations, media outlets—any way to get his picture out to the public. I'm so grateful to be a part of the press who are diligent in helping bring Sawyer home."

Elise linked arms with Wesson and they turned back to the house. Agent Rodriguez opened the door. Senator Boone turned and tried to join them. Elise slowed. "I'm sorry, Senator Boone, did you need something?"

"I'm here to help." His smile reminded her of the Cheshire cat's, although she'd always liked the cat.

Agent Rodriguez stepped outside. "That's wonderful, Senator.

We've just set up some additional phones so some of our volunteers can take tipsters information as they call in.

For a split second, Elise thought the senator would refuse. He glanced over his shoulder at the news crews, sighed, then held out his hand to the agent. "Of course. Anything I can do to help. I do have contacts all over the state that I'm happy to call in favors to get information."

"I think we're good on that end." Agent Rodriguez motioned him inside. "But we'll get you set up at the call table. We really appreciate it."

Elise caught the agent's grin at her before he led the senator into the kitchen.

Wesson shut the door and glanced out the blinds. "Good, they're leaving." She rubbed her hands together. "Ready to head to Conway as soon as they're all gone?"

"My car's in the garage. I'm pretty sure all the agents' vehicles have me blocked in."

Wesson smiled. "Ahh, but mine isn't. Mine's parked on the street across from your house. We can get in and away before anyone notices we're gone." She looked back out through the blinds. "Only two more vans to go, then we're home free."

Elise nodded. "Let me grab my purse." She went into her bedroom and jerked her purse off the chaise at the foot of the bed. She was torn—stay here in case Sawyer was found, or go with Wesson and get some answers. She'd been here twenty-four hours waiting for word from Sawyer. She had her cell phone. Should she tell Noland and Mary Ellen where they were going? It wasn't like either of them knew anything more about Alice Poe than they did. No, they needed the rest. She'd update them when they got back.

Moments later, they sprinted across the street and jumped into Wesson's car, a little Mitsubishi Eclipse. It was a silver baby, with pink racing stripes over the hood, roof, and trunk—very noticeable and identifiable, just like its owner. Wesson plugged the address from her source into her phone's GPS program, then they were on their way.

Wesson opened the sun roof, letting in the April air. Elise closed her eyes and leaned back in the seat. Even though she'd had a good nap hours ago, it felt so good to close her eyes and let the sun warm her face.

A gentle shake of her shoulder brought her eyes open.

"Hey, we're here." Wesson smiled at her.

Elise bolted upright, then unfastened the seatbelt and wiped the sleep from her eyes. "I slept the whole way?"

Wesson chuckled. "Yep, and you snore, by the way."

"I can't believe I slept again." Elise flipped down the visor and checked herself in the mirror.

"Well, you're stressed and your body needs to recharge."

"I guess." She flipped the visor back up and looked at where they were. Wesson had parked on the street in front of a little A-frame house that looked like it'd seen much better days. A shutter had disappeared from the front window and the paint peeled. An older black Mazda sat under a tired carport whose roof leaned heavily on the support of a makeshift post. "Is this it?"

Wesson nodded. "This is the address and that's the car registered to her."

"I have no idea what to say to her." Elise's heart pounded until she could hear it echoing in her head.

"Why don't we see if she's here first? Then we can show her what Senator York sent and explain what happened to her. Maybe that will encourage Alice to talk to us." Wesson checked her own reflection in the rearview mirror. She pressed her lips together, then opened her car door.

Elise stepped out of the car, her mind racing with scenarios and questions. She didn't have too much time to think because they'd barely pressed the doorbell when the front door opened.

A young woman cracked open the door. As Elise stared at her, she knew two things immediately. One, this was the woman in the photograph, and two, she was scared.

"What do you want?" Her voice quavered, confirming the fear.

Elise smiled. "Hi. I'm Elise Carmichael and—"

"I know who you are. What do you want?" She didn't make an effort to smile, or if she did, she failed miserably.

"I'd just like to talk to you. My mother-in-law, Lilliana York, sent me your picture and information just before she died. I wanted to talk with you about that."

Alice cut her eyes to Wesson. "Who are you?"

"My name is Wesson Kelly, I'm a reporter with—"

"You're a reporter?" Alice's eyes widened. "I don't want to talk to any reporter. You all should leave." She started to close the door, but like Wesson had once done to Elise, she shoved her toe in to block the closing.

"Just wait a minute. If you don't want to talk with me present, that's fine. I'll wait in the car. But you need to talk to Elise here."

Elise leaned a bit closer. "You don't have to worry about Wesson, either. She doesn't report anything unless you give the okay. I know this because she's been open and honest with me. You can trust her."

Alice looked from Elise to Wesson, then back to Elise. "I can't trust anyone," she barely whispered.

"You can trust us." Elise held her breath as Alice seemed to consider them both. Finally, she eased open the door. "Come on inside before somebody sees you on my step and recognizes you and I get asked questions I have no intention of answering."

Elise and Wesson stepped into a very close, very cramped living room. A sofa, rocking chair, and entertainment center with a twenty or so inch television filled the room. Despite its crowdedness, Alice had tried to make it homey with framed pictures of her son and bows on the curtains covering the dirty windows.

Alice led them into a kitchen the size of a butler's pantry. The table and three chairs, along with a high chair, crammed the galley-style kitchen. "I have coffee if you're interested. If not, I have Kool-Aid and water. That's it."

"Water would be nice. Thank you." Elise took a seat at the table.

"Nothing for me, but thank you." Wesson sat opposite Elise, so Alice would have to sit between them.

Alice pulled out a glass, dropped in a couple pieces of ice from the tiny over-the-refrigerator freezer, and then filled it with tap water. She set it in front of Elise, then leaned against the counter, sipping coffee from a logoed mug. "So, what do you want to know? Understand that I don't have to tell you anything."

"Oh, I know. I thank you for just taking the time to talk to me, period." Elise pulled out the two pages from her purse. "I think you knew my mother-in-law, Senator Lilliana York?"

Alice set her cup on the counter. "I admired Lilliana. She was the type of person trying to make a difference that I hoped to one day be. I'm assuming since you're here you know I knew her. That we met when I was clerking at the statehouse. She was very kind and never underappreciated the female clerks and interns like so many of the senators do."

Wesson nodded. "That's how it used to be in the news business. Everyone thought a female could only deliver the news that someone else fed them." She shrugged. "Some still think and act the same way, but we're making progress."

"I'm sure you heard Lilliana was murdered." Elise spoke softly.

"I did. I know nothing about that, I promise." Alice stiffened.

Elise shook her head. "Of course not. I just wanted to tell you what wasn't reported on the news. Just before she died, as her last act, she sent two files to my son's tablet." Elise held up the papers to her. "These were what she sent."

Alice's hand trembled as she took the sheets of paper.

"She sent them to my son's tablet, knowing that he never checked the email but that I did and cleaned it out. I can only assume she wanted me to find these. Find you." Elise studied Alice's face as she looked at the papers.

Alice sniffed and handed the papers back to Elise. "Well, you did. You found me."

Elise waited a moment for Alice to continue, but she didn't. She cleared her throat. "I'm assuming that paternity test is for your son?"

"Yes."

Again a pause. Once again, no elaboration.

This was worse than getting a root canal. Elise was tired of hemming and hawing. "Look, I'm just going to lay it all out for you because I'm a desperate mother. I read lips and I saw a conversation from a man making a threat against Lilliana. The next day, she was dead. I reported what I saw to the FBI. That day, I got a threat. I identified the man, who was murdered the day I identified him. I worked with a sketch artist to ID the other man. He died. Now, the day we buried Lilliana, my son was kidnapped. From my own backyard, with the FBI at my house. So I'm desperate."

"I saw you on the news. I'm very sorry about your son, but I don't know what you want me to do. I'm not involved in that." Alice took another drink of her coffee. "And I'm not going to get involved."

Elise let out a slow breath. "But you were involved with something that Lilliana felt was important enough that she sent me those files—possibly her last act on earth—so I would find you." She paused. "I'm asking you what that connection is, because whatever it is, it got Lilliana murdered and my son kidnapped."

"I'll tell you, but understand that I have no intention of making a statement or coming forward. My life is all about my son right now."

Elise understood, totally. "I'm trying to save my son, which is why I'm even here in the first place."

Alice set her cup down again and gripped the side of the counter. "The senator had been following up on some reports about a politician and his sexual abuse and assault of young women in the state building. He used his power to make us feel like we had no choice but to do as he wished, or he would kill our careers. As he'd destroyed a couple of women before, we all believed he would do what he threatened."

She let out a slow breath. "Senator York had talked to many of us. Most admitted what had happened, but wouldn't stand up to him. He scared many of us because some of us didn't have a relationship with him willingly. Some of us, well, he took what he wanted, regardless of our protests and trying to shove him off of us."

Elise and Wesson looked at each other, then back to the younger woman who continued. "Some girls he paid off just to leave. Another got pregnant and he paid her to have an abortion and disappear with a nice little chunk of change to start over."

And just like that, Elise knew where she was going. "But not you." It wasn't so much a question as it was a statement of fact.

Elise hadn't guessed wrong. Alice shook her head. "I couldn't. About three months after he assaulted me, I found out I was pregnant. He made the appointment for me and everything, but I just couldn't do it. I was raised in the church and I wholeheartedly believe abortion is wrong. I left the clinic and didn't even tell him." She let out another long breath. "But then, three days later, he called me. Furious. Told me he'd made me another appointment and if I didn't go through with it that time, he'd make sure it was taken care of. I was terrified."

"So you went to Lilliana?" Elise could barely whisper the question.

Alice shook her head. "Not at first. I left town and went to stay with a friend of mine in Shreveport, Louisiana. I had my son there, and planned to stay there—did for over a year. Me and my son built a life there, until the day I saw one of his security detail following me. I knew he had found me. I was scared and didn't know what else to do."

Elise could only imagine the fear this poor woman felt.

"I moved here and contacted Senator York. She was so very kind to me. She helped me get the paternity test by having one of her aides get his DNA sample off of his coffee cup. Once she had proof of his paternity, she told me I had to come forward. It would be the only way he would be stopped. I knew she was right."

Elise felt a little sick to her stomach.

But Alice was on a roll, like she had kept the truth bottled up for so long that once she'd started talking, it all spilled out. "She was the one who contacted him and told him she had the DNA proof that he'd fathered my baby and my statement that he'd assaulted me. She told him she was going to expose him for the rat he was. He tried to deny it—even said I'd seduced him and then tried to blackmail him by threatening to go to his wife. Senator York didn't buy it, and told him just that. She gave him the option to get out of politics, or she'd go public with the proof." Alice sniffed. "Two days later, she was dead."

Elise's throat tightened until she felt like air couldn't pass through.

"Who was he?" Wesson asked.

"You don't know?" Alice blinked, her eyes filled with disbelief. "I figured you knew and wanted me to come forward against him, which I won't do."

"No, we don't know who he is. I don't think Lilliana had time to type a message when she sent the files to me."

Alice shivered.

"So who is he?" Wesson whispered.

"Grady. Senator Grady Boone."

CHAPTER TWENTY-NINE

The car ride from Conway to Little Rock seemed to fly by. Or maybe Elise just felt that way because the conversation with Wesson never lagged, even if they found themselves repeating one another.

"It all makes sense now. Mary Ellen said Lilliana had detested Senator Boone. No wonder she wanted to destroy him." Elise shook her head.

Wesson pressed her foot harder down on the accelerator as they raced down I-40. "Especially since he's made it known he intends to make a bid for himself in the next primary."

A bitter taste crept up the back of Elise's throat. "He had Lilliana killed, then used her murder as a political ploy. That's brazen."

"He believes he'll get away with it."

Elise's cell phone vibrated. She glanced at the text message that had just come in from Mary Ellen: ARE Y'ALL OKAY?

Elise quickly texted back: WE'RE FINE. FILL YOU IN WHEN WE GET BACK. HEADED THAT WAY NOW. ETA LESS THAN 30 MINS. She turned to Wesson. "Sorry, text from Mary Ellen. I told her we'd fill her and Noland in when we got there. Don't want to take a chance on putting anything about Alice in a text message. Just in case my texts are being monitored."

"Could be." Wesson nodded.

"Back to Grady Boone. He's probably connected more to Sam Edwards because I bet if we check, Sam Edwards was on the senator's Capitol Police duty."

Wesson nodded. "Yep, and Sam probably brought in Marcus Tate because he was local, and they were already friends."

"Then, following that connection," Elise continued, "Marcus Tate probably brought in Fred Otto to make the deliveries because of their connection."

"Makes sense." Wesson sped a little more.

"Now Marcus Tate and Sam Edwards are both dead. It was probably Senator Boone's plan all along to take out Marcus Tate because he was the person who actually murdered Lilliana. I don't think he planned to lose Sam Edwards because he trusted him, but he probably accepted that he was expendable if need be."

"Right. When the FBI showed up and Sam Edwards was killed, then Senator Boone probably thought he was home free. That explains how he could show his face at your mother-in-law's funeral and at your house."

Elise held up a finger. "But wait, there's still Fred Otto that's a loose end. If he doesn't have Sawyer, he's a liability to the senator. He can connect Marcus Tate and Sam Edwards to the crimes, and now that they're gone, he has to be getting orders from Senator Boone directly."

Wesson tilted her head. "But that isn't to say that he knows who Senator Boone is. Maybe he doesn't know his name or anything, just a phone number—maybe the senator uses an alias with him." She paused a moment. "Or Grady Boone is so arrogant that he can't fathom any peon like Fred Otto, who works as a stocker at a box store, would dare give his name."

Elise shook her head. "The senator probably does think that, but I don't think he'd take the chance with someone like Fred Otto. Too much of a risk. He's only used Fred as a delivery boy, probably instructed to deliver the box given without even looking inside." And now that she knew who was calling the shots, Elise wasn't so sure that Fred Otto did have Sawyer.

If that were right, *who had Sawyer?*

"We've figured the connection between Fred Otto and the rest was Marcus Tate, but Marcus was the first person taken out of the equation." Elise's head started to pound.

"Probably by Sam Edwards."

"Okay, but now that Sam is out too, do you think the senator is giving orders directly to Fred Otto? I'm scared that Fred Otto's only connection to the plot was through Marcus Tate and then Sam Edwards. Now that both are gone, is he getting directions straight from Grady Boone?" Elise's mind spun in a multitude of different directions. "Even if he doesn't know who the senator is, he must know he was the man in charge."

"And the man with the money," Wesson added.

"Fred Otto seems to have disappeared. He's either got Sawyer and is hiding on instructions from the senator, or Grady Boone had Fred bring Sawyer to him, is hiding him somewhere, and has gotten rid of Fred Otto." Just thinking about her son with Grady Boone made Elise want to be sick.

"I don't think Senator Boone has Sawyer, Elise. For one, it'd be too hard to hide. Too many people are always around the senator. He wouldn't take a chance on Sawyer being found anywhere near him."

That made sense. Elise's lungs loosened their hold on her breathing capacity. "And Senator Boone wouldn't take out someone himself. He won't get his hands dirty. He probably doesn't want to add another person into his plans because he keeps losing them."

"So I'm still going with Fred Otto having Sawyer." Wesson whipped the car off the interstate. "That's why no one can find Fred— the senator has put him and Sawyer somewhere in hiding."

Elise rewound Alice's statement. "Alice said she was fine in Louisiana until she saw one of Senator Boone's security detail men."

"I'm betting that was Sam Edwards. He probably was on the senator's detail either here or in DC."

"You know that most senators don't have security detail when they aren't in DC, right? I mean, if they're in the statehouse here, the state capitol police are there, but when they're at home, they usually don't have a detail."

Wesson shrugged as she steered her little Eclipse toward where Elise lived. "Maybe he hired him personally. That would make sense."

Elise snapped her fingers. "Wait a minute. Senator Boone's the Democratic whip. He has a detail all the time."

"He's the party enforcer? I can see that."

"Yeah. It's just his speed. And since he is, I'm sure he believes he's a shoe-in for his party's nomination as presidential candidate." Elise shivered at the thought of a man like that in the White House. Not that all the past presidents have been fine, upstanding men, but for a man to be such a cad before he goes into office and to be willing to murder anyone in his way. . .well, Elise didn't want anyone like that in the Oval Office.

"And that would make him all the more determined to keep his secret."

Elise nodded. "And right now, he's in my house, pretending to be concerned about bringing my son home when he's the one who had him kidnapped." She balled her hands into fists in her lap, grateful she wasn't the one driving. "He stood up and bemoaned Lilliana's murder, crying that justice needed to be served, when all the time, he was the one responsible. It makes me furious."

"Oh, me too." Wesson turned down Elise's street. "But we need to be smart about confronting him. Alice has already said she won't admit he assaulted her."

"I don't want to take a chance on putting Sawyer in jeopardy by confronting him. Not until I know my son is safe and where he is. I don't trust Grady Boone not to panic and make a stupid decision that I'll regret forever."

Wesson pulled the car along the street, across from Elise's house. The black SUV the senator had arrived in was still parked in Elise's driveway. "So how do you want to play it?"

"Until we can find Sawyer, I don't want to confront him at all."

"Okay, then that's what we'll do. I'll keep my sources checking all of his properties, or places he goes with others like camps and leases and hunting lodges." Wesson turned off the engine and opened her door and stepped out. Over the roof, she nodded to Elise. "I'll start trying to hunt down the money trail. I know the FBI looked into Marcus Tate's accounts and couldn't find anything, but I'd be willing to bet that he got something before he murdered Senator York and the balance would be wired. I'll look into Senator Boone's accounts as best I can."

Elise slammed the door and hitched her purse strap over her shoulder. "Bob Parker should be here by now. This ought to be interesting."

"That's something else. How is he connected? I mean, we know he got the information from Agent Wright, but who did he give it to?" Wesson led the way across the street.

"Do you think he went to Senator Boone himself?" Elise couldn't imagine someone as arrogant as Grady Boone talking or explaining anything to an entry level civil servant. "Or do you think he had someone as a point person?" This circle seemed to keep getting wider and bigger. The more that were involved, the messier it became. That meant it was riskier for Sawyer.

"I don't know. Maybe if Parker is here, we can watch and see how he interacts with Senator Boone. If they don't give off a vibe, I'd bet there was another point person."

Elise took in a cleansing breath, squared her shoulders, then opened her front door. Noland and Mary Ellen rushed forward, but the FBI agent spoke first.

"Where have you been?" Agent Rodriguez looked like a teenager's dad waiting up when she's late for curfew.

But Elise wasn't a teenager, and this was her house. "Not that it's any of your business, but I just needed to get out for a little while."

"To Conway?"

She narrowed her eyes. How did he know where she'd been? "Do you have a tracker on me?" She was about to lose her cool in a hundred different ways.

"No." His blush gave him away.

"Do you have a tracker on me or my car?" Wesson crossed her arms.

"No, we don't." He wouldn't make contact.

Elise wasn't playing games. Not after what she'd learned today. She took two steps forward, deliberately invading his personal space. "Then I'll ask one more time. . .how did you know where we went?"

"We just want to make sure you're okay, Mrs. Carmichael. That if we need to get in touch with you about your son, we know where you are."

She shook her head. "You had me followed."

His blush deepened. "Again, it's for your safety."

"Hmm-mmm." She wasn't buying it, but realized having her followed probably wasn't his decision to make. "Well, I'm back, safe and sound. Is there anything new?"

Agent Rodriguez glanced over his shoulder, then back to her. "Nothing as of yet. We're still looking for Fred Otto and have his home and work staked out."

Good. She'd made the right call to follow a lead instead of just sitting around doing nothing but worrying. She knew she needed to fill Mary Ellen and Noland in on what Alice had told her and Wesson. "Is there any fresh coffee? I could sure use a cup." She made sure her voice carried.

"Of course." Noland touched her arm. "Why don't you all go sit on the back porch and I'll bring coffee out?"

Mary Ellen grabbed her purse. "I'll go put this away then meet you outside."

Elise and Wesson headed out the back door, striding right past Agent Rodriguez without further conversation.

"That was weird," Wesson commented as soon as they were outside on the porch.

"That means Noland and Mary Ellen have something to tell us."

"Oh. Okay."

They took their seats, then Mary Ellen and Noland came outside, Noland carrying a tray with her old French press and four cups. Mary Ellen shut the door behind them, then dropped to the chair beside Elise. "Okay, here's the scoop. Bob Parker is here. Agent Rodriguez has him gathering a ton of supposed DNA samples. From Sawyer's room, yours, the guest room, just about everywhere. I hope you don't mind that I gave permission, but you were gone."

"Of course it's fine. Anything that might help bring Sawyer home is certainly fine." Elise nodded as she spoke.

"I figured you wouldn't mind. But then I realized he didn't really need any samples. I mean, think about it—Sawyer was taken from the backyard. Not from inside the house." Mary Ellen's eyes grew rounder as she spoke.

Noland took the last vacant chair and picked up the story. "So we surmised that Agent Rodriguez was only having Bob Parker do busy work. We just needed to find out why."

"And we did." Mary Ellen dumped cream and sugar absentmindedly into her coffee. "Noland overheard Agent Rodriguez talking on the phone to his partner. He told her that he needed her here to do some computer work. She's supposedly on her way now."

Elise took a sip of her black coffee. "So he really is looking into their relationship." At least he wasn't just glossing things over.

"What about Senator Boone? We saw his car was still here. Is he still manning the calls?" Wesson asked.

Mary Ellen snorted. "Please. He slipped out the back door soon after you two snuck off. He wanted to appear to be here, working tirelessly, so he had one of his aides come pick him up, leaving his SUV here."

Elise set down her coffee cup very slowly. "Was there any talk in the house about us being in Conway, specifically?"

Noland nodded. "In the kitchen. Agent Rodriguez got radio

reports from the agent following you. That agent gave turn by turn directions."

That bad taste was back in Elise's mouth. "Think carefully, please, because this is important. Did Senator Boone leave before or after the report came in about where Wesson and I were?"

Mary Ellen and Noland locked stares, then both said. "After. Why?" It was almost as if their response was rehearsed it was so much in unison.

Elise looked at Wesson before she began telling Mary Ellen and Noland all about their visit with Alice.

"I've got someone on their way to Alice's now," Wesson interrupted. "She'll move them and stay with them. I trust her to make sure Alice and her son are safe."

"Thank you. I never meant to put her in harm's way by visiting." Elise finished telling her sister-in-law and Noland everything. When she'd finished, it was quiet on the porch. Barely a breeze filled the silence of the afternoon.

Finally, Noland quietly spoke. "So that's why Lilliana was murdered? Because she wanted to help this young woman and bring down Grady Boone?"

"I think so, yes." Elise put her hand over Noland's. "I'm so sorry."

"No, this is what Lilliana would choose to do. She was adamant about standing up for those who couldn't stand up on their own. It was her life's work, so it is fitting this is the reason for her death." But he blinked several times and even Elise felt the tears burning her own eyes.

Mary Ellen took his other hand. "This sounds just like Mom, a champion for the defeated and downtrodden."

"Yes, Lilliana was a defender. She's a hero to many, and now, in death, a hero forever."

"But what do we do with the information? If we can't expose Alice and her son, and we can't confront Grady Boone, what do we do?" Mary Ellen asked.

"I haven't figured that out yet. Wesson has people checking out the places Senator Boone would feel secure having Sawyer kept at, but nothing in his name to lead back to him."

"The hunting and fishing places, right?" Mary Ellen asked.

"Yes. And anything else we might be able to find out. Especially if there's a link to Fred Otto as well."

Noland jumped to his feet. "I'll call in favors from some of my old sources. See if there are any financial connections on properties that the senator is a silent owner on." He rushed inside.

Mary Ellen sat straight, stone-faced.

"What are you thinking, Mary Ellen?" Elise asked.

"I want Sawyer found and brought home, safe and sound."

"Me too." Elise waited for the *but*.

She only had a moment to wait. "But once he is, I'm going to take up Mom's torch and expose Grady Boone. Not only for the kidnapper and murderer that he is, but also for what he's done to many young women. I will see him in ruins."

Elise took in the seriousness of her sister-in-law's face. "Then I will help you. With everything I can, I will stand by your side."

"Me too," Wesson chimed in. "Not because I care about you two, although I really do, and not because I want a byline, although I'd be lying if I said I didn't want one, but because Grady Boone is the scum of the earth and should be destroyed."

There it was—a serious pact of three women. Elise smiled. They were going to get Sawyer back and finish Grady Boone's reign of abuse.

CHAPTER THIRTY

The doorbell rang and the lights flashed.

Everyone tensed as Agent Rodriguez made it to the front door of Elise's before she did. He glanced through the peephole before unlocking and opening the door. Agent Wright crossed the threshold, her eyes wary.

Elise gritted her teeth and retreated back to the couch in the living room. It was bad enough that agents were letting people in and out of her house all the time, but add to that the fact that it was a woman Elise detested. . .well, it was almost too much. Yet she knew that this was a test of sorts to see the interaction, if any, between Agent Wright and Bob Parker.

She'd made sure to sit at an angle that she could see the chair where Agent Rodriguez had set up a little logging station for Bob Parker. This way, she wouldn't miss seeing their reaction to one another.

And what a reaction it was!

As soon as Agent Wright turned the corner into the kitchen, Bob Parker lifted his gaze, then froze a split second before he smiled at her. Her face went as red as the Hawaiian Punch Noland had poured them and she all but tittered. Agent Rodriguez lowered his head, but not before he made eye contact with Elise. He knew she'd been right.

Elise turned back to Wesson. "Did you ever find a connection for Bob Parker to Marcus Tate, Sam Edwards, or anyone?"

Wesson hopped on her phone, just as Elise's vibrated. She glanced at the caller ID before answering. "Hello, Arabella."

"I saw you on the news. I'm so sorry, Elise. Is there any update on your son?"

"Nothing concrete. A lot of tips are coming in, so I guess that's good."

"Any idea why he was kidnapped?"

Elise watched as Agent Rodriguez led Agent Wright out the kitchen door onto the porch. "A box was left in the backyard where Sawyer had been playing. It was full of pictures of me working with the FBI and a note that said I was warned."

"Oh Elise, I'm so sorry. Is there anything I can do for you?"

"I don't think so." If only there was something any of them could do.

"I'll be praying. If you need anything, you call me. Okay?"

Elise nodded, even though Arabella couldn't see her. "I will. Thank you." She disconnected the call and stood. "I think I need to load the dishwasher." There was a window right over the kitchen sink that conveniently looked out into the backyard and porch.

Mary Ellen grinned and stood as well. "I'll help."

They went to the kitchen and the sink of dirty cups. Elise turned on the water and rinsed a mug out before passing it to Mary Ellen who placed it in the top shelf of the dishwasher. They moved slowly as they stared out the window and watched the two partners.

The pair were clearly at odds. Agent Rodriguez leaned against the porch side, his hands resting on the railing on either side of him. Agent Wright had her hip resting on the back of one of the chairs, her arms crossed over her chest, clearly in defensiveness. The matching expressions on both of their faces reflected accusations and distrust, emotions not welcome in law enforcement partners.

Suddenly, Agent Rodriguez pushed off the railing and pointed his finger at Agent Wright. She responded by jabbing her finger into his chest.

"Should we intervene?" Mary Ellen whispered.

Elise just shook her head, not able to stop watching the drama unfolding in her own backyard. The two agents seemed to have reached an impasse as they both stood facing one another, hands on hips, without speaking. Finally, Agent Rodriguez pointed toward the road. Agent Wright paused, gave him a final look, shook her head even as she dropped it, then she descended the porch stairs and headed to the street.

"Wow. Did he just make her leave?" Mary Ellen asked softly.

"I think so." Elise handed her the final cup. "I'll be back." She dried her hands on the dish towel she carried to the back door. She walked outside where Agent Rodriguez stared off into the distance.

"Are you okay?" Elise eased alongside him. While she didn't like Agent Wright and knew that the leaks had come through her, she didn't like that Agent Rodriguez had gotten caught up in the deception.

"You were right. She admitted to telling Bob things about the case when he asked her, all to impress him."

Elise twisted the towel. "He asked her about the case?"

Agent Rodriguez nodded. "According to her, yes. She says he sought her out and flirted with her, asking her questions. She knows she shouldn't have told him details, but pointed out that he was with the bureau, so it's not like she put the information out into the public."

"How long ago did you say Bob started working for the FBI?"

He shrugged. "A few months, maybe. Why?"

"Well, if he took the job to be able to get information about the case, then that shows a whole lot of premeditation, wouldn't it?"

"I guess." He leaned against the railing again. "What were you doing in Conway, anyway? I surmised it had to do with the case and be important or you wouldn't have gone."

The truth was going to come out soon enough. "We found the woman in the picture Lilliana sent to Sawyer's tablet."

His eyes widened, then narrowed and he crossed his arms over his chest. "What? Why didn't you tell us? This is critical to the case."

She nodded slowly. "Yes, but we weren't sure who she was and the connection. That's why we needed to go talk to her." She held up her hand. "And before you say anything else, she won't talk to you or anybody else in law enforcement. She's had enough threats and been scared enough. She's a terrified young woman trying to protect herself and her son, and I won't give any information that will jeopardize that safety."

"We'd protect her."

Elise fisted her hands on her hips. "Really? Because working with the FBI led to mine and Sawyer's safety, right? Do you want me to remind you how that's working out?"

"Mrs. Carmichael, this could jeopardize our case, and getting your son back. I know you don't want that."

"Let me give you the overviewing details of what I learned. I'm just not going to give you her information. And yes, I know you had me followed so you have her address, but I believe the man responsible for Lilliana's murder and my son's kidnapping overheard as well. She's already being moved and protected."

"Fair enough." He listened intently as Elise told him about Alice, not using her name even once. She told him about Lilliana defending the young woman, and finally, her threat to Senator Grady Boone just before she was murdered.

Agent Rodriguez's arms fell to his sides. "If this is true. . .Elise, this is huge."

She nodded. "And that's why I can't give you the girl's name. It would put her and her son in too much danger. To protect himself, Grady Boone has already paid off many, many young women. He's had Lilliana murdered, then Marcus Tate. He sent someone, I can only guess it was Sam Edwards, to find this young woman in Louisiana. Luckily, she was aware and alert and ran. Senator Boone's actions then got Sam Edwards killed."

Elise kept twisting the towel. "He's had my son kidnapped. We have no idea where Fred Otto is, so for all we know, he could be dead.

Before we make any accusations, we have to get Sawyer back, because there's no telling how he'd retaliate."

"From my standpoint, we'd need proof of it all, not supposition."

"That's the DNA paperwork. That alone is enough to prove he fathered a child. I'm sure there's more of a paper trail. There has to be a money trail somewhere to show where he paid off these young women and paid for their abortions. That alone would be enough to stop him on his bid for the White House, and probably more."

"I need to update my supervisor, not only on the status of Agent Wright, but also on this information."

Elise nodded and untwisted the hand towel. "I'd strongly suggest you go and tell him in person. We can't take a chance that Senator Boone doesn't have ears everywhere. Like Bob Parker. According to your partner, he instigated the conversations about the case. He might very well be a plant for the senator."

He nodded. "I'll head there momentarily, after I check in on my guys here. I think I should have Bob Parker come with me back to the office, to go over evidence, of course."

She smiled. "Of course." The smile slid off her face. "I'm sorry about your partner."

Agent Rodriguez shrugged. "She knew the rules. I think she was more miffed that she got played, which doesn't bode well for her career in the bureau."

"Either way, I'm sorry." Elise turned and headed back inside.

Wesson stood in the hall just outside the guest bedroom as Elise made her way back to the living room. Wesson's frantic waving pulled her down the hall. "What's going on?" Elise noticed Mary Ellen and Noland in the guest bedroom.

Wesson gently tucked her in the room and shut the door behind her. "I heard back from one of my sources. He's found a possible money trail from Marcus Tate to Senator Boone."

"The FBI missed finding a payment?" Elise couldn't believe they'd be that inept.

Wesson shook her head. "No. It was a stock purchase in Marcus's name made the day before Senator York was murdered. A large stock purchase that's valued at about twenty-five thousand dollars. And while the purchase was made through a company, owned by a company, owned by yet another shell corporation, my sources have found that Senator Boone's wife sits on that board."

Mary Ellen dropped into the rolling chair companion to the desk. "I'm not even sure the FBI looked to see if he had acquired anything recently. I think they were only looking for cash deposits or wires into Marcus Tate's accounts."

Noland sat on the edge of the wingback chair and leaned forward, almost to the edge. "Here's the thing, the senator's wife has no clue she's listed on any business mast."

Elise sat on the end of the bed. "How do we know that?"

Wesson thrust a tablet into her hands and pressed PLAY on an internet video.

"I interviewed her just before Lilliana and I married and I retired. This is part of that video." Noland pointed to it.

Onscreen, the wife of Senator Grady Boone, Marla, stated she devoted all of her free time to volunteering. "I sit on no boards, I own no stock in any private or public business. . . . I volunteer and that's what I do."

Wesson turned the video off and took the tablet. "See?"

"Could she have been lying?" Elise asked Noland.

"Anybody could lie, of course, but I don't think Marla was. She appeared to be genuine. Of course, since then she's had a little mental issue or two, so even if she was lying and was on any business's board, that would have been rectified immediately after her first mental breakdown."

"Mental breakdown?" Elise hadn't heard this before.

Noland patted her knee. "Oh, yes. About seven years ago, she showed up at Baptist Health Hospital, claiming to be in labor."

Elise sat up straighter. "In labor?" While Marla wasn't old, she had to be in her fifties back then, beyond normal childbearing years, and as far as Elise knew, Grady and Marla didn't have any children.

Noland nodded. "Yes, that's what she told the ER nurses. Obviously, she wasn't pregnant—she'd had a hysterectomy several years prior, but she truly believed she was in active labor. They finally admitted her to the psych ward and called the senator. Oh, it was so very sad. She stayed for a couple of weeks, then was released. She had outpatient therapy in her home for a few years, then that ceased. That's just before the senator began making noise about looking forward to the White House."

"But if Mrs. Boone isn't well mentally. . ."

"You've lived here all your life, right?" Noland asked.

Elise nodded.

"But you didn't hear about it, did you? And your mother-in-law was in politics."

He had a point.

"Oh, the senator did a marvelous job of covering it up. Most were told that she'd had a virus that affected her mind, but she made a full recovery."

"A virus?" Mary Ellen shook her head. "I don't remember even Mom saying anything about this."

Noland smiled. "Like I said, the senator did a remarkable job of covering it up. I told Lilliana the truth, of course, but she felt so sorry for Marla that she never said a word. She pitied the woman who had to live with such a man and his philandering ways. She didn't want to bring more harm to the poor woman."

"But if she exposed him, and she was fully prepared to do so, wouldn't that have hurt Mrs. Boone?" Wesson asked.

Noland smiled again. "Everyone assumes that Grady is wealthy and prestigious."

"He does have a lot of money, Noland," Mary Ellen said.

"Yes, yes he does seem to because he has access to a large amount of money. Marla is a trust fund baby. She has millions." Noland sat back in the desk's chair.

"It's *her* money he's using?" Elise didn't know whether to be more shocked over Marla's illness that no one seemed concerned with, or that no one had already exposed Grady Boone for the using jerk he was.

"Lilliana knew it would hurt Marla, but also knew Marla wouldn't tolerate adultery. Especially not when they were unable to have children. You see, Grady had contracted a sexually transmitted disease that he passed unbeknownst to Marla. She thought she contracted it in college and it was just undetected. At any rate, she required a hysterectomy. If the truth came out, mentally unstable or not, she would leave the senator."

"But in a lessened mental state. . ." Elise said.

Noland shook his head. "Marla has two sisters who aren't fans of the senator. From what I know, and trust me, my sources are very accurate, they've begged Marla to leave him. He apparently even made a pass at one of them. She slapped him and told Marla. When Marla confronted him, the senator told her that he'd been teasing and her sister had taken it out of context. The sisters haven't been back here to visit. They live in San Antonio, Texas, and stay far away from the senator. But if Marla were to leave him, even with her issues, I guarantee her sisters would be here and on him faster than he could blink."

"So, we have enough on the senator to take to the FBI." Elise made the statement, but her mind warred.

Do the right thing and expose him and ensure the safety of Alice and her son? Or, hold off to ensure Sawyer's safety? Although there was no guarantee Sawyer was safe, even now.

"What do you want us to do?" Mary Ellen asked softly.

"It's your call, Elise." Noland nodded.

"I don't know." It was like a no-win situation for her. For Alice. For Sawyer.

Wesson shook her head. "He's so arrogant and he thinks he's

gotten away with everything. He makes me sick, but I know we have to find Sawyer first."

Arrogant.

Elise snapped her fingers. "That's it, Wesson. Let's use Grady Boone's arrogance against him. We can force his hand and get Sawyer back, then expose him for the scum that he is. It's a win-win."

CHAPTER THIRTY-ONE

"Okay, fill me in." Wesson had stopped pacing and leaned against the wall of Elise's guest room. "Because I'm not seeing how we get your son back and expose Senator Boone."

Elise nodded. "The senator has been using this family's trials and grief, the ones he brought on us in the first place, to play to the public about what a caring man he is, right?"

Mary Ellen nodded. "His press conferences make me want to hurl."

Elise rolled her eyes. "Yeah, me too. He even goes so far as to come to my house and pretend to be helping field calls, even after he slipped out the back, because he wants his public image to be so shiny and prestigious, right?"

"I'm following you," Wesson said.

"Then how about I give him the best opportunity there is?"

"What's that?" Noland asked.

"Give him the opportunity to be responsible for my son being returned to me unharmed. Imagine how that could play out in the press. Senator Boone helps bring deaf son home to grieving mother. Tell me that wouldn't guarantee him the Democratic Party nomination for president."

"Oh, I'm sure he'd be interested in that, I'm just not sure how you plan to achieve such a goal." Mary Ellen rolled the office chair closer to Elise.

"Well, if he really does have Sawyer put away somewhere, then he can pull him out, right?"

Noland nodded. "I see where you're going. Smart."

"So, if I can play into his hand, let him know that he'll be able to have a press conference about his critical role in having my son returned to me. . ."

"That's dicey for you," Wesson said. "You'll have to do that persuading very carefully. Not tip your hand that you know he's involved, but play one hundred percent to his ego."

Elise smiled. "I think I can handle it."

"Seriously, Elise, it can be tricky," Mary Ellen agreed with Wesson. "You can't just flirt with him because he'd know you were up to something immediately."

"Oh, I'd vomit if I even tried to flirt with that ape." Elise shivered just thinking about that. "But I'm pretty sure I can play to his political ego. I can play the poor pitiful widow whose son is missing and how much I want him back and how the public wants my son to be found."

"I have no doubt you're smart enough. I just worry that he won't take the bait. He's got to be extremely cautious right now," Wesson said.

Elise nodded. "I think he's looking for a way to get rid of Sawyer now that it's so public." It hurt just to think that, much less say it aloud. "His plan has failed so now he needs to know what I know, and he can let Sawyer be found due to something he does. It can work."

"It can, but it can also backfire on you," Mary Ellen said. "Because you know a lot."

"I do, but also, my son is on the line so you can bet I can give an Academy Award performance of not knowing even a fraction of what I do."

Noland shook his head. "It's almost too risky, Elise. For you and for Sawyer. Grady Boone is an experienced liar and manipulator. He's been doing this for a long time, and getting away with it. I'm worried despite your best acting, he'd see through you, putting both you and Sawyer in danger. We should find another way."

"I don't think there is another way. Not one that we can execute quickly." Elise glanced at her watch. "It's been almost thirty hours since Sawyer was kidnapped. I have to do something soon." Everything in her screamed that she had to act and act now.

"I'm with you." Wesson nodded. "If we let much more time pass, then the senator might get restless, especially if he has no backup plan."

Mary Ellen brushed her jeans with her palms. "We've been praying for God's intervention. Perhaps this is His plan." She looked at Noland. "I'm at peace with this. Truly." She looked back at Elise. "Are you? Have you prayed about it and feel peaceful over the decision?"

Elise resisted the urge to squirm. "I don't think God's into answering me much these days, Mary Ellen."

"Oh, that's not true. Maybe you just haven't been willing to have conversations with Him." Mary Ellen smiled so softly. "Even though you're mad and disappointed, you still have to talk to Him, Elise. Trust me, He can take all of your emotions."

"Thank you for praying for us." Elise forced the noncommittal smile. "I'm okay with my decision to move forward."

Wesson pushed off the wall and began pacing again. "So what's your game plan?"

Elise hadn't really thought about specifics. "I'm just tossing ideas out here, so everyone feel free to jump in with thoughts or ideas. Maybe I call him and ask him to come stand with me at a press conference?"

Wesson stopped pacing and wrinkled her nose. "You kinda blew him off with that already. He'd smell that was a setup."

Mary Ellen nodded. "Yeah. He wouldn't buy a quick change like that."

Elise knew they were right. "Any suggestions?"

"How about a work around?" Noland asked.

"What do you mean?" Elise asked.

"Well, what if you had another press conference by yourself.

Pleaded for Sawyer to be returned. Asked that anyone who could help, to please do so. Maybe even offer a reward," Noland suggested.

"He doesn't need the money," Mary Ellen huffed.

Elise thought about what Agent Rodriguez had told her. "Well, he may or may not need the money, but it might be enough that he sees it as an opportunity to do a little glad-handing and getting himself in front of the public as a savior of sorts." Now that really made her stomach turn, but to get her son back, she'd fight through the nausea.

"Hey, it's worth a shot," Wesson added. "Anything you can do that will pull him into having Sawyer *found* will work."

Elise stood. "Then this is what we'll try first. Hey, it can't hurt anything. At least it'll get Sawyer's picture in front of the cameras again."

Noland shook his head. "No offense, Elise, but I don't know if everyone will come again. I mean, you had a conference this morning, then the senator had his. . . . I'm not sure they'll come again without there being something new to report."

"I didn't think of that, but he's right," Wesson said.

"So, let's think of something new to give them." Mary Ellen stood, then sat back at the desk. "There has to be something the public doesn't know yet that is newsworthy that we can tie into Sawyer's kidnapping."

"We can go with a reward. That might play into the senator's public appeal," Wesson said.

Elise did a quick mental rundown of how much money she actually could get her hands on quickly. "I think I could come up with ten thousand, but that's not much."

"Oh, don't worry about the money, sweetheart. I've got you covered." Noland smiled. "I can use the money from Lilliana's life insurance. I'm sure she'd want us to offer it all to get Sawyer back home safe and sound."

Heat filled Elise's face. "I can't ask you to do that."

Noland grinned. "Then it's a good thing you aren't asking and I'm offering." He rubbed his chin. "What do you think? A hundred thousand?"

Elise gasped. "That's way too much."

"We need it to be attention grabbing to get the media involved, and to really entice the senator to go for it." Noland stood. "I'll call my contacts again, you too, Wesson. Let's set this conference at five, so it can run live on the five o'clock news? Hit everyone on their way home from work or having dinner."

"I'm on it," Wesson nodded.

Noland squeezed Elise's shoulder. "Talk to Agent Rodriguez and tell him what you're going to do. Invite him to be a part of the conference and share any information he can."

She nodded. "I will."

"Also," Noland continued. "Call and invite your attorney. She might need to be in on the wording of how the reward will offer." He took out his cell and sat back down, starting to make his calls.

Wesson was already on the phone, pacing as she spoke.

Mary Ellen stood and smiled. "Why don't you call your attorney, then go talk to Agent Rodriguez? You'll have a little time to yourself before the conference. I'd suggest you seek a little quiet time, maybe in your room. Just to center yourself. Pray, maybe."

Elise nodded and pulled out her cell. She called Arabella, explained what was going to happen, and Arabella said she would be right over. While everyone else was on the phone, she went into the kitchen to seek out Agent Rodriguez. She led him onto the back porch for privacy.

"What's up, Mrs. Carmichael?" He sat opposite her in one of the patio table chairs.

She told him the plan. Well, not the whole plan, but that she was offering a reward and about the press conference.

But he wasn't fooled. "You said you believe that Senator Boone is the instigator of your son's kidnapping, so why offer a reward? You know he can never come forward to claim it."

"No, but he might *recover* Sawyer and then publicly denounce the reward to gain public popularity. The deadline for declaration of intent to run as a candidate in the next presidential election is coming up soon. This would almost make him a shoe in for the party's support."

"Perhaps."

Elise didn't want to be talked out of doing this. "Or, he'll have Sawyer released and one of his underlings collect the reward, which will then be processed and eventually end up in his hands anyway. That's not my first concern, which is, and has always been, getting my son back."

"I understand completely." He stared out over the backyard, silent.

"My attorney will be here shortly to write out the conditions of claiming the reward. Will you work with her on that?"

"Of course."

"Thank you." She couldn't help but stare at the soccer net in the back corner. Her throat tightened and she forced herself to look away. "Is there anything new you can add at the conference, or anything you'd like to say?"

"Nothing new, but I'm happy to stand with you and answer questions."

"Thank you." She stood, and for the first time, noticed the wedding band on his left hand. It made her wonder. "Do you have children, Agent Rodriguez?"

He nodded as he stood. "A boy and a girl. Ten and eight, respectively."

"Then you understand how I feel. If it were your son or daughter, your first and foremost goal would be to get them safely home, right?"

"It would be. I do understand, but I also have a job to do that involves not only seeing your son safely returned, but that the criminals—all of them involved, be brought to justice."

"Oh, they'll get justice, I can assure you of that." She turned to go back inside.

Agent Rodriguez stepped in her path. "What do you have planned, Mrs. Carmichael?"

"I told you. The press conference."

"That's it?"

"Well, I told you what I thought would happen."

He rested a hand on his hip. "And that's it?"

"That's all I have planned for today." She held up her hand. "Scout's honor."

Agent Rodriguez relaxed a fraction. "Were you even a girl scout?"

She chuckled as she opened the door. "I'll never tell." Elise headed down the hallway toward her bedroom. Wesson stopped her in the hall. "Noland and I have all our contacts coming, even a few more than this morning. The enticement of such a large reward is news."

"Thank you, both of you. I'm going to freshen up for a few minutes. Will someone let me know when Arabella gets here?"

"Of course. Take your time," Mary Ellen said, smiling.

Elise nodded her thanks, then retreated to her bedroom, shutting the door behind her. She kicked off her shoes and went to her closet. She would at least have to change blouses. It wouldn't do to wear the same shirt to both press conferences. She flipped hangers until she found one of Judson's favorite shirts of hers. It was white with pink orchids all over it, and made from the softest material. He said just seeing her in it made him happy. She'd wear it for the conference and maybe feel closer to Judson somehow.

Oh, how she wished he was here right now. He'd always known the right thing to say and do.

After she freshened up and changed shirts, she sat on the side of the bed—Judson's side, and stared at the framed photo of her, Judson, and Sawyer—the last snapshot of them as a family. Lifting the picture, she traced her finger over the image. Her throat burned, but she didn't find the anger rising up in her chest. She set the picture back on the nightstand, then slowly opened the drawer.

Judson's Bible laid there, as if waiting. It'd been there since the day they moved in. Oh, it'd been taken out, carried to church, read all over the house, but it was always put back in Judson's drawer. He said he liked to read the Word first thing in the morning to set his day off on the right path, and last thing at night so he could be thankful for his many blessings.

Elise carefully lifted the worn Bible. As she set it on her lap, she found a bookmark she'd never noticed before. She flipped open to the pages and lifted the bookmark. It was one of Judson's many prayer cards that he loved so much. He'd read the scripture off the card, then look it up in his Bible and read the whole passage. Often, he'd pray that exact scripture and make a note in the margin of his Bible of date and prayer. Many of his pages were filled with the scripture they'd prayed over Sawyer before he was born, and after.

Elise gasped as she read the scripture card of Psalm 34:18, "The Lord is near to the brokenhearted and saves the crushed in spirit." Her body went tense as she read Judson's handwritten note on the opposite side of the card:

> *Father God, I pray for my wife, Elise, and son, Sawyer. I know there will come a time when they go through heartbreak. I pray You will comfort them and save them as they ache from being crushed in spirit. I believe in Your promise written in Jeremiah 24:7 that says, "I will give them a heart to know that I am the Lord, and they shall be my people and I will be their God, for they shall return to me with their whole heart."*

Her mouth went dry. If she'd been looking for a sign of God's love in her life, there was nothing better than this. In Judson's own handwriting, even before his death, he knew she'd be heartbroken and crushed in spirit, and prayed for her to return to God and be comforted by Him.

Unable to deny the tears burning her eyes, she sank to her knees beside the bed and bent her head. She began to pray with all her heart for forgiveness, acceptance, and comfort, and so much more.

Chapter Thirty-Two

Rap. Rap. Rap.

Elise stood and put Judson's Bible back in the nightstand drawer. Mary Ellen cracked open the door. "Elise? Arabella's here."

"Oh, thanks." She swiped at the tears drying on her face. "Let me wash my face and I'll be right out."

Smiling as if the Holy Spirit had given her a heads-up as to what had just happened in the room, Mary Ellen nodded. "No rush. She's sitting down with Noland and Agent Rodriguez to go over the terms and get it all written down."

"Thanks."

Mary Ellen shut the door. Elise let out a heavy breath, but she felt lighter than she had since before Lilliana had been murdered. She splashed cold water on her face, dried it, then ran a brush through her hair. It looked limp and lifeless, but she couldn't do anything about that right now. She flipped her head over and pulled her hair up into a messy bun on the top of her head. Hey, it was the fashion these days and it hid a multitude of hair-care sins.

No one was in the guest bedroom as she made her way down the hall. No wonder, they were all in the living room.

Arabella jumped up and hugged her as soon as she entered. "I'm so sorry for what you're going through. I'm so happy I'm able to help out in some small way."

Elise gave her a genuine smile. Arabella was going to turn out to be a friend instead of just an attorney. "Thank you so much. . .

for coming, for doing this."

"Not a problem."

"We've about finished up the details." Agent Rodriguez stood, handing her a piece of paper. "These are the specifics. We think it's probably best for me to read this part after you make your plea because it has to do with the details of claiming the reward."

"Whatever y'all think is best is fine with me. I just want someone to see or hear this and help bring my son home."

Wesson handed her Sawyer's picture again. "Here, hold this up while you're talking. Keep holding it so everyone gets a good long look at Sawyer. I took the liberty of sending this picture to the news stations for them to keep putting his photo up there. All of the stations have posted it on their social media accounts too."

Noland nodded as he stood. "There should be a lot of viewers for the five o'clock newscasts. I've seen the stations giving teasers about your live broadcast."

Mary Ellen appeared out of nowhere with a bottle of water she pressed into Elise's hand. "You've got this. Just remember to talk about how much you want and need your son returned. Beg, plead, and remind everyone that he's deaf and mute. Then mention the one hundred thousand dollar reward for Sawyer's safe return and then introduce Agent Rodriguez to go over the details of said reward."

Elise let out a little breath. "Okay. I got it."

Wesson handed her an index card. On it were bullet points of what Mary Ellen had just told her. "In case you get nervous or anything."

Elise couldn't help but grin as she read:

BREATHE. #BringSawyerHome. Please bring him safely home. Deaf. Mute. Dad and Grandmother dead. All you have left. One hundred thousand dollar reward. Agent Rodriguez.

"I think I can do this. Thanks, everyone, for all your support and help. I really do appreciate it very much."

"Honey, I think it's time." Mary Ellen moved to the front door.

Elise took another long drink of water, then followed her sister-in law-outside. Wesson, Noland, Arabella, and Agent Rodriguez followed her, then formed a semicircle behind her as she faced the group of reporters and camera crew. Several print reporters stood with recorders in the air at the ready.

She smiled as she approached them. "Thank you all so much for coming again. It's been a very long day, and I greatly appreciate you coming back and helping me get the word out about the reward affiliated with my son, Sawyer's return." She held up his picture. "Sawyer is seven years old, is mute and deaf. Right now, he has a cast on his right wrist following an injury on the playground, which hinders his ability to communicate with others to almost nonexistent. You might remember that his father died while serving in the Marines, and his grandmother, US Senator Lilliana York was just murdered. We had just come from her funeral and he was playing in the backyard when he was kidnapped."

Some of the reporters jostled for better angles.

"It has been about thirty-six hours since he was kidnapped from our own backyard. My family and I are offering a one hundred thousand dollar reward for his safe return." She held up her hands as the questions started. "Agent Rodriguez will go over the terms of that reward shortly, but I beg of you, anyone, if you can help in any way to bring my son home, please. It might be something you've seen, or someone you know, or even just something you think you know—it may be the thing that helps bring Sawyer home."

She let the tears out, even though she'd usually hold them in. "Even if you don't know anything for sure, but you were told something by someone who heard it from a friend. . .it all matters. Please, anything that anyone can do. . .if you have influential friends who can look, call them. Whatever it takes, I just want my son home." She sobbed a little, then sniffed. "He's just a sweet little boy who can't hear and can't speak."

"Have you received a ransom note or call?" a reporter called out.

While Elise hadn't planned to take questions, maybe it would help. She glanced at Agent Rodriguez who gave her a shrug. She'd take that as permission to give her details. "No letter, no call. No contact at all."

"Does the FBI think this has to do with Senator York's murder?" asked another reporter.

Elise glanced at Agent Rodriguez again. "I can't say what the FBI thinks, but me, personally, I do think there is a connection."

"Has your son always been deaf and mute?" someone asked.

Elise nodded. "Sawyer was born deaf and mute. We don't know the cause, might never know, but he never lets it slow him down. He signs flawlessly, when his wrist isn't in a cast, of course, and he—"

"He's a sweet and special boy," Wesson interjected to the reporter, which confused Elise for a moment since Wesson had never actually met Sawyer. Under her breath, she whispered to Elise, "That he can read lips isn't something you want the kidnappers to know at this juncture."

She hadn't even thought about that, but it was a great point!

"Mrs. Carmichael, we saw Senator Boone give a press conference of sorts here earlier today. Has he continued to be a sign of support?"

Oh, this was priceless. She needed to make sure she said the right thing. Elise paused to take a sip of water before she answered. "I appreciate any and all help in bringing my son home. Senator Boone has many contacts, and I hope he'll use his relationships and his own influence to help bring Sawyer safely home."

From the corner of her eye, she made out Wesson's nod. Good, at least she hadn't blown that.

"Mrs. Carmichael, I can only imagine your emotional despair at the moment. Are there search parties being formed?" The reporter pushed her microphone closer to Elise.

"We aren't forming search parties because he isn't missing or lost—I know he was kidnapped."

"How can you be positive?" someone asked.

Elise glanced at Agent Rodriguez, who stepped up beside her. "While we can't release certain information because of the ongoing investigation, there is confirmation that Sawyer Carmichael was kidnapped."

She smiled her relief as he kept speaking. "I'm sure you can understand Mrs. Carmichael is exhausted, both physically and emotionally. If you'll excuse her, I'll be happy to give you the details regarding the one hundred thousand dollar reward." He gave her a nod.

As if they'd made the plan before, both Mary Ellen and Noland flanked her while Wesson led the way to the front door. Arabella hung back with Agent Rodriguez.

Once the door was shut, Wesson spun around. "That was perfect. I could have kissed that reporter when she asked about Senator Boone."

Elise sank to the couch, aching as if every muscle in her limbs had ten-pound weights hanging from them. "Truth be told, Wesson, I thought maybe you had asked that reporter to ask the question."

Wesson chuckled as she dropped into the chair. "Well, I couldn't be that obvious, but I did mention Senator Boone several times in our chat, hoping the subliminal message would go through. Guess it did."

Noland laughed, stretching his legs out from his seat on the couch. "You're going to be a really great journalist, Wesson."

She blushed. "Thank you. I mean that. You were one of the really good ones. I followed a lot of your career. So much of it was an inspiration to me."

It was Noland's turn to blush. "Well, thank you. Anytime you have something you want to chat over, you know where to find me."

Elise smiled to herself. Despite the horrendous reasoning, there were many friendships that would come out of this nightmare.

"How long do you think it'll take Senator Boone to respond?"

Mary Ellen sat on the couch beside Elise.

"Knowing him? He's probably already on his way over here." Wesson shook her head. "Probably racing so he can get on the five o'clock."

"I really don't care." Elise leaned her head back on the couch. "Whatever helps bring Sawyer back home is all I care about."

The front door opened and Arabella and Agent Rodriguez rushed inside. "Whew, reporters can get to be like vultures." Agent Rodriguez shut the door. He looked at Wesson and Noland. "No offense."

Noland smiled. "None taken. Some of them are just like vultures, ready to expose any and everybody for the sake of the story. Sometimes, they don't even bother to fact check." He shook his head. "I hate that a handful can give the whole field a bad reputation."

"Ha." Arabella came and squeezed on the other side of Elise. "Try being a lawyer. That's always fun."

Agent Rodriguez grinned and went into the kitchen with the other agents. Wesson jumped up and headed down the hall. Noland pushed to his feet as well. "I know it's been a long day, but with the reward being offered. . .well, let's just say that I expect it to be a long evening. I'm going to put on a pot of coffee and see what I can make for dinner without having to go to the market."

Mary Ellen shook her head. "Don't worry about dinner. I heard from Pastor Evans that the food patrol will start delivering at six."

"The food patrol?" Arabella asked.

Mary Ellen nodded. "My mom's church, our church here, they know in times of crisis the family might not feel like cooking or have time to go to the store or have extra people at the house. The food patrol is a group of volunteers who cook meals for the house and deliver them, so the family doesn't have to worry with it. They do it for deaths, funerals, serious hospital stays, new births. . .any and all of that."

"That's really nice."

Elise nodded and smiled softly. "I'd forgotten. They brought food for a week when Sawyer was born. Same when Judson died. It was such a blessing."

Mary Ellen shared a smile with Elise. "It will be now too."

Wesson practically exploded back into the living room. She perched on the coffee table right in front of Elise and lowered her voice. "I heard back from one of my sources. About properties that the senator is affiliated with, but there's no paper trail of it. It's a camp of sorts. A friend of a friend of a friend. Apparently, no one claims ownership, but it's a real bachelor pad. Meaning, married men take their mistresses there."

Elise sat upright. "That sounds right up Grady Boone's ally."

"Even more is that my source, while he was checking it out, says that there's been activity inside the camp, but no vehicles are parked there and there haven't been any women seen. According to him, it looks like someone's hiding out there."

Elise's heart nearly beat out of her chest. "Where is this camp?"

"Wattensaw. About forty minutes from here."

On her feet in a flash, Elise put her hands on her hips. "So, do we dare go, or should we stay and wait to see if Senator Boone shows up?"

"Why don't you speak to Agent Rodriguez first?" Arabella asked. She held up her hands to ward off the collective groan from Wesson, Mary Ellen, and Elise. "Just a minute. He's a good guy. I know it's frustrating when he has to follow the FBI's way of doing things, but he didn't make those rules, he just has to abide by them."

Elise nodded. Her lawyer was right. "Let me bring him in here." She went into the kitchen and motioned him to join them in the living room. Quickly, Wesson told him what she'd learned from her source.

"So, we're not sure if we should stay here and wait to see the senator's next move, or if we should go and at least check it out."

"I will send a unit out," Agent Rodriguez offered. "Then, if they see anything, they can let us know and we can get a warrant and—"

"No offense, Agent Rodriguez, but I'm not waiting that long. If there's a chance my son is there, I'm going." Determination set Elise's jaw, her mind now already made up.

"I'm ready," Wesson said.

"Me too," Mary Ellen added.

"Okay, let's think about this for just a moment." Arabella pointed at Agent Rodriguez. "I know the bureau has policies, but in this case, wouldn't it be better for you to ride along with these ladies, just to ensure there were no laws broken?"

He cocked his head to the side. "We're usually told to halt one of the parties, but in this case, I don't think I can stop Mrs. Carmichael. It's her son." He hesitated another moment, then nodded. "So, yes, it would be better for me to take them."

"Mr. York and I can stay here and wait in case Senator Boone does something. We can all stay in constant contact via our cells, right?"

Agent Rodriguez nodded, as did Wesson, Elise, and Mary Ellen.

"Then I think that's our plan." The lawyer smiled.

"Then let's roll." Wesson tapped her cell phone. "I'm loading the address into my GPS now."

"Ladies, I must insist that I drive."

Elise shrugged. "Fine by me."

"I don't care." Mary Ellen gave Noland a quick hug.

"Whatever. I've got it loaded." Wesson pocketed her phone. "We have an estimated forty two minutes until arrival."

Agent Rodriguez pulled out his keys and passed them to Elise. "Go ahead and get in the car. I'll let my team know I'm following up on a lead."

Elise took the keys and headed out the door. She raced toward the agent's car, but her heart raced faster. This was it—she just felt it. God willing, she'd be holding Sawyer in her arms in an hour.

Please, God.

Chapter Thirty-Three

The forty-something-minute car ride provided time to discuss their game plan.

"Remember, none of you are law enforcement. You cannot just barge in there." Agent Rodriguez sped the packed sedan down the interstate.

Wattensaw in Lonoke County sat east of Little Rock in Arkansas, and was one of the hunting and fishing secrets in the south. There weren't many permanent residents in the Wattensaw area, but there were plenty of camps, lodges, and other part-time draws to the area.

"I'll be respectful of not barging in, unless I find without a doubt that my son is being held there. If that occurs, all bets are off."

"I think perhaps you've been focusing so much on finding your son that maybe you've chosen to ignore the fact that he was kidnapped, which means, there is someone, probably heavily armed, who is with him." Agent Rodriguez glanced at Elise seated in the front seat, then put his concentration back on the road. "You don't want to do anything to make a kidnapper jumpy. Not safe for your child."

Elise's stomach sat in knots. She'd managed to avoid seeing Sawyer with a gun or knife to his temple or his throat. But now that they could very well be facing such a scenario, she wanted to vomit. Her mouth had gone as dry as the Mohave Desert.

He cut his eyes at her for a moment. "Look, I'm not trying to scare you, I'm just trying to prepare you for the reality of the situation."

"So what is our plan?" Mary Ellen asked.

Wesson slapped the seat. "I thought maybe, just maybe, I could approach and knock. I'm a reporter and blah blah blah. It would give me a chance to maybe see inside. I could come back and report what I've seen."

"That's good, but, again, you aren't law enforcement." Agent Rodriguez gave her a glance in the rearview mirror.

"Then what do you suggest?" Mary Ellen asked.

"I'll approach and see if I can get inside."

Wesson let out a half snort, half-dry chuckle. "Like you aren't intimidating or anything."

"Why don't I go knock on the door? I'm searching for my son. Maybe I can appeal to him if Sawyer's inside."

"And if you think your son is inside and you try to rush in, you can put either yourself or your son at risk." Agent Rodriguez shook his head. "I don't think that's a situation any of us want to find ourselves in."

Frustration hung heavy and thick in the car. Everyone went quiet, working their mind over ideas that might work. Most were ruled out as too risky or impossible.

"Look, I had my team call the state police who are assigned to work in that area. A team is at the ready, standing by for me to call for their assistance if needed." Agent Rodriguez gripped the steering wheel as he pushed a little harder on the accelerator. "They assured me they could be at the address Wesson gave us in less than ten minutes."

"Ten minutes. No offense, but if my son is in danger, that might as well be ten hours." Elise just couldn't imagine waiting ten minutes, knowing for fact her son was with someone who had a weapon on him.

Agent Rodriguez nodded, but kept his eyes on the road. "I understand, but in such a case, ten minutes is actually a very quick turnaround."

Mary Ellen leaned forward, like a kid in the back seat on a long trip who kept bobbing up between the parents to ask the age-old question, *Are we there yet?* "I'm wondering if we can kind of meld several ideas of ours together. I do agree with you, Elise, that the good agent here is very intimidating and perhaps could be perceived as a threat."

"Then what do you propose?" Agent Rodriguez asked.

Now that she had the floor, so to speak, Mary Ellen leaned back against the back seat. "Why couldn't Elise and I knock on the door and just say her son, my nephew, was kidnapped so we're asking all the area people if they've seen him? That comes across as if we don't suspect anyone in that home of having kidnapped Sawyer, but that we're asking for help."

That was a good—no, great idea. "I like it. It gives us the opportunity to see if we can catch a glimpse of Sawyer, but not accuse if he actually does have him."

Wesson nodded. "Since we know he won't confess and just hand your son over, when we walk away, he'll have to call Senator Boone or the middle person between them and ask for instructions. I'm pretty sure that if we show up searching for Sawyer in the area, he's going to be a little panicked and want reassurance and instruction."

Elise could see this working. She touched Agent Rodriguez's arm. "And if we do know he has Sawyer, we can have you call in your backup of the state police. They'll probably arrive about the same time he'll get in touch with the senator or the go-between person, so it's not more of a threat to Sawyer." Yes, this could work! "Also, he won't be as jumpy because if he has Sawyer held in a different room, there's no chance Sawyer would hear us knock on the door or anything."

"Right." Mary Ellen leaned forward again, just not as far. "So that wouldn't put Sawyer at any more risk."

"Unless Sawyer's in the main room," Agent Rodriguez offered.

Wesson grunted. "Then he's the most stupidest kidnapper ever to hear a knock on the door, look out a peephole or window or something, see the kid's mom who has been on several news broadcasts today, and not put Sawyer in a different room."

"Kidnappers aren't always the brightest crayon, you know." Agent Rodriguez shot a look at Wesson in his rearview. "This one is probably less savvy than the average kidnapper because he's just taking orders. I'm pretty sure he wasn't involved in the initial planning, because I don't think it was ever a plan to kidnap your son, Mrs. Carmichael."

"Yet, here we are." She stared out the front windshield and chewed her bottom lip. Her nerves felt like they were sitting on top of her skin, all jumbled into a wad—even breathing hurt.

Mary Ellen squeezed Elise's shoulder. "It's going to be okay. Remember, God's got this and Sawyer."

Elise nodded. "I know. It's just a little scary right now."

"For me as well. I've been praying Philippians 4:6 ever since we left. 'Do not be anxious about anything, but in everything by prayer and supplication with thanksgiving let your requests be made known to God.'"

Elise reached and put her hand over Mary Ellen's. "Thank you." She let out a long breath and pushed herself to pray.

Dear God, I'm so anxious about Sawyer and his well-being. That's probably a sin to be anxious because it means I don't trust You. I don't know. If it is, I'm sorry. But, Lord, with my heart full of gratitude for you letting me have Sawyer to begin with and be his mom and love him so much, I'm asking—no, begging, that You keep him safe and let him come home safely. Please. In Jesus' precious name I pray, amen.

"I guess it could work. It's the best idea we've come up with yet," Wesson said.

Wesson's GPS on her phone gave the instruction to exit the interstate.

Agent Rodriguez steered the car to the off-ramp as he slowed down. "I still don't like it. What if he answers with a gun?"

Elise licked her lips, which suddenly felt even drier than her mouth. "I was assuming you would be close enough with your weapon in the event it all went sideways anyway." Well, not entirely, but now that Agent Rodriguez had brought up such a scenario. . . .

He pulled the car to a stop at the end of the ramp at the stop sign and then followed the GPS's instructions and turned. "I suppose that's the best we can go with, but I still don't like the idea of you ladies being vulnerable, even for a few minutes."

Elise touched his arm again. "Thank you. And I promise not to try and provoke him, no matter what."

Mary Ellen leaned forward a little. "And I promise not to belt him on-site if Senator Boone is actually there."

"Do you think he could be there?" Elise hadn't considered that as a possibility.

Wesson shook her head. "Very doubtful. I imagine he's trying to figure out a way to get Sawyer released to a safe place without anything coming back to him. Being at the location where a kidnapped child is being held would be bad for him. Very bad."

"If he is there, or you even suspect he is, you are to immediately stop whatever conversation you are having and get back to the car." Agent Rodriguez cut his eyes first to Elise, then to both Mary Ellen and Wesson in the rearview. "No discussion, period. Because if he's there and we've shown up. . .well, he'll know he's busted and that will make him desperate. Trust me on this, desperate people usually do the worst acts if they feel their back is against the wall."

Mary Ellen nodded. "He already had Mom murdered because he felt threatened by what she could expose. This is even worse."

Elise closed her eyes and sent up another quick prayer for guidance, wisdom, and divine intervention if needed. She had a strong feeling she was going to need it all.

The robotic voice of the GPS announced they had two more turns and then they would arrive at their destination.

"There aren't many homes, camps, or whatever close to each other, so it will make sense that we arrive in a vehicle," Wesson said.

"Should you get out with us?" Elise asked Agent Rodriguez. "Or what?"

"I still don't like it, but considering it's the best option at the moment, I would suggest that you two ladies approach the door. I'm sure if someone's there, they'll look out when they see or hear the car drive up. While you are approaching, I'll get out and discreetly move alongside the house to be able to take a place near the door, but out of the line of vision." Agent Rodriguez turned as directed by the GPS.

The sun had set behind the trees, leaving only fleeting remnants of itself—streaks of orange and reddish across the darkening sky. A cool breeze danced through the woods that they had entered two turns ago. Not visible from any road, definitely no 911 address, much less a postal address. Soon, night would take over the area, extinguishing all light and spilling tendrils of pitch black into the already dark recesses.

Elise gripped her hands in her lap. She would either get Sawyer soon, or. . .well, she didn't want to go through a consideration of an alternate ending. In her mind, it was either get Sawyer, or nobody was there. She had to face the very real possibility that Sawyer could not be there. She'd be devastated if that happened. She could only pray Sawyer was there, safe, and that she would be able to get him and bring him home, safe and sound.

Pray.

Funny how she'd avoided it for several years, but now she'd managed to fall right back into the habit of praying. Thinking it, and believing it—her faith bursting inside of her. As such, she was going to believe that God was in control and that He would keep her son out of harm's way.

Agent Rodriguez made the final turn, steering down a half gravel, half dirt. . .*road* was too generous of a word for what they were on. More like a long drive. Decades-old trees canopied over the drive. Butterflies swarmed Elise's stomach as the camp came into view.

She wasn't sure what she had expected, but it wasn't this. Nestled into the primitive setting of trees with a designated four-vehicle carport sat a log cabin. There was no water coloring of the exterior wood. In fact, it looked like the wood had been treated consistently and well cared for. There was a flag pole in front that boasted the American flag rippling in the April breeze. The grass areas around the building itself looked recently cut and trimmed, with little overgrowth even in the wooded areas on either side of the house.

Agent Rodriguez pulled up on the carport, but on the other side of a truck, using it to block the line of vision from the house's front door and big front window to the car. He twisted, facing Elise in the passenger's seat and Mary Ellen and Wesson in the back seat. "Remember, no heroics. We don't know what we're dealing with." He handed Wesson a business card. "That's the contact information for the state police units who are on standby, just in case I can't take the time to call for backup. I put my badge number on there, so you just give that and they should pick up immediately."

Wesson took it, nodding. "Got it." She looked at Elise and Mary Ellen. "Okay, time to do this. Can't sit out here for long without somebody growing suspicious and possibly coming outside. And remember, you don't know how many are inside, so stick to the plan."

Elise let out a long breath and locked stares with her sister-in-law. "Ready?"

Mary Ellen nodded and opened her door. Elise followed suit, carrying the picture of Sawyer that they'd had at all the press conferences and posted on social media. Her steps were a little wobbly as they made their way around the truck.

Elise felt like she was going to be sick. No, she was not. She was going to walk in faith and be strong for her son.

Mary Ellen took her hand. "We've got this," she whispered as they reached the door.

Elise nodded, then knocked on the door. The knock sounded firm and steady, not nearly as weak as she felt. She straightened, waited a moment, then knocked again.

She caught Agent Rodriguez inching his way along the wall, coming closer to them. His hand rested on the butt of his gun.

Elise knocked again, a little harder. She could hear movement inside the house.

Sounded like a person or two walking on a wood floor. Maybe dragging.

Her heart leaped into her throat.

A door shut inside. Then footsteps.

Impatience lifted her hand and she knocked again. This time, she called out, "Hello? Is anybody home?"

CHAPTER THIRTY-FOUR

The door whipped open and a man wearing jeans and a plain red T-shirt stood there. Elise took a step back. She was pretty sure it was Fred Otto, but it was really hard to tell. Fred Otto, as Wesson had described, had dark hair that brushed the top of his shoulders while this man sported a platinum-blond flattop. Fred Otto had a thin mustache and partial goatee. This man at the door was clean shaven.

"What do you want?" His voice came out nearly as a snarl. It was the way his lip curled as he spoke.

Elise lifted the page with Sawyer's picture. "I'm not sure if you've seen me on the news today, but my son, Sawyer, was kidnapped." She held the picture out to him. "He's deaf and mute, has a cast on his right arm so he can't communicate well right now."

He glanced at the picture, then back to her face. "Kidnapped, you say? Then what are you doing here? Do you think I kidnapped your kid?" He sounded tough and angry, but the bobbing of his Adam's apple screamed his uncertainty and fear.

"Oh, of course not." Elise forced herself to act shocked. "Not at all."

Mary Ellen smiled. "My sister-in-law and I are out canvassing areas that maybe have trouble getting television reception or only watch cable. We're asking people for their help. People might have seen him, or heard someone say they saw something…really anything."

Elise nodded. "I'm a widow, and my son just lost his Nana last week." She opted to use the name Sawyer had called Lilliana, hoping to appeal to his sympathy. "Matter of fact, we had come home from her funeral and he was playing soccer in the backyard when he was taken."

"My nephew loves soccer. He used to play with my brother before my brother, a Marine, was killed in the line of duty." Mary Ellen laid it on just as thick. "My nephew and I are all my sister-in-law here has."

"Aren't the police or FBI or somebody in charge of such an investigation?" That he mentioned the FBI, well, sure meant he knew who some of the players were, but the wariness in his voice as well as the animosity that seeped from him gave Elise a hunch.

She played it. First she snorted, then rolled her eyes. "My son was kidnapped from our own backyard while *FBI agents were in my house!* That's how inept they are." She cut her eyes to where Agent Rodriguez was pressed against the house. She hoped he would understand why she was saying these things, especially since she remembered the hurt expression he'd worn when she'd said something similar to the press earlier today.

Mary Ellen let out a very loud sigh. "Law enforcement isn't being very helpful. They won't even update my sister-in-law on her son's case. They haven't kept me updated about my mom's murder, either."

"They aren't very trustworthy, in my opinion." Elise lifted a hand and covered her mouth. "I hope you aren't in law enforcement. If you are, my apologies."

Now he snorted. "Me? In law enforcement? Not hardly." He let out a humorless laugh. "I'm with you, sister. I don't trust any of them." He nodded at Elise, seemingly more relaxed now.

She plastered on a smile. "Oh, good. I mean, I don't want to offend anyone, but the agents I've been dealing with. . .they leave a lot to be desired." She tossed Agent Rodriguez a quick, sheepish look. "Anyway, have you seen my son or maybe heard something? He's my entire world, and I'm lost without him." A quick flip of emotions, but maybe it would play on his sympathy.

He leaned against the doorjamb, the side with the hinges, which pushed the door open wider. He was definitely more relaxed, and if she didn't know better—which she actually didn't, she would say he was flirting with her and Mary Ellen. The thought disgusted her, so she shifted her attention from his face. She could see just over his shoulder into a common area of the house. A television played, sound muted, to one of Sawyer's favorite cartoons.

Despite her heart lurching, Elise forced herself to look back into his creepy eyes. "Anything you might know would be helpful."

"There's a reward for helping with his return too," Mary Ellen added. "A large reward."

He turned his attention to Mary Ellen. "A reward you say? How much of a reward?"

Elise used his change of focus to glance into the house more. Hope blazed against her chest as she saw a juice box on the counter, as well as what looked like remainders from a peanut butter and jelly sandwich.

Sawyer had to be inside!

"It's a one hundred thousand dollar reward."

"A hundred thousand dollars! I've not heard about that." His cover slipped for that moment, then went back up. "But I haven't seen your son." He looked back at Elise. "I'm sorry."

Elise made herself make eye contact with him. "Me too." She let out a loud breath and shifted to Mary Ellen. "I guess we should go to the next house."

"And I saw a little convenience store down the road. We should talk with them too."

Elise nodded. "Even if they didn't see Sawyer, they might have seen something that was strange to them. Like a grown man buying stuff a kid likes to eat—like snack cakes, peanut butter and jelly, juices. . .that kind of thing." She turned her attention back to him quick enough to catch the panic on his face. Bingo!

"I thank you for taking the time to look at the picture." Elise spoke directly to him. "If you do see anything unusual, please do call the number at the bottom of this page." She forced the picture into his hand.

Mary Ellen held out a card that Wesson had given them. "This is who to contact for more details about the reward, just in case you do see something, or you remember seeing something out of place or anything."

"I will." He nodded at Elise. "I hope you get your son back."

"Oh, I will. I have no doubt about that. Thank you." She turned away as he shut the door.

"Sawyer is in there," she whispered under her breath to Mary Ellen.

Mary Ellen nodded as they moved down the carport. "I know. I saw the cartoons."

Agent Rodriguez had already made a move toward the car when inspiration, or maybe it was desperation, hit. Elise let go of Mary Ellen's grip. "Wait right here, don't go to the car just yet. I'm going to try something. Don't let Agent Rodriguez or Wesson be seen."

"Elise, no," Mary Ellen hissed.

But it was too late. Elise walked faster back to the front door. She knocked confidently on the door.

The man swung the door open, just as Elise had suspected he would. She guessed he would be staring out the windows to make sure they left before he did anything. "Was there something else?" he asked.

"May I please use your restroom? My sister-in-law and I have been driving and I've been so upset that I've been drinking a lot of coffee and water to keep hydrated and, well. . .may I please use your bathroom? I promise I won't be but a minute."

He hesitated, as if weighing his options. "Hang on." He shut the door.

A minute passed. Then another.

Elise wondered if he was just going to leave her out here until she would have to leave. Just as she started to turn back to the car, he jerked open the door. "My brother's asleep in the room at the end of the hall. He worked all day, so I can't have him woken up."

"I'll be quiet as a mouse, I promise."

He opened the door wider. "The bathroom is the second door on the right."

"Thank you." She rushed past him, making a point to notice that he didn't seem to have a gun on him. She hadn't seen one in easy reach to him either. That was promising.

She made it to the bathroom and eased the door open, then shut it quietly behind her. He had to be keeping Sawyer in the room at the end of the hall. How could she get to him without the man seeing or hearing her? She looked around the bathroom for. . .well, she didn't know for what. She saw a marker. Maybe she could write Sawyer a message. He *was* an advanced reader.

Elise pulled out a strip of toilet paper and wrote: *Mommy coming, Sawyer. Be strong.*

Footsteps sounded in the hall.

She flushed the toilet and turned on the water in the sink, looking around. There was no place to leave the message that the man wouldn't see. Elise turned off the water and made a final look around. She folded the toilet paper message and put it in her pocket. It'd been a hope, but now it was gone.

He waited at the end of the hall. She had no choice, she'd have to leave, even though every instinct inside her screamed at her to do something.

She wavered like a drunken sailor.

"Hey, what are you doing?" He started for her.

She needed to think fast, but not a single logical thought came into her head. She did the only thing she could think of: she burst into sobs and fell on the floor.

He stood over her. "Lady, what are you doing?"

"I–I'm sssso sorry. I just miss my son sooo much. I think I'm having a heart attack."

"What?"

There, she'd go with that. Elise gripped her chest over her heart. "I think I'm having a heart attack. Please. Can you call an ambulance for me?"

"Uh, I don't think—"

"I might die right here on your floor. Please. Help me."

"Let me get your sister-in-law. She can drive you to the hospital or clinic. We don't have ambulance service out here. Wait here."

Just what she wanted, but she hoped that Mary Ellen had done as she'd asked and not gotten back into the car and wouldn't let Agent Rodriguez or Wesson be seen. She let out a pitiful moan.

He turned and rushed down the hall and out of the house.

She jumped to her feet and went to the door at the end of the hall. It was locked. She twisted and turned it, but it was locked.

Think fast, Elise.

She took the toilet paper message and slid it under the door.

The front door banged. "Elise, are you okay?" Mary Ellen's voice carried.

Elise moved to the bathroom door and leaned against it just as Mary Ellen and the man rushed to her.

"I don't think I'm okay, Mary Ellen. I think I need a doctor."

Mary Ellen took one side of her and motioned for the man to take the other, and they lifted her to her feet. "Our friend here gave me directions to the closest clinic. You'll be okay." They walked her to the door. Mary Ellen smiled at him. "Thank you for everything." She pulled Elise's arm from around him and "helped" Elise toward the car.

The last vestiges of daylight were gone. The night sky darkened as each minute passed. At least the darkness helped with keeping Agent Rodriguez and Wesson from being seen from a distance.

"What have you done?" Agent Rodriguez growled from the back seat where he and Wesson were scooted down.

"Shh." Elise and Mary Ellen got in the front seat, Mary Ellen behind the wheel. She started the engine and turned on the headlights.

"You can't drive an FBI vehicle. Only authorized agents are allowed to drive them."

Mary Ellen put the car in REVERSE. "Well, when there's a man watching us to make sure we leave to go to the clinic, and he thinks it's just me and Elise, there are no other options. Stay down, both of you." She put the car in DRIVE and started down the drive.

"Once we're out of his line of vision, pull over." No mistaking the anger in Agent Rodriguez's tone.

But Elise didn't care. She knew her son was there, and alive. Yes, she finally allowed herself to say what she'd feared—that Sawyer could be dead. Dead children didn't eat peanut butter sandwiches, drink juice boxes, or watch cartoons. Agent Rodriguez could be as angry as he wanted, but Elise was too filled with thanksgiving to care much.

She only hoped that Sawyer had gotten her toilet paper message before that man saw it.

Chapter Thirty-Five

Agent Rodriguez refused to drive any farther until Elise and Mary Ellen told him everything said, seen, and heard at the log cabin. "That's enough for us to get a warrant to get into the house. Let me make the call." He pulled out his cell phone.

Exhilaration filled the car with something akin to an electric charge. Elise turned to Wesson. "You will get an exclusive. Write down everything you see and hear tonight so you can write it up for tomorrow's headlines. I just know that we'll have Sawyer home safely tonight."

"If you're sure, I can call my editor and tell him to hold me a spot."

"Of course I'm sure." Elise smiled at the reporter.

"Agent Wright is getting a judge to agree to the warrant, then will fax it to the state police here for them to bring. I'm calling them now to set it all up." Agent Rodriguez showed more excitement than he ever had on this case.

"I need to update Noland and Arabella." Mary Ellen pulled out her cell.

Elise realized she should update Hallie. She made the call and brought Hallie up to date on everything. She asked Hallie to go to the house to be there if they brought Sawyer back.

No, not if. . .*when* they brought Sawyer home.

"There's news on Senator Boone," Mary Ellen announced as she slipped her cell back into her back pocket.

"What?" In the excitement of knowing she was this close to

having Sawyer back, Elise hadn't thought about the weasel.

"He did come forward and tell the good people on the news, via a statement his office distributed to all the press outlets, that his office was working on finding any possible lead and would take immediate action when any viable lead was uncovered. He promised to do everything in his power to see mother and child reunited."

"Maybe he's called Fred Otto and is telling him to take him somewhere to release him. Maybe that convenience store we mentioned." Mary Ellen's eyes were wide.

"You know, Fred Otto hadn't heard about the reward. Maybe he'll turn him loose on his own to collect."

Then, when time should have felt like it was dragging, everything started happening at once. The state police called Agent Rodriguez that they had the warrant and were en route to their location. Agent Wright and two other FBI agents were on their way to assist as needed. Agent Rodriguez retrieved his Kevlar vest and put it on. "I'll park the car as close as I can risk without your safety being in jeopardy," he told Elise. "But I must have assurance that under no circumstances are you to get out of the car. Any of you. Is that understood?"

They all mumbled, but he stood beside the open driver's door. "I mean it. I will have an agent drive you all to the end of the drive to secure your safety if I can't trust you to stay in the car."

"We understand." Elise bit her bottom lip as he got into the car. If he made them stay there, she'd run all the way to the log cabin. She was not going to miss getting Sawyer as soon as humanly possible. No matter what.

Before anyone could say anything, a silver truck shot past them, barreling down the road toward the cabin.

"Was that any of your people?" Elise asked Agent Rodriguez.

He shook his head and lifted his cell to his ear.

Elise's mouth went dry again. Was this nightmare ever going to end? Ever?

Before Agent Rodriguez got off the phone, two cars flew down the drive, filling the air with dust. He continued to talk.

"That's three additional. What's going on?" Elise clenched and unclenched her hands.

"Maybe it's peons the senator sent to get Sawyer and bring him to a safe place for his return to show that he can move mountains and is amazing and blah blah blah," Wesson said.

"Could be." Elise worried her bottom lip. She could see him doing something like that. Especially if it was Fred Otto in the log cabin and Grady Boone wanted a couple to pick up Sawyer and say they "found" him or something, then one to tie up the loose end of Fred Otto. It all made her stomach tie in knots. Sawyer had to be terrified.

Unless he didn't see any of them.

Another truck sped down the drive to the log cabin. Four. That was four more people, and that was if there was only one per vehicle. Elise's already frantic panic had shifted into overdrive. Her fear for Sawyer's safety choked her. She tried to pray, but could only think two words.

Please. Help.

Minutes later, two state police vehicles came to rest beside theirs. Agent Rodriguez rushed to them, and the five law enforcement officers huddled up.

Elise just wanted them to do something quickly. There was no telling what was happening at the log cabin, and she felt like she could jump out of her own skin at the moment.

Agent Rodriguez returned and slid behind the steering wheel. He started the car, keeping his headlights off as did the two state police cars. "Here's the deal, we don't know what's going on with the other vehicles. It could be as Wesson suggested, but we don't know that. I, along with the four state police officers will approach with the warrant. At that time, we hope to be able to get into the house and recover your son." He slipped in behind the second state police cruiser.

"What do you mean, 'hope to be able to get into the house'? I mean, isn't that what the warrant is for?" Elise demanded.

"Sometimes when people are served with a warrant, they make a bad decision and refuse, sometimes with a show of armed force."

Elise's heart crashed against her ribs. "You mean, they shoot? With guns?" Well, of course with guns and not bow and arrows. Her mind was a tangle.

"I've alerted the two teams that this is a kidnapping case and that we have every reason to believe your son is inside. We will use caution and back away if we are met with any resistance, and one of the FBI agents already on the way is an authorized hostage negotiator, so that's what this will be moved to—a hostage situation."

Elise was going to vomit. Sawyer, a hostage.

"Look, I know it's scary, and I hope it doesn't come to that, but we are prepared if it does. I'm telling you everything so you know. Once we get there, things might happen quickly, one way or the other, and I might not have time to explain, so I want you to know first."

"I appreciate it. I really do. Thank you." Elise's voice cracked.

"I'm still praying, Elise. God's got this. Trust Him." Mary Ellen reached and squeezed her shoulder.

Elise nodded, but she knew if anything happened to her son, she wouldn't make it. She'd have no reason to live, and just thinking that scared her.

They approached the carport. The three dark cars inched behind the other vehicles at the carport. The four state police officers and Agent Rodriguez crept toward the door, hands on their guns. Two of the state police officers pulled their guns and held them at the ready, pointed at the door.

Agent Rodriguez held the warrant. He pounded on the door and then yelled, "FBI. Open the door. We have a search warrant to enter the premises." He pounded harder on the door. "FBI, open up."

The two windows on either end of the front of the house crashed and glass flew outside. A flash of light filled both.

Pow! Pow! Pow! Pow!

Agent Rodriguez and the officers retreated behind the cars at the carport. "FBI. Stop shooting and put down your weapons. Come out immediately."

Another set of rapid gunfire.

Elise pressed her fingers against her lips to keep the screams inside. Mary Ellen was in a similar position, but Wesson held up her cell as she recorded.

The officers and Agent Rodriguez regrouped beside where Elise and the others sat.

"I counted five with guns," one of the state police officers said. "It's now a hostage situation."

As if on cue, Agent Wright and other agents pulled up and joined the huddle. They were quickly brought up to speed. Agent Louis, the hostage negotiator, got a bullhorn from his trunk and moved closer to the front of the cabin. They quickly and quietly moved their vehicles in a row to face the log cabin. All of the officers turned on their headlights, blinding the front of the log cabin. Two of the state police, guns drawn, headed around to the back of the house.

"This is Agent Louis with the FBI. I'm here to help this situation be resolved peacefully. What do you want?"

"For all of you to die," a voice from inside the house yelled through one of the broken windows. "Stay away, or the deaf, dumb kid dies."

Elise covered her whole mouth with her hand, muffling the scream filling her chest. Confirmation Sawyer was in there with at least five people with loaded weapons.

"Now, you know we can't just die or leave. What do you really need? Let me try to help you get what you need." How Agent Louis kept his voice so steady and calm, Elise would never know. She'd never be able to do that.

"Give us the reward money for the kid, and let us go," someone hollered.

"That I might be able to work on. Give me a few minutes. But we need proof that the boy is actually in there and okay before I can get anybody to agree to anything. Can we see him?"

Elise watched for any movement or response. *Please, God.*

And then there he was.

Sawyer.

Only the top of his head, down to his mouth, but he was there, living and breathing and blinking against the brightness of the cruisers' headlights on high beam.

Just as quickly, he was gone from view. It took everything in Elise not to bolt out of the car and run to the house.

"Okay, you saw him, now get us the one hundred thousand dollars, then you leave and let us go. We'll release the boy in a public place when we are sure we aren't followed."

"Let me see what I can do." Agent Louis walked back to the group. They all formed around the back of Agent Louis's sedan, except for the two officers who were in the back.

Elise couldn't wait any longer. She joined them, standing slightly behind them so as to not be easily noticed. She wanted to hear their thoughts and knew they'd most likely guard their statements if they knew she was there.

"The sad thing is, had they just come forward and said they found the Carmichael kid, they could have claimed the reward and we wouldn't be in this mess." Agent Louis leaned against his open trunk. "Now they've gone and made it more complicated."

Elise bit her tongue again. She tried to focus on anything else. She started with the contents of Agent Louis's trunk. Two other Kevlar vests. Several shotguns.

"Look, I know this family. They'll willingly pay the reward money even knowing that it's a hostage situation. They just want the boy back safely, and quickly."

Elise remained quiet and continued listening and inventorying the trunk. Several sets of earmuff-style ear protectors. Spotlights that slip into the car charging plugs. Were those waders?

"And it might come to that." Agent Louis rested his hip against the side of his car.

"Can we try the tear gas?" one of the other agents asked.

Agent Rodriguez shook his head. "Not when a young minor is involved. Too much of a risk to a kid."

"I guess that leaves storming the place out," another agent said.

"Um, yeah. We can't put this boy at risk by trying to take the location by force." Agent Rodriguez sounded as disgusted as Elise felt.

"Everything we have in our arsenal is too much of a risk with a young kid involved." Agent Louis shook his head. "We have to go with the negotiation attempts and see where that takes us."

"So we have no other options," another agent asked.

"None that I can see," Agent Louis said.

"But there is another option," Elise said. Excitement surged through her veins, only matching her anxiety.

"Mrs. Carmichael, what are you doing out here?" Agent Rodriguez frowned at her. "You were told to wait in the car."

"I couldn't help it. I just wanted to get the game plan, but didn't want to interrupt. But you do have something you can use that won't put Sawyer at any risk, but will disable the men in the house with him."

"Do tell." Agent Louis shifted his weight.

She took a few steps forward to his trunk and pointed at something. "The LRAD."

Agent Rodriguez glanced at the machinery, then back at Elise. "The what?"

"I can't remember exactly what it stands for, but basically, a sound cannon."

Agent Louis explained further. "It's a portable speaker designed for crowd control and anti-rioting."

"It makes noise?" Agent Rodriguez looked as confused as he sounded.

"Yes, very loud. It's kind of like pressing your ear against a car's hood while the alarm is going off. It's a big amplifier."

Elise nodded. "Humans begin suffering from permanent hearing loss with a sustained sound louder than ninety decibels. Eardrums will burst, literally, at one hundred and sixty decibels. The LRAD can reach, I believe it's close to a hundred and fifty."

Agent Louis nodded. "You're really close. It can reach about a hundred and fifty-two. Enough to cause loss of hearing, but it's the intense pain it causes that makes it most useful."

"We can use it against the people in the log cabin?" Agent Rodriguez asked.

Elise nodded. "It won't affect Sawyer at all. He's totally deaf." The flame of hope fanned in her chest. "But it will render the men in there with Sawyer unable to do anything but either run away or try and cover their ears to stop the pain." She nodded at his trunk again. "I can put on the ear protectors and run into the house and get Sawyer while you and the other agents secure the men."

"That just might be the best idea I've heard all day, no pun intended." Agent Louis looked into the trunk. "I have three pairs of the ear protectors."

"Are those like the ones we use on the shooting range?" Agent Rodriguez asked.

Agent Louis nodded.

"I have a pair in my trunk."

"I do too," said one of the other agents.

"Me too," another chimed in.

"Then we have plenty for all of us and one extra." Agent Louis gestured with his thumb toward Agent Rodriguez's car. "But one of them, and you state boys, will need to move to the end of the drive to protect yourselves."

"I'll drive us to a safe distance," one of the police officers replied.

Agent Louis handed Elise a Kevlar vest from his trunk. Let's suit you up."

"Can Mary Ellen use the other vest and ear protectors?" Elise made eye contact with Agent Rodriguez. "He's her nephew and she just lost her mom. She'll stay out here with the cars."

He nodded. "Explain quickly. I want to get them cuffed before they come up with an alternate plan."

"Yes, sir."

Chapter Thirty-Six

Elise stood at the edge of the carport, crouched down behind one of the trucks. The agents wearing the ear protectors gave each other the thumbs-up sign. Agent Louis held on to the portable machine they'd set on the roof of the car and turned to her. She gave a thumbs-up and pressed the protectors tight against her ears.

Agent Louis held up five fingers.

Four.

Three.

Elise held her breath. *Please, God, let this work.*

Two.

One.

She could hear the sharp siren, but the piercing didn't penetrate the earmuffs.

Agent Rodriguez held up five fingers and did another count down. He led the charge to the door, gun drawn, the other agents on his heels. He opened the door and two men spilled out and fell to the ground, holding their ears.

Two agents pulled out handcuffs. The other agents followed Agent Rodriguez inside. Elise was in last. She made her way to the end of the hallway. Agent Rodriguez moved beside her. She tried the door and it was still locked. Agent Rodriguez knocked it down.

Sawyer slept in the bed, completely unaware of anything happening. Elise's heart lurched as she touched his face. His eyes fluttered open. It took a moment for awareness to come, then he was clinging to her neck.

Elise held him tighter than she ever thought she could and followed Agent Rodriguez out of the house. Mary Ellen waited in one of the cars, engine running. Elise jumped in, still holding Sawyer in her lap. Mary Ellen put the car in gear and headed toward the end of the road.

Sawyer leaned back and signed, "Why are y'all wearing those headphones?"

She laughed and hugged him again, then kissed him half a dozen times. "Are you okay?" she signed.

He nodded, then smiled. "I got your note. On toilet paper." He crinkled his nose like Judson had, and laughed.

Elise laughed and cried at the same time. He was going to be okay. Everything was going to be okay.

** [SECTION BREAK] **

Five days later, Sawyer made the soccer team. Elise couldn't have been prouder. They went out for ice cream before she took him over to Noland's. She picked up Mary Ellen and headed to the courthouse.

Mary Ellen had exposed Senator Grady Boone with not only the documents Lilliana had lost her life for, but also the statements by Alice, who had decided to come forward to honor the US senator who had fought so hard for her.

His wife had left him, he had resigned immediately from the senate, and he'd been indicted. His lawyer had told the judge that he was going to plead guilty and requested a quick hearing and sentencing due to his inability to afford living accommodations. The judge had granted the request—for today.

Mary Ellen and Elise held hands as they slipped into the back of the packed courtroom. They saw Wesson and slid into the space she'd held for them. "They just finished waiving the reading of all the charges, just the main counts."

"How do you plead?" the judge's voice boomed into the microphone.

Standing with only his lawyer at his side. "I'm guilty, Your Honor."
Murmurs filled the air.

The judge banged the gavel. Silence fell over the courtroom.

"Grady Boone, I hereby sentence you to ninety-four years."

The judge kept talking, but Elise stopped listening. She and Mary Ellen hugged, then they included Wesson in their hug before they rushed out of the courthouse. Wesson made her call into her paper as she was officially covering the case. Now that Sawyer was home, her editor had approved her *story behind the story* exposé idea. All she had been waiting on to conclude the story was the court ruling. Her story would run tomorrow: font page, above the fold.

"Can you believe it? Ninety-four years. He'll never be free." Mary Ellen's eyes glimmered with tears. "Mom would be so proud."

Elise felt the same relief, glad the man couldn't hurt another child or woman, but right now, she just wanted to get back to her son. Her sweet Sawyer who had made the soccer team.

She'd had a few days to come to terms with everything that happened, and how it all worked out. God *did* always have a plan. Sawyer's deafness had saved his life. She would forever be thankful to God for providing seven years ago what would save her son's life this week.

"As for you, you meant evil against me, but God meant it for good, to bring it about that many people should be kept alive, as they are today."

Thank You, God. Thank You.

Dear Reader:

Welcome to Arkansas!

I must admit, when my husband's job brought us to Little Rock some 20+ years ago, I came with great hesitation. I'd been a Louisiana girl from birth, and loved (and still love) my home state, but now, I'm so glad we were able to enjoy a second "home" state. Arkansas is filled with beautiful parks, four real seasons, and a capitol city with all the good and bad sides included. I enjoyed using it as a backdrop for Elise and Sawyer's life, and I hope you enjoyed a little visit to the Natural State.

For many years, my mom was a single mother, raising three daughters. It was a lot of work, guilt from not being able to be at home with us kids, and emotionally trying, at best. But my mom was and is a strong woman, even after marrying my dad, and I used many of her strengths when I created Elise. My hat is off to all the single moms out there who work every day to make their kids' lives better.

Family dynamics can be some of the most complicated relationships ever—I know this from personal experience. As this story came to life, I wanted to show how many instances can bring a family together. . .or tear them apart. Thank you for letting me share these insights with you as the characters worked out their family issues.

I hope you enjoyed reading *Dead Silence*. I would love to hear from you. Please visit me on social media and on my website: www.robincaroll.com I love talking books with readers.

Blessings,

Robin

Acknowledgments:

Each book marks the accomplishment of an entire team who made it possible. I'm so grateful to the entire team at Barbour Publishing, but especially Annie Tipton, Jessie Fioritto, Shalyn Sattler, and Liesl Davenport. From acquisitions to contracting to editing to cover design to marketing, you are all awesome and I'm grateful to work with you. Each of you have my sincerest gratitude.

I can't express enough how in awe I am of the AMAZING cover for this book. The design is perfect and I couldn't be happier or more grateful!

Thanks to my agent, Steve Laube, who manages to keep me on track and sane in this ever-changing industry.

This book was brainstormed with some pretty amazing writers and an agent at a private retreat in beautiful Arizona. My thanks for their input and excitement: Colleen Coble, Carrie Stuart Parks, Karen Solem, Lynette Eason, Voni Harris, and Pam Hillman. I had the best time hanging out with y'all and always look forward to being able to brainstorm with you. Thank you to Kara & Mark Davy for letting me visit and play with Elijah & Silas. Thanks to Dave Coble for carting us around and making sure we didn't get lost—which is NO easy feat when I'm involved.

Huge thanks to my beta readers who don't let me get away with much of anything. . .Lisa Burroughs, Tracey Justice, and Heather Tipton. My books are much better because of you!

To my immediate family who help me brainstorm, plot, and cause havoc in my poor characters' lives: Casey, Remy, and Bella—THANK

YOU for taking the active part in my stories. I can't tell you how much it means to me for y'all to rock the fiction process with me.

Lots of love for my family's encouragement. I so appreciate your continuous support: Mom, my grandsons—Benton and Zayden, daughter Zoey, Bubba and Lisa, and Wade (because you are more family than not).

Thanks to Carrie Stuart Parks for being invaluable in helping me write realistic scenes regarding forensics and the sketch artist process. You, my friend, have no idea how awesome you really are!

Big thanks to Colleen Coble for always being my mentor and friend and loving me enough to give me the hard truth when I need it. I love you so much and am so grateful to have you in my life.

To my hubby, Casey. . .what on earth would I do without you? Thank you for loving me despite my writer-moods, and letting me chase this dream of mine. I love you to the moon and back again, a thousand times over!

Finally, all glory to my Lord and Savior, Jesus Christ. I can do all things through Christ who strengthens me.

About the Author

Robin Caroll grew up in Louisiana with her nose in a book. She still has the complete Trixie Belden series, and her love for mysteries and suspense has only increased with her age.

Robin's passion has always been to tell stories to entertain others and come alongside them on their faith journey—aspects Robin weaves into each of her published novels.

Bestselling author of thirty-plus novels, Robin Caroll writes Southern stories of mystery and suspense, with a hint of romance to entertain readers. Her books have been recognized in several awards, including the Carol Award, HOLT Medallion, Daphne du Maurier, RT Reviewers' Choice Award, and more.

When she isn't writing, Robin spends quality time with her husband of nearly three decades, her three beautiful daughters and two handsome grandsons, and their character-filled pets at home in the South.

Robin serves the writing community as Executive/Conference Director for ACFW. You can find out more about Robin by visiting www.robincaroll.com.

OTHER BOOKS BY ROBIN CAROLL

Darkwater Inn Series
Darkwater Secrets
Darkwater Lies
Darkwater Truth

Stratagem

Justice Seeker Series
Injustice for All
To Write a Wrong
Strand of Deception
The Christmas Bell Tolls

Torrents of Destruction

Weaver's Needle

The Evil Series
Deliver Us from Evil
Fear No Evil
In the Shadow of Evil

Hidden in the Stars

The Bayou Series
Bayou Justice
Bayou Corruption
Bayou Judgment
Bayou Paradox
Bayou Betrayal
Bayou Blackmail

Dead Air

For Middle Grade/YA Readers
Samantha Sanderson Series
Samantha Sanderson At the Movies
Samantha Sanderson On the Scene
Samantha Sanderson Off the Record
Samantha Sanderson Without A Trace

JOIN US ONLINE!

Christian Fiction for Women

Christian Fiction for Women is your online home for the latest in Christian fiction.

Check us out online for:

- Giveaways
- Recipes
- Info about Upcoming Releases
- Book Trailers
- News and More!

Find Christian Fiction for Women at Your Favorite Social Media Site:

 Search "Christian Fiction for Women"

 @fictionforwomen